Irena Karafilly is a Canadian-educated writer whose fiction has won several literary prize Magazine Award and the CBC Literary Award. Her short stories have been broadcast, anthologised, and published in several countries; her articles have appeared in numerous newspapers, including the *New York Times* and the *International Herald Tribune*. Karafilly is the author of three acclaimed Canadian books and two Greek novels, one of them a national bestseller.

The
Captive
Sun

Irena Karafilly

PICADOR
Pan Macmillan Australia

First published in Australia 2012 in Picador by Pan Macmillan Australia Pty Ltd
1 Market Street, Sydney

National Library of Australia
Cataloguing-in-Publication data:

Karafilly, Irena.
The captive sun / Irena Karafilly.

ISBN: 9781742612089 (pbk.)

A813.54

Cover and internal text design by Nada Backovic
Typeset in 12/15.5 pt Adobe Garamond Pro by Post Pre-press Group
Printed in Australia by McPherson's Printing Group

For Eleni, Toula, Ranya, and Ben

Over the weeping shores
of invaded dreams,
the sun, captive,
refuses to shine.

Pericles Alexiou, 'Occupation'

Author's note

Molyvos is the Turkish name of a coastal Greek village situated on the northeastern Aegean island of Lesbos. Although its official Greek name is now Mythimna, the former name is still in vernacular use. The island is separated from Turkey by the narrow Mytilene Strait and was part of the Ottoman Empire until 1912. In Greece, Lesbos is pronounced 'Lesvos' and is often referred to as Mytilene, after its capital. The spelling of all transliterated names varies from source to source.

The Captive Sun is set in the twentieth century, during the most turbulent era of modern Greek history. Although the characters and plot are all fictitious, the historic events on which the story is based have all been thoroughly documented. The reader may find it helpful to consult the historical highlights and glossary at the back of the book.

PROLOGUE

The day on which the stranger appeared in the village was a snapping, spitting day in March; the sort of day on which men were wont to grouse about their arthritis and gout and to bicker with everyone in their household before heading down to the *kapheneion*, where they could, for a time, forget all their troubles. It was 1935 and only the devil could have masterminded the current state of the economy. This was the one thing everyone seemed to agree on.

Despite the belligerent weather, all the regulars were there when the gypsy turned up: playing cards or backgammon, gossiping over drinks. Philippas Adham, the headmaster, sat discussing Hitler's denunciation of the Treaty of Locarno with his friend, the doctor. He had just ordered coffee and was about to light a cigarette when the gypsy tramped in, tailed by two scruffy boys with shoes so large they had to be half-dragged across the threshold. The stranger looked slatternly but imperious, closing the door behind her with a decisive toss of wet plaits. She wore a colourful skirt and a faded green sweater; a small crimson scarf was tied around her neck, as beguiling as a poppy in a field of thorns.

'Good afternoon.' The gypsy stood peering through the haze of smoke, a bale of tablecloths draped over her arm. 'Good afternoon, gentlemen!'

The greeting was grudgingly returned by a handful of men; others went on staring at the stranger with mute interest. She was an attractive woman with nutmeg-hued skin and a beauty spot on her left cheekbone. The children had found a vacant table and sat with their bare legs dangling, staring at the rain. It was growing dark.

1

'Look here, gentlemen! I've got tablecloths – fine tablecloths all the way from Athens.' The gypsy plucked off the protective oilcloth and cast it aside. 'I invite your offers!' She stood surveying the room: the men toying with their worry beads, the blazing pot-bellied stove. The fire crackled and hissed, spitting out an occasional spark. One of the lamps on the wall flickered, running out of oil.

'Do I hear an offer?' The question was cast over to the right, where Mimis Lyras, the village wit and football champion, sat bantering at the fishermen's table. One of the few fair-haired men in the village, Mimis was idly picking his teeth, staring appraisingly as the gypsy danced her way towards his table.

'How 'bout you, sir? I bet your wife could use a nice tablecloth for thirty drachmas, eh?'

Mimis took a lazy drag on his cigarette, gazing at the stranger. 'What's your name?' he asked, his tongue testing his inner cheek.

'Amalia. Amalia the fortune-teller's what they call me.'

'Well,' said Mimis, his eyes full upon her. 'Look here, Amalia. I'd gladly pay thirty drachmas – maybe even sixty – but the God's truth is I don't have a woman.'

'What?! A handsome *palikari* like you!' The gypsy cackled. 'You pay me sixty drachmas, sir, and I'll find you two wives for your money!' She winked, flinging back her plaits, while Mimis's companions guffawed and Hektor the fool hooted in the background. Someone called out, demanding a coffee reading. Only the *kapheneion* owner appeared impassive, slowly stirring beans in a steaming cauldron.

'Your own wives couldn't match this with their nimble fingers!' the gypsy was saying. Someone – the doctor or the headmaster – had ordered a plate of beans for the rawboned boys. The *kapheneion* owner's father-in-law set the plates down with a sour look. The men had all but abandoned their games; the shop, entitled to ten per cent of all winnings, was beginning to lose money.

'All right: only twenty-three drachmas and your fortune free!' The gypsy stood warming her hands at the wood stove, scanning the crowded room.

'I'll tell you what!' she cried at last. 'I'll read one man's fortune,

2

one man's only, then—' She paused dramatically. 'If he wants – *if* he wants – he can buy one of these lovely tablecloths. How's that?'

The question was aimed at one of the fishermen, who'd recently lost two fingers while fishing with dynamite.

'Why . . . why don't you try the Alexiou brothers here?' The gnome-like man made a flustered gesture, then buried his maimed hand in his lap. 'They've got money to burn, those two. I . . . I'm just a poor fisherman,' he stammered.

The Alexiou brothers were seated in the corner, lingering over their coffee. The gypsy glanced over her shoulder, then made her way towards them, her teeth flashing.

'Don't be afraid . . . there's nothing to be afraid of.' She pulled out a chair and sat down, theatrically overturning one of the coffee cups. The cup belonged to Iason Alexiou, the village merchant's middle son. He was in his mid-twenties, with sparkling blue eyes and the sleek, tender skin of a pampered adolescent.

The fortune-teller studied Iason's features, waiting for his coffee dregs to settle. The rain was still falling but its fury had gradually been exhausted. At the back of the room, Hektor the fool swatted a fly, snickering to himself.

'Well!' exclaimed the gypsy, wagging her head. 'This is a fine – an excellent – cup. Excellent!' she repeated, her eyes sweeping the surrounding men, as if every one of them stood to benefit from her pronouncements.

'You don't say.' Iason half-smiled, fumbling for his pack of cigarettes. He seemed about to add something, but his older brother stopped him.

'We've already got us a fortune-teller in this village!' he tossed out, his pugnacious jaw pulsing. Anyway, I'm sure you'll do better with the women – much better,' he reiterated.

'He's right,' said Iason. 'Our women, they give us nothing but pocket money for a drink or two.' He paused, eyes round with mock innocence. 'What? You don't believe me?'

The gypsy let out a hoarse little laugh. 'And what would you know about it, my friend? I don't believe you're even married yet, are you?'

The merchant's son smiled, but did not contradict her.

'He's looking for a wife, is Iason!' screeched Hektor. He squinted towards Iason's table, tittered, then clamped his hand over his mouth, like an irrepressible child during Sunday Mass.

'Is that so?' The gypsy shifted her attention to the coffee-smeared cup, tilting it this way and that, intent on its spotty motifs. Iason remained silent, but the village wit muttered something that made the fishermen howl with laughter. One of them rose to leave, slapping Iason's shoulder in passing. The rain had ceased, but the wind went on gusting in the thickening dark. Soon, the headmaster and the doctor also paid and left, the headmaster trudging uphill, the doctor heading down. Dr Dhaniel was not a regular at the *kapheneion*, but had darted in after being caught in the downpour.

'Well,' the gypsy was saying, 'every man needs a wife. You don't need Amalia to tell you that.' She spoke in a husky, seductive voice, smiling deeply into Iason's eyes. 'But you, my friend – you are destined to marry the girl of your dreams!'

'In the dark, every woman's a dream,' Mimis put in.

The men laughed again, but the gypsy remained unfazed. 'In the dark, maybe. But this man . . . this man shall have a truly beautiful girl! The most beautiful girl any of you have seen!' she pronounced, glowing with satisfaction.

'Ca-Cal-liope!' screamed Hektor the fool. He jumped out of his chair like a jack-in-a-box, scratching at his crotch. 'She . . . she's the most . . . the most beau-ti-ful girl in the whole wide world! She's got di-di-dimples!'

Calliope Adham was the headmaster's daughter, still unspoken for at the age of twenty.

'As for that, I can't say.' The gypsy shrugged, glancing up as the *kapheneion* owner came to refill the guttering lamp. The two young boys had finished their beans and were rolling soft, leftover bread into little pellets.

'So!' said the gypsy with abrupt resolve. 'Will any of you gentlemen be buying a new tablecloth for Easter? We'll make it only twenty drachmas, since the women hold the purse strings here. What d'you say?' She turned and winked at Iason.

'Well, let's see now.' Iason leaned in to examine the hem on one of the tablecloths. 'All right, I'll take three of them,' he finally said, reaching into his pocket.

'He . . . he's gonna sell them in . . . in the *pantopoleion*!' shrilled Hektor. 'He—'

'Ach, shut up, Hektor!' Iason's brother swore, but before Hektor could summon a retort, the *kapheneion* owner told the gypsy it was time to go.

'It's stopped raining,' Rozakis pointed out, gesturing with his chin. He had a heavy chin and a long nose, but his most striking feature was a kidney-shaped birthmark on his left temple. He beckoned the gypsy boys over, offering peppermints. 'Anyway, this is no place for a woman with young children.'

'Ach, you're right there!' conceded the gypsy, rising. 'Perfectly right, my friend.' She stood gazing into Rozakis's eyes, as if mesmerised by something in their weary depths. Suddenly, she reached out and lightly touched his birthmark. 'But how 'bout you, sir?' she said, as tender-voiced as a mother. 'Might you want to know something 'bout your own future?'

Rozakis just looked at her, stolid and impassive in his smoke-blurred kingdom.

'Time tells the end of a story, lady.'

☙

Time, people said, was not going to wait for the headmaster's daughter. They said she was too headstrong for her own good. They said she read too much. They said she might go blind before she found a suitable husband. She was bold and dreamy and much too outspoken. She was oddly indifferent to her own single state – a hen hoping to lay eggs without a rooster in sight! Some said Philippas should have known better than to let his daughter become a schoolmistress, cramming her head with useless knowledge: French, German, poetry! Her poor mother. She'd done her best to teach Calliope to sew and cook and embroider, but her father was the only one the girl seemed to heed. The headmaster was widely respected, but who could fathom what went on between an educated man's ears?

The Adhams' windows overlooked one of Molyvos's public fountains, so the headmaster's wife had heard the neighbours whisper that very afternoon. She wasted no time repeating what she'd heard, for there was a new suitor she had been pressing her daughter to consider. An Athenian wine merchant.

'Uncle Kleanthis says he's still quite young,' Mirto ventured over supper. 'He says—'

'Ach, Mama! I said I'd think about it, didn't I?' Calliope glanced at her father, pleading for support. And then she changed the subject.

But she did think about it. In the morning, waiting for her class to copy an exercise, she sauntered over to the window, mulling over the little she knew about her latest suitor. She imagined him as just a younger version of her mother's brother. Uncle Kleanthis was a banker; a childless, overfastidious man who had about him the slightly perplexed look of someone awakened from deep slumber. The only thing that interested Calliope about her Mytilene relations was their library. Could the wine merchant possibly be a bibliophile?

Two mangy tomcats were roaming the dusty school grounds, stopping now and then to eye the new swallows' nest under the schoolhouse eaves. The cats appeared restless, as did the schoolchildren. After six consecutive days of wind and rain, the sun had emerged, the choppy sea had grown placid. It was only late March, but the warm weather had blown in a heady reminder of the long, voluptuous days of summer. Every time a dog barked or a sheep bleated, the children would twist around on their scarred benches and gaze at the windows, eyes dilated with longing.

'Very well, you can close your books. Go out and play for a while.' Calliope put her book down. She clapped away chalk dust. But the children only gawked at her, blinking in disbelief. 'Well? What are you waiting for? Go – quietly, please – before I change my mind!'

She threw open the door, flattening her back as her pupils stormed out. Sunlight danced on the classroom walls; children's laughter wafted in from the schoolyard. One of the youngest boys stopped to pick his nose, dreamily watching the schoolmistress pause to adjust her belt. The belt was handloomed, splitting a paisley dress whose principal colour conspicuously matched her plaited auburn hair. Another moment was spent pinning a stray tendril, then Calliope Adham padded into the midday glare, breathing in the penetrating scent of rain-soaked earth, of blossoming honeysuckle.

The school had two classes, one of them taught by the headmaster. Soon, Philippas Adham let his own pupils out and went to join his daughter, skimming newspaper headlines with one eye and watching the children play with the other. There had been a recent outbreak of measles, so the groups were unusually small. The girls in their blue smocks played skipping rope; the boys chased each other along the picket fence. Only Pericles Alexiou, the *pantopoleion* owner's youngest son, seemed to be alone. When Calliope beckoned to him, the boy shuffled over, a melancholy ten-year-old with the world's sorrows weighing on his shoulders.

'Yes, *Kyria?*'

'I was just talking here to the headmaster and we couldn't agree on the German capital. Can you perhaps . . .'

'It's Berlin, *Kyria.*'

'Not Munich, eh?'

The boy was obsessed with world capitals; Germany was on Calliope's mind because Hitler's recent decision to expand his army had violated the Treaty of Versailles. It was all in her father's paper.

'No, it's Berlin, *Kyria,*' Pericles repeated, smiling down at his own scuffed shoes.

Calliope thought the smile sublime, though the child's bookishness often left him out of children's games, as she herself had been. Whenever she thought of her own childhood, what Calliope saw on her mental screen was her young, plain self gazing longingly at a cluster of giggling girls.

'Book-eater!' boys would jeer at her, greedy hands snatching whatever she happened to be reading and casting it in the air, ripped pages whirling down like chicken feathers. *'Book-eater! Book-eater!'*

'How about the capital of Romania?' the schoolmistress asked her pupil. There was something in the paper about a new Bolshevik movement in Romania.

'It's Bucharest, *Kyria*. Not Budapest . . . Budapest's in Hungary—'

'Yes . . . yes, I see. It's easy to confuse those two, I suppose?'

Pericles shrugged. He never seemed in the least confused.

The headmaster patted the boy's shoulder. A pale, hulking man, he had ferocious grey eyebrows but the gleeful chuckle of a four-year-old who has just managed to win a game of marbles against an older sibling. His daughter had no formal qualifications. She'd been invited to take over the younger class when the new schoolmaster engaged from the mainland had died of malaria.

'The boy will go far,' said the headmaster, smiling to see Pericles Alexiou dodge a flying ball. But soon the smile faded. Philippas Adham sneezed, pulled a handkerchief out of his pocket, and forcefully blew his nose. 'I hope I haven't caught the measles from one of the kids,' he grumbled.

Calliope cast him a sceptical look. 'Didn't you have it as a child?'

'Ach, I don't know,' Philippas said and sneezed yet again.

He was still sniffling, still blowing his nose, when the whistle sounded. The children were sent home, scattering in all directions like hens released from a coop. The headmaster and his daughter strolled companionably towards the *agora*: Philippas to get a haircut, Calliope to buy laundry soap. It was Friday afternoon. Easter would be late this year, but the village houses, with their red roofs and colourful shutters, were being readied for Independence Day. Olive cans had been painted to hold basil and geraniums; courtyards and privies were being swept and whitewashed.

'So, what about the wine merchant?' Philippas asked at length. 'You promised your mother you'd think about it.'

'I thought about it.'

'And?'

'I'm not interested.'

He looked at her for a moment. 'Just like that? Why?'

'I prefer goats' milk to wine!' Calliope tossed out, letting go of her father's arm. She had just spotted a fisherman's cap, which the wind had blown from a balcony onto a roadside bush. She plucked the cap from the oleander branch, arranging it on her own head with a small, theatrical moue. 'What do you think? Would the Athenian like me in this?'

'*Ach, koritsi mou, koritsi mou!*'

The village was perched on a hill, its maze of stepped streets overlooking fields and mountains and sea. The main street led steeply to the wisteria-shaded *agora*, then gradually sloped down towards the fishing harbour. In the heart of the *agora*, between the barber's and the main kiosk, was a small *plateia* with a mulberry tree and a faded bench that had been there as far back as anyone could remember. The tree, too, was ancient, its leafy canopy offering shelter on hot summer days.

On that clear, spring-perfumed afternoon, two men were idling under the mulberry tree, bantering in loud voices. One was the kiosk-owner, the other a local man who had prospered in Melbourne and had just returned to marry off his two sisters, and possibly find a bride for himself. Johnny the Australian. Calliope had been at school with his younger sister, but the fisherman's son could now almost pass for a foreigner.

Calliope met Johnny's curious gaze, smiled vaguely, then stepped aside to let a mule-riding farmer go by. Then she saw the gypsy.

The stranger was standing next to the barber, laughing, as sprightly and colourful as a tropical bird. Calliope's father had entered the shop, stopping to greet two children waiting to have their hair cut. They were not Molyvos boys. Calliope watched for a moment, cast a final glance towards the green-eyed Johnny, then sauntered towards the *pantopoleion*.

It was a cluttered general store, selling everything from rice and sugar to bolts of silk and cotton. The shop was owned by Pericles's father, who had recently fallen ill. It was being run by his two grown sons. Vangelis was married and often wore the churlish air of a man displaced in his wife's affections by too many children. Iason, more genial, seemed to enjoy teasing Calliope.

'And what would our little teacher like today?' he would ask, clasping his hands to his chest like an obsequious Turk at a carpet bazaar. 'Can I possibly be of service?'

Calliope was almost as tall as Iason: a solidly built young woman with thickish eyebrows and bright, unflinching, amber-hued eyes. Hektor the fool was not the only one who thought her the most beautiful girl in the village, yet she had never been kept under lock and key. And now there was the new teaching post, conferring even more liberties denied other girls. Not even the boldest of them would have been permitted to wander alone through the village the way Calliope was prone to do day and night, accompanied only by Socrates, her beloved dog. As if keeping a dog was not bad enough! The neighbours had long since given up issuing dark warnings to the headmaster's wife: Mirto was obviously under Philippas's sway, letting her daughter do exactly as she pleased!

It pleased Calliope to shop at the *pantopoleion*, which often had something new for sale: toiletries or ribbons, imported caramels or bananas. Crammed with crates and boxes, and jute sacks bulging with legumes and spice, the store had a musty-sweetish smell, slyly evocative of distant lands: foreign ports, mysterious alleys.

Philippas Adham had an older brother, who lived in Paris, and who was in the habit of sending fine chocolates every Christmas. For Calliope, the pleasure of the annual treat was eclipsed only by the collectable photographs enclosed in the box: the Eiffel Tower and the Taj Mahal, the Statue of Liberty, the Egyptian Pyramids. As a young girl, she would often clamber up a giant plane tree and hide for hours among its leafy branches. She was Amelia Earhart, bold and free! She was a young stowaway headed for exotic shores!

She was a twenty-year-old schoolmistress, but the arrival of spring could still stir up the familiar yearning – for what, she could not say. Some obscure but transcendent event. Some sublime revelation.

Nothing of the sort seemed to be in the offing that Friday afternoon. Calliope entered the *pantopoleion* planning only to buy laundry soap, but soon found herself tempted by a pair of beaded, butterfly-shaped haircombs. She had been paid that day and could afford to indulge the impulse. But then, at the last moment, another item caught her eye, though this one would serve neither domestic necessity nor feminine vanity. She refused to tell Iason what she intended to do with her purchase, but left the store bemused, her eyes flicking towards the *plateia*.

Johnny the Australian was gone. Some invisible creature was stirring in the leafy tree, strewing tiny, unripe berries onto the empty bench. It was growing warm. In front of the kiosk, two schoolgirls stood blowing soap bubbles, watching them drift up towards the cloudless sky and, one by one, explode into nothing.

∽

The idea of keeping a journal, like so many of Calliope's ideas, had been inspired by something she had read in a foreign novel. The fat notebook she had just purchased had stiff black covers edged in red, with a medallion holding a single red rose. It was the rose that had first caught her eye at the *pantopoleion*.

That very afternoon, after a short siesta, Calliope went into the blossoming garden, bearing a small cup of coffee and her brand-new journal. Her father had left for the *kapheneion*; her mother to visit her sister, Elpida, the new mayor's wife. No interruptions for at least an hour! There was a stone bench in the grape arbour and that was where she sat, mentally reviewing the day's events as she sipped her coffee. The setting sun was the colour of a blood orange.

A stray kitten came from behind an oleander bush, meowing plaintively. Mirto had issued countless warnings about ringworm, but Calliope scooped up the kitten and hugged it to her chest. Socrates, snoozing by the doghouse, opened his eyes, blinked a few times, then went back to sleep; the kitten began to purr. Then the mother cat came leaping over the stone fence and the kitten scrambled away and went sidling up to its mother.

It had been an interesting day. Calliope began by writing about the gypsy she had seen at the barber's, going on to recall a childhood trip to Athens, where she had encountered entire families camped on the sidewalks: mothers with their breasts thrust out to nurse their children, fathers sleeping like dishevelled islands amid urban traffic. Next, she recorded her impressions of Johnny the Australian. It was hard to pinpoint the subtle change that came over a man after a decade spent living abroad, but there was unexpected satisfaction in the attempt;

a thrill, almost, in being able to express herself without any need for self-censorship.

The following day, Saturday, Calliope was back in the grape arbour. As there were no exceptional events to record, she wrote about her pupils, going to some length to describe her favourite. Little Eleni Bastia reminded Calliope of herself as a girl, incessantly asking impossible questions.

'If God made the world, who made God?' the blacksmith's daughter had demanded only that morning. Then, 'If there was nothing before He made it, what was nothing like?'

That she'd had no satisfactory explanation to offer had left Calliope feeling vaguely disgruntled, as she often was when answers eluded her. She felt particularly protective towards Eleni, whose family life was almost as bitter as that of Stendhal's Julien Sorel. The poor child not only had twin brothers who liked to torment her, but a brutish father given to slapping her around.

'How fortunate I am to have my doting father,' Calliope wrote in her journal, 'even if he can be a bit of a nag sometimes. And a *malade imaginaire*,' she added for good measure. She had, a little earlier, seen Philippas take his temperature, fussing over what seemed like a common cold. He had gone down to the *agora* as usual but, barely an hour later, returned, coming in through the garden gate with a complicated expression on his florid face.

'I didn't go to the *kapheneion*!' he announced hoarsely. 'I went to the clinic!'

'The clinic?' An afternoon coffee in the *agora* was one of her father's daily rituals. Calliope closed her journal. 'And?'

'Well, the doctor examined me. My mouth, my ears, everything.'

'And?

'And! And! I was right, of course!'

'What, you've got the measles? Did the doctor say so?'

'You never believe me!' Philippas complained, though without much heat. 'But it's like I said: I must have caught it from the children!' With this, the headmaster bent slightly so his daughter could examine his scalp. 'You see anything? Dhaniel says that's where the rash usually starts!'

'I'm sorry, *Baba*,' Calliope said.

'We'll have to find someone to take over my class on Tuesday,' he said at length, turning to go indoors. Monday was Independence Day, which gave them an extra day to find a substitute. 'Ask the mayor to phone Petra if necessary.' Petra was Molyvos's sister village, but as yet only the town hall and the police station had telephones.

'Yes, yes, I'll go immediately.'

Mirto greeted them in the hallway, wringing her hands on hearing the news. '*Ach, Panaghia mou!* Didn't you have it as a child?' she asked.

'Dhaniel says I couldn't have,' Philippas said, overcome by a cough. He then turned back to Calliope, who was putting on her street shoes, slipping the journal into her handloomed satchel. 'The retired schoolmaster in Petra, what's his name? Maybe he can come.'

'Please don't worry, *Baba*. I can handle both classes if I have to.'

'Ach, no. Try to find someone,' Philippas said. He stationed himself before the hall mirror, with Mirto squinting and craning her neck to look into his mouth. He had opened his mouth wide, stretching it with his fingers in search of more telltale symptoms. 'I can't see any spots!' he said in an aggrieved tone. 'But Dhaniel ordered immediate bed rest!' he added, as if to ward off any suspicion that he might be malingering.

'Go to bed, *Baba*. Don't worry about a thing,' Calliope reiterated.

She kissed her father and watched him plod away, supported by Mirto, who was slightly lame from childhood polio. Her father certainly looked unwell, yet somehow, at the same time, almost – there was no other word for it – triumphant. As if his symptoms were the consequence of some exceptional effort, she said to herself, some stupendous achievement. She remembered one of her young pupils, who had come to her recently, proudly displaying his scraped, iodine-stained knee.

'How odd men can be sometimes,' she was to write later in her new journal. 'I don't know who created God. I'm not even sure I believe He exists, but I hope He does, because no one else could possibly understand the extraordinary two-legged creature He is said to have created in his own image.'

1939–1942

'How glorious it is – and also how painful –
to be an exception.'

Alfred de Musset

ONE

~ 1 ~

The first time they dug up Philippas Adham's grave, the exhumed corpse had been found to be insufficiently decomposed. The gravedigger had opened the casket, then hastened to shut it, scowling. They would have to wait at least a year before trying again, he stated.

The custom of disinterring a loved one's remains had been explained to Calliope in early adolescence. She understood it had to do with the shortage of burial ground. All the same, when, in the spring of 1939, Fanis the gravedigger finally lifted her father's skull from the rotting coffin, the cloudless sky grew abruptly blurred, and the dripping cypresses, impassive as sentries, went spinning around the graveyard.

Shored up by her husband, Calliope shivered as Fanis began to pick mud out of the dead man's eye cavities, reaching in with his gnarled fingers to retrieve the gold coins meant to pay for the journey to Hades.

An old copper vat stood waiting by the graveside. Tradition dictated that the disinterred bones be carefully washed and rinsed, then sanctified with wine before being placed in an ossuary, ready for their permanent resting place. Weeping, Calliope kept struggling against the rising stench of putrefaction. Another moment and she saw scraps of her father's flesh clinging to his spine, like bits of cod on a discarded fish skeleton.

And now the entire universe was wobbling. Bolting to the edge of the graveyard, she stood emptying her stomach into a tangle of weeds crawling with giant snails. It had rained much of the previous night.

'Oh . . . please go back. Go help my mother,' Calliope heaved, pulling away from her husband's comforting hand. Even as a child, she had hated to be observed retching. 'I need to be alone right now.'

'Call me if you need me.'

The afternoon was starting to fade. Somewhere beyond the fence, a dove began to call, intermittently heard above the taunting wind and the professional mourners' wails.

When, at length, Calliope rejoined the women, they were starting to gather her father's scrubbed bones, piling them with the absorption of children building a matchstick house. Only her mother's hands were idle. Mirto had abandoned her wifely task and sat slumped over her knees, a black-clad widow surrendering anew to the enormity of her loss.

Calliope got down to her knees, looping her arms around her mother's shoulders.

~ 2 ~

Some families were lucky and some unlucky. It was as simple, as obvious, as that. This was what the Adhams' neighbours were still saying four years after the headmaster's untimely demise. Long before Philippas Adham contracted the measles that inflamed his brain, those who made it their business to know such things had noted that the Adhams' home had nothing by way of protection against the evil eye. It came as no surprise to anyone that the evil eye should have aimed its malevolent gaze at what was, after all, the headmaster's most valuable asset. But some maintained that Philippas's decline had been precipitated by the scandal his daughter had sparked on Independence Day, compromising herself with Johnny the Australian. What good is a man's intelligence if he can't rein in his unmarried daughter?

All this was widely rehashed the day of the disinterment.

When Philippas's bones had been laid to rest, Iason returned to work and poor Mirto, utterly drained, lay down for a nap. Left to her own devices, Calliope sought solace in a brass-studded chest that had once belonged to her father. She kept the chest under her bed, along with her journal. The Turkish chest was stuffed with Philippas's personal possessions: his silver cigarette case and tie pin, his nail clippers, notebook and magnifying glass, a half-empty bottle of French aftershave, a tiny jar of eucalyptus ointment he liked to use in winter, to clear nasal passages.

Calliope still kept a journal, pressing secrets into its pristine pages as she had once pressed wild flowers, weighing them down with tomes from her father's encyclopaedia. The journal helped her sort out her thoughts and feelings, but the old chest provided the spiritual relief that, she supposed, others sought in church. Some evenings, waiting for her husband to come home, she would take out the green chest and place it on her bed. She would uncap the aftershave bottle or eucalyptus jar and inhale deeply, the vibrant smells conjuring up her father more vividly than any photograph ever could.

She had only one snapshot of him as a young man. It had been taken in Constantinople, shortly before his parents were slaughtered in their own courtyard, trapped by frenzied nationalists bent on ridding Turkey of its ethnic populations.

Philippas and his brother had been at university when the carnage took place in coastal Phocaea. The Greek island of Lesbos, only recently independent of the Ottomans, was some seven miles off the Turkish coast and this was where the two orphaned brothers eventually landed, as would hundreds of other refugees in the years to come. It was 1914 and, what with the recent draft, twenty-nine-year-old Philippas Adham was soon offered a teaching post in the village of Molyvos. His younger brother, who had studied French literature, had by then left for France.

In time, the schoolmaster found a close friend in the village doctor, a more recent victim of political upheavals. The grim statistics were known to anyone who read the newspapers. By the early 1920s, over a million Greeks had been forced out of Turkey; close to half-a-million Turks had been expelled from Greece.

'That's how it is,' Calliope had overheard Dr Dhaniel say to her father. 'When two bulls tussle, it's always the grasshoppers that suffer.'

The past haunted Calliope as it had her father. Sometimes, in an especially bleak moment, she would clutch the faded sepia photograph and sit whispering in the dark, as she had once done with her child-hood dolls. Lately, what she mostly whispered about was her apparent inability to conceive. It had been her father's deathbed wish that she settle down and have children. There had been a recent assault on their Socrates, a shocking dismembering whose perpetrator would remain unknown for years. Philippas feared that the dog was just the begin-ning. He pleaded with Calliope to help him depart in peace.

'A woman . . . a woman like you, *koritsi mou*, will only make people want to hurt her,' he said. He entreated her to make up her mind and accept one of her fine suitors. There was the Athenian wine merchant, as well as a new banking colleague of her uncle's. Closer still, there was Iason Alexiou, who had recently shown up in person, asking for Cal-liope's hand. His proposal had come as something of a surprise, though not an unwelcome one. Marriage to the merchant's son would ensure that Calliope remained in Molyvos, and was well provided for. Iason might not be a bibliophile, Philippas conceded, but he was a clever, hardworking boy who had made it clear he would allow his wife to go on teaching, if she so wished.

'Doesn't . . . doesn't that tell you something about him, my dear?'

This exchange had taken place on the ninth day of Philippas Adham's illness, but Calliope would not believe her father was dying. Sitting on the edge of his bed, she had argued and argued with him, until all at once he stopped her, frantically gesturing for the chamber pot. He vomited into it several times, then fell back against the pillows with a long, ragged breath. Mirto had gone downstairs to answer the door: the doctor had arrived. Calliope sat dabbing at her father's stub-bled jaws with a washcloth, listening to the murmur of voices below. There was the smell of vomit in the air, of smoking oil and sticky medicine bottles.

She was about to go empty the chamber pot when her father stopped her, reaching for her wrist. Slowly, he brought her hand to his lips, gazing at her all the while with dark, eloquent eyes. He seemed intent on conveying something of vital importance; had parted his lips to speak but seemed unable to produce a single sound. Another moment and the doctor's footfall was heard on the landing. There was a knock at the door. In the garden below, a passing bird called, its odd querying cry ripping through the night.

~ 3 ~

But what had he meant to say? What was it that had made him surrender to the gods' caprice in the small hours of the morning? Was it her argumentativeness that exhausted him beyond endurance? Her reckless behaviour on Independence Day? How did something so ill-deserved, so irrevocable, befall a robust fifty-year-old man? She had been right there, sitting at his bedside! How could she not realise he was about to be snatched away from them? *How could she let it happen?*

In the weeks that followed, Calliope's thoughts kept returning to her father's last hours with a feverish obsessiveness that bordered on madness. She could see what was happening – to her, to her mother – but could no more arrest it than she could the setting of the sun or the waning of the moon. The apathy of the universe seemed more astounding with every passing day; an eternal outrage.

Mirto had become a tight-lipped, aloof woman, moving about the house like a sleepwalker, rejecting all offers of help or solace. Calliope sensed *she* was being blamed for her father's demise. Mirto would not say yes, she would not say no. Her sigh-filled conversation had gradually shrunk to household requests, the occasional muttered rebuke. She was only in her mid-forties, but whiled away her evenings polishing brass and silver as if her very survival depended on it. Calliope's own survival, she was starting to realise, largely depended on her ability to escape the perilous fog of her mother's grief. By midsummer, she had begun to frequent the beach, reading or watching children splash in the azure sea. Only the sound and smell of the sea seemed to soothe her. The sea and the books that the mayor – her godfather – had brought back from a trip to Athens.

One late-summer afternoon, Calliope went to the *pantopoleion* to buy candles. Iason, who was unloading a new shipment off a mule's back, watched her cross the *plateia*, a sea breeze ruffling the hem of her black summer skirt. He paused, lit a cigarette, then smiled a little, blowing a ring of smoke.

'You've lost weight,' he observed at length.

'I suppose,' she said.

She had lost her appetite after her father's death and must have looked downcast, because Iason hastened to turn his casual observation into a compliment.

'Never mind,' he said, 'you're so light on your feet you make other women look as if they were treading grapes for homemade wine.'

'What?!' For a moment, Calliope was too surprised to utter another word. Iason appeared abashed, as if the words had tumbled out of his mouth against his better judgement. Years ago, sitting behind her at a puppet show, he had tugged on her plait, looking utterly innocent when she turned around. He was still given to teasing, but not to flattery. 'Have you been drinking?' She laughed.

And then, abruptly, she stopped. It was the first time anyone had managed to make her laugh, as much in delight as in astonishment: she had not thought Iason capable of poetic whimsy. But that was the thing about Iason. He often surprised her; had always known how to make her laugh.

After a while, she began to stop at the *pantopoleion* on her way home, even when there was nothing she really needed to buy. What she urgently needed was to find her way back to the sun. She could not discuss poetry or philosophy with Iason, but he did make the clouds of her rage against the fates gradually dissipate.

The months went by, season after season. A year after her father's death, Calliope consented to marry Iason Alexiou. She did so in a spirit of growing affection and hope, relieved to be able to stay on the island, grateful to find herself cajoled across the stormy river of her filial grief. Even after all these months, hardly a day went by when she did not feel her father's presence. On her wedding day, standing before the altar, she reminded herself how happy he would have been to see her finally garlanded. She greeted him in her heart. She asked for his blessings.

But when the wedding festivities were over and she was finally alone with her husband, it became imperative to banish Philippas's ghost from the flower-festooned bedroom. They had been given her parents' sombre matrimonial room, the very bed in which she had been conceived and born. Mirto was spending the night with her sister.

It was Iason who finally succeeded in chasing off the paternal phantom; Iason's roaming hands, his voracious lips. Calliope felt shy, but also curious, as intrigued by her husband's manhood as an avid child stumbling upon some rare, fascinating creature.

'It looks so proud of itself,' she heard herself say, bemused, perched next to Iason on the edge of the scented bed. Two candles were burning on either side, a pair of watchful sentries.

'Proud?' Her husband laughed at her words.

'And wilful. Is this what it's like when you have your clothes on?'

'If you kiss me, yes.' He smiled. His gaze slid from her face down to his own exuberant member. 'Sometimes it's enough just to think of you.' His eyes sparkled.

She laughed like a schoolgirl. She reached out and touched the pulsing crown with her fingertips: lightly, teasingly.

'It's the strangest thing I've ever seen,' she said and bit her lip. It seemed to have its own life, its secrets. And then she laughed again, and averted her eyes. He was regarding her closely, stroking her cheek, her neck.

'You're not afraid, are you?'

She considered the question. 'A little,' she admitted.

He put his lips to hers. 'Don't be afraid. Touch it again.'

There was no denying she felt vaguely threatened. She reminded herself: *my husband*. He had reached out and was tugging at the strings of her nightie – a long bridal shirt embroidered by her mother. His hand slipped in and caressed her breasts, first the left, then the right. His breathing was growing harsher.

'I *am* afraid,' she whispered. She would not look at his face, would not meet his eyes. 'Are you sure it's going to fit?' she asked. 'Is . . . is it normal—'

His lips brushed her ear. 'It just wants to get to know you better.'

She pondered this for a moment. 'Yes, but—'

'Don't worry: it'll fit perfectly . . . I promise.'

He kissed her collarbone. His hand slid between her legs, bold with a husband's beguiling prerogative. 'Why don't you take off your nightie?'

She turned to him. It was not his words that had stopped her breath, but her own volatile flesh. She was trembling, her deepest secrets just beginning to unfurl. In the garden, the crickets were singing.

'Don't be afraid,' he whispered in her ear. He reached out and took hold of her hem and began to lift it, planting moist little kisses all along her perplexed abdomen. Her heart was flapping against her ribcage. Her gaze kept sliding towards his thighs.

'It – it looks like it's trying to tell me something,' she said, suppressing a nervous giggle. Her voice kept surprising her, like an echo in the wilderness.

'It's making you a promise,' he was saying in her ear.

'Oh, yes?' Her cheeks grew hot again. These were her own breasts, exposed to the light – to a relative stranger's eyes. He had been her husband for barely six hours. 'What's it promising?' she brought out at last.

'I think it's promising you some lovely surprises.'

'Surprises?' she said. 'Like what?'

'You'll see,' he said, smiling complacently. 'I promise.'

~ 4 ~

He had the face of a man accustomed to taking forgiveness for granted; the manner and walk of someone running late for some consequential appointment. Now and then, going about his business, Iason resembled a man being propelled forward by an invisible force, oblivious to potential devastation. And yet, there was something endearing, something faintly roguish, about the way his small ears curled ever so slightly forward. He had an overlapping upper lip that Calliope found inexplicably stirring, especially when his gaze said that he meant to kiss her.

He continued to make her laugh. Her golden eyes, he told her, were like the eyes of a tiger lolling in the sun. He said she had the look of a woman harbouring some secret surprise or pleasure. She was. She could feel herself being towed towards the shores of love.

Only Mirto remained reluctant to abandon her sorrowful island. Although she had strongly supported Iason's proposal, she seemed to have little to say to him, once he was living with them. She continued to clean and do the laundry and prepare meals, but had turned her back on every conceivable pleasure. She ate next to nothing, and rarely left the house, except to visit her sister or Philippas's grave; sometimes to light candles to the saints.

Seeing her plod by, the neighbours clucked their tongues. '*Poh poh poh*,' they said to each other, 'she'll be blown away by the wind, she will, if she keeps this up.'

Calliope went on teaching. She did the daily shopping, going to the harbour for fish, the dairy shop for cheese and yoghurt. She despaired of helping Mirto regain her spirits. And, in time, even the high-spirited Iason seemed in danger of succumbing to the pervasive gloom. He was unfailingly courteous to his mother-in-law but, a year into the marriage, began to spend most evenings playing cards in the *kapheneion*, as his father had done throughout his married life. Calliope tried her best to be as tolerant as her mother-in-law had been. Night after night, she lay awake in the dark, a restless question mark longing for her husband's answers.

No answer – no persuasive answer – was forthcoming when she finally broached the subject. Nothing was wrong, Iason insisted, turning her question into a joke about the pitfalls of thinking too much. He was, Calliope was beginning to perceive, the sort of man who hid his own grievances behind a wall of facetious humour. She could laugh at her own culinary failures, her occasional clumsiness, her squeamishness at the sight of blood. But there were some things she hated being chaffed about.

One day, she was reading by the window when she spotted her husband's nephews playing by the public fountain. Iason was getting ready to return to work. When she realised that the two boys were preparing to set fire to a cat's tail, Calliope dropped her book and stormed out, shouting at the top of her lungs. She was going to tell their mother; would have them expelled from school, she threatened, waving her arms like a fishwife who had just caught street urchins stealing her sardines. Iason, coming down to see what the fracas was all about, stood scratching his head.

'They're boys, Calliope. Little boys are cruel.'

'They're not all cruel!' she snapped, thinking that children who tortured animals grew up to be Attilas and Ghengis Khans. 'Why should it be a thrill to see a helpless creature suffer?'

'Why? Why?' Iason made a vaguely exasperated gesture. This, his arm said, was a typical example of thinking too much.

'I'm just trying to understand! What makes them want to do it?'

Iason appeared to ponder the question, then his mouth curled. 'Are boys in foreign novels always good little tykes who obey their teacher?'

'No! Boys in novels can be just as vile but that doesn't mean I have to approve of what they do, does it?'

'You don't have to approve, only to accept. God works in mysterious ways,' he said, smiling into one cheek. It was something his mother was given to saying; a conversational quirk he occasionally mocked behind her back.

Calliope fell silent. Her husband didn't understand her, but then, she didn't understand him either: his Royalist sympathies and flippant humour, his inordinate joy in amassing money. She might have understood the latter if, like some Dickensian orphan, he had been raised in poverty. But Iason's family was one of the richest in the village, and there were those who said it was the Alexious' wealth that had persuaded the headmaster's daughter to finally settle down.

Calliope was not immediately aware of these speculations. But when the gossip eventually reached her ears, her aversion to Iason's mercantile devotion only seemed to intensify. It was unreasonable and unfair, she conceded in her journal; yet she could neither help it nor deny it.

And then the evening came when she stopped at the *pantopoleion* on her way home from a pedagogical meeting. The *agora* was virtually shut for the night. Iason sat hunched over his desk, counting the day's takings. He was flicking through the bills with mesmerising speed, occasionally bringing his index finger to his tongue for a spot of saliva, but not stopping, not offering so much as a smile.

There was something intensely private about the nocturnal scene: the hushed interior, the flickering candle flame, the *pantopoleion*'s cat chasing a tiny mouse across the dusty floor. Iason himself suddenly seemed like a furtive stranger muttering an incantation. Calliope, a reluctant voyeur, was both repelled and spellbound.

Iason locked the store and they headed home together, crossing the *agora* in the thickening dark. Iason was jangling the loose change in his pocket, a habit that made Calliope want to leap out of her skin. It was an utterly innocuous habit, yet it never failed to set her teeth on edge. Her murky antipathy made her ashamed of herself, but it was hard to broach the subject, for when it came to his own character, his habits, Iason's sense of humour would evaporate like a child's promise. She had heard rumours that both he and Vangelis were given to shortchanging elderly customers. Envy, Calliope reminded herself, often made villagers vicious. All the same, she eventually found herself comparing her husband to the village doctor, who often treated patients without exacting payment. One thing she was sure of: in his entire childhood, the doctor had never tortured so much as a fly or spider.

~ 5 ~

Elias Dhaniel had become Calliope's only confidant. The friendship had blossomed unexpectedly, after the doctor's wife had died tragically, giving birth to her fourth child. When Calliope and Iason became the boy's godparents, the doctor began dropping in for coffee when passing through the St Kyriaki neighbourhood. Iason was usually at work when the doctor turned up and, in time, Calliope found herself airing a personal concern: could her failure to conceive be what was gnawing at her husband?

'He's been drinking a lot,' she offered reluctantly. 'He never used to drink much before we were married. The only time he played poker was on New Year's Eve.'

The doctor asked questions and offered suggestions, but months went by and Calliope continued to menstruate, albeit somewhat erratically. The neighbourhood's old women took to teasing her, pinching her hips with their claw-like hands. 'Skin and bones, Calliope!' they cackled. 'Skin and bones. Nothing here for a man to get a handle on!'

She was not as bony as her mother, but she was still thinner than she'd been before her father's death. And there were those who said that the evil eye was not yet done with this family. Why else would a young bride fail to conceive after all this time? Others went so far as to wonder whether Calliope was even fulfilling a wife's chief duty.

It had turned out not to be a duty. What had she expected? Calliope hardly knew, but remained grateful for the conjugal blessings even after she and Iason had begun to quarrel over the nightly card games. There were village men, wealthy landowners, who had lost their entire family fortune playing poker. Calliope was not privy to her husband's financial affairs, but one day her aunt reported that Iason had just lost a small fortune, playing poker at a neighbour's house.

The irony proved harder to digest than the loss. That a man so hard-working, so enamoured of lucre, would allow himself to lose thousands of drachmas in a single night's game! A man who had reproached *her* when, during a rare trip to Mytilene, she had splurged on a fine dress she did not especially need.

Another spring went by; another summer followed.

One autumn day, a few months after Philippas's bones had been laid to rest, it became apparent that Mirto might not be quite as oblivious as she appeared.

'You're not behaving like a proper wife,' she told Calliope as they stood clearing the dinner dishes. It was the last day in October, the name day of Iason's best man. Mirto's comment had been provoked by her daughter's reluctance to pay the traditional name day visit. Calliope was dutifully polishing her husband's Sunday shoes, but her tongue would not rest. She hated the stiff formality of name day parties. Why should she have to attend an event she had no interest in? Iason was out alone every evening. Could he not pay his respects to the olive mill owner's family without her hanging onto his arm?

Mirto remained silent for a moment. She was picking through a tray of fresh almonds, preparing to set them out to dry in the sun.

'Life is not about satisfying our whims,' she pronounced at length.

'Well, it certainly seems to be for some of us!' Calliope shot back.

Iason had left them to have a nap, after a long night in the *kapheneion*.

'Ach.' Mirto heaved a sigh, refraining from further comment.

When she finished buffing Iason's shoes, Calliope set them down by the door, then went to listen to the neighbour's wireless. Spyros Balliou, the *hamam* caretaker, owned one of the few radios in the village, a gift from an American relative. The schoolmistress, he often said, was the only Molyvos woman who understood politics. Not only had the recent referendum on the monarchy been rigged, but the King had appointed Ioannis Metaxas as Prime Minister. The appointment had left both Spyros and Calliope seething. Metaxas was a ruthless Right-winger; a man who now had the King's blessing to do as he pleased. How could Iason remain a Royalist supporter?

In recent days, however, Hitler's expansionist ambitions had begun to eclipse all other political concerns. Calliope would have liked to share the latest news with Dr Dhaniel, but there was no wriggling out of the name day visit. Dimitris Stephanides was Iason's closest friend. They had gone through school and army together.

So Calliope set about ironing a jacket, then lingered before the vanity mirror, critically studying her own reflection. Her new dress had puffed sleeves and a dainty scalloped collar, its mother-of-pearl buttons going all the way down to the belted waist. It was a lovely frock, the colour of ripe cherries. If only her mouth were more dainty, her large hands a little more feminine.

Mirto was outside in the garden, cutting roses for the name day visit.

A swallow flew in, flapped about blindly for a minute or two, then found its way out again. There was the scent of ripening quince and decaying leaves, the soul-bruising smell of approaching winter.

~ 6 ~

The village fool was coming up the street, weaving his way through the *agora*. An orphan from nearby Stipsi, Hektor worked as a messenger and rubbish collector, trudging through the village every morning with the municipal horse, ringing a bell to announce his passage. By two o'clock he was usually done. Unless there was an urgent message, he would promptly head down to Fotini's *kapheneion* in the harbour, where he passed his time drinking and bantering with idle fishermen. Sometimes he would find a shady tree and lie down for a nap. In the late afternoon, he would rise, relieve himself in the sea, then trudge uphill towards the *agora*.

There was no telling where Hektor might turn up after a drinking bout. He was given to roaming the village, occasionally climbing a tree to free a stranded kitten or help himself to someone's ripening fruit. A few days earlier, walking her dog, Calliope had come upon him in the hilltop fortress, spreadeagled on the ground, trying to count the stars. The villagers were indulgent towards Hektor, who was obviously soft in the head, even if he did seem to be in on everything happening in the village. He was thirty years old but wore an old man's Turkish breeches; often a turban and a cummerbund as well. He seemed to have no relatives and no home, except for a garden shack Zenovia the fortune-teller let him have, rent free.

Calliope and Iason were on their way to Dimitris Stephanides's party when they ran into Hektor, who was heading towards Rozakis's *kapheneion*.

'*Kyria* Calliope!' he spluttered, his hair standing on end like a cockscomb. He had stationed himself in front of the cobbler's shop, and waited with his arms stretched out, the smell of stale urine coming off his clothes. '*Kyria* Calliope, I—'

'Ach, let us pass, Hektor,' Iason said irritably. Hektor was stamping from side to side, his eyes swimming in their bloodshot sockets.

'*Kyria* Calliope, I . . . I wish to say something, *Kyria* Calliope!'

'Well, say it, for heaven's sake, Hektor.'

'I wish, *Kyria* Calliope, that you . . . that you was cross-eyed . . .'

'Cross-eyed!' Despite herself, Calliope smiled.

'Y-yes,' stammered Hektor. 'I . . . I wish you was cross-eyed so . . . so your eyes could see how beautiful they are.'

'Listen to that!' said Iason. 'I suppose—'

'Cross-eyed!' Hektor repeated, scratching his groin. 'Bea-u-ti-ful, beauti-ful,' he muttered, then plodded on without another word. Calliope and Iason exchanged looks, then burst out laughing, the tension between them lifting.

~ 7 ~

They arrived to find Iason's brother and his wife already seated, along with Dimitris's fiancée and her tiresome parents. The host being the proprietor of Molyvos's olive mill, there was the usual interest in the olive crop about to be harvested. Everyone present owned at least one orchard.

Eventually, the talk turned to Italian aggression and the possibility of yet another war. The Italians had recently sabotaged several fishing boats in the Ionian Sea, then sank a Greek warship on a sacred Orthodox holiday. In spring, both Dimitris and Iason had been called up for military exercises. A national draft was beginning to seem all but inevitable.

Serving homemade brandy, Dimitris's mother did her best to divert the guests. She was a pale, fleshy woman, with an opulent bosom that seemed to be leading her wherever she went. Perfumed and squeezed into a tight corset, Polyxeni bustled about, assisted by Dimitris's simpering fiancée.

When talk of the military draft dried up, Dimitris's future mother-in-law launched forth into the details of a controversial land dispute involving St Kyriaki's priest, who had reportedly tried to swindle the new harbourmaster from Kavala.

'Imagine: a man in his position! Jesus Christ rode a donkey, but our priest will soon be rich enough to buy himself a motorcar!' said her husband, to widespread laughter. A building contractor, Seraphim Lemos was one of the wealthiest men in the area, but the only villager to own a motorcar was a man nicknamed The American, who had recently returned from the United States and purchased a taxicab.

The laughter died down, but not the interest in *Papa* Iakovos, whose soul, the hostess was soon saying, was blacker than his cassock. 'I wouldn't be surprised – not in the least surprised – to know he's got his hand in the church till,' she added.

'Ach, the whole family's a bunch of hypocrites,' the host stated, reaching for the bottle of brandy. 'They say the rascal even paws the occasional widow who comes in for confession.'

At this, an exasperated sound escaped Calliope's throat. 'Who's *they*?' she heard herself ask. 'Has anyone actually seen him do it?'

She turned to face Loukas Stephanides and found him looking stunned, like a child robbed of a treat he'd been about to bite into. *Papa* Iakovos happened to be Calliope's neighbour, and no one would ever catch *her* kissing his greedy hand. Still, she had come to loathe the way a casually dropped word would start rolling about the village – a tiny pebble that sometimes grew into a lethal stone.

Loukas was still looking flushed, still defending his unnamed sources, while his wife did her best to steer the conversation in less controversial directions. Calliope resolved to withhold further comment, except to compliment Polyxeni on her cherry preserves. She then made an effort to engage her sister-in-law in small talk. Ioanna was seated beside her, but seemed intent on communing with her own occupied womb.

'Are you all right?' Calliope asked.

'Yes. Yes, the baby's kicking, that's all.' Ioanna was only a year older than Calliope but already carrying her fourth child. She was considered a blessed woman, having snagged the merchant's eldest son despite a negligible dowry.

Calliope returned to her private musings, but her ears pricked up when the talk turned to Johnny the Australian's younger sister, who had emigrated to Melbourne with her husband but was reportedly planning to return to Greece. Nikki, who had once been Calliope's classmate, was said to be pining for Molyvos.

At this, Dimitris let out a little chortle. 'Why would anyone want to leave the island anyway?' he demanded, twirling his moustache. The black, devotedly waxed moustache reminded Calliope of a trapeze artist she had once seen at an Athens circus. Dimitris's speech, however, was as measured as a politician's. 'Has anyone ever gone hungry on this island?' he continued. 'Fish in the sea, fruit on the trees. What else could one possibly want, I ask you?'

'Well, Dimitraki,' Polyxeni addressed her son, while passing a fresh napkin to his maladroit father, 'Some people just prefer city life, you know. Nikki's sister-in-law, for example – what's her name – the pretty one who married Johnny?'

'Kristina,' prompted Loukas, wiping torte cream off his gabardined thigh.

'Kristina, of course! Well, they say she's taken to city life like a bee to fresh thyme. Isn't that so?'

The hostess turned to the pregnant Ioanna, who happened to be related to Kristina's family. 'I hear they've got a second shop now, *and* a newborn son?'

'Yes.' Ioanna shifted her pregnant bulk, casting a nervous glance towards Calliope. 'Yes, that's right.'

Nothing else was said on the subject, but it was not hard to guess why Polyxeni had contrived to slip Kristina's name into the conversation. Back in 1935, Calliope had been spotted going into the pine wood with Johnny the Australian. Without a chaperone! She had been only twenty at the time; had run into Johnny on her way back from a distant beach. He said he wanted to talk to her and she followed him into the resinous wood, abdicating thought. Although she hardly knew Johnny, she knew the rest of his family. What could he possibly want from her?

He wanted her to be his wife, to go to Australia with him. To Melbourne! Oh, she might have been tempted by France or America, but Australia? A land of ex-convicts and hopping kangaroos?

And yet, she had let him kiss her, her sun-licked body feeling oddly alien, as if, lying on the beach, she had been squeezed into some wanton stranger's skin. She had been reading Stendhal, had devoured love scenes in other foreign novels, but never before had she found herself ensnared by her own lust.

All the same, she had turned Johnny down. And, within days, he went on to ask for the cobbler's sister. Kristina was a pretty sixteen-year-old girl, but stupid as a brick, Calliope thought. She had felt confused on first hearing about the engagement: a little hurt, vaguely insulted, but ultimately vindicated.

She managed to keep all this to herself at the name day party, realising that Polyxeni could not resist trying to settle the score. Her husband had just been challenged in public: by a young woman! Calliope had no one but herself to blame. She was incorrigible. Her own mother used to accuse her of having no sense of discretion, of voicing whatever crossed her mind. As a child, Calliope had told her mother's sister that none of them enjoyed the European dishes she liked to prepare on Sunday; she'd told her aunt Lydia that her visits made Mirto as nervous as a cat about to give birth. And there she was, a married woman, still unable to control her tongue!

Nothing made Calliope want to weep as predictably as awareness of her own character flaws.

~ 8 ~

Iason had made no reference to the name day visit on the way home, but as soon as they arrived, he followed Calliope into the kitchen and made for the ouzo.

'There's something I'd like to discuss with you,' he said.

Calliope stiffened. She lowered herself onto the day divan, mechanically groping for the book she'd been reading. 'What?'

'I want you to listen to me, Calliope.' Iason fell into a chair. He frowned at the book. 'Are you listening?'

'Of course I'm listening!' She tossed the book aside. 'I'm all ears!'

Iason lit a cigarette. He inhaled deeply. Finally, he spoke.

'I was wondering what . . . what you'd say to adopting Vangelis's baby,' he said, reaching for his ouzo.

'*Vangelis's baby?*' Calliope swallowed, watching Iason blow smoke through his nostrils. 'Are you serious?'

'Yes, I . . .' Iason averted his eyes. 'I thought that—'

'Absolutely not!' The response was accompanied by a scandalised little sound. The mere idea, Calliope's expression suggested, was too preposterous for words. In truth, the adoption of a sibling's child was not uncommon on the island, either because a family had too many mouths to feed or, as sometimes happened, because God had not seen fit to bless a couple with children of their own.

Calliope sat struggling with her inner havoc. 'We're still young. I'm only twenty-five,' she said at last. 'Anyway—'

'What?' said Iason.

She hugged herself in silence, listening to the clock tick in the foyer.

'Anyway what?'

'I don't like Ioanna's brats!' she finally blurted, her thoughts flying back to the day she had seen Ioanna's sons preparing to set fire to a neighbourhood cat.

'Ioanna's brats? We're talking about a newborn, Calliope!' Iason protested. 'Ioanna might be a little too easy on her kids – all right, she *is* too easy – but the child . . . he wouldn't have to be a brat if you brought him up from infancy, would he?'

Calliope raised her gaze, filled with intense but not quite diagnosed feelings. What if the child took after the parents? She disliked the irascible Vangelis and didn't much like the bovine Ioanna. 'I can't do it. I'm sorry – I can't.'

'But why, in God's name? Just give me one good reason and—'

'I don't want someone else's child!' Calliope erupted. 'I already have a godson I love dearly. And a dog,' she added with a wry smile, having recently adopted a stray black puppy she had named Sappho. Suddenly, Iason's use of the masculine pronoun registered. *He wouldn't have to be a brat if you brought him up from infancy.*

She regarded her husband for a moment. 'Has it ever occurred to you the child might be a girl?'

'Of course it's occurred to me! A girl would be better than nothing, wouldn't she?' said Iason. He raised his glass to his lips. 'Well? Wouldn't she?'

Calliope closed her eyes. 'I don't want to raise someone else's child,' she said at last, overcome by unbearable weariness. 'I'm sorry. It's out of the question.' She picked up her book as she had seen her mother pick up a dish of peas to be shelled or a skirt to be hemmed, making it clear the subject was closed. Briefly, she wondered whether her mother might be eavesdropping upstairs.

'You're so stubborn!' Iason said, reaching for an ashtray. 'Like a mule!'

'Fine, I'm stubborn.' Calliope was determined to say no more. Not another word. A moment went by. 'I can't help it, Iason!' she suddenly cried, her hands flying towards him, pleading for understanding. 'I can't help the way I feel, can I?'

Iason said nothing. The only sound was that of Hektor the fool singing out on the street, prompting Sappho to raise her head with a whimper of recognition. In the foyer, the clock struck nine times, then fell silent.

Calliope rose and lumbered past Iason, heading for the bread box. Across the garden, their neighbour had turned on his wireless, as he did every evening.

It was as the news wafted into their kitchen that a startling thought came to Calliope: Iason is worried about Albania. He's afraid of dying! The insight struck her with the force of abrupt revelation. All at once, she could feel her will starting to weaken. But does he want a child to avoid being drafted, she wondered, or does he just want to ensure that he has an heir?

Slowly, mechanically, she put down the bread and turned to face her husband.

'Look, Iason . . . let me think about it, all right? I *will* think about it, but . . . please, I'm not making any promises. It's not easy, taking another woman's child.'

Iason made a vague gesture, then rose, stopping to down his ouzo. 'I want an answer now,' he said. 'I told Vangelis I'd let him know tonight.'

'You what?!' Calliope stared. 'It's no use,' she finally said, lapsing into silence. She resumed slicing the bread loaf, the air in the room thickening.

Suddenly, she slashed her finger. She stood blinking at her oozing blood, tears flooding her eyes. When it came to blood, she was as squeamish as her young pupils. Nauseated, she hurried to the sink and rinsed her hand, sobbing soundlessly. Iason, who had been pacing, stopped. He had never seen her cry, except at her father's burial. He stood watching her for a moment, then let out a small, exasperated sound.

'Fine, be like that!' He wheeled about and stormed out of the house, slamming the door behind him.

Calliope finished her solitary meal, then went to bed, something she had recently begun to do whenever she felt unhappy.

~ 9 ~

In the morning, Iason ignored all her overtures. Calliope prepared rolls and coffee. She said he was behaving like a sulky child, but Iason did not deign to answer. What was he thinking? Was he hoping to wear her out with such juvenile tactics?

After breakfast, they both went to work, Calliope to school and Iason to the *pantopoleion*, which he now owned in partnership with Vangelis. Their father had died soon after Philippas passed away.

When her husband didn't come home that night, Calliope decided to lock him out – teach him a lesson once and for all! It was by then past one o'clock in the morning. She barred both entrances, then went to bed, waiting for sleep to transport her to a calmer realm. Let him go and sleep at his mother's house! Let him cry on her ever-available shoulder!

She was awakened by loud banging. Iason was hissing her name, rattling the knocker, kicking at the door. Calliope sat up, drawing the quilt up to her neck. Rain was again pelting at the windows. He would not want to go to his mother, would be too ashamed to turn up, drenched, in the middle of the night. Her own mother slept like the dead, but they were surrounded by inquisitive neighbours. Sooner or later, someone was bound to be awakened by the fracas, and hasten to spread the gossip.

And still she dithered, listening to the slurred curses at the front entrance, the wind whining in the garden. Finally, she fumbled for her robe, slid off the bed and lit a candle. The pounding was growing louder. Barefoot, she stumbled across the bedroom, her shadow bouncing in the candlelight. She would not speak to him; would open the door, then head straight back to bed. Let him curse! Let him stay out every night! She would not stoop to answer a drunkard's ravings.

Cupping the candle flame, Calliope padded downstairs and across the foyer, shivering within her flannel robe. Through the rain came the sound of night birds, of waves assaulting the shore. The pounding went on and on.

Steeling herself, Calliope reached out and unlocked the door.

'Aaagh!'

She had sprung back, executing a chaotic jig. She had never before been physically struck; not even as a child. Her father had been passionately opposed to corporal punishment and her mother had not dared cross him. There would be fewer wars in the world, Philippas liked to say, if only people did not teach their children to respond to provocation with physical force.

Calliope stood paralysed, her left hand still clutching the candle, the right sheltering her stinging cheek. A spurt of blood was trickling down from the corner of her mouth. Gingerly, she touched it, recoiling from the sight of her own bloodied fingers.

What now?

The question kept repeating itself as, at last, Calliope left the foyer. It was now well after two. Reeking of ouzo and stale cigarettes, Iason had disappeared towards the outhouse but was now bumbling back, crashing onto the divan. His eyes were bloodshot, the fly on his trousers unbuttoned. Almost instantly, he began to snore.

Calliope found herself lifting kitchen utensils at random, clutching them for a moment as if trying to recall their precise purpose, then replacing them with a shaky hand – on the wall, the shelves, the scarred kitchen table. There was something maddening about the kitchen's irreproachable order: the hanging plaits of garlic, the gleaming copper pans, the dry bouquets of wild herbs.

The clock in the foyer went on ticking. Soon, it struck three. The room was damp and silent, except for the rain striking the windowpanes. Dazed by her own impotence, Calliope left the kitchen and, heavy-footed, began to mount the stairs.

Her bed was waiting for her. Her mouth had stopped bleeding, but something within her had begun to ebb away and could not be arrested.

There was no turning back. The knowledge came creeping towards her, stunning with its icy clarity. The bedroom was frigid, its walls staring back at her with mute disapproval. Out in the garden, the rain went on falling. An owl began to call, then abruptly stopped.

~ 10 ~

She did not go back to sleep that night. At the first crack of light, Calliope rose and started the fire, ignoring her mother's sighs. Iason was still snoring on the kitchen divan, evincing no awareness of morning. Calliope and Mirto sat drinking coffee, as laconically polite as strangers sharing a cabin on a ferry.

'It's stopped raining,' Mirto observed at length. The neighbour's wireless was already on. She would stop in the *agora*, Calliope decided, and get Vangelis to come and rouse his brother out of his stupor.

Shivering under her wool cape, she trudged down the cobblestoned steps, the early-morning mists whorling above the rooftops. Many of the houses were still shuttered but, here and there, she could hear fragmented talk and children's cries, the clatter of dishes behind kitchen windows. The sky hung low, bloated with clouds. A stray cat sat on a stone balustrade, resolutely licking its fur.

In the *agora*, Vangelis was rolling up the shutters when Hektor came galloping up the street, his turbanned head thrust forward, his arm jabbing the air. 'Va-va-van-gelis! Va—'

Iason's brother turned. Hektor was making odd guttural sounds, his left hand clutching the top of his breeches, the right gesturing frantically.

'What is it, Hektor?' Vangelis glanced towards Calliope but did not greet her. 'Well, spit it out for heaven's sake, Hektor!'

Hektor was rolling his head, blinking furiously as he tried to convey some momentous news – something he had just heard in the *kapheneion*. There was mention of the Prime Minister, but Hektor's speech was more fractured than ever. 'He woke him up. He . . . he . . .'

Something about a message. Something he'd heard over the wireless.

'What happened, Hektor?' Calliope asked. 'Please look at me. Tell me.' Hektor was blinking furiously, scratching at his groin.

'Me-ta-xas,' he croaked. 'Metaxas . . . said . . . said no!'

Calliope and Vangelis exchanged mystified glances.

'No to what?' Calliope asked.

'No to the Italian envoy!'

These words were unexpectedly tossed out by the *hamam* caretaker, who was huffing towards them, his empty sleeve flapping in the wind. A decorated war hero, Calliope's neighbour had lost an arm in the Balkan trenches. He seemed at least as excited as Hektor, but far more coherent.

And, at last, Calliope understood. All the time she and Iason had been engaged in their domestic confrontation, all the time she had been stumbling about, grappling with her private chaos, a historic event was taking place in Athens. In the early hours of the morning, Mussolini's emissary had paid an urgent visit to their own ailing Prime Minister, demanding an immediate right of passage through strategic Greek territory. Entrenched in Albania, the Italians ostensibly wanted to ensure Greek neutrality.

'They gave us three hours to decide!' Spyros was saying. 'Three hours, the bastards. But—'

'Me-Metaxas said no!' Hektor managed to bring out at last. 'He—'

'He said no?' Calliope echoed. 'But the Italians have the Germans on their side!'

'Well, he said no anyway.' Spyros heaved a sigh. 'We're in for it now! It's war for sure now, *Kyria* Calliope!'

But Calliope was already spinning away, muttering over her shoulder. She had to tell the doctor. Outside the *kapheneion*, several men stood listening to the blaring wireless. Hektor had got it right: Metaxas had conceded Italy's superior strength, but had refused to yield. Mussolini's troops were already invading northern Greece.

Calliope sped on, dry-mouthed, a muddled prayer rising in her brain. Turning a corner, she almost ran into a woman bearing a large aluminium platter meant for the communal oven. Three schoolgirls traipsed behind her, giggling, satchels clinging to their narrow backs.

'Go home!' Calliope blurted without slowing down. 'Tell everyone to go home!'

More children stopped on the street and gaped after the schoolmistress, like newborn goats discovering the light of day. The church bells began to peal. A stray cat darted out of an alley and scrambled up a pomegranate tree. It was going on eight o'clock. The morning bus had just arrived and a gypsy peddling yoyos stopped and sweet-talked the cat, who was meowing from the top of the tree. The street was quickly emptying. A stonemason shouted to his partner, then hurried down, wheelbarrow clattering on the cobblestones. The church bells went on tolling and tolling.

~ 11 ~

A week after October's call to arms, Calliope's uncle, the mayor, suffered a heart attack, but the controversial Ioannis Metaxas had overnight become a national hero.

'We'll beat the stuffing out of those cocky bastards!' the draftees had promised their weeping women. 'We'll show Mussolini what we Greeks are made of!'

The women shed tears, but wasted no time taking over fields and orchards. With the sudden shortage of hands, Calliope and Mirto, too, had to pick their own olives. Every morning, Mirto would mount a mule and set out towards rural Eftalou. The hamlet was a kilometre away. In the afternoon, she would be replaced by her daughter and Eleni Bastia, Calliope's erstwhile pupil.

There were sunny days in November but, more often than not, rain would pelt the grey countryside. Since the trees offered scant shelter, the women went on working through the downpour. They beat the ripe olives off the tree branches; they sat on their haunches for hours, gathering the fallen fruit into giant baskets. Although the work was arduous, Mirto's newly found purpose was making her cheeks rosy. She had begun to laugh again.

The adjacent orchard was owned by Zenovia the fortune-teller, who had roped in her tenant, Hektor, to help with the olive harvest. He might be a fool and a drunkard, but Hektor saw to it that the solitary old woman never ran out of food or firewood, and that her cats were fed whenever she felt indisposed.

'You have to take the wind as you find it,' Zenovia stated during a picnic lunch under the olive trees. It was an unusually balmy afternoon and the women were resting in the sunshine, mulling over the changes brought on by the recent draft. 'That's one thing life teaches you: take the wind as you find it!'

Calliope nodded vaguely, fondling her snoozing dog. The old woman's advice might be perfectly sound, but it offered scant help in dealing with one's emotional chaos.

Leaving the ageing women to their talk and sighs, Calliope and Eleni scrambled up and began to do cartwheels under the olive trees. Eleni was barely fifteen, but already engaged to marry the village telegraphist. She would have been picking her own olives had her blacksmith father not lost his assets in a poker game shortly before the draft.

There had been no letters from the front, but the new headmaster, whose brother was a career officer, had reported that the Italian troops were trapped in the mountains, mired in mud; that the Greeks had not yet suffered a single casualty. If this was patriotic hyperbole, it was one the villagers warmly welcomed, especially as it had come from the punctilious new headmaster.

Philippas Adham's successor hailed from the village of Aghiassos but affected the refined manners of an Athenian intellectual. He was a slight man with weak eyes and a bullet-like head. His habitual squint irritated Calliope, if only because she had come to associate it with his barely suppressed disapproval.

Stamatis was not much older than Calliope, but he was better qualified, and increasingly sceptical of her idiosyncratic approach to pedagogy. She was considered a fine teacher, but one given to neglecting official curriculum in favour of Aesop's fables or a Hans Christian Andersen tale.

Calliope, for her part, thought her colleague a pompous pedant, capable of putting even his keenest pupils to sleep. He was fond of sprinkling his lessons with pithy proverbs and classical allusions, and his choice of words could make the most banal utterance sound like ancient Greek.

'Would you please transfer your weight to an alternate seat!' she overheard him bark one day, ordering an unruly pupil to move. 'An alternate seat, if you please!'

How she laughed at that! Secretly – a little guiltily – she wished that Stamatis, too, had been drafted. The headmaster was obviously myopic but, stopping in the *agora* to have her shoes repaired, Calliope wondered why the cobbler, a strapping young bachelor, had been draft-exempted as well. The doctor refused to tell her but, as the islanders liked to say, 'You can keep a secret from everyone, except God and a village.'

~ 12 ~

The doctor sat on a velvet settee, pensively jiggling the brandy in his glass. It was St Basil's Day, the beginning of a new year.

'A man grows rather attached to someone whose life he saved,' he was saying.

'Really?' Calliope said. 'Not the other way around, Uncle?'

Elias Dhaniel looked up with a little smile. 'No, *koritsi mou*. Take it from me: nothing perishes faster than gratitude. Nothing, whereas . . .' He stopped and glanced at his children, who were on the floor, squabbling over a new game.

'Whereas?'

'Whereas most people are loath to relinquish any reminder of their own virtue.'

Calliope dimpled. The exchange had been prompted by the mention of a note from a Turkish grocer who had risked his own life to save Dhaniel from a band of raging Turkish patriots. Once a year, just before Christmas, the Turk wrote to the doctor, to wish him a happy new year, and offer news of his own family. There had been no one to save Elias Dhaniel's family, who had perished in Smyrna, in the 1920s.

The doctor was by now in his early forties: a sandy-haired, rumpled-looking man who, Calliope thought, resembled a poet more than a physician. Not that she had ever met a poet, but she'd read about them in foreign novels. There was something vaguely ascetic about Dhaniel's features, but his expression suggested a man listening to a joke with one ear and to some melancholy narrative with the other.

Dhaniel had paused to reprimand his bickering children.

'It may sound strange,' he went on, 'but you're far more likely to encounter goodwill among people who've done you a good turn than those you yourself have helped in any way.'

Calliope mulled this over. 'People don't like to feel too indebted, I suppose?'

'Precisely.'

They both chuckled. This was the kind of conversation she had seldom had since her father's death, and was enjoying on this first day of the new year, with the four boisterous children gathered about, absorbed in their new games. Calliope had travelled to Mytilene just before Christmas, returning with gifts for the doctor's children. She had helped her mother prepare a sumptuous chicken dish with walnuts and pomegranate seeds, accompanied by sultan's pilaf.

After dinner, Mirto had gone upstairs for a nap, so it was Calliope who served the doctor his brandy, slipping into a discussion of Bulgaria's potential alliance with the Axis powers. The children went on playing on the floor. There was a threadbare Turkish rug inherited from Calliope's grandparents. A shining large copper brazier stood glowing in the centre of the room.

It was beginning to rain when a knock came at the entrance door. The butcher's son had been sent over to say that his sister's newborn had fallen ill. He begged the doctor to examine the child.

Dhaniel left immediately. He was gone for an hour, during which Calliope put the kitchen to order. Soon after, Mirto came down, calling the children to come to the kitchen. She sat all four of them at the dining table, then gave them leftover dough to play with, along with a dish of raisins and almonds to be made into eyes, noses, ears.

They were still playing when the doctor returned. He stood rain-splattered in the doorway, shaking his umbrella. A pale moon was drifting across the sky, trailing thunderclouds. Calliope closed the door.

'Another brandy?'

'Please.' Dhaniel lowered himself onto the settee, his eyes coming to rest on the Alexious' wedding photograph. Calliope traced the doctor's gaze and her thoughts flew towards her absent husband: Iason preparing to leave for the front, Iason hunkered down in some Albanian trench, with the snow falling, falling.

At that moment, as if to distract her from her melancholy musings, Calliope's godson ran in from the kitchen. A cherubic-looking toddler, little Aristides had huge hazel eyes and pale, silky hair yet to be cut. Frightened by an owl's cry, he clambered into his godmother's lap, thrust his thumb into his mouth and promptly fell asleep. Dhaniel and Calliope exchanged fond smiles. Not for the first time, the thought that the child had never known his mother sent a spasm of pain through Calliope's chest, though she could not imagine loving the boy any more passionately had he been her own.

The six-week-old infant the doctor had been called to treat was not breathing when Dhaniel arrived at the butcher's house. He'd been nursed and put down to sleep, then found dead a few hours later.

The doctor had been unable to establish the cause of death. Babies, he told Calliope, sometimes died for no apparent reason. He had arrived to find the infant's grandmother shrieking about the evil eye, while her daughter sat rubbing the dead infant's body with olive oil, sure that the doctor would be able to revive her baby.

'You have no idea how discouraged I feel sometimes!' Dhaniel sipped his brandy. 'We live with one foot in the Middle Ages, the other in the twentieth century,' he said, gazing at his sleeping son. 'The thing is, I don't even know if they're telling the truth,' he added after a moment. 'For all I know, they'd given the child something they won't tell me about. Something to make him nurse better, or grow fatter. Who knows?' He sighed, swirling the amber liquid.

Ever since the pharmacy opened in Molyvos, the villagers had been buying drugs as if they were Turkish Delights, there being no law requiring a prescription. If a neighbour had been helped by some medication, someone else would be sure to hurry and buy it. Why waste time and money on a doctor, they reasoned, gulping down heart pills for gout, antispasmodics for blood in the urine.

'Incredible.' Calliope crossed her legs, unintentionally waking her godson. She was wearing a pair of new, very light stockings and her favourite cerise dress, with a matching velvet ribbon around her neck.

Mirto came in, bearing a tray of cookies baked by the doctor's mother-in-law. After his wife's death, Stella Gravari had come from Mytilene to raise the children, but she spent the holidays in the capital, with her elder daughter's family.

Mirto served the cookies, then the doctor said it was time to go.

'Oh!' cried Calliope. 'We haven't made our new year's resolutions yet!'

Elias Dhaniel smiled. When he was about her age, he said, he'd resolved never to make new year's resolutions, since he invariably failed to keep them. 'But if you must do it, I'd like you to make an extra one – just to please me.'

'What?' Calliope smiled over her godson's head.

'I think it's time you stopped calling me "uncle," don't you? It makes me feel as old as Alekos,' he stated. Alekos was Molyvos's oldest man, rumoured to be a hundred.

'Oh, go on with you!' Mirto interjected. 'You hardly look a day older than the day you arrived from Smyrna!'

The doctor smiled at Calliope. 'Your mother should resolve never to flatter foolish old men,' he said.

Aristides slid off his godmother's lap to join his sisters on the floor. Calliope noted that he had a chocolate smudge on his new sailor collar. For some reason, the dark stain tugged at her heart. Mirto, meanwhile, had refilled the empty brandy glasses, poured herself a drink, then stood with her glass raised in a holiday toast.

'Here's to a happy new year!' she said solemnly. 'May it be better – much better – than the last. And may it bring our Iason back safe and sound,' she added.

They all drank to that: Mirto, Calliope and the pensive-looking doctor. The children sat cross-legged on the faded carpet, absorbed in licking chocolate cream off their sticky fingers.

~ 13 ~

The year started on a melancholy note, with the sudden return of two gravely wounded men. Eleni Bastia's uncle had come back with his head swathed in bandages; Mimis Lyras, the football champion, had his leg amputated below the knee.

Although the Italians had failed to repel the Greeks, both Mussolini's and General Papagos's troops had been thwarted by Albanian weather. The *kapheneion*'s wireless, which had once blared out exultant reports of Greek victories, was now broadcasting bulletins listing the names of the dead and wounded. As Easter approached, many believed the Germans were preparing to send reinforcements.

'They're allies after all, they've got to help Mussolini, like it or not!'

'They are allies, but if they planned to help them Italians, wouldn't they've done so by now? Why didn't they send their troops all winter if they wanted to help, eh?'

'Why? Because they know those Italians are bumbling fools, that's why! Their fathers must have been singing arias while they fucked their mothers!'

The men guffawed. A joke was a joke, but there was only one fact from which to draw a modicum of hope: Churchill had offered to send expeditionary forces to Greece, to buttress the country's defence against potential German aggression.

One night Calliope had a dream: Iason had returned home from Albania, brain-damaged and blind, with his manhood blown off by flying shrapnel.

Flinging back her blankets, she scrambled out of bed, her heart wild. For a moment she paused, muddled, then swept straight across the room, towards a massive wardrobe she had shared with her husband since their wedding day. The house was at its coldest just before dawn, but Calliope ignored the chill, propelled by a mysterious force. Perhaps she was still dreaming?

She became aware of her own laboured breath, of an odd taste clinging to the back of her mouth. Standing before the wardrobe, she reached out and opened the creaky pine doors with their floral motifs; then stopped, suddenly hesitant, as if some malevolent spirit might come leaping at her from behind the suspended garments. For a moment, she was about to retreat and dash back to bed, but found herself instead leaning deep into the old wardrobe, pressing her face into her absent husband's abandoned clothes: his trousers, his shirts, his faded blue cardigan.

Iason. What was she doing? What was she searching for?

In the years to come, Calliope would say that she must have had the sort of premonition Zenovia the fortune-teller claimed to have experienced before her son perished in the Balkan trenches. Calliope did not believe in premonitions, but there it was: impossible to believe it; impossible not to …

'Forgive me,' Iason had said, gazing at her humbly, deeply. 'Please forgive me.'

He had been all but ready to leave for the front; had clasped her hand and stroked her fingers, waiting for absolution. He made no attempt to kiss her. They stood facing each other outside the wind-swept town hall, surrounded by a noisy, overwrought crowd. There had been announcements, and speeches, and patriotic songs. The military transport trucks were waiting. The women and children were saying goodbye to their men, whom they might never see again.

What was there to say? Everything and nothing. The hand strok-ing Calliope's fingers, her cheek, was the hand that, only a few hours earlier, had viciously slapped her face. She could still feel both sting and insult, but, at the same time, a small, unexpected surge of wifely tenderness.

Her feuding emotions had left Calliope stunned, too muddled to respond to her husband's apparent contrition. Though her rage against Iason would take days to dissipate, awareness was already dawning that solicitude could be almost as unsettling as rage.

But she was only twenty-five that autumn of 1940, still getting to know herself, still resisting inner contradiction. What she longed for, in those final moments with her husband, was emotional clarity. Unable to find it, she stood barely breathing, inwardly agitated, out-wardly as impassive as the façade of the freshly painted town hall.

Everyone's farewells were necessarily brief. But, in the years to come, Calliope would always recall how, in that short, chaotic inter-val, she had stood dry-eyed amid the lamenting wives and mothers, trembling a little, enveloped in silence.

Oh, she had wished him well as he turned to go. She had done that much. But no, she had never answered his final plea. Iason had marched away towards the waiting trucks with death in his eyes. Unforgiven.

It would take a long time for her to forgive herself.

TWO

~ 1 ~

The day the Germans arrived in the village was not the first time the *kapheneion* owner's daughter was seen weeping in public. She had been known as Dora the weeper ever since her fiancé, who had been hospitalised in Athens for injuries suffered in Albania, cancelled their matrimonial plans.

Dora's younger sister had been betrothed to the former football champion, Dora to the baker's brother. Before the Albanian war ended, however, Dora's fiancé wrote to say that he'd had the misfortune of getting a nursing auxiliary in the family way. Sadly and apologetically, he begged Dora to release him from his engagement vows.

Dora did not write back. In the years to come, she would often be observed weeping, not only for her own melancholy fate, but for the entire world's sorrows. Even after the war, she would continue to be known for two things: her remarkable ability to start bawling at the slightest provocation, and her refusal, after being jilted by the baker's brother, to eat baked products ever again.

On that spring morning in 1941, Dora and her father were on their way to the *kapheneion* when they spotted a motor vehicle roaring towards the village. A German jeep, raising dust and stones, almost running over a stray dog snoozing on the gravel road. It promised to be a fine day. Dora was about to help in the *kapheneion* because her grandfather had contracted bronchitis. Dora's mother had her hands full caring for the old man; her sister was busy helping her future mother-in-law. And so it fell to Dora to accompany her father, and be the first to spread the momentous news.

'They've come! The Germans have come!' she announced, darting from shop to shop, spilling out the news to merchants, shoppers, hawkers. She was a seventeen-year-old girl, with mellow eyes and long, narrow nostrils that gave her the look of someone perpetually trying to sniff out some peculiar scent.

'We saw them with our own eyes, me and my father! They're here – in Molyvos! They're here, I tell you!'

There were no Germans around the *agora* but, having alerted everyone in her path, Dora fled to her father's *kapheneion*, her headscarf askew. 'Ach, Holy Virgin, what's to become of us?' she sobbed. 'Why would God free us from the Turks, only to let us fall into the Germans' clutches – why, *Panaghia mou*?'

It was a question neither the Virgin nor her father seemed likely to answer. A man of few words, Yannis Rozakis was often sought in times of dispute or trouble. If there was a solution to a conflict or problem, the *kapheneion* owner was sure to find it. The one thing he seemed utterly helpless against was the sight of a weeping woman. He fled to the balcony, which was as far as he could get from the sound of his daughter's sobs. And there he stood, leaning over the sea, puffing on a cigarette, while Dora pursued her unanswerable questions.

By noon, the shopkeepers had all abandoned the *agora*. Housewives had stopped hanging laundry and shaking rugs, and bolted indoors with their whining children. A telegram had just come through, but Tomas Kafatou could not find anyone to deliver it. The wire had been sent by Johnny the Australian's sister and her husband, who had just come back from Melbourne.

Surveying the street, Tomas spotted the *kapheneion* owner and his daughter, who were locking up early. Would they do him a favour and take the telegram down to Dimitris's elderly mother? Fotini lived down in the harbour; Rozakis and his family lived halfway down, but Dora said she would be glad to deliver the message and read it to Fotini.

Tomas thanked her, scratching through his thinning hair. He was a tall, loose-jointed young man – an epileptic – with keen eyes set in a long, freckled face. Even on an ordinary day, he had a deeply alert air, like a dog hearing a distant whistle.

Tomas was still at his post when classes ended and Calliope came sweeping uphill, followed by a cluster of pupils. She had been singing along as they approached the shops, but all at once stopped, taking in the empty *plateia*, the deserted *agora*. The afternoon was eerily quiet. You could hear the mulberry leaves stir in the breeze, a stray dog rooting through an abandoned grocery crate.

Seeing Tomas, Calliope motioned her straggling pupils to wait while she found out what was going on. But in her marrow, she already knew. A week earlier, The American had reported seeing a German troopship dock in Mytilene, accompanied by two destroyers flying Italian flags.

'I think I'll take the kids home,' Calliope muttered to Tomas. Then she turned away from the telegraph office with her arms spread, like a mother hen uselessly flapping her wings to protect her chicks.

~ 2 ~

The *kapheneion* owner had forbidden his daughter to go to the harbour alone. He would grab a cheese pie, then walk down with her, to deliver the telegram and see what was what. His wife stopped him to brush dandruff off his shoulder. His daughter Anna was preparing liquorice root for Mimis's cough. Dora waited, looking out the window. Much later, she would recall that, right after she left the house with her father, they found a dead crow lying in their path, and that she forced her father to turn around and take another route to the harbour.

As they made their way down the acacia-lined street, Dora and her father encountered Ourania the seamstress, who was taking a plate of freshly laid eggs to her elderly aunt. The doctor's mother-in-law was chasing little Aristides, a bowl in one hand, a spoon in the other. The village artist – a young deaf-mute who never left the house without her drawing pad – was seated on the carpentry shop's threshold, sketching, as usual. Further down, just before the downward turn to the

harbour, Michalis the sexton had stopped to greet the building contractor's father, who had recently suffered a mild heart attack. The old
man's wife had outlawed tobacco, so he was smoking at the gate, doing
his best to entertain passersby.

As Rozakis and Dora approached, Lemos was narrating the story
of his nephew's amorous pig, which had been choked to death by an
unwilling sow.

'Ach, females are often in a foul mood, aren't they?' The old man
cackled, picked a thread of tobacco off his lip, and turned to say hello.

Rozakis returned the greeting, but said nothing about the invaders.
Dour-faced, he shuffled on with Dora, until they reached the harbour.

And then, abruptly, father and daughter stopped.

On the wharf, directly across from Fotini's *kapheneion*, stood a
German officer, his binoculars aimed at the distant mountains. In
front of the harbour guard office, two soldiers were squatting by a
parked jeep, replacing a tyre. A helmeted guard stood watching, a rifle
slung across his chest.

'*Kalimera!*' The officer had wheeled about and was striding towards
Dora and Yannis Rozakis, a look of resolute goodwill pasted on his
face. He was tall and straight-backed and, as Dora would eventually
tell her sister, so courteous! So dashing! His uniform, she would report
breathlessly, perfectly matched his eyes!

Despite the confident greeting, it soon became apparent that the
German possessed a Greek vocabulary of barely a dozen words. Fishing a folded note out of his tunic pocket, he went on to read a sentence
which he mispronounced but which they understood to be an enquiry
about Mayor Metrophanis.

Neither Rozakis nor his daughter responded to the question.

'Where-is-the-mayor?' the officer repeated, spacing out the words.
'*Kyrios* Metrophanis,' he said yet again, his r's like the sputter of a
motorcycle engine.

The lieutenant's Greek might sound atrocious, but when he aimed
his clear, enquiring gaze at Dora, the young woman found herself
placing her clasped hands under her tilted head: the mayor was ill,
she mimed.

The officer nodded; he seemed to understand. 'Police,' he said then, still speaking Greek. 'Where-is-the-police?'

Rozakis kept his gaze on the German's polished boots, but Dora began to gesture, doing her best to answer the foreigner's question. The police station was up in the village. You got there by taking the long harbour road, then turning left uphill, then left again, almost as far as the cemetery.

The officer glanced up towards the village. It must have occurred to him that he might not readily find what he was looking for in the maze of streets on the looming hill. 'Come with me,' he said to Dora in German. 'Please.'

The girl did not understand the request, but her father seemed to. Speaking Greek, Rozakis said that village girls did not walk about with men, especially not foreigners.

The German looked fleetingly at a loss. He summoned his adjutant. Turning back to Rozakis, he motioned towards the hill, asking to be guided to the police station. He said 'please' again. He introduced himself in German. '*Leutnant* Lorenz Umbreit.'

Rozakis hesitated. He instructed Dora to deliver the telegram and stay with Fotini until he came to get her. Then he turned his back on the sea and began to shuffle uphill, with the air of a man heading to the gallows.

The lieutenant and his adjutant followed. The sea lay on their right, frothing with tiny white wavelets. On top of the seawall, a cat lay curled up in the sun, its tail twitching, its eyes slitted with sleep. Rozakis walked with his hands clasped behind his back, pressing his worry beads all the way to the police station. Inside, the chief was seated at his desk, trimming his new moustache before a small mirror set against the black telephone. When he looked up and saw the Germans, Christopoulos dropped the scissors, jumped to his feet and sent the mirror flying. He then uttered the only foreign words he knew.

'*Nasil yardimci olabilirim?*'

'What, you expect them to understand Turkish?' Yannis Rozakis sputtered. 'Turkish, you blockhead?!' He stood for a moment, his birthmark throbbing. 'And why would you offer to help them anyway?'

He shook his head, made a hopeless gesture, then turned on his heels and tramped back towards the sunlight.

~ 3 ~

There were still no Germans around the *agora* but, having dropped off the last of her pupils, Calliope became aware of her heart as a discrete organ. It felt like some panic-stricken creature, a swallow or a mouse, trapped inside a chimney. The sensation slowed her down as she began to climb home, stopping to catch her breath halfway up the hill. All around her, the neighbours' houses stood mute and shuttered, except for one derelict Turkish house which had long since lost all its windows.

For years, whenever she thought about their erstwhile Turkish neighbours, Calliope would experience a spasm of remorse, recalling how she and her young cousins would amuse themselves by hiding the shoes left at the entrance to the village mosque. The Turks would come out, blinking against the sunlight. They would search and search, swearing away in Turkish, while three pairs of childish eyes peered through gate cracks, hands clamped over gap-toothed mouths.

Despite such childish pranks, there had been no animosity between the Greek and Turkish Molyviates. They had not worshipped together and had not intermarried, but the men had worked and played checkers together, and the women exchanged household tips and helped each other through countless domestic crises.

Then, one day, they were all gone, forced into sudden exile. By the time Mussolini had started to flex his muscles, the Turkish house in Calliope's neighbourhood was so decrepit there was talk of building a cinema on the site. Iason had been one of the men championing this proposal, but now he, too, was gone.

Missing on the field of honour.

This was the official euphemism offered during the Albanian war. Calliope, scanning the Ministry of War's telegram, had been assailed by a vision of Iason's body decomposing on alien soil, maggots swarming through his wounds, vultures pecking at his lifeless eyes.

A peculiar odour had accompanied the vision: acrid and vaguely familiar, like the smell of freshly slaughtered lamb dangling from a butcher's hook.

The telegram had arrived just before Easter, but the lurid images had not yet lost their power to ambush. Calliope, recognising the warning signs, had turned her back on the derelict Turkish house, only to find her legs revolting against her own weight.

Flying from the hilltop fortress, fluttering in the sea breeze, was a German flag. A bold black swastika, a red-and-white background, overlooking the blue Aegean.

— 4 —

At the town hall, German and Greek flags were flying side by side. Calliope had stopped at the gate, gazing up at the two flapping banners. There was the familiar scent of roses planted by a Turkish pasha's wife, the sound of an aggrieved child whining over some parental injunction. Two stray kittens were toying with a bird fallen out of a nest. Chickens squabbled in some nearby courtyard.

All this was so commonplace Calliope would have hardly registered any of it had it not been for the presence of German sentries. Two young, armed soldiers scowling beneath their metal helmets.

A morning like any other. A morning like no other.

The megaphone was blaring out the German national anthem, loud enough to be heard all over the neighbourhood. *Deutschland, Deutschland, über Alles.* Calliope realised she had forgotten to bring her dictionary, but she was often forgetful. It was the German anthem that was making her stomach churn: *Germany above all others!*

I must go in, she told herself. I have no choice.

She had been summoned through the chief of police, after Rozakis had turned up at the station, flanked by the two Germans. Unable to make sense of what the officer wanted, Christopoulos had sent Sergeant Floros to fetch Dhaniel from the clinic. He had always thought the doctor knew German, but Dhaniel claimed he didn't.

Lieutenant Umbreit, however, turned out to have a much better command of French than he did of Greek. They had been given an interpreter, he explained to the doctor, but the young recruit knew only Classical Greek and had proven virtually useless. They were waiting for a replacement, but had been led to believe that Molyvos's mayor spoke German.

'Only a little,' Dhaniel said. 'Anyway, the mayor's had a heart attack. He wouldn't be much use to you now.'

'Anyone else?' the lieutenant asked. 'We need someone . . . someone to act as a liaison officer.'

'Liaison officer,' the doctor echoed, looking uncertain.

'An intermediary between us and the villagers,' the lieutenant elaborated.

'Yes. Yes, I see.' Elias Dhaniel sighed, paused to reflect, then – as he would later tell Calliope – decided it might actually be advantageous to have her working for the Germans. He gave her name to the lieutenant. Calliope Alexiou.

The German raised an eyebrow. 'A village woman?'

'A schoolmaster's daughter,' replied the doctor. He studied the floor. 'Her German's adequate, but . . . well, she's the schoolmistress now. She's busy—'

'Do not worry, doctor. I'm sure we can arrive at some sort of arrangement.'

Dhaniel quietly translated the ensuing exchange. The police chief must see to it that the schoolmistress presented herself at the town hall in the morning, when Major von Herden was expected to meet with the village council.

It might have sounded like a request but, calling on Calliope that evening, Christopoulos made it clear: this was an order. 'Not mine, you understand. I had nothing to do with it. It's those bloody Germans. They want you there at ten o'clock.'

And so Calliope came. She arrived a few minutes late, pausing outside the town hall garden, her palms damp with sweat. A praying mantis had landed on one of the rosebushes and sat there, eyeing her with its sceptical eyes.

She opened the gate, adjusting the satchel over her shoulder. *I have no choice.* The two sentries watched her climb the front stairs: a tall, black-clad young woman wearing an old widow's kerchief, her golden eyes bright with anguish.

They must have been told to expect her. Hearing her name, one of the sentries promptly escorted Calliope indoors, announcing her to his superior.

'Guten Morgen!' The officer introduced himself. Unlike the stiff-necked sentry, he appeared as relaxed and amiable as a social host dealing with some last-minute party arrangements, pleasantly surprised to be interrupted by a friend's early arrival.

Calliope did not return the greeting. She merely nodded, eyes riveted to the eagle-and-swastika badge above Lieutenant Umbreit's breast pocket. Eventually, she looked up. She noted that the German's eyes were the colour of a wintry sea; he had a dented chin resembling her father's, though the officer's face was more angular, as high-coloured as a mountaineer's.

The German anthem had ended, giving way to the Greek. The lieutenant ushered Calliope into the former pasha's reception room, where the village council was already assembled. Kyriakos Himonas, The American, was sitting in for the ailing mayor. The doctor and headmaster were lodged on his right, along with *Papa* Emanouil; the *kapheneion* owner and the olive mill owner were on the left, as restive as schoolchildren during a prolonged lesson. They were all waiting for the major, who was said to be on his way.

Coffee was served. Dhaniel did not touch his, but the olive mill owner spilled some on his carefully knotted tie. The German lieutenant had stepped out and was conferring with his adjutant. Calliope stared at her own hands with sudden astonishment. They were trembling like the hands of an old woman. They didn't seem to belong to her, to respond to her inner commands.

She hid the hands in her lap. The Greek anthem came to an abrupt end. There was the sound of clicking heels, a flurry of *Heil Hitlers* at the front entrance. And then the lieutenant threw open the conference room door. Major von Herden had arrived.

— 5 —

The major was older, shorter, and darker than Lieutenant Umbreit. Calliope had never met anyone with such pale, pale eyes; eyes virtually colourless except for the thin grey rim encircling the iris. A wolf's eyes, she said to herself, recalling a picture book she had recently bought for her godson. And had she got the German's first name right? Could it really be Wolf?

It turned out to be Rolf. Calliope realised her error when the major rose to give an introductory speech. He cleared his throat, letting his eyes sweep over the Molyvos council. The Germans, he stated, had not come to the island as enemies but as well-meaning friends. *Gut meinende Freunde.*

'The occupation of this island is temporary,' he went on, waiting for Calliope to render his words into Greek. 'Our purpose here is to protect you against a British attack.' The major paused. The young lieutenant was taking notes, as was the village doctor. Now that the loudspeaker had stopped blaring, birds could be heard, twittering in the garden. A distant goat had begun to bleat.

'Naturally, we shall not interfere with your authorities,' the major was saying, 'nor molest anyone – provided the Occupation is not challenged, of course.' *Voraus-gesetzt natürlich, dass die Besetzung in keiner Weise eine Herausforderung darstellt.*

The proviso was added as an afterthought. Calliope, translating, saw Dhaniel exchange looks with the acting mayor. Kyriakos's tie was askew, his hair in utter revolt, as if he had forgotten to comb it on getting out of bed. She thought of her own husband as he used to look on waking in the morning, and a wave of helpless tenderness washed over her heart. Momentarily distracted by her own musings, she missed the major's next words – something about a speech Hitler had recently given.

'And I can tell you the Führer singled out the Greeks for special praise,' he was saying emphatically. 'No other nation – not one – fought with the valour and tenacity of your Greek soldiers!' The major went on and on in this vein, but eventually got down to spelling out German demands.

For, of course, there were demands. He spoke of an evening curfew, the necessity of adhering to the blackout guidelines. 'All the required materials will, of course, be provided.' The major paused, briefly scanning the Greek councillors' faces.

'Needless to say, all firearms must be surrendered,' he continued. 'But there are other . . . other important measures we'll have to ask your people to respect. We're preparing a list, but for now, all night fishing must stop. Stop,' he repeated emphatically. 'In a few days, permits will be issued for daytime fishing.'

Permits for fishing! Calliope saw amazement spread on the councillors' faces. This was a fishing village! Its inhabitants had lived off the sea from time immemorial!

A charged silence followed. The birthmark on Yannis Rozakis's forehead had visibly swelled; the acting mayor kept running his hand over his face, as if trying to decide whether a shave was called for. When she turned back, Calliope found the major wearing the pained expression of a parent forced to renege on a promise.

'School attendance will be cut to two hours daily,' he was saying, 'six days—'

'Two hours?!' Calliope blurted.

The major spread his palms. Calliope stared for a moment, then swallowed and turned to translate his words for the council's benefit. 'At least they're not demanding we conduct our classes in German,' she added without expression.

The statement was aimed at the headmaster but, turning back to the major, Calliope became aware of the young lieutenant's querying eyes. He appeared faintly amused, as if he'd guessed the nature of her aside. Did he understand more Greek than he let on? she wondered uneasily. He had a deliberate, distracted way of raking his hand through his hair, like a man absorbed in solving an intricate problem. The hair was wheat-coloured, as fine as a boy's.

'Any questions?' If not for his uniform, the major might have been a stern professor scanning his students' faces. His listeners were looking more restive than ever; they had been forbidden to smoke indoors. 'Please feel free to voice anything on your mind,' the major said: polite, encouraging. 'Anything at all.'

The *kapheneion* owner was the first to speak, asking about travel in the days to come. He didn't state the reason for his personal concern, but Calliope guessed it had to do with Rozakis's ailing brother in Mytilene, or perhaps his son, who had failed to return from the Albanian campaign. For weeks, there had been reports of families travelling to Epirus, to scour the battlefields for their missing relatives' remains.

The major said that trips around the island should present no problem, but travel by sea would henceforth require an official permit.

'Rest assured, you'll have permits for everything, including the usual trade with the mainland.'

Saying this, von Herden consulted his watch, conferred with the lieutenant, then went on to announce a brief interval. He must have a quick tour of the village, then hurry back to headquarters. Lieutenant Umbreit would conduct the second part of the conference. He would also be responsible for carrying out all further directives.

This, too, Calliope conveyed to her fellow villagers, wondering what 'further directives' could possibly mean. Her anxiety had not quite evaporated but, stepping outdoors with the doctor, she was conscious of a surge of relief: she had never expected foreign invaders to be so civilised.

'He even thanked me for my services!' she told Dhaniel, speaking of the major.

They went to sit on a garden bench. The other council members strolled about, smoking and arguing. They lingered by the fishpond, trying to decide how best to disseminate the Germans' demands.

The doctor was not taking part in the discussion. He could not, he said, think clearly, with all of them babbling together. He seemed, all at once, uncharacteristically testy. When Calliope spoke of German civility, he made a small, disgruntled gesture.

'Don't confuse fine manners with friendly intentions, *koritsi mou*,' he said.

'What? Would you rather have them flashing swords like the Turks?'

Dhaniel sighed, his eyes wandering around the garden. Suddenly, he reached out and plucked a coral-hued rose from one of the pasha's bushes, as if searching for consolation in the flower's beauty. He brought the rose to his nose, held it there for a moment, then passed it to Calliope.

'The garden is technically theirs now,' he said, 'but why should they mind? After all, they're only here to protect us from the British.'

Calliope paused. 'You don't believe them,' she said, scanning the doctor's face. She had enormous respect for Dr Dhaniel.

'Ach, Calliopitsa. They're here to protect their own interests. They think the Allies might try to land here from the Turkish coast.'

'But why should they ban night fishing? Do they think our fishermen might collaborate with the Allies?'

'Exactly. Or try to escape to the other side.' Dhaniel anticipated her next question. 'To join the Brits,' he said. 'Or our own forces in Egypt.'

'I see.'

Calliope mulled it over, watching the German major and his minions briskly stride away. Just before his heart attack, her uncle, the mayor, had voiced the possibility that Iason might be fighting in Egypt. It was widely known that some Albanian draftees had joined the Free Greek Army, but even Iason's mother didn't think her son was likely to be among them. Iason had hated army life. He would have sailed home the moment he got his discharge papers, she said.

And, for once, Calliope agreed with her mother-in-law. Reading Iason's letters, she had sensed he was rather anxious about her fidelity. On the other hand, what did she know about the changes a man might undergo after the horrors of a battlefield?

In the town hall garden, the councillors had reached a decision and were coming up to share it with the doctor. *Papa* Emanouil had undertaken to speak to *Papa* Iakovos. The two priests would announce the new measures after Sunday Mass; the acting mayor would see to it that notices went up in the *agora*.

The discussion was still in progress when the German adjutant appeared on the threshold. Lieutenant Umbreit was ready to resume.

~ 6 ~

The first thing to disappear from store shelves was bread. It was mid-June and, walking home from her new duties at the town hall, Calliope came upon a gaggle of women gathered outside the shuttered bakery, clucking like distraught hens. They stood huddled together in the midday glare, gesturing towards the sign Petros Morales had posted on his bakery door: NO BREAD.

There was no bread because there was no flour anywhere on the island. There was no flour because sea transports from the mainland had virtually stopped. Morales could have stayed behind to explain all this to the women, but had chosen not to.

'There's no bread,' Calliope told her mother. She went to the cistern for a glass of water. 'No one knows when – no one knows if – we'll have bread again.'

'No bread!' Mirto crossed herself. 'Mother of God, what next?' She was stirring a pot of thick lentil soup, which was not quite ready. Calliope was hungry and irritable, itchy all over in her mourning clothes.

'We can always eat cake, I suppose,' she said.

Mirto, alas, had never heard of Marie Antoinette. 'How can we bake cake when there's no flour?' She shook her head with well-practised forbearance. 'May their bones rot in pitch, Hitler and his cohorts!'

Calliope sat down to prepare her lessons. She taught only two hours a day now, but spent at least five at the town hall – usually in the late morning, but sometimes in the evening as well: translating the Germans' communiques, the acting mayor's questions, the villagers' complaints about permits, house searches, shortage of boat fuel. Even Hektor the fool had a grievance: there was too much rubbish put out by the Germans; he was now having to make extra trips to the village dump.

The dump was all the way up behind the fortress, not far from the watchtower the Germans had constructed to survey the sweep of sea between the Turkish coastline and Eftalou. A military seaplane was frequently seen hovering over the village; German boats kept patrolling the sea, on the lookout for British submarines, contraband, Greek Resistance fighters.

The Germans remained polite, but they didn't hesitate to requisition anything they needed, including Fotini's *kapheneion* in the harbour. The shop had become a German canteen, though Fotini was duly paid for serving the Wehrmacht soldiers.

Lieutenant Umbreit had settled into a spare room at the back of the town hall; his adjutant was billeted in the cellar, next to what used to be the servants' quarters but was now a detention cell. Eight recruits were lodged in the abandoned Turkish house, in Calliope's own neighbourhood. They had slept in tents while the house was restored and cleaned, with a skill and efficiency that left the neighbours agog.

There had been little left of the Turks' possessions, but the Germans had burned whatever they found. They disinfected every corner, they requisitioned mattresses from the villagers. Within a week, a huge swastika was posted above the entrance. The place seemed deserted during the day, but sometimes, sitting at her window late in the evening, Calliope would hear the German soldiers sing their melancholy songs.

The town hall had come to house both Greek and German administrative offices. Calliope spent much of her time running between floors, working at the desk she'd been assigned in the mayor's office, keeping at bay any thoughts of Iason. In the *agora*, villagers who had once detained her to enquire about their children's progress were stopping her now to pose questions she could seldom answer. Questions about produce or leather quotas, about confiscated fishing boats or relinquished gold. Gold was one of the commodities the Germans had demanded upon arrival; hoarding it was liable to the death penalty.

There was little gold around. The few villagers who possessed precious valuables did not hesitate to voice their resentment, as if Calliope were personally responsible for their confiscation.

'But it's not right – surely you can see it's not right,' her own mother-in-law protested. 'Expecting me to give up a family heirloom as if it was a sack of potatoes!'

Katina Alexiou was a widow in her late forties, with creamy, sumptuous flesh and blue eyes perpetually lit by the fire of indignation. Since her husband's death, much of Katina's energy had been expended in search of someone to blame for her various vexations. She would have continued about the gold had it not been for the timely arrival of Pericles: Katina's favourite son, with his sparkling blue eyes and unruly hair. Every day, the young man would comb and comb his black hair, resolutely flattening it, only to have it spring up again an hour or so later.

The boy plopped himself into a kitchen chair, to munch on olives and chat with his former teacher. They both had a passion for salty black olives. As a child, Calliope could seldom be bribed with sweets, but would have done anything for a handful of shrivelled black olives.

Pericles was going on seventeen now, but his attachment to his former teacher seemed undiminished. With his brother away, he often came around after school, offering to chop wood, or prune a fruit tree, or get rid of a large spider. Unlike his older brother, Pericles never mocked Calliope's arachnophobia. All he asked in return for his devotion was that she look over a new poem he had just written; often, two or three of them. Sometime around puberty, Pericles's interest in world geography had begun to fade, giving way to a new, lasting obsession with the power of words.

~ 7 ~

What the Occupation demanded above all was cunning. Due to the recent requisitioning of livestock, a medical certificate was required for the purchase of meat. Calliope's mother seemed healthy enough, but the doctor officially diagnosed anaemia, offering the false document with a little ironic flourish. Oddly, as soon as the certificate was issued, Mirto began to complain of real weakness in her legs and arms; sometimes of a malaise she could neither describe nor pinpoint.

Calliope was physically stronger than her mother, but her job as a go-between was proving to be far more complex than teaching. She found it as difficult to mediate between the Germans and the Greeks as she did between her own conflicted selves.

The Germans confused her. She pulsed with resentment against their authority, yet could not help admiring their competence and their courtesy. She bristled at the exclusion of Greek history from the school curriculum, at being obliged to facilitate the invaders' purpose, yet could not deny the pleasure derived from the daily challenge. She would not admit this even to the doctor, but there was undeniable satisfaction in improving her command of a language that her father had taught her, and that she'd seldom had occasion to practise, except with her godfather when his mayor's duties permitted it.

But now her uncle was bedridden and The American continued as acting mayor. He had time on his hands. Too much time, Kyriakos grumbled, now that his taxi stood virtually idle because of fuel shortages.

The American did his best to emulate Mayor Metrophanis. He never left home without donning a carefully knotted tie, never used a simple word if a longer one could be ferreted out of his meagre vocabulary. He had brought a miniature of his own patron saint to the office, dusted it with his tie, then set it conspicuously on the massive desk, next to a cherished American souvenir: the Statue of Liberty.

While still a young man, the stonemason's son had left the island and sailed away on a merchant ship. He worked in Chicago for some years, then returned to marry the well-dowered cousin of a Kaloni man with whom he had shared a sea cabin. Suddenly, Kyriakos was a man of means and status. His achievements were widely applauded and envied, but a few drinks, and especially the company of some passing stranger, soon had Kyriakos lapsing into a boastful mood.

'I'm not like you aristocrats,' he was given to saying in the presence of his social superiors. 'I've sweated buckets for everything I've got. Buckets, believe me!'

It was easier to believe this than the stories of Kyriakos's youthful exploits, especially those involving women in various ports of call. He was, when the Germans came, in his mid-forties; a solidly built man blessed with what was generally regarded as American drive and vigour.

Sharing the mayor's office, Calliope was often amused by Kyriakos's affectations; occasionally, she found it hard to suppress a sardonic comment. Nevertheless, she liked to hear Kyriakos reminisce about his travels, and thought him both amiable and good-looking – in a rugged, primitive sort of way.

~ 8 ~

Petra's Church of the Sweet Kissing Virgin was where Molyviates traditionally went on the Holy Day of the Assumption. Before the Occupation, most villagers would take the bus or hire the mayor's taxi. Some rode a farm cart or a mule, but virtually everybody went: it was one of the most sacred days on the Orthodox calendar.

In that first summer of the Occupation, most Molyviates made the pilgrimage to Petra on foot. It was five kilometres down an unpaved road but, what with the fuel shortage, the bus was no longer running.

The acting mayor had been granted a small quantity for medical emergencies. On that mid-August day in 1941, he had just enough fuel left for one round trip to Petra. He was taking his own family but, at the last moment, his father complained of an aching back, so Calliope's lame mother was invited to take the old man's place.

Mirto went, leaving Calliope to her own devices. Around six o'clock, after a long swim and a nap, she took Sappho for a walk. At the entrance to the village, two German soldiers were leaning against the sea wall, keeping an eye on things.

The harbour was deserted. There was the sound of breaking waves, of seagulls swooping above the rippling water. A rare moment of peace, of exquisite solitude. The sun was still beating down on her head, so Calliope removed her black headkerchief. Settling down on the bench outside the harbour guard office, she reached for her satchel and brought out a novel sent by her French relatives. Sappho scampered about, stopped to nuzzle Calliope's feet, then went tearing after a cat.

Half an hour had gone by when Lieutenant Umbreit came strolling into the harbour. He paused by the canteen, his eyes sweeping the deserted quay. Absorbed in her novel, Calliope was as yet unaware of his presence.

'*Guten Tag, Fräu Alexiou!*'

The officer had finally crossed the wharf, his cap in his hand. Though both voice and face conveyed nothing but friendly intentions, the greeting sent a dart of anxiety through Calliope. Had she overlooked some request yesterday? Had she forgotten to hand in something before going home? She was a hard worker, but occasionally absent-minded.

'*Guten Tag.*' She swallowed. She crossed her right leg over the left, clutching her book. Her eyes took in the pistol in the lieutenant's holster, the binoculars around his neck. She looked up slowly, her hand at rest on her open book.

'Beautiful day,' he said genially, eliciting a small inner sneer: a beautiful day in mid-August was hardly worth commenting on.

But his scent intrigued her. It was a fresh, soapy smell, vaguely reminiscent of her father's shaving cream. He must have showered just before setting out. What was he doing here? His hair was the colour of hay, gleaming in the sun. Absently, Calliope's fingers were stirring of their own accord – opening, closing, opening, closing – on top of the printed page. The lieutenant glanced down at her hand and smiled.

'What are you reading?' He had a way of crinkling his eyes, an expression that gave his face an amused, benevolent look. Not the look of a conqueror.

'A French novel.' Calliope picked up the book and turned it over, letting him see the dust jacket for himself. Polite but impassive. In four months, they had barely exchanged a single sentence beyond the absolute requirements of her job.

'*L'Assommoir!*' Surprise flickered across the German's face. 'And in French!' He stood looking at her with his clear, foreign eyes.

'Well, why not?' Calliope said, mastering her irritation. 'As a matter of fact I've already read it. Long ago, but . . .' She shrugged, letting the statement dangle.

'But?'

'I have nothing else to read,' she stated dryly. There had been no new books since the start of the Occupation, but she resisted the urge to express resentment. 'I'm re-reading everything in our library,' she said.

The lieutenant regarded her for a moment: her full lips set in an expression of apparent displeasure, her plaited crown gleaming in the sun. 'Have you read the sequels?' he finally asked.

'No.' Calliope glanced up. He was probably somewhere in his late twenties – not much older than she herself. 'Not yet. Have you?'

He nodded. He smiled. A German soldier who had read Zola!

'I'd really like to read Flaubert,' she suddenly said, speaking mostly to herself.

'Well. I'm sure you will some day.' He made a small, ambiguous gesture, hesitated, then turned to go.

'Have you read Balzac?' Calliope blurted, surrendering to curiosity.

Umbreit paused and turned to face her. He had studied literature and philosophy; had read all the French authors. 'At Heidelberg University,' he told her.

'I see,' she said, then fell abruptly silent. *Heidelberg University!* She lifted a hand, then dropped it, feeling herself flush. Umbreit stood gazing at a soaring seagull.

'I miss my student days,' he said suddenly. There was no mistaking his sadness. And yet, he seemed to be in a relatively relaxed mood today. Calliope was accustomed to seeing him bustle about, always clutching some urgent document, issuing orders, talking on the phone. He was unfailingly courteous but also preoccupied, officious.

He stood, now, regarding her closely. 'Have you read any German books?'

'A couple.' Calliope had finally risen, mechanically smoothing her black skirt. Her godfather had once been an ardent Germanophile. When Princess Frederica married the Greek Crown Prince, he had given Calliope two Herman Hesse novels for her name day. Reading them had been something of a struggle. 'My vocabulary's still very small,' she told Lieutenant Umbreit.

'Not that small.' He smiled. One of his front teeth slightly overlapped the other. 'Your German's surprisingly good,' he said. 'Really.'

She managed a vaguely grateful smile. *'Danke.'*

She did not see him again until the following afternoon, when she came into his office to hand in an official record of olive oil production in the past three years. She knew why the Germans wanted the olive mill's records. It was the only way to determine how much oil they could reasonably expect in the coming season. Umbreit took a cursory look at the sheaf of onionskins obtained from the olive mill. He tossed the file down, reaching into a drawer.

'I have something for you.' He brought out a heavy black book embossed with gold letters. 'You may borrow it if you like.' He paused, looking into her eyes. 'Nietzsche,' he said, the hint of a smile hovering around his mouth. Was he mocking her? Was he waiting for her to say, 'Who's Nietzsche?' It so happened she did know the German philosopher's name.

'It's kind of you, but—'

'It's all I have here,' he put in, palms spread in apology.

'*Danke schön.*' Her gaze veered away, sweeping over Umbreit's wall map; a German map of her own island, with red pins marking Wehrmacht garrisons along the coast. 'Unfortunately, there is little time and – well, as I said, my vocabulary's really . . .' She broke off, letting the dangling sentence convey the hopelessness of the proposed challenge. 'It's kind of you to think of me.' She had spoken politely, but not without a smidgen of satisfaction. Somehow, her rejection of the book seemed to compound the pleasure of the surprising offer. A Greek village girl being offered a philosophy book by a German officer!

Whatever his motives, Calliope concluded he had not meant to mock her. He was no longer smiling, but regarded her with a slightly perplexed expression.

'Wouldn't you at least like to try it?'

She shook her head. '*Danke sehr,*' she said yet again.

'Very well.' He tilted back in his chair, swivelling very slightly. 'You're free to go, *Fräu* Alexiou.' He opened the drawer and put the book away.

She left his office and went down to the Greek quarters, struggling with herself. Should she have accepted the book? Was it churlish of her not to?

All afternoon, she kept weighing the question, torn between complacency and regret. She would have greatly liked to read the lieutenant's book; would have at least liked to try, as he had suggested. He'd caught her off-guard and she had reacted instinctively: he was the enemy after all!

Calliope tried to find vindication in this inner reminder; kept trying to settle her internal confusion with the memory of the way he'd looked at her yesterday, standing in front of the harbour guard office – his widening eyes, his raised eyebrows – when he first realised she was reading Zola.

It was the surprise she could not forgive.

～ 9 ～

One day, a dispute broke out between the acting mayor and Captain Yorgos, the former football champion's father. The Lyras family's new caique was the finest in the village, so it came as no surprise that the Germans had commandeered it for the transport of island produce. The supplies were to go by sea to Salonika, then by cargo train to the German Reich.

'The fucking bastards!' the captain fumed, storming into the mayor's office without so much as a greeting. '*My* boat to fatten up Hitler!'

He was a thickset man with flashing eyes and a mouth agleam with gold. Looming over the acting mayor, he went on to demand that the village council intervene with German authorities. They – their Italian allies – had already got his son's leg, he pointed out in his thundering voice. 'Mimis is crippled for life, and now the motherfuckers want my boat!'

Kyriakos listened, toying with his moustache, as attentive as a newly ordained priest at his first confession. He let Yorgos have his say, then leaned back and tried to explain: the village council had no leverage with the Germans. 'None, I regret to say.'

The statement was made in a grave and collected manner, as befitted the dignity of a mayor's post. But Kyriakos's restraint only inflamed Yorgos. Soon, he was waving his hammer-like fists, insisting that a meeting be called to resolve the issue.

Kyriakos regarded the fisherman from under his bushy eyebrows. 'Can't do that, Captain,' he said, faintly apologetic. 'Anyway, the council—'

'The council should at least try to squeeze them!' Yorgos insisted. 'They—'

'But that's just what I've been trying to tell you: we've got no authority over the Germans! They take—'

'They take whatever they want because you let them! The Germans spit in your face and you say it's raining!' roared the captain. He was an ardent Communist and Germany had just invaded the Soviet Union, compounding his outrage. He turned and spat on the floor. 'What are you, a man or a jellyfish? Is that what they taught you in America, to be the Germans' puppet?'

'What did you say?' The mayor sprang up, sweat running down from his eyebrows.

Calliope, who had tried to ignore the quarrel, glanced up from her desk. 'Gentlemen, please! I'm trying to work!'

The men's voices were running into each other like hawkers' cries at Mytilene's central market. Kyriakos was jabbing his finger at the captain's chest; Lyras's sunburned face was contorted with rage.

'Stop now, both of you!' Calliope commanded. 'You're behaving like children!' She had failed to catch the mayor's last words, but the words tumbling from Yorgos's lips made her bounce up from her chair.

She came around her desk, jumping back to dodge the captain's flying spit. Were they going to end up punching each other like two brawling sailors? Right there, in the mayor's office? Kyriakos was accusing the captain of cheating Mytilene fishmongers; the captain was scoffing at everything connected with the mayor, from his politics to his long-dead mother's honour.

He was still waving his fists when Umbreit's adjutant happened to pass the office. Alfred Reis glanced at the two feuding men, nodded stiffly, then hurried on towards the staircase, as if nothing untoward was happening in the mayor's office.

Calliope sighed, her inner distaste giving way to a surge of shame. The German had said nothing; his glance had been brief and impassive.

But oh, the disdain in those frosty eyes; the suppressed contempt for two Greeks ready to go at each other's throats in a public space – in a woman's presence!

'Go ahead!' she spat out as the men went on trying to outshout each other. 'Kill each other for all I care!'

She snatched the document she was working on and swept out of the sweltering office. She wished she could go home, but had promised to hand in her finished translation for typing and duplication. Would Umbreit be able to hear the men's voices in his upstairs office? she wondered, her glance flying upwards. Oh, maybe not: his office was in the back, overlooking the courtyard.

Calliope collapsed onto the garden bench, perspiration trickling down her face. Her widow's weeds made her feel smothered in the rising heat. The dye seeped from her collar and into her bra. It left black stains on her neck and breasts. It made her want to scratch in intimate places.

The men went on shouting. Kyriakos was in no position to accede to the captain's demands, but he could have handled the situation more tactfully. Calliope was sure *she* would have, had she been in his shoes. But then, who would ever consider electing a woman to serve as mayor? Or, for that matter, even a village councillor?

THREE

~ 1 ~

At the end of that first, torrid summer of the Occupation, Calliope woke from an afternoon nap and, succumbing to heat and impulse, decided to burn her widow's weeds. Hearing her mother stir, she hastened to gather every mourning garment she owned: the black dress and skirts, the stockings and blouses, the traditional widow's kerchiefs. She then hurried out into the garden, hugging the hateful tangle with the look an overworked maid might wear while disposing of a soiled diaper. Soon, Mirto came shuffling out and found Calliope standing at the firepit.

'Do you realise what you're doing, daughter?'

Calliope struck a match. 'Yes, Mama, perfectly.'

'Perfectly, eh?' Mirto wrung her arthritic hands. She let a silent moment go by. 'Did you stop to think what people are going to say about you?'

Calliope jerked back from the leaping flame. 'Let them talk! I don't give a button anymore!' She stood watching the sizzling clothes, her face set in ferocious resolve. There was the smell of burning dye in the air, a foul odour that somehow seemed to vindicate her own rebellious impulse.

Mirto, too, was gazing at the flames. 'Ach, my daughter, you still think you can go through life doing whatever you like, eh?'

Silence. The implicit argument was nothing if not familiar. Watching the fire devour her clothes, Calliope found her thoughts drifting towards her wedding day: the musicians accompanying her all the way

to St Kyriaki, playing their violins and accordion, the children skipping alongside the bridal entourage, the old women waving kerchiefs
through the open windows, calling out their blessings.

But Mirto was going on with her melancholy rant.

'You heap scorn on everything I say, then—'

'Not everything,' Calliope broke in. 'Only the superstitious nonsense you keep trying to brainwash me with.'

'Superstitious nonsense, eh?' There was a glint in Mirto's eye.
'That's what you said when I warned you . . . didn't I warn you when
you broke the mirror?'

'The mirror? Oh, God, not that again!' Calliope's eyes turned
heavenwards. The mirror in question had been broken six years earlier,
but Mirto seemed unshaken in her belief that all their woes had been
brought on by her daughter's carelessness.

'Did the Germans invade all of Europe because I broke the mirror,
or is it just Greece I'm responsible for?' Calliope's lips were twitching.

'Yes, laugh! Laugh all you want!' Mirto picked up an old garden
broom and set about sweeping the leaf-strewn path. 'Most widows shut
themselves up and cry their eyes out, but you—'

'Well, I'd much rather laugh than pretend to weep for a husband
I didn't really love!' Calliope retorted, surprising herself no less than
her mother.

She had spoken the truth, but it was a truth she had repeatedly
averted her mind from. She had, at first, found it hard to believe that
Iason was never coming back. It was only recently, having failed to
receive any sign of life, that she knew Iason must be dead. Only then
did she find herself willing to examine her innermost feelings.

'I can't help it, Mama!' she blurted now, her eyeballs starting to
sting. 'I did my best to love him. I did, but . . .'

'But?'

'But I refuse to be a hypocrite now he's dead! It's not going to do
Iason any good, my wearing black for the rest of my life, is it?' She met
her mother's baleful gaze, then looked away, watching Sappho go in
pursuit of a cat.

'I can tell you one thing,' Mirto said after a long silence. 'It isn't going to do *you* any good to shed your mourning clothes so soon.' She set the broom back against the stone wall, then busied herself picking acacia threads out of her coiled hair. 'Just think what your mother-in-law's going to say when she sees you tomorrow.'

'I don't care – I don't care, I tell you!'

She had worn black every time she visited her mother-in-law; had done everything expected of her, yet it all seemed futile before the blue accusation in Katina's eyes. *If only you had not been barren, if you'd borne my son children as you were meant to do, Iason would not have been drafted. He'd be alive today!*

Although the hateful words had never been voiced, Calliope had heard them as plainly as Katina's polite platitudes.

'She acts as if I was personally responsible for Iason's death!' Calliope reached out and sullenly plucked a ripe plum from a sagging branch. 'She hates me, Mama!'

At this, Mirto turned and stood for a moment, scanning her daughter's face. Then she sighed again, more deeply than ever. 'We shouldn't have pushed you to marry. You were not born to be a wife and mother,' she stated.

These words stopped Calliope's breath. They made her long to hug her mother; wrap her arms around Mirto's narrow shoulders and bawl like a child who, lost in a seemingly endless forest, has stumbled upon a small, unexpected shelter.

～ 2 ～

Winter came early that year, evicting a brief, blissfully sunny autumn. One morning in late November, Calliope came down and found a rat heaving in the kitchen. A grey rat the size of a half-grown kitten. The dying creature must have crept up from the cellar, perhaps scouting for food, or just a warm place to die. Inexplicably, it had crawled into one of the garden clogs kept at the entrance door.

Calliope had been on her way to the outhouse, had taken off her slippers and was about to thrust her foot into the wooden clog when her sleepy brain came abruptly awake: the shoe was not empty! The chamber pot in her hands was half full. It had been used by her mother, who was in bed with flu, and who, in subsequent days, would be made to swear on everything she held dear never to breathe a word to anyone about the dropped chamber pot or expiring rodent.

Since the end of summer, there had been numerous sightings of domestic rodents, probably due to the shortage of rat poison or the gradual decline of the cat population. Were villagers beginning to eat cat meat? Had the cats starved to death? In Athens, there had been reports of cat meat being passed for rabbit.

Breakfast was out of the question now. Cleaning up as best she could, Calliope sent for Hektor the fool to come and dispose of the expiring creature. She sent another message to the headmaster: she would be late today. Would he please give her class an assignment and ask them to work on it until she arrived?

Driven by some stubborn vestige of professional pride, Calliope carried on as if these were normal times, though her pupils' attendance had become erratic. Some, she knew, came only because of the corn bread she occasionally gave them; a piece the size of a seagull's egg, which they would swallow without chewing, blinking at her damply as they bolted it down. It was the first winter of the Occupation. The children's eyes were beginning to retreat into their sockets, their teeth huge in their shrinking faces.

The school was warmer than most private homes. A small stove stood between the two classrooms and burned for one hour each morning. The children sat huddled in layers of clothing, their fingers swollen with chilblains, their faces grey as trough water. Some mornings, half of them would drift off with their heads on their desks, scratching at their inflamed skin, muttering in their dreams.

Calliope let them sleep so that they might find the strength to go and sift through the Germans' rubbish, scavenging for scraps of food in the endless rain, perhaps a bit of kindling. Most villagers were by now using mule droppings as fuel.

Just before the end of the year, Calliope's godson came down with whooping cough. All over the village, people were coughing, sniffling, spitting into gutters. There would be no holiday celebrations this year, no children singing Christmas carols. Every day, pregnant women swooned, climbing up the hill. Their infants were born underweight, some with shortened limbs, without fingernails. When both Molyvos's and Petra's midwives fell ill, people said it was from grief at bringing such pitiful specimens into the world. Molyvos's midwife had suffered a mild stroke; Petra's died from some kidney ailment. All at once, women in both villages had no choice but to call on the doctor when their labour started.

It was the worst winter in living memory. The country had become isolated from the world, yet somehow the dire news kept trickling in: Hitler's armies had overrun much of European Russia; Japanese troops were triumphing in Southeast Asia.

Calliope and Mirto began sleeping together, clinging to each other under a heap of blankets. The walls of their house were half a metre deep, but the cold and damp seeped in all the same. The winds came sweeping all the way from the Siberian steppes, howling day and night at the shuttered windows.

On the first morning of the new year, snow began to fall.

Calliope spent most of the day at the kitchen hearth, reading and sipping sage tea, and blowing her nose as she burned the last of the kindling Hektor had managed to find somewhere beyond Eftalou.

The doctor and his family lived on the other side of the village, but Calliope swore she could hear Aristides cough and wheeze. The thought of her godson's suffering pierced her more deeply than the bone-curdling cold. She recalled the last time Aristides had come to spend the night; the way his ribs stood out as she bathed and dressed him. The village children had never seen snow, but even the elderly couldn't remember snow that didn't melt soon after it hit the ground.

The snow that fell on that first dawn of 1942 began as a languid dance of feathery flakes, but in no time at all turned into a tempest. By mid-afternoon, the entire village was cowering under the white onslaught. No one went to church. No German aircraft appeared in the sky.

By suppertime, Calliope and Mirto's kindling was gone and Mirto, who seemed to have a perpetual cold, wept as she opened a can of

Christmas ham sent by the Germans. Calliope hugged her mother, started to say something, then spun and strode upstairs, her hand cupping a flickering candle.

She opened the study door, shivering yet taut with purpose. This used to be Philippas's favourite room. It was so cold Calliope could see her own breath billow out of her mouth. There was the familiar smell of old printing ink, of dusty book jackets. She began to scan the book spines, hands buried within her armpits.

There were numerous novels and poetry collections on the shelves but no, not those, she decided. She was just beginning to consider the essay collections when her eyes fell on her father's old encyclopaedia. So old, she reasoned, that much of the information was probably out of date. The encyclopaedia had been published in 1910.

One of the first entries in the *A* volume was *Allemagne*: French for Germany. She dropped into a chair and began to skim the closely printed page. 'Allemagne. A German Empire . . . its territories occupied by peoples of distinctively Teutonic race and language.' No mention of the first World War, let alone the one that had brought the Wehrmacht to Aegean shores. Not a single line hinting at German aggression!

Calliope returned to the kitchen hugging a wobbly tower of Morocco-bound volumes. Quickly, before she could change her mind, she tossed the first volume into the hearth, then stood before the fiery choreography she had set in motion, batting at her stinging eyes. The pages had promptly caught fire, the singed edges curling like evening primroses surrendering to the sun.

'Don't say anything,' she cautioned her mother. 'Come . . . come and sit with me. Just don't say anything, Mama!'

They sat together then, huddled in private thought, while the sparks went flying, volume after volume devoured by the hissing flames. Before long, Calliope's eyes began to water. She thought of the Mongols' destruction of Baghdad's House of Wisdom. She had read about it in the very encyclopaedia she had just sacrificed; remembered her youthful astonishment on learning that the waters of the Tigris were said to have run black with ink for several months. *Months!* Calliope trembled, as much with suppressed repugnance as with the chill clinging to her bones. Over and over, she begged her father's forgiveness.

~ 3 ~

The following morning, Mirto limped downstairs and began to shriek. Shattered roof tiles littered the kitchen floor; chunks of rotting masonry lay strewn over the sink, table, counter. The ceiling had caved in under the weight of snow, leaving the kitchen awash in dust and fetid water. Sometime in the night, the snow had begun to melt.

'*Aman!*' The exclamation, which the villagers had picked up from their Turkish neighbours, was apt to slip out during domestic crises. '*Aman, aman!*' Mirto crossed herself, hobbling about with the air of an earthquake survivor emerging to survey the ruins. 'Calliope!' she called out, clasping her head. 'Calliope, come down! Quick now – quick, my daughter! Oh . . . may the saints preserve us. Cal-li-o-pe!'

Calliope was just getting out of bed. Arriving in the kitchen, she found Mirto frantically pulling at the roots of her hair, the way professional mourners did, wailing at a graveside. For a moment, Calliope stood on the threshold, unable to move a muscle; then she spun about, bolting for the laundry tub.

Ordering her mother away, she set the zinc tub directly below the ragged aperture. It was roughly the size of a manhole. The ceiling went on dripping, the foul water pattering against the metal with a dreary throb. Mirto could not stop coughing.

'We'd better send for Seraphim,' Calliope said, gazing at the ceiling. Seraphim Lemos was the building contractor, though the Germans' arrival had brought construction to a virtual standstill. All over the village, houses stood abandoned in varying stages of construction, as bleak as rotting teeth in elderly villagers' mouths.

By noon, it began to rain. The temperature had risen several degrees, but the house was as frigid and damp as an outdoor privy. Mirto was napping when Seraphim arrived. He leaned back from the waist and threw his chin in the air.

'Ach, ach, ach!' he said, contemplating the gaping ceiling. 'Ach, ach, ach!'

'Well?' Calliope did not trust Seraphim, who was prone to exaggerate problems in order to justify his inflated rates. Above all, she resented his restless, suggestive eyes.

'I can't do it – not right now,' the contractor was saying.

'Why not? Don't tell me you're too busy because—'

'No! What d'you take me for?' Seraphim cocked his balding head, looking offended. 'I wish I could say I was busy, but this . . . this here roof,' he said with a flick of his chin, 'it can't be fixed in this weather, *Kyria* Calliope. I'll need three days – three dry days – before my men can get up there.'

'Three dry days!' Calliope echoed. The weather in January had always been unpredictable. This year, it seemed to be in cahoots with the Germans.

'At least three.' Seraphim lingered in the kitchen, eagerly elaborating on the job at hand. 'You never know, we might get lucky with the weather,' he said.

They were not lucky with the weather. There was the occasional sunny day, but then the rain would return, flooding the tub in the kitchen, bringing down showers of dust and crumbling masonry. Calliope and Mirto had begun having their meals with Aunt Elpida, but they still slept at home. Uninhabited houses were often invaded by rodents; the tub had to be bailed out at regular intervals.

It was February before the sun emerged, sparkling on the aquamarine sea, drying up rain puddles. Calliope sent a reminder to Seraphim Lemos, who had promised to return once the weather cleared.

When the contractor didn't come, Calliope asked Umbreit for permission to leave early so she could nab Seraphim before he sat down to the midday meal. She would finish her translation later, she promised, explaining the problem. If she didn't get the roof repaired, they might run into another long spell of rain, and then what?

The building contractor lived on the village outskirts, next to his vegetable farm. Calliope found him working his field.

'Welcome, *Kyria* Calliope! How are we today?' Seraphim leaned on his pitchfork, watching Calliope pick her way through the neat rows of green cabbage. 'To what do I owe the honour?' He grinned extravagantly, like a frisky, jovial horse in search of a playmate.

'Have you forgotten? You promised to come when the weather—'

'Promised? Did I promise?'

Seraphim clapped a cigarette into his mouth, his eyes travelling around the contours of Calliope's body, as if assessing how much weight she had recently lost.

'Well, you did say you needed three dry days, you said—'

'Three days would be right,' Seraphim cut in with a judicious nod. 'But I did not promise, *Kyria* Calliope. Please don't offend my soul!' Calliope was silent. 'How could I promise such a thing?' Seraphim flared up, gesturing towards the cloudless sky. 'You can see for yourself, the sun's shining! There's work to be done in the fields right now!'

'Are you saying you can't do it?'

Seraphim raised his eyebrows and clicked his tongue in a gesture that was commonly understood as no, then gave her a long, speculative look. 'On the other hand,' he said, 'I have no objections to discussing it further, at least not—'

'Discussing it? What's there to discuss?' With a spasm of disgust, Calliope finally registered what Seraphim was after. 'Can you or can't you do it?'

'Ach, ach, ach, *Kyria* Calliope . . . be reasonable. I have to do everything myself these days – everything! The world's going to the dogs with those German bastards! You know that as well as I do.'

Calliope hesitated. She opened her mouth, closed it, then pivoted and stalked off across the field, her lips clamped together.

She did not cry often. Increasingly, she felt herself retreating into a grim, private realm. But that afternoon, when Umbreit enquired about the damaged roof, Calliope horrified herself by bursting into tears.

She had for months resisted complaining to the Germans about anything connected with the Occupation, held back by some delicate sense of pride. As if to complain would be tantamount to an admission of weakness – or worse, an appeal for pity. But on that day, Calliope told Umbreit the building contractor had refused to come. So had the two stonemasons she had approached.

'They say they have no supplies,' she said. 'Only Lemos has them.' She paused, struggling against the sudden threat of tears. 'I don't suppose you have any construction materials?'

The lieutenant looked at her. 'I'll see what I can do,' he said.

A restless night followed. Calliope went to school in the morning, then to the town hall, where neither she nor Umbreit mentioned the roof. She was beginning to regret having appealed to him. Though their relations were far more cordial than they'd been back in the summer, the lieutenant seemed exceptionally busy. She decided she would try to get Odysseus the beekeeper to take her to Petra in his mule cart. She would look for a building contractor there.

When she arrived home in the afternoon, however, Calliope found the ceiling intact.

'Oh . . . so he came after all!' she squealed, clapping her hands. She glanced at her mother. 'What's the matter?'

Mirto was bustling about with averted eyes, as if she'd had to pay with her honour for the roof repair.

'The Germans did it,' she finally said.

'The Germans?' Calliope's eyes flew to the ceiling. '*They* fixed the roof?' She stood with her hand over her mouth, trying to digest this extraordinary news.

'They came early this morning, right after you left.'

'And fixed it . . . just like that?' No one in the village ever fixed anything without making a song and a dance about it.

Mirto shrugged. 'They had a work order from Lieutenant Umbreit.'

Calliope dropped into a kitchen chair. 'I don't believe it!' she kept muttering.

'Well, you won't be the only one,' Mirto said and sighed.

Within three days, the entire village knew about the German roof repair. Naturally, Seraphim Lemos heard about it too, though days would go by before he happened to spot Calliope, who was hurrying past the public urinals, on her way up from school. The contractor hastened to button himself.

'I hear you got your roof fixed *tchick-tchack*,' he said, sounding at once wounded and reproachful.

'Yes . . . yes, I did,' replied Calliope. She had, after the roof repair, found herself wavering between gratitude and what she recognised to be an unreasonable flash of resentment. It was not her vague sense of indebtedness that irked her – she knew the Germans were squeezing her for all she was worth – but the speed and efficiency with which the repair had been completed. Neither Seraphim nor anyone else in the village could have accomplished as much in one morning.

'You wouldn't come!' she suddenly flared up, stopping in mid-stride. 'I pleaded with you and you said—'

But Seraphim wouldn't hear her out. '*Kyria* Calliope.' He drew himself up, eyeing her severely. 'I can't help it if you'd rather deal with the enemy, can I?'

~ 4 ~

Oh, she would have liked to tell Seraphim the truth! What she wouldn't have given for the satisfaction of watching the bastard flail and flounder, trapped by his own insinuations! Yes, indeed, she would have been willing to offer quite a lot, but the one thing she could not disclose in her own defence was the simple truth: she had recently joined the Resistance. She had kept the news even from her mother, partly because those were the rules, but also because Mirto's perpetual anxiety might have led Calliope to lose heart as well.

She was a secret coward; had been one as far back as she could remember – a coward and a ninny, howling at the sight of her own blood! The very idea of someone like her being asked to help the underground had almost made Calliope laugh when the doctor had broached the subject.

'I can't believe you're asking me – me!' she said. 'I'm a spoiled, selfish woman. Ask my mother.' She smiled a little. 'She'll tell you it's all my father's fault.'

'Maybe so, but I don't have to ask your mother,' he said. 'I've known you since you were eight years old.'

'Then you know—'

'I know we need you,' Dhaniel interjected.

'You mean you're so desperate you'll take anyone?'

The doctor, Calliope thought, was probably blinded by memories of her young self playing with her male cousins, climbing trees, leaping from rocks and sea walls. And yet, deep in her heart, she already knew she would end up consenting. It was not the first time she'd observed herself weighing a situation, scrutinising it from every possible angle, when a decision had already been reached in some other, barely examined chamber.

But how shrewd Dhaniel's timing was! Just last week, she'd found her hair starting to fall out in clumps; yesterday, her youngest pupil had fainted in class and they'd had to summon the doctor to revive him.

'We need someone like you,' he was saying now. 'Someone strong and decisive and quick-witted. Someone trustworthy.'

Calliope was silent, wondering whether she was being recruited because of her liaison job. Would it make her less likely to fall under German suspicion? She asked the doctor what would be expected of her and that was when she finally understood.

A go-between was needed to deliver a coded message to Mytilene, to a pedagogical priest named *Papa* Ioannis. She would ostensibly be going to attend a curriculum review conference; the priest was responsible for the school curriculum's religious content. As a schoolmistress, Calliope was the ideal person for this mission, Dhaniel pointed out. She would go in Kyriakos's taxi, along with two villagers in need of medical treatment. The priest would sit next to her at the conference. She would slip the message into a Bible and casually pass it to him. And that would be all. Her mission would be accomplished.

'What if there's a roadblock along the way?' Calliope asked.

'You will carry the message in your socks. Under your soles,' Dhaniel said. The plan had been carefully thought out. Of course, every mission entailed a certain risk, but it was unlikely they would bother to search her.

'Oh, I don't know,' Calliope said and sighed.

'Extremely unlikely,' said the doctor.

And, at last, Calliope capitulated. It occurred to her that courage was, perhaps, nothing more than the willingness to slam the door on one's imagination.

~ 5 ~

Every year, just before Easter, parent–teacher meetings were held at the local school. It was doubtful many parents would bother to attend this year, but the occasion could be exploited for the transfer of provisions to the guerillas. On Thursday afternoon, the headmaster had waited in vain for the parents of pupils planning to attend middle school in Petra; Friday was the day assigned for the juniors.

Tense and alert, Calliope settled at her desk, listening to the swallows flitter under the eaves. She had always had trouble waiting for things to happen; would sometimes provoke negative results from sheer inability to keep still and wait.

Without the children's presence, the abandoned desks looked sadly reproachful. Calliope waited, her ears pricking up when a passing horse whinnied. But nothing happened. The wagon rumbled on. For some reason, she felt voraciously hungry, as if every gram of nutrition had been extracted out of her body.

It was as she rummaged in her satchel for some dry chickpeas that Calliope heard the anticipated signal: the first bar of the national anthem. *We know you by the sharpness of your sword.* The whistler was a woman; the food being delivered was ostensibly meant for elderly parents living on the village outskirts.

The school was situated amid olive orchards. There was the beach across the road, but no immediate neighbours. As clandestine activities went, this one seemed far less risky than her first assignment. The coded message had been delivered to Mytilene without a hitch; no one had paid the slightest attention to the casual exchange between a schoolmistress and a pedagogical priest. But the possibility of being spotted by a stool pigeon had Calliope leaping out of her dreams in the nights that followed.

And now the fear was back, shrivelling the contours of her heart. She had stepped out to retrieve the baskets and found them, exactly as expected, behind a flowering oleander bush. It was a spring afternoon radiant with light, fragrant with honeysuckle; yet even the breeze rustling the poplar branches sounded like a portentous whisper. Calliope peered about in case a parent arrived early or some children turned up to play in the schoolyard, though both possibilities seemed highly unlikely. The parents would be too apathetic to come early, if at all; the children too feeble to kick a ball or play hide-and-seek.

There were two wicker baskets, both covered in freshly laundered linen. As she bent to lift them, Calliope's skirt became briefly snagged by a protruding branch. She stopped and released the cloth, glancing over her shoulder. What if Umbreit happened to be going by? What if he decided to send someone for the document she was expected to drop off on her way from school?

But no one came. Nothing stirred, except for birds, leaves, insects.

Breathing shallowly, Calliope strode towards the shed, where garden tools and broken desks were being stored for repair. There was no one left to do it. When people could no longer afford new furniture, the village carpenter had taken his wife and deaf-mute daughter and hastened to leave for Athens. Since then, broken furniture had been piling up all over the village. The school shed itself seemed to be subsiding into the earth.

The provisions were to be placed in an old chest at the back of the shed and eventually retrieved by another activist. The instructions were to leave the shed door unlocked. A lizard scurried by, quickly disappearing over the roof; a wasp circled over the entrance, its aggressive buzz somehow compounding Calliope's anxiety. The distance between the shed and the schoolhouse was negligible but might have been as long as the climb to the hilltop fortress.

Calliope dashed back to the classroom, back to her own desk. She was safe now – safe! Five minutes or five hours might have passed while she sat, slumped in her chair, shaking all over. Oh, she knew her dread to be overblown. True: aiding and abetting the guerillas could lead to summary execution. There had been warnings on shop windows and telegraph poles all over the village. But there was no reason to worry any longer: it was all over. She was at her own desk as she was meant to be, waiting for some stalwart parent to appear.

Gradually, Calliope willed herself into a semblance of professional composure. She checked her watch. Casting about for something to do, she took out the document she had been translating. Might as well review it once more.

The original version had been written by the verbose von Herden. The major visited the village only once a month, but Calliope's work was apparently deemed satisfactory, for much of it originated in the capital. She received formal thankyou notes from Mytilene; was secretly flattered to find her efforts praised by Lieutenant Umbreit, whom she had done her best to dislike.

She had not succeeded, for the German had a rare gift for making people do his bidding. He was the sort of man who, in times of peace, might have been called upon to settle disputes rather than issue orders. Calliope admired his manners, his air of competence and quiet authority, but their budding friendship was sadly contingent upon her own ability to maintain separate mental chambers for her endlessly clashing musings. In her wildest dreams, she would not have expected the Germans to undertake the repair of a private roof. And how ironic it was, how maddening, that they'd done so just days after she had agreed to join the Resistance!

Calliope's thoughts and feelings may have been at odds but the war was one subject she and Umbreit resolutely shied away from. To listen to them, the Occupation did not exist, hunger did not exist; there were no arrests, no Gestapo interrogations. Occasionally, when Mirto chastised her for fraternising with the enemy, Calliope would find herself engaged in an inner debate, in which the blame was laid at the feet of fate. Had Umbreit studied science or law, Calliope told herself at such times, they might never have exchanged a single superfluous word. But after their encounter in the harbour, after her rejection of the Nietzsche book, she was touched by Umbreit's evident disappointment. There was remorse. There was pride. There was the awareness of a small need to make it up to him.

In short, she had let her guard down. They began to discuss literature, to talk about this and that. They continued to address each other formally: he called her '*Fräu* Alexiou', she called him '*Leutnant*', but not without a gleam of irony. Ten months after the start of the Occupation – two weeks after the roof repair – Calliope knew Umbreit well enough not to be surprised when he came back to her with the Nietzsche.

'Your German's certainly good enough now!' He held out the book, smiling obliquely. It came to Calliope that he might be less interested in her reading the book than in testing his own belief that, this time, she would not reject it. He was a man of steely resolve, infinite patience.

She began to read with the furtiveness of a villager hoarding gold or arms. The book was *Beyond Good and Evil*, and she pored over it with the help of a dictionary, disconcerted to find herself hiding it from her own mother.

Aware of Mirto's curiosity, Calliope had always carried her journal with her. Now her shoulder bag contained the Nietzsche as well. But why? Why should she hide a German philosopher's book? Why shouldn't she enjoy a purely intellectual advantage? No one hesitated to squeeze every possible benefit out of their grim circumstances. Mirto herself had been happy to profit from the phoney medical certificate; had raised no objections to accepting foodstuffs from the Germans. What reason was there to turn down a book?

This inner debate was still going on as the first year of the Occupation drew to a close. When Easter came around, Umbreit gave Calliope – and her mother – a box of Swiss chocolates, an unheard-of luxury; she gave him her own copy of Hesse's *Steppenwolf*. She had been surprised to learn that he'd never read it. Anyway, she had nothing else that might interest him.

Umbreit accepted the book with an enigmatic smile, thanking her and promising to read it as soon as he had the time. Some time would pass before Calliope learned that in Germany, Herman Hesse was considered an enemy of the Fatherland.

~ 6 ~

The coffin was the size of the wooden crates used for storing dry cod in the winter months. As it was lowered into the freshly dug grave, the blacksmith's daughter began to utter odd little sounds, like the cries of swallows fluttering over a storm-devastated nest. Eleni's eyes, as round and shiny as black olives, were today looking opaque and droopy. Her loose hair, normally gathered into a long, neat plait, was blowing across her face.

It was late April but the afternoon was as damp and blustery as a winter's day. *Papa* Emanouil's cassock billowed and flapped, exposing his hirsute ankles. Calliope stood next to her young brother-in-law, Pericles, her gaze fixed on the gravedigger. There had been reports of villagers digging up coins and gold teeth in the cemetery, but she didn't think Fanis had anything to do with that. The gravedigger's features were more gaunt than ever; his fraying clothes hung as loosely as rags on a scarecrow.

Calliope dabbed at her eyes. Eleni had been one of her favourite pupils. She had longed to go on to middle school but her father would slap her whenever he caught her absorbed in a book. Her mother, the local herbalist's daughter, had occasionally expressed the wish that God had seen fit to bestow cleverness on her twin sons rather than on her daughter, but you didn't have to be lettered to know that God worked in mysterious ways, did you?

Glancing at the bereaved family, Calliope noted that Eleni's father and his bachelor brother had both come to resemble vultures; that her husband Tomas's dark head had begun to sprout grey hairs – a man in his twenties! Standing beside his wife, the grieving father cast a few clumps of earth onto the tiny coffin, then stood gazing into the gaping grave with his arm suspended, like a mendicant's.

The couple had already lost one child through a miscarriage. But the second pregnancy had been normal; the baby had died only because his mother's depleted body had failed to provide adequate nourishment. Calliope had done her best to help – had traded in her favourite frock for extra flour – but the infant had died after ten days of incessant howling. Standing beneath the sooty clouds, Eleni made Calliope think of a solitary tree warped by lightning. The wind went on swishing across the cemetery. It muffled the mother's heart-rending cries. It blew away *Papa* Emanouil's prayers.

It was time to leave. Calliope embraced Eleni. She shook Tomas's limp hand.

'Let's go,' she said to her brother-in-law.

It was late afternoon. She and Pericles were the only non-relatives at the cemetery, for who had the strength to attend every burial nowadays? Almost a year had passed since the start of the Occupation and the number of deaths was beginning to exceed that of births. Calliope's godfather had suffered a second heart attack and died; her mother was bedridden with pleurisy.

Pleurisy had become rampant all over the island. The little energy people could rally was spent scouring the countryside for anything edible, though there was always the risk of stumbling on a German mine. Even so, islanders were generally luckier than their urban brethren, who were said to be dropping off like flies. No one in the village had been reduced to begging; no women were prostituting themselves the way so many were said to be doing in the capital.

Molyviates had gradually learned to focus on such paltry consolations. There were virtually no medicines left, but at least they didn't have malaria on the island; the shops had stood shuttered all winter, but at least they had wild greens and sea urchins and mountain snails and, occasionally, a bowl of yoghurt sweetened with figs. There was little dairy because of the shortage of animal fodder. Meat had become nonexistent. Although fishing was theoretically permitted in spring and autumn, the fishing caiques stood idle because of fuel shortage.

Calliope left the cemetery with Pericles, her chunky footwear making a steady, mournful sound. The shortage of leather was forcing women to put on heavy clogs fabricated from carved wood and bits of cloth. The handcrafted product was not only unsightly but awkward to negotiate on the cobblestones. It was a well-known fact that Greek leather was being shipped to the Reich, along with most of the island's olive oil.

Approaching St Pandeleimon's, Calliope spotted one of her pupils, whose father had been executed for being pro-British. In recent months, the Resistance had become increasingly effective in disrupting German supply and communication lines. There had been several instances of Greek sabotage: weapons had vanished from the German cache; jeep and motorcycle tyres had been slashed in the night.

The tanner's execution had failed to deter, but his orphaned child was running around barefoot, his hair shaved against the suddenly ubiquitous lice. As Calliope and Pericles approached, Leonidas stopped in front of a fig tree, his chin tipping up. He hadn't been to school since his father's demise; had reportedly been taken in by his Petra grandparents. Yet there he was, his head tilted back, his eyes in their hungry sockets scanning the twisted tree's canopy, where a mourning dove could be heard calling. Calliope was about to speak when the boy pulled out a catapult. He ran his sleeve across his nose, then aimed the catapult at the invisible bird.

Invisible to her, to Pericles. They had stopped, she and her suddenly mute brother-in-law, and watched the stone go zipping up towards the treetop. As it hit the branch, the hidden dove came fluttering out of the wet foliage. It circled the tree for one chaotic moment, then flapped away towards the nearby church. The boy burst into tears. With a quick, furious gesture, he cast the catapult onto the cobblestones.

'Leo!' Calliope called out. 'Leo! Wait, *pedhi mou* – I want to talk to you!'

The boy ignored her calls. He bolted down the alley, vanishing around the corner. Calliope remained rooted to the spot, hand clamped onto Pericles's arm: she had, lunging towards the boy, twisted her foot in its wooden clog.

'Are you all right?' Pericles was asking.

'Yes . . . I think so.'

'Good.' Pericles was still staring up at the tree. He was by now in his last year of high school; had grown taller than Calliope. 'I must write something down before . . . before I lose it,' he said, his lips tightening. Then he rushed off to write a new poem, like a man chasing a departing train.

Calliope turned and headed for the town hall, to type a document she had been translating at home during her mother's illness. The clerk engaged to do the Germans' typing had just given birth, so Calliope had to type, as well as translate, the Germans' communiques. It would be past curfew when she finished today, but she had a night pass. Iro Balliou, their neighbour, was looking after Mirto, in exchange for the bread and soap Calliope managed to obtain from the Germans. If she was lucky today, she might get not only bread but a couple of eggs; maybe even coffee.

Despite the nutritional benefits, Calliope's thoughts were today flowing in rather hostile directions. She had just heard that high schools would soon be required to teach German as a second language. Pericles, who had passed on the rumour, was about to graduate, but the proposed language law made one thing clear: whatever they said, whatever they did, the Germans had no intention of relinquishing the Aegean.

~ 7 ~

Because of the ever-present possibility of capture and torture, Resistance members were usually kept in the dark about their colleagues' activities. Calliope didn't even know that their new office cleaner was an underground member, though they saw each other virtually every day.

Ourania Nakou had been the village seamstress. Despite a somewhat dour nature, her services had been much in demand before the Occupation. When people could no longer afford new clothes, Calliope, a regular client, had used her connections to find work for the fisherman's wife. Ourania was engaged to clean both Greek and German offices. The day of the Kafatou baby's funeral, she had just finished washing the lobby when Calliope entered, reprimanded like a careless child for leaving tracks across the clean floor.

Everyone had grown testy over the winter months. Calliope took off her clogs and was carrying one in each hand when Lieutenant

Umbreit looked up from his files and found her standing on the threshold. He smiled at the footwear, then leaned back and sat scanning Calliope's face.

'What's the matter?' he asked, gesturing towards a chair. *Was ist los?*

'Oh . . .' Calliope met his probing eyes. 'Nothing out of the ordinary,' she said, speaking with a sullen sort of irony. 'I've just seen a friend bury her newborn baby. I've seen one of my pupils try to shoot down a mourning dove with a catapult.'

Umbreit sat clicking the lid on his fountain pen.

'Don't you understand? He was only doing it because he's hungry!' Calliope blurted with sudden heat. 'The whole village is starving to death – starving – while you ransack our land so *your* people can enjoy the fruits of *our* labour! Is that what you promised us? When you first arrived – is that what von Herden told us?'

Umbreit lit a cigarette. He gazed at her from behind his desk: silent, inscrutable.

'You came here claiming to be our friends!' Calliope went on, unstoppable now. 'Is that how friends behave in your country? Is that how your mother raised you?'

At this, the lieutenant's jaw tightened. He seemed on the verge of speaking, but Calliope was not done yet.

'Now you're planning to make our children learn German – German! – when they barely have the energy to study their own language!'

She sat with her eyes fastened on Umbreit's face, perspiration oozing from her armpits. She was the only villager who could risk making such a speech, but there was little courage in it, for her friendship with the lieutenant seemed secure by now; she could afford the sour luxury of speaking her mind. And yet, oddly, the knowledge of her privileged position only seemed to fan Calliope's suppressed anger.

One of the things chafing at her was the Germans' condescension towards her people. Von Herden might claim they had come as friends but his men were forbidden to fraternise with the natives. They were not permitted to pay social visits, or drink in the *kapheneion*, and certainly not to indulge in intimate relations. Calliope and Umbreit had never had the slightest physical contact, but the affinity between them sometimes seemed stronger than that between most husbands and wives.

Having listened to the rant against the German language, and perhaps hoping to divert Calliope, Umbreit calmly pointed out the obvious advantage of being able to read German authors in the original.

'Just think,' he said, 'if you'd been teaching German all these years, your young brother-in-law would be able to read Rilke in the original.' He smiled, releasing a plume of smoke. 'Wouldn't that be a good thing?'

But Calliope was not in the mood for banter. She went on with her diatribe, speaking of the useless food coupons, the idle fishermen, the children's thwarted education. 'You take everything we've got,' she repeated, 'then, as if that's not enough, you demand that we pay your expenses – the expenses of *your* Occupation!' she spat out, then fell abruptly silent, struggling with her tears.

Twilight was coming on, flooding the office with a warm, golden light. There was a sea urchin shell resting on the lieutenant's desk. White and brittle and exquisitely patterned, it was the only extraneous item in the austere office. Calliope became aware that Umbreit was offering her something. A pristine lemon-coloured handkerchief, laundered and pressed and carefully folded. She declined it, shaking her head emphatically, as if to disclaim her own tears.

He returned the handkerchief to his pocket, then stubbed out his cigarette, waiting for her to regain her composure.

'War . . . war is never pretty,' he brought out at last, searching Calliope's face with his calm Nordic eyes; eyes that were sometimes the colour of the sea on an overcast day, other times the colour of ripening olives. An evening breeze blew in through the window, stirring the papers on Umbreit's desk. Calliope's nostrils caught the familiar smell hovering about his person – the scent of leather and ink and shaving soap. The villagers all seemed to smell foul these days. 'You know enough about history to know that, surely?' Umbreit was saying. *'À la guerre comme à la guerre?'*

Calliope turned this over in her head. *All is fair in war.* She was about to respond but stopped herself, hearing the sound of Sergeant

Reis's boots approaching the front entrance. The boots crossed the lobby, then headed downstairs, towards the cellar.

'But what?' Umbreit was asking. 'Did your generals stop to consider the Turks when they burned their way towards Ankara? Did Venizelos give a thought to the innocent victims while dreaming of a new Byzantine empire?'

Calliope sat up, her eyes flashing. 'What Venizelos dreamed of was land which the Allies had promised us before . . . before we got embroiled in their Great War!'

'Well, there you are . . . your Allies. They, too, claimed to be your good friends, didn't they?'

'They're not *my* Allies!' Calliope snapped back, knowing herself to be on suddenly shaky ground. 'Anyway,' she hastened to add, 'the point is those lands – the lands Venizelos was after – were Greek even before Alexander the Great's time. Surely you know that?' she echoed ironically.

'True,' said Umbreit, a gleam of amusement lighting his eyes. 'But how did the Greeks get to occupy those lands in the first place – have you ever asked yourself that?' He paused, regarding her steadily. 'There were ancient peoples there, you know, long before the Aryans invaded Asia Minor.'

Silence. Calliope swallowed, stumped for words.

'As for your Alexander the Great,' Umbreit continued, with his calm, relentless logic, 'when he went about founding his famed *polis* all over the map, do you suppose he did so waving an olive branch? Is that how he succeeded in building his mighty empire?'

'Oh! You . . . you're talking about an altogether different era!' Calliope flashed out, unnerved by her own inadequacy. 'This is the twentieth century – shouldn't your Hitler have learned something from history?' she demanded. 'Even Napoleon—'

'Shouldn't you?' he cut in, his eyebrows arching. 'Take a good look at human history – it's all blood and gore in the name of this ideal or that . . . often in the name of some higher civilisation,' he added, a note of disgust creeping into his voice.

'Yes!' Calliope cried. 'Exactly! But don't you see? You people pride

yourselves on being so civilised – certainly more civilised than us primitive Greeks,' she couldn't help adding: *wir, die primitiven Griechen.*
'Yet you . . . you torture innocent people! You arrest simple men and
put them through hell, just . . . just so . . .'

Calliope turned away, tears constricting her throat. She sat with her
hands tightly clasped in her lap, hearing Ourania leave the town hall
on her way home. Umbreit was gazing at her with his sad, foreign eyes.

'My dear Calliope,' he said, sounding all at once weary, seemingly
unaware of the personal salutation he had just used for the first time.
'And what did your heroic Metaxas do, I ask you. To his own people?'

'Metaxas!' she shot out. 'Metaxas was a dictator – I'll be the first to
grant you that! But I didn't vote for him, whereas you – you are carrying out the orders of a . . . a ruthless imperialist!' she snapped out. She
had almost said 'megalomaniac' but stopped herself in time, feeling a
tiny thrill of fear. Or something. She was suddenly not sure how far he
would let her go before he lost his temper. Was he angry now?

No, he appeared more rueful than angry, sitting there with his
black fountain pen in his hands, staring moodily towards the open
window. 'I wish . . . I wish I could show you pictures of my people
after the First World War,' he said quietly.

'But who was responsible for that war? Who—'

'Whoever was responsible – and scholars don't agree, mind
you – people, families like mine, did not sign the Treaty of Versailles.
They did not accept your Allies' outrageous conditions—'

'They may have had nothing to do with signing the Treaty, but
they'd chosen the leaders that signed it for them! Aren't people responsible for the leaders they elect?' Calliope demanded, doing her best to
subdue the familiar voice echoing in her head. *When two bulls tussle, it's
always the grasshoppers that suffer.*

But the doctor's words would not be ignored, so at last Calliope
stopped and mulled them over, feeling the beginning of some internal
shift. She watched Umbreit lever himself to his feet and go to the window, gazing out at the darkening sky.

'My mother was a widow with four children,' he said at last, speaking in a low, dispassionate voice. 'My father shot himself after losing

his job during the Depression. My baby sister died.' He turned to face her. He had never spoken to her of his family; she had never asked.

She sat gazing up at Umbreit, lost for words.

'I'm sorry,' she said at length, looking away. 'I didn't know. I'm very sorry.'

'So you see . . .' He detached himself from the window, his trousers ballooning above his boots, his thumbs hooked on his leather belt. 'Your people, Calliope, don't have a monopoly on suffering – I'm sorry to say they don't. And . . . well, neither do mine on ruthlessness,' he added.

A long moment passed. There was the sound of distant waves, of frogs trilling in the garden below. 'Sooner or later, we all suffer,' Umbreit said at last. He spoke with averted eyes, his gaze briefly landing on the swastika. Then he turned to face her, tall and straight and mournful, fingers nervously raking through his hay-coloured hair. '*Whose* suffering we choose to mourn is – well, it's not really a question of choice, is it? Just . . . just an accident of birth, really.'

~ 8 ~

In May, a subversive rumour spread through the *agora*: two foolhardy fishermen were said to be planning an escape to the Turkish mainland. Alerted by a stool pigeon, Lieutenant Umbreit brought in additional sea patrols, concentrating their guard along the Eftalou coast, where the fishermen had reportedly hidden their getaway boat. Night after night, the Germans patrolled the deserted shoreline, waiting for the clandestine fishing boat to fall into their hands.

The boat did not appear in Eftalou. It was in Skala Sykamnias that the father and son had actually found shelter, waiting for a moonless night, for the German patrol to pass on its first evening round, before launching their escape.

The two men were Captain Yorgos and his elder son, Kostas. They were to share the boat with an unknown Allied agent meant to join the British forces stationed across the water; the fishermen's destination was Egypt, where the Free Greek Army had its wartime base. That was as much as Elias Dhaniel would tell Calliope when they last talked, on Saturday afternoon.

It was now Sunday morning. Mirto was attending Mass, while Calliope prepared dandelion greens for the midday meal. Waiting for the pot to boil, she marvelled at the Lyras men's daring. She could not imagine ever undertaking such a bold mission; could not even imagine joining the guerillas: sleeping in forests and barns, going for weeks without a bath, bitten by fleas and lice. She had laughed over this with the doctor – her willingness to risk her life, her unwillingness to give up simple creature comforts.

What Calliope couldn't work out was how the neighbourhood women had got wind of the details; how they knew that the captain had sold his gold teeth to subsidise the escape. She had heard the women whisper at the fountain only that morning, speculating on where the fugitives had found the getaway boat.

Yorgos's own boat had been sabotaged the night before its scheduled departure, loaded with some of the finest oil in the country. The captain himself had set it ablaze, then fled to the hills, and eventually to Turkey, bearing forged documents.

The doctor had shared the news of the escape with Calliope, but only after the Lyras men had safely reached the Turkish shore. Calliope knew nothing about the Resistance movement's communication network, but Dhaniel had it on good authority: Yorgos and Kostas had succeeded in circumventing the German patrol; the insidious rumour planted by the Resistance had worked exactly as expected!

Calliope understood: For once, Umbreit had been outwitted.

~ 9 ~

The dandelions were ready to be drained. Setting them aside to cool, Calliope sat down to read Nietzsche, waiting for her mother to return from church. She herself had long since stopped attending Mass. Her mother was by now resigned to this fact; had even managed to extract a small compensation: Calliope was to prepare the midday meal. Every Sunday.

'It's the least you can do, staying home when you should be in church.'

Calliope received this with an ironic smile. 'I wonder how God would feel about such a convenient compromise,' she mused out loud.

'Oh you . . . you always have an answer to everything, don't you?'

Calliope had an answer to this as well but chose to withhold it. She was grateful to be able to stay home Sundays, reading in bed, cooking a simple meal. Today, the menu included beans and dandelion greens, which one of the neighbours had picked and bartered for sugar and German coffee. The coarse ersatz coffee most villagers drank was made of toasted barley, and offered as much satisfaction as a Lenten salad.

Calliope tasted the beans, speculating about Dhaniel's role in the Lyras men's escape. It was almost noon now. Sighing, she went into the pantry. She was getting the olive oil when her eyes fell on a jar of sour cherry preserves. Lydia, her Mytilene aunt, had given them the preserves just before the Occupation, but Mirto was saving them for an emergency. As far as Calliope was concerned, they had been living in a state of emergency since spring 1941 and might continue to do so until they all starved to death. There were, indeed, those who said that this was the Germans' ultimate goal; 'Hitler's secret weapon'.

Calliope picked up her book and went into the garden, not bothering to change out of her sleeveless house-dress. Spyros Balliou had recently died, so only Iro and sixteen-year-old Melpo could see into their garden. It was a fine morning. Sappho was slumped under a shady tree, eyes drowsily following a white butterfly. The garden was full of them, its air scented by spring blossoms. Bees were humming over oleander bushes; birds twittered and cicadas sang in leafy fruit trees. Every now and then, a breeze would rise from the sea, sweeping through the garden. Sappho kept snapping at the beanpods whorling down from the acacia tree.

There was something both comforting and maddening about nature's stunning imperviousness to human anguish. Babies died from hunger, men were arrested and tortured, but the sun went on shining, the peaches and plums ripened as wantonly as ever, most of them destined for shipment to the German Reich. As she strolled towards the grape arbour, Calliope brushed past a tray of chickpeas her mother had set out in the sun for tomorrow's meal. Legumes had become the mainstay of their diet.

'Thank God we've got something to put in our mouths!' Mirto was wont to say, as if to placate her own grumbling stomach. She served chickpea soup all too often, but why would she leave tomorrow's batch out in the sun? Calliope wondered. Fruit and vegetables were often set out to dry, but the chickpeas were dry already; what they needed was thorough soaking. Even she knew that.

Suddenly, she noticed the weevils: pale commas of wriggling flesh creeping out of the dry chickpeas, frenziedly crawling over their round, sunbaked dwellings. Was that why her mother had set the peas out in the sun, to rid them of the weevils? Back in winter, they'd heard that an old farmer had made a weevil paste, which he ate on crusts of bread thrown out by the Germans.

This memory was choked off as Calliope sprinted towards the outhouse, feeling her stomach heave. A woman approaching twenty-seven, she was still given to bouts of nausea in stressful moments. But there wasn't much to bring up just now: all she'd had was coffee and a stale crust of bread, followed by that tiny taste of dandelions. Nor did she feel the hoped-for relief after she'd stopped retching. The nausea had vanished, giving way to an odd, hollow sensation in the pit of her stomach; a strange sort of hunger that made her think of the cravings pregnant women often described, so urgent that foetal welfare seemed to depend on gratification.

Sappho rose, shook herself and padded over, sniffing the air. Calliope gave her a perfunctory pat, then returned indoors. The kitchen smelled of dill and boiled dandelions. Two flies were mating with intermittent enthusiasm, buzzing at the windows for a moment or two, then settling down again on the warm panes.

Cherry preserves!

The moment she identified the craving, a peculiar excitement possessed Calliope – an intense physical urge impelling her towards the pantry. That she should find herself drooling by the time she reached for the *gliko* jar! Drooling even as she laughed at herself. How ridiculous! How extraordinary!

The cherries were plump and thick with red syrup. Calliope unscrewed the lid. She had one teaspoonful of *gliko*. And then she had another. And yet another, the delectable sweetness sliding down her throat like ambrosia, spreading voluptuous satisfaction through her empty belly.

Oddly, though, deep as it was, the satisfaction only generated a new wave of greed, conquering her body as ardently as sexual desire. She had, at first, laughed at herself, then, all at once, slid to the edge of tears. There was something both euphoric and terrifying about the irrational power subjugating her body.

She ended up finishing the entire jar. It was not a large jar and she finished it, spoon after spoon after spoon. Out in the garden, Sappho lay with her head resting on her paws, her droopy, reproachful eyes fixed on the kitchen windows.

Oh God, what have I done?

No sooner was the jar empty than Calliope was swept by a wave of remorse. She knew her impulse must have had something to do with the time of month: she had always craved sweets just before her period. She suspected the hormonal havoc had been compounded by prolonged deprivation, but the knowledge did nothing to placate her pangs of shame. She might have wept with regret but for the heedless joy coursing through her veins. She was beginning to feel both giddy and exhausted, as if she'd spent all morning carrying jugs of water under the blazing sun.

Sighing, she lay down on the day divan. Not reading, not thinking – just trying to hold on to the exquisite sweetness suffusing every cell in her body. This, she told herself drowsily, was the first time in months that she felt thoroughly sated. So sated that she soon drifted off to sleep.

It was, it seemed, possible to feel repentant and yet, however briefly, almost divinely blissful.

~ 10 ~

Coming home from church and visiting her sister, Mirto found Calliope curled up on the kitchen divan, plunged in heavy slumber. She glanced at her daughter, was turning to leave the kitchen, when her eyes landed on the cherry jar – an empty jar standing on the floor, flies buzzing around its rim.

'I don't believe it,' she let out, stopping in her tracks. 'I . . . don't . . . believe . . . it!'

Calliope opened one eye, then sat up, struggling with her mental cobwebs. She watched her mother stoop to pick up the sticky preserves jar. 'I'm sorry, Mama,' she said. And she was; both sorry and incredulous at her own greedy impulse.

'But how could you? How could you be so selfish?' Mirto shrilled, shooing away the flies buzzing around her hand. 'An entire jar!'

'I got carried away, Mama, I'm—'

'Got carried away!' Mirto grabbed the fly swatter. 'What are you, a child? Can't you ever think of anyone besides yourself?'

Calliope hung her head. She had hoped her remorseful tone would mollify her mother, but Mirto was not one for silence once she got good and going. 'An entire jar!' she kept repeating. She was swatting at the flies with the gusto of a weary but sorely provoked warrior. 'As if there was no tomorrow!'

'Well, who knows?' Calliope rose for a glass of water, feigning sangfroid. 'There might not be a tomorrow,' she said, turning the cistern on.

'Oh, you! You and your clever tongue!' Mirto had given up chasing the flies and began to set the table with quick, nervous gestures. 'Your tongue's sharp, but your head's full of cotton, if you ask me.'

'Well, I didn't ask you, did I?'

'There you go again, trying to get around the truth with your witticisms.'

'And what's the truth, Mother?' Calliope said, her mind darting to Nietzsche's views on the relativity of all truth. 'I got greedy and ate a jar of preserves. I said I was sorry, didn't I?' Even to her own ears,

Calliope's tone sounded callow, when in truth she felt more ashamed than she had in her entire life.

'Ach, it's not just the cherry preserves!' Mirto pulled out a drawer and snapped up two cotton napkins. 'It's your general conduct. People are dying – dying – and you sit discussing books with the enemy! Philosophy!'

The last word was accompanied by a scornful glance towards Nietzsche's book, which was lying face down on the divan. Calliope had forced herself to stop concealing the book after her quarrel with Umbreit following the burial of Eleni's baby. She still felt the lieutenant was essentially misguided. At the same time, a lengthy meditation on world history had made it impossible to dismiss his views.

'Well,' she said now, mulling over her mother's last comment, 'isn't it better to discuss literature and philosophy than to kill each other, Mother? Maybe—'

But Mirto would not let Calliope complete the thought.

'You know what they say. If you keep company with a blind man, you end up squinting. Squinting, my daughter!'

Calliope disdained to reply to this patently absurd warning. She permitted herself only the tiniest of smiles, but it was enough to set Mirto off all over again. She pulled out a chair and lowered her meagre bottom into it, glaring at her daughter.

'Yes, smile . . . smile all you want!' She spoke with sudden vehemence. 'It's no wonder people are saying you're like Metaxas's daughter!' The former Prime Minister's daughter had the reputation of being so intractable she was said to have broken her father's spirit long before the Italian betrayal. 'Anyway, you know I'm right. You know you don't give a button about anyone but yourself!'

The smile on Calliope's face faded. 'No, I don't know that, Mother.'

'You don't, eh?' Mirto had put her feet up on the divan. She sat wriggling her toes in their black mourning stockings, scowling at a tiny hole on her right foot. 'The cherry preserves are just the latest example,' she said. 'All you care about is satisfying your selfish whims, and to the devil with—'

'Mother, that's not true! It isn't true!'

'Not true, eh?' Mirto wagged her head. The look on her face – the expression of pity mixed with lofty disdain – reminded Calliope of her mother-in-law. She thought of Katina's son, Pericles, whom she loved dearly, of the doctor and his children, of Eleni and Tomas Kafatou. There was no shortage of people she cared about, most of all Aristides, her cherished godson.

'No!' she heard herself say, her voice swelling. 'It isn't true! It's—'

'You're shouting because you know it is true,' Mirto broke in. 'Nothing hurts like the truth, as they say.'

'No, Mother,' said Calliope coldly. 'Nothing hurts like being mis-judged, especially by your own mother.' This might well be true, but she was not at all sure Mirto had misjudged her. She *was* selfish, or at least self-indulgent.

Mirto studied her for a moment. 'I'm misjudging you, am I?'

'Yes, Mother.'

'You didn't just gobble up a whole jar of cherries? You're not cosying up to the Germans, getting whatever you can—'

'Mother!' Calliope cut in. 'You—'

'Whatever you can get out of them,' Mirto persisted.

'Yes! Yes, Mother!' Calliope was suddenly beside herself. 'I also risk my life! I do whatever I can to thwart the enemy!' she blurted, startling herself. Resistance members were under strict orders not to discuss their activities, not even with family.

'Thwart the enemy?' Mirto stared. 'What in God's name do you mean by that?'

'Oh!' Calliope closed her eyes. She should have kept her mouth shut. She should have, but it was too late now. She wanted to tell her mother. She didn't want to tell her. She went and stood by the window, groping for a way out. Mirto wasn't stupid. It was probably better to tell her now, make sure she didn't go about asking questions. 'Do you promise not to tell anyone?'

'Y-yes.' Mirto gazed at Calliope's face, flexing her arthritic fingers.

'Not even Aunt Elpida?'

'Ach, I promised, didn't I?'

Calliope paused, then said, 'I've joined the Resistance.' She stood perfectly still, like a wayward child steeling herself against parental censure. Mirto, too, had stopped, staring with mute amazement.

'Mother of God!' she finally let out.

'Not that this has anything to do with the cherry preserves,' Calliope blurted, vaguely aware of a sudden need to change the subject, go back to bickering over trivia. 'I had a moment of childish weakness. I'm sorry!'

For a moment Calliope hesitated, then, before Mirto could rouse herself out of her stupor, she spun around, seized by an intense need to get away. Away from her own inability to control her tongue, from having to listen, now, to whatever it was her mother might have to say. Seething with self-reproach, she flung the door open and stormed out of the kitchen. The garden was a hot, hazy, pulsing blur, but she surged forward blindly, ignoring her mother's calls.

~ 11 ~

That summer the doctor came up with an unsettling proposal. An afternoon excursion to the Eftalou springs, he tried to convince Calliope, would be the perfect pretext for carrying out an urgent underground mission. She and her mother could start by collecting wild greens, then Mirto would stay at the bathhouse for a therapeutic soak while Calliope went on with the assigned task. Everyone knew Mirto to be in poor health; no one would ever suspect Calliope in her timid mother's company. It was, Calliope conceded, an inspired idea, though she was deeply reluctant to involve Mirto in any dangerous ventures. She would have to think about it, she told the doctor.

Mirto herself had turned out to be surprisingly brave. To think that she would be willing to participate in Resistance activities! More than willing: eager. As eager as she'd been to help refugees back in the early 1920s. Calliope, it seemed, had misjudged her mother no less than Mirto had misjudged her daughter. She might be a worrywart, but Mirto apparently considered some things worth worrying about.

'No sheep . . .' she'd pronounced on the evening of the cherry preserves quarrel. 'No sheep has ever saved its neck by just bleating, has it?'

It was the friendship with Lieutenant Umbreit that left Mirto shaking her head. She didn't see how it was possible to be friends with a German officer and simultaneously participate in Resistance activities. It made no sense to her, no sense at all, she said over and over, as if sheer repetition might help her grasp some small but elusive logic. And yet, Calliope had detected a note of relief that she was not quite the frivolous creature her mother had always believed her to be.

'Your father would have been proud of you,' Mirto had said once she'd recovered from the shock of hearing about Calliope's clandestine activities. 'Is there anything I can do to help?'

Calliope had muttered something noncommittal. She had no intention of putting her mother at risk. And anyway, what could poor Mirto do?

It was only in early July, when a request came through to transfer live ammunition to the guerillas, that she was forced to consider the merit of exploiting her mother's exemplary respectability.

Just before bedtime, she took Sappho to the fortress, to mull things over. It had been a long day of shrivelling heat but the moonlit night was clear and breezy, flaunting its stars across a velvety sky. By the time Calliope stepped out with her dog, half the village was submerged in sleep; the other half would be getting ready for bed behind blackout blinds.

The night seemed at its most radiant at the fortress, where the moonlight danced among the brooding stones. She sat in her favourite spot, her feet up on the parapet, while Sappho went snuffling along the crumbling walls. It was cooler here, on top of the hill, with the sea breeze sweeping across the fortress, murmuring in the trees. Sappho was chomping down on something, but had swallowed it by the time Calliope came down to see what the dog had pounced on.

She returned to the balustrade. The silence was deep and blissful. Among the surrounding trees, underneath each stone, invisible creatures pursued their nocturnal activities. There was the intermittent piping of frogs, the call of a distant nightjar.

Suddenly, there was a small, crunching noise; the sound of feet treading over twigs or pebbles – something. Calliope held herself very still, feeling her skin tingle. Sappho let out a volley of barks, then paused uncertainly, head slightly cocked.

'Don't be alarmed . . . it's only me,' Lorenz Umbreit's voice said from within the shadows. He stepped forth through a crumbling wall, tall in the light of the silvery moon. *'Guten Abend, Fräu Alexiou.'* He had taken off his officer's cap, stopping in front of her with a mock little bow.

'Kalispera,' she answered. She had recently taken to greeting him in Greek.

'I thought you were one of the sleepwalkers,' he said, a smile in his voice.

She waved away a buzzing mosquito. 'No, just a walker who should be asleep.'

For unknown reasons, several local women had taken to sleepwalking since the start of the Occupation, but she was not one of them. She had merely come out to walk her dog and to think, she said conversationally. She turned to lean over the balustrade, facing the Eftalou coast. Umbreit stood beside her.

'Think about what?'

'What, is there a shortage of things to think about?' She gave him a sidelong glance, shifting slightly as Sappho padded over and slumped at her feet. She supposed Umbreit had been at the watchtower; had probably stopped at the fortress on his way back to the stifling town hall. He stood fumbling for a pack of cigarettes.

'So,' he said, 'why *are* there so many sleepwalkers in this village?'

Calliope shrugged.

'And all of them women, it seems. I was wondering why, just the other day.'

'I don't know.' Calliope swatted the insect, scowling in the dark. 'There weren't any before. Not that I know of.'

'Before what?' Umbreit struck a match, cupping it between his hands. The flare of the match briefly illuminated his face.

'Before what? Before you arrived!'

'Ah.' He took a hard drag on his cigarette. Then they were both silent, gazing down together at the moonlit sea. A breeze stirred, trailing the scent of evening primroses across the vast fortress.

'A sublime evening,' he said and blew a puff of smoke into the balmy air. 'Sublime' seemed to be one of Umbreit's favourite words. *Hervorragend.* In recent weeks, Calliope had caught herself using the Greek equivalent with growing frequency. She was like a parrot, she told herself. It probably explained the gift she had for foreign languages. But the evening was indeed sublime. Umbreit began to say something.

'Shhh.' Calliope raised her hand. 'Listen.'

He stopped. He listened. 'A nightingale,' he said, chuckling softly.

'We used to hear them all the time,' Calliope said. 'I don't know why they stopped.' She spoke very softly. 'Strange, it's not their mating season.'

They listened together, standing side by side. It was impossible to explain why Umbreit's chuckle should move her so deeply, and not only when accompanied by a nightingale's song. His chuckle made her think of an infant essaying laughter for the first time. The nightingale went on singing below the fortress.

And then, abruptly, it stopped, and the silence was like a physical blow. It seemed, somehow, to unleash cosmic disappointment.

'Have you ever read Hans Christian Andersen?' Calliope asked.

He smiled. His teeth gleamed in the dark. 'You're thinking of the Chinese emperor, I suppose?'

'Yes.' She stood brooding for a moment, recalling her own childish indignation on hearing how the emperor had turned his back on the humble-plumed nightingale in favour of a bejewelled toy. 'I wept when I first read it,' she said, speaking into the night. 'I wonder how old I was.'

He turned his head sideways and chuckled again. 'What a sentimental soul you are.' *Eine sentimentale Seele.*

'Am I?' She stopped to ponder this, feeling vaguely miffed. She became aware of Umbreit studying her profile, the tip of his cigarette glowing in the dark, circling hypnotically as he moved his arm. He was a superb listener. She hadn't met anyone who listened so keenly since her father died. Elias Dhaniel was a sympathetic listener, but she often felt that half his mind was on his ailing patients. Umbreit listened as if nothing else existed while they talked. As if they had been cast adrift by some unexpected storm and there was nothing to do but listen.

There was a long silence. A sudden breeze brought a whiff of his scent her way.

'I'd better be getting home,' Calliope said, pushing away from the mottled wall.

Umbreit crushed his cigarette under his heel. He seemed about to speak but finally didn't. They said goodnight. Calliope turned to go, while Umbreit leaned back against the parapet, watching her stroll away under the floating moon.

～ 12 ～

One of Calliope's neighbours was Odysseus the beekeeper, who owned a farm on the village outskirts, as well as an old mule cart. It was agreed that, in exchange for soap, Odysseus would transport Mirto and Calliope to the hot springs, late on Saturday afternoon. He had tried to talk them into going early, before the day grew hot, but Calliope had to teach in the morning. It seemed best, moreover, to avoid venturing out when Eftalou was sure to be swarming with hungry women scouring the countryside.

It was past five o'clock when they climbed down from Odysseus's cart, but the sun still had teeth, the beekeeper grumbled. He had let them off in front of the Eftalou bathhouse, promising to return in two hours. He made a vague parting gesture, then swung the cart around and jolted on towards his farm, prodding his reluctant beast.

They were on their own. The bathhouse was long and narrow, with one shaft of light slanting in through a tiny window. It reeked of mould and sulphur. The walls around the shallow pool were yellow with creeping moisture. There were cracks in the walls, caused by some long-forgotten earthquake.

'There's no time to waste,' Calliope said, glancing about tensely. The room had an echo. One of the cracks in the wall had sprouted a pale green weed straining towards the light. 'Will you be all right?' she asked.

Mirto was yanking off her shoes. 'Of course I'll be all right!'

'Fine then. I'll be back as soon as I can.'

Calliope picked up the two baskets. She left Mirto soaking her feet, then hastened across the dirt road, her skirt brushing bushes of sage and thyme. The countryside had been stripped bare over the summer months. Some farmers had taken to staying up nights, on guard against thieving guerillas. The partisans were said to be worse than martens. They pounced on the little poultry and produce farmers still had, then bolted to the hills.

Calliope plodded down the dusty road. Some of her fondest memories were linked to Eftalou; the long summer days she and her cousins had spent here all through their childhood, staying at their *yaya*'s seaside cottage. On hot nights, they were allowed to sleep out in the garden, myriads of stars winking at them through the bamboo trellis, legions of crickets rioting in the bushes. In the morning, they would stuff their mouths with sun-ripened blackberries, the juice trickling down their chins, staining their hands purple. That was their daily breakfast. They would gobble up the fruit, drink some fresh goats' milk, then run off, screeching, into the frothing waves.

Musing on all this, it suddenly came to Calliope that her feelings for the village of her birth were not unlike those one might have for some close family member; someone whose shortcomings one is familiar with, is occasionally vexed by, but for whom one nonetheless feels a deep, abiding affection.

At length, she came to an abandoned field. Squatting, she picked young dandelion greens sprouting along the fence, then, walking a little further, finally found the large, crinkly leaves she'd been looking for: wild mustard. She dropped the greens into her mother's basket, shooing away a red ladybird. The countryside hummed with insects. It was still very hot. She was wearing a headscarf, but the sunrays beat down on her neck and arms. She sat up and arched her back, then got down on her haunches and resumed picking. A few feet away, a lizard lay sunning itself on a rock.

Finally, she was ready. She stood swabbing the back of her neck with her handkerchief. Her cheeks blazed, her collar and back were drenched in sweat, but never mind: she had what she needed.

Retracing her steps, Calliope trudged on along the dirt road, all the way to an isolated beach she had long regarded as her private hideaway. She stopped for a moment, keenly surveying the land, the sea. Gingerly – she was still wearing her homemade clogs – she made her way among the sunbleached rocks strewn along the shore.

She had been charged with picking up a cache of bullets intended for the mountain guerillas. She had recently been involved in the transfer of hand grenades in the village proper, but such ventures were now considered too risky.

Although the distant beach had been her suggestion, she had no idea who had hidden the bullets. It was impossible to know who could and could not be trusted. Anyone who had not visibly lost weight in the past fifteen months was assumed to be among the collaborators or black marketers. Calliope, however, knew better than to trust any rumours. She herself was probably suspected of being a collaborator.

The cache of bullets was waiting in a pit dug to the left of a tamarisk tree where she had often sat in the past, reading or daydreaming. The beach was distant enough to make the location safe, she'd assured the doctor. Yet they both knew the truth: there was always the chance of being spotted by children or some roving shepherd.

Calliope paused and looked about yet again, then shifted to dislodge a rock, feeling her skin prickle. The cache was heavier than she'd expected: a small burlap bag stuffed with lethal iron. The image of an unsuspecting Lorenz Umbreit being felled by one of these bullets surfaced in the back of her brain, and was instantly quelled. *Calm down, calm down, calm down.* Her hands trembling, Calliope transferred the clandestine bag to one of the baskets, then quickly spread bunches of freshly picked greens over the bullets.

She was almost done, was shifting the rock back into place, when she heard a noise – a small rustling sound – somewhere behind her back. It lasted only a moment, but in that short spell, Calliope's body stiffened as if pierced by an arrow. Still crouching among the rocks, she whipped her head around, eyes wildly scanning the overgrown roadside. There were rocks and weeds and thickets of dry bush among the tamarisk trees, but it took another minute to identify the culprit. *Ach, Thee mou!*

A feral, ash-grey dog was staring straight at her, a dead seagull between its jaws. A dog! *Breathe in, breathe out.* Just a hungry dog, already scampering away. *Don't panic. Don't let yourself panic.*

Calliope scrambled to her feet. She peered up and down the beach.

Nothing. Nothing but sea and rocks, the rustle of birds, the dusty, whispering trees. The dirt road was still deserted, the beach as tranquil as ever. Yet she couldn't stop trembling. Three raucous seagulls kept gliding over the shimmering water, calling to each other. The smallest of the birds landed on the crest of a wave and sat there, swaying plumply, contentedly. But the other two went on screaming, like two frenzied parents issuing unheeded warnings.

It was time to head back.

Mirto was waiting outside the bathhouse. Calliope spotted her from a distance: a small, black-clad figure perched on a flat stone, one hand shielding her eyes as she surveyed the dusty road. She had, she said, got sick of the sulphur smell, but Calliope suspected her mother had grown anxious. No surprise there. What surprised Calliope was the wave of warm feeling that washed over her as she took the last few steps towards her waiting mother.

'*Yassou*, Mama!' she said.

She said it brightly, bravely, leaning in to hug her mother's heroic shoulders.

~ 13 ~

Odysseus Pagonis had obtained his mule from a Mytilene merchant who had for years been procuring honey from Eftalou. The family had been unable to feed the mule; had been glad to trade it in for two jars of thyme honey. Odysseus's own mule had long since expired of old age. He himself was much too old to be tramping back and forth on his spindly legs.

All this the beekeeper shared with Calliope and Mirto during the early-evening ride from the Eftalou bathhouse.

'What can you do?' He sighed. 'Once you get past sixty, every day on this earth's just a gift from God.'

'Pah, and why only sixty?' Mirto demanded from the back of the cart. 'Every day from the time we're born is a gift from God!'

Odysseus made a noncommittal gesture. He was a shrivelled old man, with the melancholy eyes of an ageing bloodhound. He kept scratching himself: his arms, chest, thighs. The cart creaked and bounced. He talked, and prodded the mule, and scratched. Now and then he muttered about his eczema, or tried to entertain his two passengers, lisping through missing teeth.

'What's the difference between a Nazi master and his dog?'

'What?' Calliope said vaguely, wondering whether Umbreit had ever had a dog.

'The master lifts his arm!' Odysseus guffawed, swivelling his head back to glance at the two women. Mirto was leaning against her daughter, her hands clasped around her knees. The hands were small and delicate, but raw from years of washing family laundry. Something stirred in Calliope's chest.

'Look,' she said, pointing to the house of a man they had once hired to pick their olives. A dejected-looking child – one of Alekos's great-grandchildren – was lolling against the door of the stone cottage. The boy, Odysseus said, had been sick with measles; had not been the same since then, though the family had called in Sultana the herbalist and given her an egg-laying hen.

'Poor little sod. But at least we ain't got typhoid.' Odysseus sighed, stopping to greet two farmers who had just emerged from a roadside orchard, their shoe soles flapping up dust. The older man had once been a prosperous farmer; the younger was Lazaros, one of Paraskevas the blacksmith's nineteen-year-old twins. Christos, his brother, had recently joined the guerillas, without so much as a farewell to his own mother. Athena Bastia cried for days, Odysseus was soon saying. Women didn't understand men's need to take action in dire times.

'A woman's a woman – she can cook, she can have children – but a man's a man, not a jellyfish, eh? A man's got to defend his land!'

Calliope managed to hold her tongue. The passing farmer was one of Johnny the Australian's brothers-in-law; a man prone to grumbling about the four daughters Mina had given him. Many years had passed since Johnny had come back to marry off his sisters; exactly seven years since he and Calliope had run into each other on this very road.

Calliope sighed. Not for the first time, she found herself wondering how her life would have turned out had she accepted the Australian's proposal.

The mule cart was approaching Odysseus's farm. The beekeeper offered to take his passengers into the village, but Mirto demurred, saying they wanted to dig up some wild onions before heading home. She fished a spade out of her bag, and placed it conspicuously on top of the mustard greens. If there was time, she said, they might stop at the forest, to look for pine nuts.

'Good luck!' Odysseus said, absorbed in scratching himself. Calliope climbed down from the mule cart, doing her best to lift the heavy basket as lightly, as nonchalantly, as if it indeed contained nothing but wild greens. She did not succeed. It was a good thing Odysseus was not so sharp anymore.

Calliope paused, setting the basket down while she adjusted her headscarf. Mirto had offered to carry half the bullets, but Calliope would not hear of it. In the unlikely event that they got caught, she would insist that Mirto had known nothing about the bullets; Calliope had simply exploited her mother's need for a sulphur bath.

The women tramped on towards the wood, each immersed in her own anxious thoughts. The plan was for Calliope to go into the forest where her contact was waiting for the bullets, while Mirto sat guard on the wood's edge, as if taking a rest before climbing home. If anyone chanced to come by, Mirto would say that she was waiting for Calliope, who had gone in search of pine nuts.

But things did not work out as planned. Plodding towards the forest, they suddenly heard the roar of an approaching motorcycle. It was as yet invisible, but Calliope slowed her pace, anxiously peering up the dirt road. No one in the village rode a motorcycle these days. The police chief owned one, but there was no fuel to keep it running. The distant motorcycle had to be German.

'Keep walking,' Calliope said, her mouth going dry. Instinctively, she moved closer to her mother, fingers tightening over the wicker handle. Soon, the motorcycle was rounding the bend, drowning out the clamouring cicadas. An involuntary gasp escaped Calliope's throat: Sergeant Alfred Reis was hunched over the handlebars; Lieutenant Lorenz Umbreit sat in the sidecar, staring straight ahead through his amber goggles. Was it possible she had been betrayed?

'Try to act normal. We were just gathering greens,' Calliope whispered.

The motorcycle engine was cut. '*Guten Tag!*' The lieutenant yanked off his goggles, shifting in the narrow sidecar. He had spoken lightly, pleasantly, looking relaxed and fresh in his summer uniform. 'A walk in the countryside, I see?' he said, still conversational, still his usual affable self.

'Yes. We have to eat after all.' Calliope shrugged. She'd spoken in a consciously offhand tone, but instantly regretted her words. The reference to food must have sounded churlish, given that Umbreit saw to it that she and her mother never went hungry. It was also redundant, since he knew that she liked swimming in Eftalou. Somewhere she had read that the guilty often explained too much.

While all this was getting tossed about in Calliope's head, Umbreit's keen gaze shifted away from her face, briefly landing on her wicker basket. He then raised his sea-hued eyes and regarded her in silence, the corners of his mouth turning up slightly. Was that a smile? Maybe. He was saying something about the benefits of living so close to nature. Sergeant Reis sat waiting, his lips pressed together.

Reis did not like her. Calliope had sensed this from the start, though perhaps it was simply that she did not like him. He was unfailingly courteous, but she felt something cold – cold and condescending – behind his civilised exterior. His eyes, she'd told Mirto, were such an icy blue they might have been made of glass.

'I wish you good health, *Fräu* Alexiou,' Umbreit said in German.

He waited for Calliope to translate the message, then the motorcycle engine came to life again. *'Auf Wiedersehen!'* The lieutenant raised his hand in parting, still smiling genially, like a man who had chanced to encounter a couple of old friends on his way to work.

But could a German officer really be a friend? Calliope asked herself. He had, two days after she'd told him about the cherry preserves, brought her a jar of Bulgarian blackberry jam, telling her she was not to have so much as a teaspoon; it was all for her poor mother.

Yes, he certainly behaved like a friend. And yet, there had been something a little strained in his parting smile. Or had she imagined it? She glanced back over her shoulder, looping her arm around Mirto's elbow.

'Don't worry. It's all right, Mama.'

She had spoken as quietly, as evenly, as she could, but her flesh still felt clammy with fear. A tiny pebble had become lodged deep inside her clog, ignored for the past few minutes. 'Wait, Mama . . . just a moment, please.'

She set the basket down, her muscles knotted with pain. The pebble was chafing at her little toe. Leaning against her mother, Calliope yanked her clog off and shook it.

Suddenly, an inexplicable impulse made her turn, her foot fumbling its way into the waiting shoe. The motorcycle was too far off by then, too shrouded in dust to be seen very clearly, but it looked as though Umbreit had twisted around in the sidecar, and was gazing back across the hazy distance. Yes, that was definitely his face, though there seemed to be something – some dark object – cutting across his features. Calliope didn't think that it was his goggles. Something black, she thought, splitting his face in half. Then realisation struck: his binoculars!

Reaching down for the basket, she felt the cicadas' cries issuing out of her own skull: a shrill, maddening, derisive chorus. She darted a glance at her mother.

'Everything's fine . . . he should be there by now,' Calliope said, desperate to break the silence. She was referring to the unknown guerilla waiting in the woods. 'Are you all right, Mama?'

'Yes,' said Mirto. 'Don't you worry about me!'

'Fine, Mama. I won't.' Calliope took her mother's arm and squeezed it. It was the least she could do now. The least and also the most. Perhaps Odysseus was right; perhaps women were not meant to take part in such hair-raising ventures.

The thought circled over Calliope's consciousness like a greedy vulture.

He knows, a voice in the back of her head was saying. He knows.

1942–1945

'Love is composed of a single soul inhabiting two bodies.'

Aristotle

ONE

1

God did not seem to be on the Allies' side. By the autumn of 1942, Molyviates were starting to point this out to their priests, as if lodging a formal complaint against divine arbitrariness. In North Africa, the Axis forces had begun to sweep into Egypt; in Russia, they'd penetrated the Caucasus, preparing to launch a massive offensive against Stalingrad. American troops had landed on Guadalcanal, were still holding out against the Japanese, but German submarines went on sinking Allied ships, and thousands of soldiers had just lost their lives in the disastrous raid on Dieppe.

The Germans had confiscated all the wireless sets they could find in Molyvos. But, huddled inside a wardrobe, Stamatis the headmaster listened daily to his own clandestine broadcast, passing on the news as he saw fit. Calliope usually learned of recent events from Dr Dhaniel, who was in the habit of dropping his son off for a weekly sleepover.

The child's company offered so much consolation that, one day in early October, Calliope made the mistake of letting him stay up well past his bedtime. On Sunday, Aristides awoke in a contrary mood. When Mirto insisted that he sit down to eat a bowl of gruel, Aristides threw such a spectacular tantrum that, two decades later, he would still be teased about this early hint of his anarchistic leanings.

Mirto went to get ready for church, but Calliope was still trying to reason with her godson when *Papa* Iakovos's wife turned up to request a favour. Calliope was opposed to bribing children, but that morning she promised to take Aristides to the beach if only he'd quiet down.

123

The *papadhia* had come begging for an ointment, hoping to cure the pus-filled boils that had recently appeared on her husband's hands, and that were now spreading to his face and chest. Olympia must have been counting on Calliope's friendship with either the doctor or Lieutenant Umbreit, but Dhaniel had no medicines left and Umbreit was away that month.

All this was patiently explained, but Olympia would not be persuaded, not even when Mirto came down, eagerly jumping in with talk of her own afflictions. The doctor was their friend, she readily conceded, but he hadn't been able to help her either; not even with common female ailments.

'I've got cramps right now – *poh poh poh*, you'd think I was giving birth!' She winced, rubbing her abdomen. 'You think he'd let me suffer if he had medicines?'

The priest's wife was silent. She was a hefty woman with voracious eyes set in a face as pale and plump as dough. The pharmacist had long since closed his shop and returned to Mytilene, but Olympia was not yet ready to relinquish hope. Glancing at Calliope, she reached between her breasts and brought out a gold locket. She wiped it against her blouse, glanced at it wistfully, then held it out in the palm of her hand.

'Take it, *kale*,' she said, speaking in dulcet tones. 'Take it. I—'

'Ach, put it away!' Calliope blurted. The *papadhia* was not merely offering an heirloom; she was proclaiming her willingness to put herself at Calliope's mercy. A few whispered words in Lieutenant Umbreit's ear and Olympia would be arrested for hoarding forbidden gold. It was, Calliope understood, meant to make her feel powerful.

'What do I have to do to convince you, Olympia?! I can't get you the ointment you need—I'm sorry. I couldn't get it if I had boils on my own skin.'

'God forbid!' Mirto crossed herself.

Olympia looked from mother to daughter. Aristides was tugging on Calliope's skirt, wanting to know when they could go to the beach.

'Soon, *pedhi mou*, soon,' Calliope murmured. She did not like the *papadhia* or her husband, but reproached herself for her antipathy. The priest's boils were hideous; his wife's suffering was clearly genuine.

'Ach, ach, ach,' she was moaning now. 'What shall I do, what shall I do, *Panaghia mou?*' She sat clutching the locket for a moment, then held it out again, with the mute appeal of a whipped yet tenacious dog.

'I don't want your locket!' Calliope erupted. 'I'm not . . .'

I'm not in the habit of accepting bribes, she was about to say when Olympia's face crumpled.

'Tell me then . . . tell me what you want and I'll try to get it for you,' she sobbed, flinching when the grandfather clock boomed the half hour.

'Olympia. Olympia, listen to me!' Calliope's eyes flicked over to her mother. *Help me*, she pleaded mutely.

'Ach, we're going to be late for church!' Mirto exclaimed, leaping from her chair. She would be ready in no time, she said to the *papadhia*. Then she turned and bolted out of the room, clutching her abdomen.

Despite the theatrics, Mirto's female troubles were genuine. She had recently turned fifty-two but her periods were heavier than ever. Not only were there no medicines left, there was no cotton to be had anywhere, not even on the black market.

Like all village women, Mirto spent hours boiling her bloody rags, soaking them in lemon juice, to be bleachd by the sun. All over the island, women were cutting up dishrags and dresses and curtains, washing and rewashing them because who could tell how long this war was going to last? Melpo Balliou, the neighbour's daughter, had come upon her father's old army uniform and cut the pants into rags, to the snoopy neighbours' noisy astonishment. Melpo was a little soft in the head but her mother, said the neighbours, should have known better than to let the girl hang a war hero's ruined uniform for all the world to see. Poor Spyros must be turning in his grave, they said. That's what you got when you went looking for a bride among the *Turkospori!*'

The *Turkospori* were the Anatolian refugees who had settled in the village back in the 1920s. Many of them had a mercantile background and were said to be cunning enough to provide for their families even under the Germans, while native islanders barely managed to stave off starvation.

People were referring to the terrible days they were living through as the Black Years. Still, in their calmer moments, Molyviates conceded they were lucky, at least in comparison with people in the German-choked capital or, for that matter, even nearby Petra, where a sadistic officer named Franz Dwinger was in command of the village.

~ 2 ~

A few hours before Aristides threw his memorable tantrum in Mirto's kitchen, his father had been awakened by a farmer whose pregnant wife lay moaning in a mule cart, deep in the throes of labour. It was almost dawn. The expectant father seemed to be in an excited state. The reasons were not immediately apparent, but were soon revealed to be only partly due to obstetrical concerns. The doctor asked a question or two, his head averted from his patient, his hand probing under the tented sheet.

He had entered into conversation between contractions, hoping to distract the fretting husband, only to find himself the recipient of deeply unsettling news. With a midwife, the father would not have been permitted to stay in the labour room, but no man would leave his wife alone with a male doctor.

The Petran hovered by while his wife lay labouring. She howled. She panted. She cried out to the Virgin. Every now and then, her hands would fly up in frenzied appeal, then return to clutch at her swollen girth. Suddenly, she turned on her husband.

'It's all your fault!' she shrieked. 'I curse the day I married you, you bastard! You want me to die, don't you? *Don't you?* Ach, *Panaghia mou*, help me . . . help me!'

The husband blinked at the doctor. 'What's she saying? Why is she talking to me like that? I never heard—'

'Don't pay any attention,' the doctor said. 'They go crazy during labour.'

'They curse their own child's father?'

'Who else?' Dhaniel stepped away from the patient. 'You must admit you had something to do with it.' He achieved a smile, then steered the conversation towards Petra. Three men had been arrested there the previous day, one of them the young man's own great-uncle. The doctor wanted to know about the other two.

'The other two were Germans,' the Petran said.

'Germans!'

'Germans.' The young man fumbled for a cigarette, his gaze helplessly sliding in his wife's direction. He went on to offer details of the arrest, oblivious to the change in the doctor's mien. The labouring woman was still moaning, but more softly now. Dhaniel muttered something vaguely reassuring, then went to stand by the window, watching the morning mists drift across the mountains.

A few minutes went by. The Petran sat smoking. Somewhere in the distance, a rooster began to crow. Suddenly, the patient let out a scream and the doctor hastened back, slipping a hand under the white cotton tent.

'You're going to have twins,' he finally told the husband.

'Twins?' The young man jumped out of his chair. 'Impossible!'

'Twins.'

The farmer went on protesting but, before long, the mother herself provided incontrovertible proof.

'A boy and a girl,' the doctor stated with palpable satisfaction. He flicked a rueful glance towards the young father, who was shifting his weight from foot to foot, like a man forced to stand barefoot on scorching sand. Scratching his head, the farmer watched, wide-eyed, as the doctor slapped one infant's bottom, and then the other. He pronounced both babies healthy and quickly prepared them for their mother's arms.

'You should thank God they haven't forbidden our making babies.' The doctor chuckled at his own little joke. He clapped the young father's shoulder, then reached for the bottle of homemade brandy. 'May they live a long life!'

The farmer thanked the doctor, then downed his brandy in silence, a small hiccup escaping his throat. All at once, he began to laugh: madly, uncontrollably.

'Twins!' he sputtered, tears streaming down his stubbly face. He dashed towards the bed and leaned over his wife, laughing and crying. 'We made twins, woman! Twins! Aren't you glad they haven't forbidden it?'

~ 3 ~

Aristides was sprawled on the kitchen floor, playing with building blocks, when his father arrived to fetch him. Mirto was upstairs, resting after the midday meal. Sappho could be seen through the kitchen window, snapping at flies.

'*Baba!*' The boy leaped up, throwing himself against his father's legs. Instantly, there was the imprint of a small hand on the pale trouser cloth. Dhaniel sat down and drew Aristides onto his lap, listening to the child prattle about the beach. He looked almost dashing in his Sunday suit, but the sunlight picked out the lines in his smooth-shaven face. His hair was still thick, but the threads of grey were numerous now, giving his sandy-hued head a silvery sheen. Calliope had finally started calling him Eli at his insistence, but in her thoughts he mostly remained Dhaniel, or The Doctor.

The doctor took off his jacket. He pressed his face against his son's cheek, planted a kiss on his crown, then sent him outdoors to play with the dog. He had something to discuss with *nona*, he said.

Calliope set two coffee cups on the table. 'What is it?' she asked. 'You seem—'

'The Turks caught Yorgos and Kostas,' Dhaniel said curtly. 'The foreigner, too.'

'The Turks!' Calliope fell into a chair, banging her knee against one of the table legs. The thought that the Lyras men had succeeded in outwitting the Germans, only to be captured by the Turks, was not easily digested.

'They've been in jail all this time,' Dhaniel said. 'I just found out . . . this morning.'

Calliope regarded him for a long moment. 'What happened?'

Dhaniel couldn't say. All he knew was that the fugitives had been captured within hours of reaching Turkish shores.

'*Thee mou!*' Calliope looked away, watching Aristides frolic with the panting dog. 'What do you suppose they'll do with them?'

'They've sent them back.'

'Back? Back to the island, you mean?'

Dhaniel almost smiled. 'They must have figured the Germans would deal with them and save them the bother.'

'Have the Germans caught them?' Calliope demanded after a moment's reflection. 'Is that what you're trying to tell me?'

'Oh, no. No.' Dhaniel shook his head, as if trying to clear it. 'I'm sorry, I'm not being very coherent, am I? They've all gone into hiding. They're safe for now.'

The words repeated themselves in Calliope's head. There had been reports of villages in other parts of Greece being burned down for aiding and abetting the guerillas. 'Don't tell me they're in Molyvos,' she said weakly.

'No. The Englishman's hiding just outside Petra. Yorgos and Kostas – I don't know – some small inland village, I suppose.' There were many such villages on the island, too insignificant for the Germans to be bothered with, except for an occasional raid. 'They were lucky – very lucky,' the doctor said and sighed. He watched his son throw a stick for Sappho to fetch. The boy threw it again and again, but the dog slumped under the tree, panting, her pink tongue lolling.

'Lazy dog! Lazy dog!' Aristides chirped, waving his arms. 'Lazy!'

The child's father and godmother exchanged wan smiles. There was another silence. 'There's something you're not telling me,' Calliope said at length, holding Dhaniel's eyes. 'There is, isn't there?'

'Ach, you know me too well.' Dhaniel chuckled sadly. 'I'm afraid you're right,' he finally admitted.

Calliope blinked. 'Tell me.'

'Ach, Caliopitsa!' Dhaniel averted his eyes. Two German soldiers had been arrested in Petra and taken to Mytilene, presumably to be court-martialled. They'd been caught trading hand grenades in exchange for a slaughtered lamb.

'Lamb!'

'It was someone's birthday . . . they wanted to have a feast,' said the doctor. 'It seems even Germans enjoy lamb on special occasions.'

Calliope began to chew on a hangnail. 'Traded with whom?'

Dhaniel didn't know the man. 'Some old farmer living on the outskirts,' he said. Mirto had woken from her nap and was stirring upstairs. 'They took him to Mytilene as well. Kouches, I think he's called.'

At this, Calliope became aware of heat creeping up the back of her neck.

'I'm very sorry,' Dhaniel said, shifting his gaze towards the open doorway. Mirto was coming down in her flip-flops. Calliope's lips parted to speak but the doctor was quicker. 'Let's hope he doesn't know too much,' he said with a sigh. 'What were you going to say?'

'You stole the words out of my mouth,' Calliope said.

～ 4 ～

Umbreit returned in early October, accompanied by von Herden. The major had made it his habit to visit Molyvos on a regular basis, but was not expected before the end of the month. Why was he here now? Calliope wondered. Did the unscheduled visit have anything to do with the Petra arrests?

As soon as she arrived at the town hall from her morning classes that Monday, Calliope was asked to interpret for von Herden, who was about to interview the olive mill owner. Calliope guessed that one of the Germans' stool pigeons must have hinted that the mill's oil production statement was probably falsified, but Loukas Stephanides staunchly denied the charge.

Lorenz Umbreit – a captain now – was present during the interview, calmly taking notes, while Calliope translated the German–Greek exchange, feeling no less fidgety than the man being questioned. She had been tense around Umbreit ever since their brief encounter in Eftalou. There had been days when she felt sure he knew about her clandestine activities. Other days she thought she must be in the sway of her overwrought nerves: Umbreit's kindness had shown no sign of flagging after Eftalou.

But if Umbreit's decency seemed surprising in a member of the occupying forces, Calliope's own feelings were far more perplexing. She found, for example, that while she loathed the army whose uniform Umbreit wore, she did like the uniform itself – at least on Umbreit's elegant frame. She could not imagine him dressed in civilian clothes, but the feelings generated by the uniform thoroughly muddled her. That the bluish-grey tunic, boots and officer's cap somehow heightened Umbreit's air of vigour and authority was perhaps understandable. But there was also an undeniable – an oddly compelling – whiff of something like risk or danger, and her awareness of this often left Calliope viciously biting at her frayed cuticles.

She was doing her best not to bite them now, though she thought that von Herden's suspicions might turn out to be justified. Both Loukas and his son were known to be cunning as foxes, though Iason's best man had returned from Albania with a slight limp and a serious drinking problem. He had been separated from Iason after being wounded in a major battle and didn't know what had become of his friend. His nerves were said to be overwrought; he seldom arrived at the mill before eleven in the morning.

When the interview was over, von Herden appeared satisfied but, as soon as Loukas was gone, he asked Calliope to telephone Mytilene's olive mill and arrange a meeting. Did he want to satisfy himself about Stephanides's records, Calliope wondered, or was the Mytilinios under suspicion too?

Although no reference had been made to recent events in Petra, something in the air exacerbated Calliope's anxiety. Von Herden was habitually brisk, but today wore a feverish sort of resolve, like a man preparing for some consequential journey, determined to put his entire life in order before his departure. When Calliope finished making the arrangements in Mytilene, he dictated a letter to German headquarters in Athens, then asked her to accompany him and his men on a house search.

House searches were common enough, and Calliope was usually present, since the operation called for an interpreter. What made that day's search exceptional was the suspect's position. Grigoris Yannopoulos was the harbourmaster. At five in the afternoon, when the search unit arrived, he and his wife, Soula, had just woken from their siesta and looked dishevelled and dazed, finding themselves presented with a search warrant.

The harbourmaster's son had recently married the baker's daughter, so the ageing couple was living alone, in Calliope's own neighbourhood. Although she had explained that this was a random search, Yannopoulos and his wife trailed the soldiers from room to room, with the tense air of people who had guns and grenades stashed in their cellar.

But the cellar had already been searched, found to contain only broken furniture and crates of salt cod and root vegetables. Following von Herden's instructions, the soldiers began to strip mattresses, empty trunks, inspect chests and wardrobes. Yannopoulos was silent, absently rubbing his jaw; Soula kept wringing her hands, exhorting the soldiers to go easy on her possessions.

Calliope dutifully translated every word, unnerved by the rancorous glances both man and wife kept flicking in her direction. Did they think that she had anything to do with the search, for heaven's sake? She watched the proceedings in silence until the soldiers arrived at the storage room on the second floor.

Soula, turning to Calliope, finally snapped, 'Couldn't you at least have let us know they were coming?'

'I didn't know!' Calliope protested. 'Do you think they'd be stupid enough to share their plans with me?'

Soula made an ambiguous sound. She was a large-hipped woman who spoke with the voice of a little girl, petulant now. She was still wearing a house-dress, heaving with indignation.

'What is she saying?' von Herden wanted to know.

Calliope shrugged. 'She's upset to see her house turned upside down.'

Transferred from Kavala, Yannopoulos was renting the house from a family who had emigrated to Australia. The owners' belongings were being stored in one of the bedrooms. The door had been padlocked but the soldiers had broken the lock and were now going through the absent owners' possessions: their trunks and chiffoniere, their brass braziers, their mahogany credenza. There was the smell of dust and mothballs as they unrolled an old carpet resting against the wall.

'None of this is ours!' Soula was wailing. 'They emigrated long before the war!'

Calliope translated but von Herden offered no reply. He only smiled a little, his wolf's eyes shifting between the harbourmaster and his wife with a look that was at once indulgent and somehow scepti-cal. It came to Calliope that this was unlikely to be a random search; von Herden would not be wasting his precious time unless something serious was afoot.

She was both surprised and relieved when the Germans came up empty-handed. Yannopoulos tried to comfort his wife, who was dart-ing from room to room, clutching her head at the chaos left in the Germans' wake.

Von Herden apologised for the inconvenience, then signalled his men to go.

~ 5 ~

He did not tell her where he'd been or why, and she did not ask. She had wondered whether Umbreit's absence might in some way be related to the Germans' North African campaign; had even found herself wor-rying that he would be transferred to join Rommel's army.

It was by now evening. Von Herden had returned to Mytilene and Calliope had come up to Umbreit's office to return his Nietzsche, which she had kept for nearly six months. She was vaguely hoping he might say something that would shed light on the Petra arrests, but Umbreit seemed in a surprisingly sociable mood. He had taken off his tie; was down to his shirtsleeves.

'So, what have you been up to while I was away?'

Calliope was reaching into her handloomed satchel for Nietzsche.

She raised her eyes and offered a partial truth: she had been taking advantage of the free time to read and review her German grammar.

'Well, I'm glad to hear that.' *Ich würde dich nicht gerne in Schwierigkeiten bringen wollen.* Umbreit smiled, fiddling with his ink bottle, while Calliope paused to ponder his words: *Wouldn't want you getting into mischief just because you were bored.* This was just the sort of statement that had occasionally made her wonder how much Umbreit suspected.

'I'm never bored!' she replied loftily. She placed the book on his desk and thanked him, her gaze landing on a small collection of beautifully patterned pebbles. Umbreit had collected them on the beach and placed them in a jar of water.

'Thank you? Is that all you're going to say?' He chuckled, studying her with affable curiosity. 'Don't tell me you didn't like our Nietzsche.' He leaned back with his hands clasped behind his neck, utterly at ease.

Calliope shifted her weight. 'To tell you the truth, I'm not sure I understand everything – my vocabulary's still too limited, but . . .' Her expression wavered. He was watching her so intently she suddenly remembered that her hair hadn't been washed for a week; they had almost run out of soap in Umbreit's absence. Was it possible that she was beginning to stink, like so many of her fellow villagers?

'But?'

'But I do understand most of it, and I . . . I can't decide how I feel about him.'

Umbreit said nothing. He swivelled a little in his chair, waiting for her to elaborate. She was having trouble focusing, partly because of the subject under discussion, but also because Umbreit's attentive gaze was beginning to fluster her. He was not handsome, exactly, but his features seemed to exert an almost magnetic pull, all the more so after his month-long absence. She liked his soldierly bearing, his boyish hair and dented chin, but it was the expression in his eyes – steady, intelligent, wistful – that moved her in some deep, ineffable way.

'I mean, there's so much I found wonderful. So much I do agree with.'

'Like?' Umbreit brought down his hands, reaching for his pack of cigarettes. His hands were a working man's hands: large-knuckled, with strong, prominent veins.

'Well, his thoughts on religion, for one thing – on God and sin and all that – I agree with him there.' She paused again, plucking her journal out of her satchel and quickly thumbing through it. Umbreit was fumbling with the cigarette package.

'I also liked what he had to say about the compromises between moral theory and social practice.' Calliope said this with a little deprecating shrug: who was she to be passing judgement on the great Nietzsche?

Umbreit struck a match, then paused briefly, letting it burn. 'I knew it would appeal to you.' He looked rather pleased with himself.

'Yes . . . well.' She bowed her head, returning to her notes. 'I also liked his thoughts on the relativity of truth – I agree with that as well. I often doubt myself,' she added. 'The truth is such a slippery thing, isn't it?'

Umbreit smiled vaguely, then turned to light his oil lamp. It was getting dark outside. 'Now tell me what you didn't like.'

'Oh . . . well, quite a lot, actually.' Calliope rubbed her ring finger, where her wedding band had been. It was one of several nervous habits acquired in recent months. 'I can't understand Nietzsche's approval, his . . . his *endorsement* of cruelty, of tyranny. He speaks of these horrible traits as if . . . as if they were virtues!'

Umbreit went on smoking, regarding her through the swirling haze with that infuriating Nordic calmness of his.

'Oh!' Calliope flared up. 'I knew I shouldn't discuss this with you! I knew it!'

She stared at him for a moment, the colour rising in her cheeks. 'All that talk about the master morality and the slave morality!' She let out a small, ambiguous sound. 'As I said, I'm not even sure I understand it but . . .'

The corners of Umbreit's mouth twitched. 'You don't understand it but you know you don't approve?'

'Yes!'

'Well,' he said, 'maybe we can discuss this further some day. I could perhaps—'

'I don't think so,' she said, forestalling whatever he was about to propose without knowing why. 'We'll just end up quarrelling over your Nietzsche,' she stated. The oil lamp had begun to flicker and she watched him move to adjust the wick. Several moths had come in through the windows and were vibrating around the glass shade. Umbreit's shadow jiggled on the wall. She said, 'I'd probably quarrel with Nietzsche himself if he came to sit in your chair right now!'

'Would you really?' He chuckled and, all at once, Calliope felt obscurely vexed.

'Indeed I would! All that nonsense about women – his total rejection of women as . . . as thinking human beings.' She looked at him with a schoolmistressy sort of disdain. 'It's shameful, absolutely shameful, coming from such a brilliant man!'

Umbreit laughed.

'Why are you laughing?' She bristled. 'Do you really find it so amusing that—'

'Forgive me,' he interposed. 'I'm only amused by how right I was in . . . in predicting your reactions.'

She chewed on this for a moment. 'Well,' she said then, 'it can't take much insight to guess how offensive such views must be to any thinking woman.'

'Well, you're probably right,' he said. But the expression on his face remained amused, fuelling her resentment: he was not taking her seriously.

She hesitated, then picked up her journal and began to read one of the passages she had copied in German. 'What does woman care for the truth? From the very first, nothing is more foreign, more repugnant, or more hostile to woman than truth – her greatest art is falsehood, her chief concern appearance and beauty.' *Erscheinung und Schönheit!* Calliope repeated with sullen emphasis.

She glanced up from her notes to see Umbreit stub out his cigarette, looking wholly unperturbed – perhaps a little bored? This, she guessed, wasn't the kind of discussion he would have had with his German professors and classmates. She was just a village woman and for some reason she seemed to amuse him.

The thought riled her. All at once, she was determined to make him take her seriously, as he would a German colleague.

'Here's another one: "When a woman has scholarly inclinations, there's generally something wrong with her sexual nature."' She looked up from her open journal. 'I'd like to know something about *his* sexual nature!' she tossed out. 'He might be a brilliant philosopher, but—'

She stopped abruptly. 'Why do you keep smiling like that?' she demanded. 'You look at me as if I was a child – a naive child spouting nonsense!' She began to stash her journal away, conscious that she was losing her temper, despite her resolve to emulate Umbreit's exemplary equanimity. 'I can't understand how you can bring yourself to agree with Nietzsche,' she continued, more steadily. 'Why? Just because he's a famous philosopher? Even philosophers are only flesh and blood! They have their own problems, they make mistakes, just—'

'Calliope . . .' Umbreit cut into her tirade, amusement giving way to sudden gravitas. The room was dense with shadows, but the light from the lamp fell on his flaxen hair, his foreign face with its wintry eyes. He ran a hand over his jaw, then rose and came to stand beside her, leaning against his desk. His high boots shone, black and insolent in their German perfection.

'I don't think you understand,' he said. He paused, sighed, then, for the second time that evening, words seemed to elude him. He stood regarding her mutely, his arms folded, his eyes dilated with feeling. Calliope shifted her weight. The silence between them was a menacing cave she had wandered into in a distracted moment.

'If you're hoping to change my mind, please don't!' she said, the words erupting out of her mouth. 'You're good with words – I know you've managed to convince me before, but not this time!' She gestured towards the book on his desk. 'There really is no point in discussing this, since you're bent on agreeing with everything Nietzsche says – just because he's German!'

'Calliope.' He was beginning to sound simultaneously reproach-ful and hopeless. He stood with his legs apart, his hands tucked into his armpits. 'It so happens I *don't* agree with everything Nietzsche says – certainly not the passages you've chosen to quote.' He paused. 'My mother's one of the most intelligent people I know. I might have told you this if you'd given me half a chance,' he stated.

Calliope regarded him. 'Why then . . . why did you keep smiling like that?'

Umbreit was silent for a long moment. Something was happening; some new emotion seemed to be flickering across his face. Suddenly, he blurted, 'Your eyes, Calliope . . . your eyes are like the golden sky in Byzantine paintings.' He smiled at her sadly. 'They're magnificent when . . . when you feel provoked. Full of Greek passion. Did you know that?'

'Oh!' Calliope sprang to her feet. She had always been given to anger in moments of profound confusion. 'Here I am, trying to have a serious discussion, while you . . . you try to appeal to my vanity!' Her eyes flashed at him. 'After all, I'm just a woman . . . my chief concerns are appearance and beauty, right?

'Calliope . . . Calliope, you're not being fair!' said Umbreit. He lifted a hand and spread it through his boyish hair. 'You misjudge me,' he added, his eyes looking wounded. *Du schätzt mich falsch ein.*

'Do I?' She tossed this at him rather aggressively, then recalled that, only recently, she'd thrown the same accusation at her mother. 'How do I misjudge you?' she asked, relenting. She sat down again. She began to pick at her cuticles.

'I take you very seriously,' he said. He gave her a penetrating gaze, a look so peculiarly intimate it made her body tingle. She wrenched her gaze away and let her eyes roam over the shadowy room. Umbreit's office had two windows facing the back courtyard and, beyond it, a long, narrow alley. There were dark blinds at the windows, blocking the room's dim light, but the windows themselves were open, letting in the pulsing sound of crickets and chirruping frogs.

'Look at me, Calliope,' he was saying. 'Please, look at me.'

Umbreit's shadow stirred on the whitewashed wall. He had unfolded his arms, detaching himself from his desk. He bent forward slightly, reached over, and gently laid his fingers on Calliope's hand, which was just then fidgeting with the pleats of her summer dress. He kept his fingers there for a moment. And although his touch was light – barely heavier than the caress of a moth – it made her heart start flapping, like a trapped bird blindly beating against an unyielding wall. She sat for a while, breathing shallowly. Some sort of insect had flown in and was buzzing around the lampshade.

And still she would not speak, would not look at him. Only when he went on to press her fingers did Calliope snap out of her mental haze. She snatched her hand away, as if accidentally scalded. He was still gazing at her with his mournful eyes, but the look she gave him was opaque with fear.

She averted her face, muttering something about having to go home . . . her mother was expecting her. Something. She didn't know what she was saying. She rose and swept past him on reluctant legs, darting out of his office towards the shadowy stairs. She paused long enough to shed her clogs: too clunky, too dangerous, on a dark, winding staircase. He had never let her leave in the evening without accompanying her downstairs, lantern in hand. Once or twice, he'd offered to have a soldier escort her home but she had turned him down: she was perfectly safe in her own village.

She would not go back for a lantern. She began her escape down the stairs, feeling as she had only once in her life, when an earthquake had made the floor in her room heave, threatening to pull the ground out from under her. The marble stairs seemed icy under her feet. A moonbeam came in through a small window, but the darkness, the stillness, seemed dense with obscure menace. She ran down, clutching a wooden clog in each hand; ran towards the exit, the moonlight.

It was only when she arrived downstairs, after she had crossed the foyer and was about to open the portals, that she realised she'd forgotten her bag back in Umbreit's office. Her handloomed satchel, containing her journal!

The realisation made Calliope stop mid-stride, breathing heavily. For a moment, she stood twisted by indecision. Finally, she turned and began to climb the staircase again, berating herself for her incorrigible forgetfulness. She muttered to herself like an old woman, but there was no one to hear her; even Ourania had gone home. The only sounds were those of rats scratching behind the walls. The sentries were no longer positioned at the front entrance, but at the garden gate. She couldn't hear them, nor a single sound from Umbreit's office. Perhaps he was back at work, she thought, sitting at his desk, shuffling official papers as if nothing had happened.

And had anything happened? Had she just overreacted as was her wont? And would he see her now for the provincial she was: a twenty-seven-year-old woman behaving like a frightened hen? Her father had occasionally warned her against surrendering to emotion, but he never told her what to do should she ever find herself caught between two conflicting voices. And, yes, she had been caught! She hadn't known what to do. And so she'd fled, like a hysterical schoolgirl. Oh God.

All this was still whirling in Calliope's head as she reached the second landing. Umbreit was indeed back at his desk, but he was not working. He sat alone in a pool of light, his elbows at rest on his desk, his face buried in his hands. He was unaware of her return; did not see her pause on the threshold, her teeth biting into her lip, her hands with their clogs once more dangling at her sides. She could have gone in and snatched her bag and fled again. Instead, she waited silently in the shadows, aware of her own pulse, watching the moths flutter around the oil lamp.

This moment, too, seemed interminable, but suddenly he became conscious of her presence; had perhaps sensed her scent, her breath. Slowly, he let his hands slide down from his face. And then just sat there, staring at her in bleak, hopeless silence.

She saw that he had been weeping.

~ 6 ~

She had never allowed herself to contemplate touching him, being touched by him. To entertain such thoughts, to acknowledge the possibility of any physical contact, would have been more terrifying, more fraught with danger, than any Resistance activity. Of course, they could discuss literature and philosophy, could exchange books, the occasional joke. What harm could there be in that? There was, as she'd told her mother, little enough pleasure to be had nowadays.

If only he hadn't touched her. If only she hadn't seen him weep.

But hadn't she been warned? Hadn't her own mother tried to tell her that she was not playing with ideas but with fire?

Yes, her mother had said all this, and more. And, truly, she had felt scalded back in his office, his brief touch like a drop of hot wax on unsuspecting skin. If only she had listened! Now, there was no holding back the truth anymore. Neither the truth nor the inner keening. To think of him weeping . . . alone at his desk.

She had gone back only to retrieve her bag, had been about to snatch it off the chair, when he suddenly rose, knocking over the bottle of ink with his elbow. What had he meant to say? She supposed she would never know. The bottle had gone flying off the desk, splattering purple ink over the sea urchin, the whitewashed wall, the scrubbed pine floorboards. It rooted Umbreit to the spot. It transfixed Calliope in mid-stride, her hand on the back of the chair, eyes riveted to his face. She had let out an involuntary gasp, then stood, dazed, two unbidden words rolling off her tongue.

'I'm sorry . . . sorry.'

He muttered something she didn't quite catch, for by then she was wheeling about, once more dashing towards the exit. And then she was running again, every cell in her body surrendering to despair.

To think that, against all odds, through some random decision in the Wehrmacht's bureaucracy, her path would cross Umbreit's. What for? What were they supposed to do about it, a Greek Resistance member and a Wehrmacht officer?

The question tormented Calliope. She did not sleep. She did not go to work for three days, sending a message to say she was sick.

And she *was* sick, all her internal organs battered. She had been offered a glimpse of him, of the flower of possibility, only the better to know what she was apparently destined to lose. She thought of Iason, of how little she had been willing to settle for; how unaware she'd been of the depth of her own marital compromise.

She knew its full depth now.

And something else as well: she was a woman for whom love was as much a matter of admiration as of physical attraction. She had not admired Iason. That she could admire a man engaged in thwarting her own people seemed like some sort of perversity. But, yes, she admired Umbreit – not just his competence and intelligence, but the delicacy suffusing every look, every gesture, with a sort of benevolent grace. He seemed interested in everything, capable of observing everything in the blink of an eye. A soldier who might have been a philosopher, a novelist, an explorer. She had long since noted his virtues, but it took her much longer to concede that he had his flaws.

Perhaps hoping to bring about a change in her internal weather, Calliope allowed herself to contemplate Lorenz Umbreit's shortcomings. She had not lived with him, could not imagine his German life. But after some fifteen months of working with him, of observing him, she realised he was rather complicated. He might have steely nerves, but he could be moody and prickly and obdurate, a man who did not find it easy to admit that he might be wrong. Now and then, she had heard him pace in his office, his boots thumping back and forth, back and forth between desk and windows. He was unable to think in a chair, he had told her in one of their casual chats.

Calliope herself was given to grappling with serious dilemmas either while taking solitary walks or lying awake in bed. But after three sleepless nights she knew that neither Umbreit's approach to problem-solving, nor her own, could ever generate an answer that would come to the surface shining with the light of unequivocal truth.

And, perhaps, in his own way, Lorenz Umbreit had reached the same conclusion. For when she finally returned to the town hall, when she arrived upstairs to report for work, she found Umbreit's office door locked. A thumbtacked note said he would be in Mytilene for the next few days. Sergeant Reis would be at the office in the evening, between six and nine. And that was all. A handwritten note, a closed door, a surfeit of emotion that left her feeling paralysed.

She remained standing outside the German office, clutching a pen, a notebook. Beyond the door, the room seemed to be vibrating with something. She thought at first that she was imagining it. But no. She put her ear to the solid door. A rock bee seemed to be trapped in Umbreit's office, buzzing incessantly. The sound was so close, so loud, it might have been issuing out of her own feverish brain.

But there was something else behind that locked door: a faint, familiar smell that was just beginning to tug at her heart. Ink. The whiff of spilled ink. Three days had gone by but the acrid smell still clung to the interior of the German office. It wafted through the keyhole and under the door, gradually invading her nostrils. Vaguely, she supposed that Umbreit hadn't had a chance to get the wall whitewashed and the pine floor bleached. For reasons she could not have explained, the thought made tears flood her eyes all over again. She turned away from the office door, but the odour of ink went on clinging to her nasal membranes.

She began to make her way down towards her office. Doomed.

~ 7 ~

In mid-November, Lorenz Umbreit was transferred to Mytilene, ostensibly to replace a senior officer wounded by partisans after leaving a local brothel with his adjutant. The visit to the brothel was quickly hushed up by the German authorities; the swift reprisal was widely publicised.

Ten Mytilene natives had been rounded up at random, then publicly executed. One happened to be a friend of Calliope's uncle, but she was less interested in the coincidence than in her private turmoil. Although, with mutual resolve, she and Umbreit conducted themselves as if nothing untoward had transpired between them, she assumed that he had personally requested the transfer. She admired him all the more for his decisiveness, his masterly self-control. If only she were equal to it!

But the transfer, it turned out, was not meant to be permanent.

Umbreit informed the Molyvos council that he would likely be reassigned once the wounded officer was back on his feet. Meanwhile, Lieutenant Franz Dwinger would be overseeing operations in both Petra and Molyvos. Sergeant Alfred Reis would remain in the village to carry on routine business; Umbreit himself would be back for occasional inspections.

All these changes left the Molyviates' nerves jangled, but Calliope and her Resistance colleagues had at least one reason to feel a measure of guilt-tinged relief: Makis Kouches, the Petra farmer caught negotiating for hand grenades, had committed suicide. He'd been hauled off to Gestapo headquarters in Mytilene and thrown in jail, where he reportedly consumed pellets of rat poison. It was unclear how much Kouches had known about the Molyvos connection. The only thing Dhaniel could ascertain was that the farmer had poisoned himself *before* undergoing Gestapo interrogation.

Calliope had fallen into the habit of dropping in at the clinic after taking Sappho for a walk. Now that there were no medicines to be had, many chose to call on Sultana the herbalist; those who preferred to consult Dhaniel usually came in the morning.

One late-November afternoon, while Calliope and the doctor sat smoking and talking in the surgery, Molyvos's dispirited men were beginning to gather in Rozakis's *kapheneion*. Odysseus the beekeeper was seated by the window with Michalis the sexton and the blacksmith brothers when the baker went by with his stout, black-eyed wife. Petros Morales was widely known as a 'domestic cat', a man who preferred to stay home with his family. It was a preference that occasionally rankled, but the baker was hardly the only *spitogatos* in the village.

What irked the men was Morales's haughtiness. His looks were not imposing, but he strode with the smug air of a pasha venturing out with his wife for an evening stroll. Elektra had long since lost her beauty, but she'd passed it on to her three daughters, the youngest of whom was still unspoken for. The eldest had married a Mandamados merchant, the second the harbourmaster's son. It was to the latter's house that Petros and Elektra were heading, closely watched by the men at the window.

The beekeeper, who lived in the baker's neighbourhood, knew the family better than anyone at his table. When Paraskevas the blacksmith asked whether Morales was really a German collaborator, the old man looked up from the cigarette he was rolling and gave a reluctant shrug.

'What can I tell you?' He made a show of lighting his cigarette. 'I don't know this for sure and . . . well, you know me, I never believe what I ain't seen with my own two eyes. But . . .' Odysseus glanced at the adjacent table. He lowered his voice, speaking of a recent night when he'd heard strange noises coming from the bakery.

'It was after two and I was still awake, scratching away like a flea-bitten dog. How a man's supposed to get any sleep with this eczema, I don't know! Still, I know what I heard. Though, mind you, I ain't saying I know what it means, I ain't—'

'Ach, get to the point, will you!' snapped Paraskevas.

Odysseus shifted in his chair. He let his voice drop another octave. 'It was very late and quiet as a tomb, see? And . . . well, there I am, tossing in my own bed, when I suddenly hear a noise – someone going into the bakery!'

'At two in the morning?' The speaker was Natis, the bachelor blacksmith.

'Something like that,' Odysseus took a long sip of tea. 'So I ask myself, I ask, what would a man be doing in his shop at such an ungodly hour, eh? What with the curfew and all . . . you tell me! He hasn't baked so much as a biscuit in months!'

The four men toyed with their beads, thinking.

'So, d'you see anything or not?' asked Paraskevas.

'How could I see anything? You expect me to jump out of bed and run out in my pyjamas?' Odysseus hacked. 'Anyway, you know what they say . . . they say—'

But this thought, too, was to go unvoiced because the sexton suddenly decided to have his say. He was clutching his right jaw, talking through a toothache.

'Ach, people say all sorts of things!' He gestured dismissively. 'If you ask me, we're all getting too suspicious. If you believe everything you hear, everyone's father or brother or cousin is a collaborator and—'

'Yeah, yeah, we know.' Paraskevas patted the sexton's shoulder. 'Ach, Michal, Michal, the devil might be boiling human flesh under your nose and you'd say it was *stifadho* cooking!'

This statement generated splutters of mirth, for it was perfectly true: Michalis the sexton was a man who, even with an asthmatic son and an infected molar, was inclined to see only the best in people. Tall and gangling with slightly protruding eyes and a long neck that seemed to clinch his resemblance to an ostrich, he was known for his odd looks, as well as his fondness for salacious jokes.

'Well,' he was saying now, 'who knows, maybe he had a rendez-vous, like, with some wench, eh?'

'*Petros?* With eagle-eyed Elektra watching him day and night?' Odysseus chortled, scratching away. 'You don't know—'

'That's just it: we don't know a thing,' Michalis insisted, only to be stopped by a jolt of pain. There used to be an itinerant dentist who would come to Molyvos once a week, but all that had ended with the Occupation. 'I think,' he went on, 'I think—'

'Ach, go on with you,' Paraskevas interposed. 'Where there's smoke there's fire, as they say. Why doesn't anyone accuse *me* of being a collaborator?'

The sexton tried to argue, but the more he protested, the more strident the men became, defending their own suspicions. Soon, they were railing not only against the baker but against other villagers who did not seem diminished by the Occupation. By now, men at other tables had jumped in, each new voice fuelling the debate. Natis, the bachelor blacksmith, did not say much, but anyone who cared to glance at him would have seen the nerve pulsing in his predatory face.

Suddenly, he banged his huge fist on the table, making the glasses rattle.

'I say, why don't we go check out the bakery?' he boomed, twisting around in his chair. Fat Dinos was seated nearby with two of his cousins. 'What d'you say, *phile?*' the blacksmith called out. 'Shall we go see what the baker's been up to?'

'That puffed-up bastard?' The postman's button-like eyes flashed in his sagging face. He was no longer fat but seemed as stuck with his name as he was with the memory of his own humiliation. It was not by chance that Natis had appealed to the postman. Everyone knew that Dinos had once asked for Morales's eldest daughter and had been rejected. He had finally married chatterbox Evgenia's daughter, who had rabbity teeth and whom he was given to belittling in public.

'Well, what are we waiting for? Let's go!' Dinos hollered 'Let's all go and see!'

~ 8 ~

In subsequent days, the police chief would be able to establish only that the blacksmith brothers had been the rabblerousers. No one wanted to talk, not even Yannis Rozakis, who insisted that he'd been washing dishes when the trouble started. The police chief seemed to believe the *kapheneion* owner but, as Mirto eventually pointed out, Rozakis's elder daughter had been jilted by the baker's brother, so how was anyone supposed to know what was what?

It was a tragic muddle, there was no doubt about it. This was what Mirto said later that night, after Calliope had returned home. She had been on her way from the clinic, had just reached her own neighbourhood, when she first heard the commotion on the baker's street. Sappho was sniffing the evening air, straining towards the hubbub. Calliope followed, tense but curious.

By the time she arrived on the scene, a dozen frenzied men had rushed up from the *plateia* and were surging towards the bakery, joined along the way by others swinging pitchforks, axes, shovels. Calliope recognised Eleni's father and uncle at the head of the mob, their eyes bloodshot, the veins in their necks bulging. She drew back, scolding Sappho, who kept trying to leap into the fray. The men pressed on towards the shuttered shop, a heaving, grunting mob.

The day was quickly waning, but the men seemed oblivious to the curfew. Although Petros Morales was nowhere to be seen, they kept jeering and heckling.

'We're gonna show you . . . show you . . . show you!'

A shiver ran through Calliope. She had joined several other women, watching the pack converge on the bakery, chopping and hammering. The wind was snarling over the men's heads, snatching at their hair. Fragments of shattered metal began to fly towards the roof. It was almost dusk now. The sky was a low canopy, swollen with thunder-clouds. There was no thunder yet, but suddenly, a triumphant cry rose from the maddened throng, followed by stunned silence. And then whoops of delirious joy.

'Ach, the bastard!' someone croaked over by the entrance. 'Look at these shelves, will you? Coffee, sugar, jam—'

'The jam's Bulgarian!' someone else piped up. 'How did the pig-fucking bastard manage to get jam from the Bulgarians anyway?'

'How? It's clear as day, you muttonhead: the Bulgarians are Hitler's allies . . . oh, look at that: cigarettes!'

It would not take the police long to work out that the baker had been in cahoots with the harbourmaster, who must have bribed the soldier in charge of foodstuffs. The harbourmaster had an office on the waterfront; Morales, whose daughter was married to the harbourmas-ter's son, had ample storage space. It all made perfect sense.

The mob, however, had no interest in speculation. Within minutes, people were storming out of the bakery, gleefuly clutching packages, boxes, jars. By now, the entire neighbourhood had come out to inves-tigate the uproar. A handful of housewives had elbowed their way in, egging each other on.

'Don't just stand there!' the beekeeper's wife shrieked at Calliope. She stooped down to retrieve an accidentally dropped package. 'Leave your dog and go grab something before the Germans get here!'

Calliope didn't budge, but it would later occur to her that had she been as deprived as her neighbours, she might well have been tempted to join in the looting. As it was, the only other person who remained empty-handed was Hektor the fool, who kept jumping up and down as was his wont, hooting with excitement. Finally, Calliope headed home, but she'd barely rounded the corner when Hektor's voice was heard, screaming: 'Fire! Fire! Fire!'

Fire? Calliope spun around. Flames were darting out of the bakery windows, snapping at the thickening dark.

'*Aman, aman,* they've set fire to the bakery!'

'Holy Mother! My husband's still inside!'

'Mine, too – oh, the saints preserve us!'

A dozen looters were jostling to get out: coughing, shouting, clutching packages and boxes. Tendrils of smoke were beginning to purl towards the livid sky.

The women were still shrieking, the crowd still gabbing, when a cry rose from some distant woman's throat; a high-pitched wail instantly recognised by Calliope. It was the voice of Iro Balliou, the *hamam* care-taker's widow. In the frenzied rush towards the exit, sixteen-year-old Melpo, Iro's daughter, had been trampled down. Skinny little Melpo, with her potato nose and big goofy smile!

All at once, everyone's interest shifted away from the burning shop towards the unconscious girl. A neighbour stood waving her arms, shrilling at her son to run for the doctor. 'Hurry, *kale*, hurry! Tell him to come at once!'

In the terrible excitement that had gripped the crowd, no one noticed the wild-eyed baker. Morales had finally turned up; had briefly stopped on a shadowy corner, then took to his heels. It was later said that he must have been fleeing to Mandamados. The last man to see him alive was *Papa* Iakovos, who had been ministering to the dying gravedigger on the outskirts. The priest would later report that the baker had been running for all he was worth. But as the *papadhia* would say over and over in the days to come, 'When your fate's chasing you, neither God nor the devil can save you from its clutches!'

Morales's fate was to be blown up by a German mine. Molyviates had learned to recognise the danger signs, but it was a dark night, and Morales had not been in a state to exercise caution.

Eventually, both the police and Lieutenant Dwinger arrived on the scene. Some of the men who had participated in the looting were now doing their best to stop the flames from spreading. By midnight, everyone had heard about the torched bakery.

Only two men seemed wholly indifferent to these goings-on: Michalis the sexton, whose toothache was to torment him all night, and Stamatis the headmaster, who had his ear pressed to his wireless, intent on far more momentous events. For while Morales's bakery was going up in flames, General Montgomery's troops were fighting a triumphant battle in Egypt, finally forcing the Germans to retreat.

It would turn out to be the first decisive Allied victory.

~ 9 ~

'I told them!' the fortune-teller croaked from under her crumpled bedclothes. 'I *tried* to tell them, but no one would believe me!'

She was speaking to Mirto and her sister, Elpida, who had stopped for a visit. Old Zenovia was down with shingles but, several months earlier, had anticipated a surprising turn in the tide of war. 'No later than Christmas,' she had predicted.

The vision had come to her on Good Friday, at church, and her neighbours had nodded sceptically, and said, 'Ach, *kale*, from your lips to the ears of God!'

Christmas was still about a month away, but Zenovia's prophecy seemed to be coming true, even as her own condition appeared to be worsening. Mirto, cooking in her own kitchen, told Calliope that Zenovia might benefit from some boiled cod soup; the latest news from Russia, she added, might go so far as to provide an instant cure!

The Germans were losing the battle in Stalingrad and, perhaps to vent his frustration, Lieutenant Franz Dwinger conducted a raid on Yannis Rozakis's *kapheneion*. Rozakis himself happened to be at a town hall meeting, but his elderly father-in-law and half a dozen customers were arrested and detained without formal charges.

This was by now a familiar tactic, compounding the loathing both Petrans and Molyviates harboured towards Franz Dwinger. Calliope was not the only villager to wish that Umbreit had not been transferred to Mytilene, but she was almost certainly the only one who kept trying to persuade herself that it was all for the best. Some days she succeeded; other days her inner suffering seemed in some odd way like her due punishment. Punishment for what? She could not say, exactly. But she knew that, one way or another, others in the village were being punished far more severely.

The baker and poor Melpo were not the only villagers to die in recent days. Fanis the gravedigger had also passed away, as had Athena Bastia, Eleni's mother. The blacksmith's wife had grown passive after her son had run off to join the guerillas, but the arrest of her husband and brother-in-law must have seemed like the last straw. Still, who would have expected a herbalist's daughter to mistake a Destroying Angel for the common button mushroom? Was it possible that Athena's death was no accident? That she had simply had enough of the bone-wearying struggle?

Such were the snatches of conversation Calliope caught everywhere she went. The villagers mourned Fanis, Athena, and poor, backward Melpo, but none had grief to spare for the baker's widow. With no one to provide for her and her young daughter, Elektra had been forced to trade in Marika's bridal house, in exchange for a winter's supply of flour and potatoes. Farmers growing their own food could name their price nowadays. After all, you couldn't eat mortar and stones, could you?

Elektra relinquished the house, then shut herself up with poor Marika. And, no matter how people had felt about the baker, it seemed as if the torching of his shop had awakened some pernicious spirits, threatening to slip across every threshold.

All this oppressed Calliope as she passed Marika's former house, on her way to the fortune-teller. It did not seem possible to endure yet another winter, especially not without the daily consolation of Lorenz Umbreit's presence.

Calliope turned the corner. She stooped down to pull up her socks, then rapped on Zenovia's door. There was no response, but most people didn't lock their doors while at home; certainly not during the day.

Thinking that Zenovia might still be napping, Calliope decided to leave the soup jar on the kitchen table. It was just after six o'clock. She opened the door, recoiling from the stench. The old woman was becoming increasingly eccentric, living alone with an ever-growing feline tribe. Her only son was dead; her philandering husband had long since departed for Salonika. Calliope had been a child when the marriage broke down, but the villagers had immortalised the scandal in a little ditty echoing the national anthem: *We know you by the sweet perfume* . . .

The perfume had reportedly originated in a Mytilene brothel, which Zenovia's husband had been frequenting monthly. One night, arriving home late, he found the door barred and his personal possessions strewn around the garden. Pyjamas and shirts were draped over fruit trees, trousers hooked on bushes, belts, socks and shoes scattered on the ground, amid rotting pears and ant-infested peaches. For days, Hektor had babbled about a full chamber pot being tossed onto the notary's balding head. Years later, whenever some womaniser's name was mentioned, Hektor could still be heard singing the catchy little tune.

— 10 —

There were cats everywhere: on faded cushions and fraying rugs, on chairs and shelves and chests and tabletops. Cats blinking and swishing their tails, cats curled up in sleep, cats energetically licking each other's fur.

'*Kyria* Zenovia?' Calliope stopped at the foot of the stairs, her skin prickling. The stench seemed more penetrating than usual, but there was something else in the air that was not quite right. She thought she'd heard something: an odd gulping sound that seemed to be coming from upstairs. Had she imagined it?

She took off her wooden clogs and set her basket down. '*Kyria* Zenovia?'

She began to ascend, certain now that the intermittent gasps were coming from upstairs. She followed the sound – an odd, muffled noise – all the way to the master bedroom. She paused on the threshold. The door was half-open and she gave it a slight push, holding her breath against the nausea tugging at her stomach.

The old woman's bedroom had four large windows but every one of the shutters was closed. There was a faint smell of lemon geraniums and stale urine, but also some other, vaguely familiar odour Calliope couldn't quite name. She took another step, casting her eyes about until she made out the large murky bed standing across the room. Was the old woman trying to bury her sobs in the pillow?

'Are you all right, *Kyria* Zenovia?' Calliope padded across the bedroom, accidentally stepping on the tail of a cat curled on the bedside rug. The cat snapped at her ankle, hissed, then vanished under the bed.

'Panaghia mou!' Overwhelmed, Calliope spun and threw herself at one of the windows, flinging the shutters open. She stood leaning out, breathing hard, filling her lungs with air. When the nausea subsided, she turned around, took a step or two towards the brass bed, then shrank back with a hoarse exclamation.

In the tangle of sheets and blankets lay Hektor the fool, his arms wrapped around Zenovia, his head pressed against hers on the embroidered pillows.

'Hektor?' Calliope whispered. 'What are you doing here?'

No answer. Calliope moved closer. She repeated her question. Hektor raised his head, his face blotchy with grief. He was dressed in his outdoor clothes, but his hair stood up as if he had spent all night tossing and turning. All around him, all around Zenovia's inanimate hump, lay a dozen or so cats, some dozing, some languidly turning their heads to blink at the intruder.

Hektor went on sobbing. Fresh tears kept spurting out of his eyes, gushing down his stubbly jaws, while Calliope stood transfixed, her stomach knotted with intense but not quite coherent emotions. An early-evening breeze came up from the sea and was stirring the fetid air. The stench was coming from a chamber pot underneath the bed.

Hektor seemed to have forgotten all about Calliope. He was touching Zenovia's face with his fingertips: her pale, parchment-like cheeks, her withered mouth, her broad, furrowed forehead. His own face wore the reverent expression a priest might wear while unwrapping some religious relic, or the most ordinary of mortals on first stroking the face of his newborn child.

Another moment passed. Then Hektor stirred and reared himself up, letting his eyes travel from the old woman's face towards Calliope's. He had finally stopped sobbing, and was now gazing at her imploringly, his mouth jerking with the effort of conveying his impassioned message.

'She . . . she . . .' he kept sputtering with a sort of hoarse hiccup. 'She . . .'

But Hektor could not quite bring out the fact of Zenovia's death, and it didn't matter, for by now Calliope knew all there was to know. She came up closer to the bed, then reached out to the quivering, blubbering man.

'It's all right, Hektor,' she said. 'It's all right. I understand.'

TWO

～ 1 ～

Lorenz Umbreit was still in Mytilene when the troubles in Petra started. The island had by then been occupied for almost two years. Calliope would eventually say that had Umbreit still been in charge, the tragic events would never have taken place. There were many Petrans who shared this view; others said that had Achilleas Makris's wife not been sleepwalking the night before, had the schoolmaster had a proper night's rest and had less weighing on his mind, he would have surely used the brains God had given him and not stuck out his neck for the Germans to axe.

Petra's schoolmaster was a heavy-set man who had spent much of his life avoiding physical exertion. He had turned thirty-eight that spring but there was something childishly comical about him – the ruddy complexion perhaps, or the bulbous nose. It was not an appearance to command respect, but the schoolmaster was nonetheless esteemed for his wide-ranging knowledge, as well as his apparent affection for his charges. If he chanced to see a mother berate her child, or a father box his son's ear, the schoolmaster was sure to intervene with all the authority invested in his position. Molyviates who had married into Petra families said he reminded them of Philippas Adham, God sanctify his soul. Their Petra relatives grumbled but took Makris's meddling in their stride. A childless man could not be expected to understand anything about raising children, much less keep his nose out of people's business.

But Makris had his own worries. Soon after Lieutenant Franz Dwinger had been posted to Petra, his wife, Alkesti, had become a sleepwalker. The night before the events leading to Makris's death, she had left the house after midnight and went strolling along the beach. There were those who thought there was something suspicious about these walks. It was a well-known fact that Achilleas Makris, fourteen years older than Alkesti, was even more besotted with his lovely wife than with the schoolchildren. It was equally well known that no good ever came from immoderate love for one's spouse, especially one who had been forced to marry against inclination.

Makris found his wife shortly after midnight. He ushered her home and put her to bed, singing her to sleep as one would a child. But he himself could not sleep, and spent half the night reading Babylonian myths. In the morning, he went to school, doing his best to impart wisdom and knowledge to his charges. School attendance had improved in the past year, thanks to the relief program organised by the Red Cross. With flour flown in and soup kitchens set up, the children were no longer in danger of starving; some even seemed hardy enough for occasional mischief.

The schoolmaster permitted himself only one indulgence, which was a glass of ouzo on his way home. The day after he found his wife on the beach, Makris locked the school door, waved to the children playing in the yard, then headed to the *kapheneion*. A housewife painting her fence later recalled his asking after her ailing parents; a young mother joggling her infant in the doorway remembered his pausing to pinch her son's cheek, commenting on the delicious smells wafting from her kitchen. Makris said something about hungry bears not being able to dance, and went on his way.

As he turned the corner, the schoolmaster spotted two schoolboys crouching next to a German motorcycle. The vehicle had a sidecar and was routinely used by the Germans between Petra and Molyvos. As a rule, it was parked outside the Wehrmacht's well-guarded headquarters. But Dwinger and his adjutant had just learned that Lakis the hunchback was a Resistance member, and had gone into his house to investigate.

Old Lakis was no more than fifty but had looked aged for years, having no wife, sister or daughter to look after him. He was a sickly, rather timid man who had been persuaded to join the Resistance, only to have his name disclosed under torture.

Dwinger and his adjutant could not have expected to stay very long, but it was long enough for the two schoolboys to spot the parked motorcycle on their way home. They looked like children retrieving a ball or chasing a stray kitten, but something about the scene stopped the schoolmaster in his tracks.

'Yassas, pedhia!' Makris lumbered down the alley, demanding to know what they were doing. The two boys took to their heels, accidentally dropping the knife they'd been using to slash the motorcycle's tyres. The *kapheneion* owner's grandson managed to escape but his classmate, a local fisherman's son, tripped and went sprawling across the alley. For a second or two, he lay stunned on the cobblestones, then scrambled to his feet and seized the abandoned pocketknife. At that precise moment, Dwinger and his adjutant emerged, dragging the chalk-faced hunchback between them.

The boy was attempting to flee when the shot rang out. It reverberated beyond the alley, followed by a child's scream, the schoolmaster's cry of protest.

'Fass ihn nicht an!' Dwinger's voice answered.

The command not to touch the boy pinioned Makris in mid-stride, his face wobbling like a drowning man's.

The fisherman's son lay crumpled in the alley, clutching his leg. Makris had fallen silent but the fracas had drawn a knot of men out of the *kapheneion*, their fists hanging like dead birds at their sides.

The schoolmaster was doing his best to control his body. Dwinger had let go of the hunchback, and was shoving his pistol back into its holster: calmly, deliberately. He regarded Makris through half-closed eyes, his mouth lifting at one corner.

Even without the faintly mocking expression, Dwinger's was not an endearing face, his flinty eyes suggesting intimate knowledge of everyone's worst secrets. As it happened, he knew Makris better than he did other villagers, since the schoolmaster was the Germans' interpreter.

'He's a child . . . just a child, for heavens' sake!' Makris's voice quavered, speaking the enemy's language. He made a frantic motion towards the bleeding boy. 'He needs help . . . he needs medical attention!'

The German regarded the gesticulating man for a moment, bared his teeth in something resembling a grin, then slid his whistle into his mouth. And blew.

Instead of reinforcements, a young man in a suit was seen shouldering his way through the swelling crowd. 'I'm the doctor!' he kept repeating. 'The doctor!' In fact, the closing of Greek universities had left Panos Gazetas short of obtaining a medical school diploma, but the villagers had welcomed him with open arms when he arrived from the capital, to be betrothed to the Petra mayor's daughter.

But Gazetas, too, was promptly motioned away. There was a bleat of dismay from the crowd, promptly silenced by a threatening gesture from Franz Dwinger. A gust of wind blew someone's hat off, but the hat went unclaimed, lying on the stones between the crowd and the whimpering child. The young doctor took a decisive step forward.

'Halt!' Dwinger spat out. 'Halt!'

When the doctor ignored the order, the German pulled out his pistol. He smiled his fiendish smile, took careful aim, then shot the writhing child into abrupt stillness.

'Eeeegh!' The onlookers lurched forth, then stopped with their mouths open, like an impassioned chorus arrested in mid-song. The doctor's face had lost its colour; Lakis the hunchback went abruptly limp.

Dwinger whistled again, whipping around to face the restive crowd. He shouted out a warning, then turned to help his adjutant haul the hunchback up to his feet.

Makris, meanwhile, appeared to be drowning in a sea of loathing. His face wobbling, he flung himself at Dwinger, lunging for his bullish neck. For a beat, the cluster of onlookers froze, their eyes bulging. Not a word was spoken. Then they all spun as one and scattered like cats fleeing from a splash of water. There was no telling what the authorities might do if Dwinger lost so much as a single hair.

The German escaped unscathed. The schoolmaster's attack had been foiled by the adjutant, who had let go of the hunchback and swiftly wrestled Makris into a headlock.

At that moment, three soldiers came barrelling down the alley. Dwinger was shaken, but possibly less so than the fleeing villagers. If they had any doubts about what awaited Makris, it was only because of the schoolmaster's knowledge of German. His command of the language was not always adequate, but Achilleas Makris was all the authorities had in Petra. And there were those who would later suggest that Dwinger had deliberately provoked Makris so as to get a better interpreter; maybe force the authorities to let him summon Molyvos's schoolmistress?

Petra's school was housed in an old Turkish residence, with a spacious yard graced by an ancient acacia tree. A couple of farmers came by just as Makris was being roped to the tree. The boisterous children had been ordered off the school grounds, but stood watching from behind the fence, along with the dazed farmers. It was this cluster of witnesses that later reported on the schoolmaster's melancholy end.

The end would come with a single bullet aimed at Makris's impetuous heart. But not immediately. Not until Dwinger himself strode to the schoolhouse, his black boot viciously kicking at the entrance door. He stopped and peered into the dim interior. Glancing over his shoulder, he called to his adjutant, who hurried away, then returned with a jerrycan full of fuel, wisps of acacia blossoms drifting onto his military cap.

Dwinger stepped aside, smiling a bit as the soldier splashed the fuel across the threshold. Then Dwinger himself struck a match, as smugly theatrical as a stage magician. The children let out a strangled gasp. A rooster poised on the roof flapped away, cackling dementedly. Dwinger and the bound schoolmaster stood mutely beside each other while the flames spread their arms, snapping up windows and doors, blackboards and desks and children's exercise books.

It did not take long. Seeing the windows burst into flames, Makris exercised his only remaining power. He squeezed his eyes shut, grief blotching his cheeks as black jets of smoke strove towards the azure sky. There was no shutting out the hissing and spitting and crackling of the spreading flames. Nor, for that matter, the sudden howl of a fisherman's wife who had just found her only son dead in a deserted alley, between two gloriously blossoming lilacs, one purple, one white.

Achilleas Makris died two hours later. Old Lakis the hunchback was found in his jail cell, dead from cardiac arrest. Franz Dwinger was the only man in Petra who had any reason to celebrate that Easter, but the failed attempt on his life would eventually bring about significant changes in Petra, as well as in Molyvos.

$$\sim 2 \sim$$

Calliope's personal life was among those destined to be touched by the Petra tragedy, as well as by other, equally unforeseeable, events following the Lyras men's aborted flight to the Turkish coast.

The foreigner who had masterminded the fishermen's escape plan was a mysterious Allied agent named Rupert Timothy Ealing. After the Turks had sent the fugitives back to Lesbos, Ealing was taken in by an elderly widow, an abbot's sister residing just outside Petra. When Franz Dwinger's terror campaign began to intensify, the abbot had the Englishman transferred to his monastery. The war was not expected to last much longer. The Germans had finally been defeated at Stalingrad. Japanese troops had been crushed in the Bismarck Sea. Axis forces had surrendered in North Africa. In Italy, Mussolini had at long last fallen from power.

In the summer of 1943, however, an earthquake shook the island, causing several deaths and widespread devastation. The hilltop monastery of St Mathaios remained standing but would require major repairs before winter set in. There would be church officials and municipal inspectors and workmen coming and going. It would be madness to let Ealing stay on, the distraught abbot told his Resistance contact.

When he learned that Molyvos had escaped virtually unscathed, the abbot sent an urgent message to *Papa* Emanouil, who offered to shelter the Englishman until his Aghia Paraskevi in-laws arrived for their annual visit. Yannis Rozakis agreed to take Ealing in before St Thekla's Feast, then someone else would have to be found. It was considered too risky for a fugitive to stay too long with any one family.

One stormy evening in early October, Elias Dhaniel stopped to have coffee with Calliope and Mirto, stunning them with the revelation that the Englishman was now in their midst. Ourania Nakou, the former seamstress, was meant to take in the foreigner that week, but her house had just been searched, so there was reason to believe that she, or perhaps her son, had fallen under suspicion.

'So, here I am,' said the doctor. 'Your company's as delightful as ever, but I confess it's not what brings me here on this dismal evening.' He sipped his coffee, looking from mother to daughter, waiting for them to absorb the news. Would they consider sheltering the Englishman next? he finally asked. That this was a risky arrangement hardly needed to be stated; that their house was probably the safest in the village was immediately understood.

'We would take him in ourselves, but the children—'

'Of course, it's out of the question!' Mirto interjected.

Calliope hesitated, then turned to her mother. 'Are you willing to—'

Mirto made a disgruntled gesture. 'If you're willing, I'm willing!' she snapped. 'He'll have to stay in the cellar, of course.'

'Of course,' said the doctor. 'He speaks French, by the way.'

'Well, I can certainly use the practice,' Calliope said.

And so it was settled. Rupert Ealing moved in towards the end of November. Mirto cleared out the storage room because the cellar had become too damp. The storage space had a staircase leading into the cellar, where the thirty-four-year-old foreigner was instructed to disappear the moment he heard anyone knocking at the front door. He was a quick, wiry man with a thick head of curly hair and the gleeful eyes of an adolescent who has just dreamed up some delightful prank for an unsuspecting parent. What with the religious texts in the monastery and Calliope's foreign novels, he joked, his education would be much improved by the time the war ended.

When he wasn't reading or sleeping, Ealing offered an occasional, rather eccentric, English lesson. Perhaps because he missed his children, he liked to amuse himself by teaching Calliope limericks and nursery rhymes. He sang or recited them, then wrote the words down with a French translation, instructing Calliope to memorise them.

I'd rather have fingers than toes
I'd rather have ears than a nose
And as for my hair
I'm glad it's all there
I'll be awfully sad when it goes!

That was how Calliope began her acquaintance with English humour and grammar while still trying to perfect her German. She had never considered studying a third foreign language, but was only too happy to sing or recite Ealing's offerings and let herself be diverted by his English jokes. The news that the former seamstress's house had been ransacked kept gnawing at Calliope. She knew that, in the event of an arrest, Ourania would not be able to withstand Gestapo interrogation. She also knew that, should she herself become compromised, Umbreit would not have it in his power to save her; certainly not with his icy-eyed adjutant lurking about.

Lorenz Umbreit was back in Molyvos, having been transferred after a second failed attempt on Franz Dwinger's life. Umbreit was now in charge of the coastal region, doing his best to placate the volatile Petrans. He divided his time between the two sister villages but, through some tacit agreement, he and Calliope continued to avoid being alone with each other.

Mirto was relieved that her daughter was now doing much of her work at home, but it wasn't long before her anxiety over Umbreit gave way to a new concern. She readily conceded the pleasure of the Englishman's company. She especially enjoyed Rupert's imitations of Hitler, Churchill, Mussolini. But if she'd known that the foreigner was young, and would be engaging Calliope in lengthy discussions, she would never have agreed to take him in. Never!

The Englishman was married, with three young children, but Mirto's anxiety erupted one Sunday after the church bells had fallen silent. Calliope had stayed up late the night before, talking and laughing with Rupert. Mirto herself was about to go off to church, leaving her daughter alone with a hot-blooded foreigner under her own roof. She didn't like it, didn't like it at all, she kept saying.

'How do you know he's hot-blooded?' Calliope asked.

'How do I know? How do I know? I know you'd rather stay with him than come to church with me!' Mirto shot back.

'But Mama!' said Calliope. 'I stayed home Sundays long before Ealing came!'

'That's true as far as it goes, but now you have a much better reason!'

This was the sort of circuitous logic that used to madden Calliope, but now it only made her laugh, for Mirto's maternal intuitions had fallen wide of the mark: she was not at all attracted to Rupert Ealing, if only because her heart had long since declared its allegiance to another. Despite everything, she still felt that everyone in the world spoke one language, while she and Lorenz Umbreit spoke another.

But there was no doubt about Ealing being an exceptional man. They discussed everything, from the progress of the war to some of the philosophical questions she had been grappling with since she'd read Nietzsche. Ealing might have an irreverent side, but he, too, seemed omnicurious, as interested in Mirto's family photos and Sappho's canine psychology as in the nature of power, truth, justice.

When, just before Christmas, the time came for the Englishman to move on, a forged ID was discreetly delivered by the mayor's brother. With his light brown hair dyed black and his jaws unshaven, Rupert Ealing could easily pass for a stonemason named Vassilis Roufos. Assuming he kept a low profile, he should have no trouble blending in with Mytilene natives.

The Englishman was to stay with *Papa* Ioannis. The only hitch was his paltry knowledge of modern Greek. Ealing had studied Classical Greek, but had been advised to play deaf-mute rather than risk being denounced. He was evasive about his precise purpose in the Aegean, but was known to have studied history and linguistics before the war. On his last evening in Molyvos, he revealed that he had also acted in amateur theatricals, back in his Oxford days.

'Well, my friend, here's your chance to put your talent to the test,' Dhaniel said, in his accented French. The Englishman kept clowning for his hosts, cracking skittish jokes. It was evidently easier to do this than to contemplate tomorrow's venture.

The tension, alas, was allayed neither by jokes nor by the spinach pancakes Mirto had made with some of the recently donated flour. The efforts of the Red Cross had immeasurably eased Molyviates' lives, but Mirto herself showed little appetite. She kept biting her lips, wringing her hands, exchanging tense looks with the doctor. Dhaniel was eating heartily, offering bits of advice to the Englishman, like an anxious father sending his young son out into the world.

Ealing would be travelling to Mytilene in the mayor's taxi, along with three passengers who had legitimate reasons for going to the capital. There would be Yannis Rozakis, whose Mytilene brother was known to be terminally ill; Stella Gravari, the doctor's mother-in-law, who spent Christmas with her elder daughter; and the doctor himself, who needed to consult a cardiologist. Dhaniel's occasional chest pains were genuine, but his trip to Mytilene was carefully timed: his presence made it unlikely that the car would be searched should they run into a roadblock.

Calliope had become so accustomed to living with dread it was hard to imagine a normal sort of existence. But then, there were so many things none of them could have imagined before the Occupation. Who could have foreseen that she and her mother would some day find themselves harbouring a British fugitive? The entire experience seemed like just another wartime dream.

On the Englishman's last evening in Molyvos, after the doctor had gone home and Mirto to bed, Calliope and Rupert stayed up alone for the last time.

'We'll miss you,' Calliope said, ready for a final goodnight. She was holding a small dish of oil with a single burning wick. 'Write to us . . . when it's all over. Please?'

'I will . . . I promise.' Ealing crossed his heart. He apologised for having no gift to offer for their many kindnesses. 'But, here . . . I've written something for you.' He held out a folded sheet of paper torn out of an exercise book supplied by Calliope. On it were written two English lines.

'I can't understand this!' Calliope laughed. The only words she recognised were *is* and *know*. 'What is it, a quotation?'

'Yes. It's by John Keats, a famous English poet.' Ealing's eyes twinkled.

'So, aren't you going to tell me what it says?'

'No!' Ealing looked playfully smug. 'But I want you to promise me something.'

'What?'

'I want you to promise that you'll learn English, and when you do . . .' He tweaked the tip of her nose.

'When I do?'

'When you do, I want you to send me a translation of these two lines. It'll be your final assignment.'

Calliope's gaze flicked down to the sheet in her hand, and then back to Ealing.

'You mean I have to live with the suspense until I've mastered English?'

'Oh, you won't have to master it to understand this.' He grinned. 'There are basically only two key nouns here and one key verb. That's all you need to know.'

~ 3 ~

The doctor's mother-in-law had brought blackberry jam sandwiches and a bag of dry figs for the three-hour journey. Having passed safely through Kaloni, they stopped at a pine wood to answer the call of nature and to let Ealing out of the boot before going on. The German interpreter in Kaloni was an inquisitive corporal, often present during random roadblocks. It seemed prudent to keep the Englishman out of sight until they left the region, and also just before entering Mytilene. If there happened to be a roadblock along the way, there would likely be only rank-and-file soldiers.

But there just might be someone with a smattering of French; some show-off chap who would want to know what a stonemason from the capital had been doing in Molyvos. Should this come to pass, the doctor would explain that Vassilis Roufos had come to the village hoping to do odd jobs for Stella Gravari, who had occasionally hired him back in Mytilene.

While all this was under discussion, Rupert Ealing was nestled inside the black Ford's boot. When at length they stopped to release him, the Englishman clambered out, peering about with a long, theatrical scowl.

'Why are there never any Germans when you really need them?' he quipped in French. He had his hands at his waist and was rolling his head, as if to relieve a stiff neck. 'I'm sure they would provide a more comfortable mode of transport!'

'*Certainement.*' Dhaniel's mouth curled. 'All the way to Gestapo headquarters!'

They laughed. Dhaniel translated their exchange to his mother-in-law while the mayor and the *kapheneion* owner trudged into the woods.

'There are some things one must never joke about,' Stella Gravari said to the doctor. She was a woman who had been raised to conduct herself with good cheer and flawless decorum, but who had grown dour and anxious after her daughter's death. A gust of wind had come soughing through the pines and she shivered dramatically. '*Poh poh poh*, how cold it is suddenly!'

It was two days before Christmas. Stella's cheeks were colourless, her lips resolutely compressed. Kyriakos and Rozakis emerged from the woods, to find Ealing standing in the pine-scented air, thoughtfully staring at a clump of trees while biting into his sandwich. A bird was trilling somewhere in the wood. Ealing listened with an air of acute attention, soon identifying the melodious bird as a common crossbill.

'*Un bec-croisé, des sapins,*' he said to Dhaniel. He swallowed the last of his sandwich, then sauntered into the woods, his hands thrust into his pockets. The doctor gazed after him with undisguised affection.

'This foreigner seems to know something about everything,' he said.

Kyriakos chortled. 'I know he's going to get his nuts frozen if he takes too—' He stopped. He turned and, looking flustered, apologised to Stella.

The Englishman came back, settling in between Rozakis and the elderly widow. Soon, they were on their way. There were villages, fields, orchards, then the scenery became a monotonous silvery blur. Nothing but cringing olive trees. The sky was as empty and bleak as if the wind had swept every ray of sun to some unknown realm. Ealing busied himself poring over Kyriakos's map. Soon, he drifted off, as did Stella Gravari and Yannis Rozakis. Only the doctor and the mayor remained awake, their eyes fixed on the perilous road ahead.

— 4 —

The farmer, an old man riding a mule cart, was not from Mytilene but from Pamphylla. All the same, he'd heard that things were tense in the capital. Two days earlier, anti-Fascist flyers had been distributed all over town and the Germans had failed to capture the culprits. The bastards were now clamping down on all Mytilene residents, the farmer told Molyvos's mayor. Kyriakos had hailed the stranger on the empty road, hoping for news from the capital. This was not the news he had hoped to hear.

'May they drown in their own piss!' he spat out in parting.

He drove on, raising dust and gravel, speculating about the flyers. Eventually, a sign marking the capital appeared in the distance. As if on cue, Ealing sat up and glanced at his watch. Stella woke as well and began to burrow in her oversized bag.

'Better move the Englishman before we hit the checkpoint,' she counselled.

'Ach, *Kyria* Stella,' Kyriakos twisted away from the wheel. 'What d'you take me for? I'm the mayor, for heaven's sake!'

'What, can't a woman say what she thinks anymore? You would think—'

'Please, let it go, Mother,' the doctor cut in. 'It's his nerves. Try to understand.'

'Well, I have nerves too, you know!' Stella retorted, powdering her nose. 'I'll have you remember that four children are dependent on my surviving this venture.'

'I remember, I remember.' Dhaniel sighed. 'Only—'

'Ach, stop, all of you!' Rozakis, awake now, gestured irritably. 'How can we keep our wits about us if we don't stop bickering?'

Everyone nodded at this, except for Rupert Ealing, who blew his nose, then tapped Stella on the shoulder, asking to borrow her compact. He sat scrutinising his own altered features, as if to reassure himself that his English looks had not somehow triumphed over those of the putative stonemason.

'Hm,' he said, raising an ironic eyebrow. His unwashed hair and stubbled jaws made Ealing look not only unlettered but somehow ineffectual. It would take little effort to imagine this man hefting stones and buckets of mortar.

He handed the compact back to Stella, stabbing his own chest with theatrical pride. *'Me Greek palikari!'* he said.

'Yeah, well, just remember not to sing the national anthem,' Kyriakos quipped. He braked and was about to open the door when the doctor stopped him.

If the Germans were busy rounding up suspects, he mused out loud, their interpreters were almost certainly engaged in extensive interrogations. It was extremely unlikely they would run into any Greek-speaking Germans. 'On the other hand, they're probably hoping to find more of those flyers—'

'So?' Kyriakos said.

'So, they're likely to be inspecting boots. Maybe we should let him stay with us after all,' Dhaniel suggested.

This idea was tossed back and forth until all agreed the doctor had a point.

All except Stella, who feared that Ealing might give himself away.

'He may look Greek,' she argued, 'but he blows his nose like an Englishman!'

168

'Don't worry, Mother.' Dhaniel expelled a forbearing breath. 'We'll tell him not to blow his nose if the Germans stop us.' He said something in French to Ealing, who did his best to soothe Stella in his fanciful ancient Greek.

But Stella would not be soothed. 'And what if he sneezes?' she said, addressing the back of her son-in-law's head. The doctor had a way of rubbing the bridge of his nose whenever his patience was being sorely tested. He turned, and was about to say something, when Rozakis roused himself, bestowing a rare smile on the fretting widow.

'Now, now, *Kyria* Stella,' he said, leaning towards her across Rupert Ealing. 'If there's one thing an Englishman does just like the rest of us, it's sneeze. Believe me, I've heard him do it many times while he stayed with us.'

'Well . . .' Stella flicked him sceptical glance. 'If you say so.'

Ealing closed his eyes. He appeared to be dozing again when, approaching the town's outskirts, they spotted the dreaded checkpoint: a red-and-white barricade running across the road. There was a small hamlet on their left, a ravine on their right. There was nowhere to go but forward. In the distance, three soldiers could be seen, attired in long winter coats, carabines slung over their shoulders. Stella shrank in her seat, muttering under her breath.

'Get a grip on yourself, Mother!' the doctor snapped. 'Try to act normal.'

The mayor screeched to a halt, peering through the windshield.

'Dokumente!'

A German soldier was leaning into the driver's window, his eyes sweeping the passengers as they fumbled for their IDs. Perhaps because of Stella's perspiring forehead, or the capacious bag she was clutching, the soldier stopped to scrutinise her face, as if suspecting a male rebel in disguise. He gave the men's IDs a cursory look, but studiously examined Stella's. The old woman's face was utterly drained of colour. She couldn't have looked more anxious had hand grenades been stashed in the depths of her bag.

The corporal threw the driver's door open. 'Out!' he ordered. 'All of you!' A young man with cornflower-blue eyes and an epicene nose, he spoke and moved in a jerky, self-conscious way, like a disgruntled adolescent determined to assert his independence. As the passengers clambered out of the car, he said something to the two privates.

'Relax,' Rozakis said to Stella, in the tone a father might use to calm a child at the dentist's. 'They just want to inspect the car . . . it's normal.' For all his size, there was something delicate, almost feminine, about Rozakis. It might have had something to do with his disproportionately small hands, or perhaps his thoughtful, measured tones. Whatever it was, Stella collected herself, while a tall, reed-like private busied himself searching the car's interior.

The corporal ordered Kyriakos to open the trunk; the second private stood looking on, his carabine at the ready. A few feet away, the five passengers clustered on the roadside, doing their best to look bored and indifferent.

Suddenly, an old woman came toddling out of the hamlet, gesticulating wildly. She was shouting as she crossed the road, her voice scratchy, as if from excessive use.

'What's she yattering about?' the carabine-brandishing private asked, scowling ferociously. He was a good-looking young man whose expression suggested he would rather be anywhere in the world than on this foreign, windblown patch of earth. For all they knew, though, this could be a Resistance plot. The old peasant might be there as a diversion; the passengers could be guerillas waiting to strike.

'She's lost her lamb,' Elias Dhaniel said, forgetting he was not supposed to understand German. It was too late. The crows in the tree shrieked, as if in sudden glee – *krrah, krrah, krrah.*

'Her lamb?' The soldier gave the old woman a sceptical going-over. She was dressed in black from head to toe, was wringing her hands, tearfully demanding whether any of them had seen the straying animal. Getting neither help nor clues, she turned away, peering into the ravine with her cloudy eyes. She was muttering to herself, alternately appealing to the Virgin and calling to her lost lamb.

'Where are you, where are you, my little rascal?'

There was a bleating sound from within the ravine.

'Ach, there he is, the trickster!' The old woman's face broke into a toothless grin. 'Come, you little rascal!' she shrieked, scurrying off on her crooked legs. 'I can see him now! He's there!' she cried. 'Come—'

'Tell her she mustn't go into the ravine,' the bored-looking private cautioned, cutting into the old woman's calls. Dhaniel translated the German's words, but the villager blundered on, flapping a reassuring hand over her shoulder.

And then, both the soldiers and the passengers became distracted. The corporal was slamming the trunk door, his disgruntled expression leaving no doubt: he had fully expected to find some kind of contraband in this village taxi. He glanced at Stella Gravari, looking undecided, then set about inspecting the car all over again. He ordered the private to frisk the passengers, starting with the old lady. In the distance, they could still hear the bleating of the lamb, the old peasant's voice calling, calling.

When Stella understood that the soldier meant to search her person, she uttered a wail of protest. The doctor let out a martyred sigh. The soldier looked tense, waiting for Dhaniel to persuade his mother-in-law to calm down and let him do his job. Stella wasn't going to make it easy. She was still protesting when something exploded in the ravine, sending blasts of smoke towards the wintry sky.

'Ach, *Thee mou*, a landmine!' Rozakis's fingers were tugging at his jowls.

'A landmine?!' Stella crossed herself, then began to jabber away. The others froze, then bolted towards the edge of the ravine. The air was thick with smoke and dust but, all at once, the lamb was heard bleating again: a faint, plaintive sound rising from the bed of the seething ravine.

The soldiers were still peering down, still scratching their heads, when a second explosion was heard – a deafening sound drowning out the crows' cacophony, the lamb's pitiful bleat, the Greeks' cries of dismay, the Germans' confused exclamations. Both travellers and soldiers had flinched back from the edge of the ravine, muddled by stench and dust. For a moment, no one uttered a word, until the corporal turned to speak to the lanky private. Dhaniel was the only one paying attention.

'Don't worry,' the soldier was saying. 'Her family will thank us . . . one mouth less to feed.' He was about to add something but, catching Dhaniel's look, stopped and cleared his nose, fidgeting with his cap. For a short spell, perfect silence hung over the dust-shrouded roadside. The entire universe seemed to be holding its breath, as if waiting for some divine power to wash it all away and make it new again.

~ 5 ~

Kyriakos Himonas and Yannis Rozakis had been drinking for over two hours when the gypsy entered the Mytilene *kapheneion*. The Molyviates had come down to celebrate their successful mission, and to pass some secret documents to Orestes Fotiadis, who'd owned the Molyvos pharmacy before the Occupation.

The *kapheneion* was pleasantly warm, tantalisingly scented by coffee and roasting chestnuts. There was a constant hubbub, a spirit of bonhomie sharpened by the dropping temperatures. Rozakis had never shed the forlorn air that had come over him when his son failed to return from Albania, but Kyriakos was in high spirits, especially after Orestes joined them with a carafe of ouzo. With the shortage of medicines, the pharmacist no longer opened his shop, but he belonged to a landowning family and did not appear to be wanting. In the third year of the Occupation, he was still fat-bellied; still had the soft, plump hands of a complacent bishop.

But there was nothing complacent about Orestes. His small eyes might resemble raisins pressed into a fresh bun, but they were as keen and alert as a spy's. He happened to be watching the entrance when the gypsy came in, tossing her long plaits. He recognised her instantly; recalled buying a yoyo from her back in Molyvos.

Rozakis remembered her as well, but the mayor didn't.

'Amalia, eh?' Kyriakos was ogling the stranger. 'Good name for a dishy wench,' he said, belching into his ouzo.

The gypsy had come to peddle Christmas chocolates. She was offering one to the *kapheneion* owner's son when Orestes and

Kyriakos rose to go to the urinals. Rozakis stayed behind, to keep an eye on their table. The *kapheneion* was packed. Rumours were flying that a German ammunition truck had just been blown up near the harbour.

Kyriakos and Orestes disappeared behind the utilities door. The secret documents quickly passed from the mayor's hands into the ex-pharmacist's. Orestes slid the papers into his pocket, patting Kyriakos's shoulder. The urinals stank, but the mayor seemed determined to share every detail of that morning's mission. Orestes listened.

By the time Kyriakos finished his story, the gypsy had worked her way towards the back of the room, where Rozakis sat alone, smoking in the corner. She cast a casual glance in his direction, stopped, then sauntered towards him, a yelp of recognition escaping her throat.

'I remember you!' she crowed. She stood scanning his features, her head canted as she strove to place him. The *kapheneion* owner had aged since the Albanian draft, but some things remained the same: the long nose, the birthmark on the left temple.

'You're from Molyvos, aren't you, my friend?' The gypsy stood beaming. 'You own the *kapheneion* there, don't you?'

'I do.' Rozakis dragged on his hand-rolled cigarette, then tapped off the ashes, barely glancing up.

'Sure, I remember you,' the gypsy was saying. 'One of your men bought three tablecloths. You were very kind . . . you offered us mints, eh?'

Rozakis shrugged.

The gypsy remained standing, a box of chocolates pressed below her breasts. 'So, what brings you to Mytilene?'

'Family matters.' Rozakis swished the ouzo in his glass. He watched Orestes and Kyriakos squeeze their way back among the marble-topped tables.

'Well, sir,' said the gypsy, 'how would you like to buy a chocolate or two? Pure milk chocolate, top quality and—'

Rozakis cleared his nose. 'No, thank you. I don't like sweets,' he stated.

'But didn't you just tell me you had a family?' The gypsy had stepped back to make room for Kyriakos and Orestes. 'A wife, children? St Basil's Day is just—'

'Here, I'll buy one . . . for my grandson,' Orestes said, reaching into his pocket. 'How much?'

'For you, sir, one thousand drachmas.'

'Ach, go on with you!' Orestes's flaccid cheeks trembled with amusement. 'Here, this is as much as you'll get from me. Take it or leave it.'

They finally settled on five hundred drachmas. The gypsy stashed the bills between her breasts, winking at Kyriakos. The mayor might occasionally drink too much, but women were nonetheless drawn to his flashing eyes and leonine head of hair. Rozakis rose from the table.

'Where are you going?' asked Orestes. 'It's still early—'

'A friend of my brother's just walked in. I'd like to have a word.' Rozakis's brother had died several months earlier, but his death had gone unreported so that the family could benefit from the extra food coupons issued by the Red Cross.

'How 'bout you?' the gypsy was asking Kyriakos. She had slid past Rozakis's chair and was leaning forward, thrusting the chocolate box out towards the mayor.

Kyriakos appeared indifferent to the boxed sweets. His gaze was riveted to the gypsy's breasts, which were pushing out roundly against her brick-coloured sweater.

'I don't care for chocolates,' he said, reaching for his glass.

'Huh?! What is it with you Molyviates?' The gypsy let out a small sound, half teasing, half disdainful.

'There's a war on, lady,' Orestes said with abrupt irritation. 'Not everyone can afford to blow money on sweets, you know.'

The gypsy turned, her tongue darting over her lips. 'True enough, sir,' she said, looking sage and playful. 'But it's holiday time. Even in wartime, there must be a little sweetness, no?'

Orestes made an ambiguous gesture. 'You're wasting your time, lady,' he said.

'Ach, what's time, sir, when you're in good company?' The gypsy cackled again, turning to smile into Kyriakos's eyes. 'Aren't I right?'

The Molyvos mayor was grinning foolishly, like a tipsy, tongue-tied adolescent.

All at once, the gypsy reached into her box and plucked out one of the chocolates. She peeled back the silver wrapper, then bent forward and popped the chocolate straight into Kyriakos's mouth.

'You might think you don't care for sweets, sir, but you've never tasted Amalia's, have you?' She grinned. She held out a finger and flicked a tiny speck of chocolate off Kyriakos's chin.

Orestes drained his glass and pushed away from the table. 'I'm going home!' he announced, doing his best to flatten himself between tables. The *kapheneion* owner was beginning to roll down the blackout blinds.

'Don't worry, this one's on me,' the gypsy told Kyriakos. Neither she nor the mayor had taken any notice of Orestes's departure. Other men were leaving as well, though in recent days the Germans had become lax in enforcing the evening curfew. Rozakis was threading his way back to the corner table.

'Believe me,' the gypsy was crooning in Kyriakos's ear. 'I could make your life much sweeter than this, sir.'

'Is that a promise?' Kyriakos smiled, glancing up as Rozakis approached.

'I'll be here until curfew,' the gypsy said with sudden resolve. 'If you like, we could leave together.'

Kyriakos slapped the edge of the table. 'Well, why not? I agree!' he said, drawing himself up as Rozakis settled down beside him. He watched the gypsy's retreating back for a moment, then refilled his glass.

'That . . . that was a damn good chocolate!' he said at length. 'Where does she get chocolates like that anyway?'

'Where do you think? She's probably fucked half the German army.' Rozakis waved away a cloud of smoke. 'Listen,' he said suddenly. 'Remember Manolis the barber?'

'Yeah? What about him?'

'She fucked him too, years ago. He let her stay in the back of the shop and, guess what, she ended up pinching his money.'

'Well,' said Kyriakos, 'I'm not a fool like Manolis, am I? Keeping money with a floozy around!' The mayor belched. 'You're forgetting that I . . . I've been around the world, while Manolis . . .' He slapped the back of his hand in a gesture commonly understood to signify stupidity. 'Manolis never even made it to Athens!'

'So?'

'So, I've got experience, my friend. Experience!' Kyriakos repeated. 'You name a foreign place and I've probably been there!'

'Still and all,' said Rozakis. 'I'm telling you, you better—'

'Japanese, African, Melanese, you name it!' Kyriakos went on. 'I've had them all, but you know what—?'

Rozakis rose to his feet with sudden resolve. 'Come on, let's go!'

'Wait!' Kyriakos glanced at the clock hanging over the *kapheneion* counter. 'I'm not ready yet!'

'Come on,' said Rozakis. 'It's almost curfew time. We're meeting Dhaniel at six in the morning.'

'So? There's almost . . . almost twelve hours yet!'

Rozakis puffed his cheeks. He pushed his iron-grey hair back from his forehead. 'Are you coming or not?'

'They say gypsies are real hot-blooded,' Kyriakos mused out loud. He shot Rozakis an appraising glance. 'Maybe we could all—'

'I'm not interested!'

'Well,' said Kyriakos. 'You go then. Go to sleep. I'll see you in the morning.'

'No.' Rozakis spoke calmly, like a sorely tested but intractable parent. 'I'm going to the toilet, then we're leaving . . . before the Germans start patrolling.'

Kyriakos made a vague gesture, watching impassively as Yannis Rozakis headed towards the urinals.

The *kapheneion* was more than half empty now. Rozakis strode across the room, absent-mindedly tousling the hair of the *kapheneion* owner's son, who was sprawled under the counter, reworking a cat's cradle.

He ended up having to wait for a urinal, listening to two men argue about the recent sabotage. It wasn't a long wait, and Rozakis relieved himself as fast as a man with a full bladder possibly could. When he came swinging through the utilities door, however, Kyriakos was gone.

'Fuck!'

Rozakis dashed out, but the street was dark and empty and cold. He stood slightly hunched, swearing under his breath. The moon was high but the entire area looked deserted. A few languid snowflakes were drifting down, melting as soon as they hit the pavement.

Suddenly, a woman's laughter rang out from around the corner; a bright, echoing laughter, eloquent with a playful, exuberant intimacy.

Rozakis sprinted across the street, but all he could see in the moonlight was an old drunk shambling towards him, his head thrown back, his mouth wide open, intent on swallowing the snowflakes whirling around his head.

~ 6 ~

'Is your name really Amalia?'

'Certainly. Why? Isn't yours Kyriakos?'

'Kyriakos Himonas. I'm the Molyvos mayor.'

'Is that so?' The naked gypsy rolled onto her side to scan Kyriakos's face in the candlelight. Her huge eyes were shadowed. 'Mayor, eh?'

'What, you don't believe me?'

'Sure, I believe you. But you bargain like a Turkish camel trader.'

Kyriakos made a small noise between his teeth. 'I've been around.'

'Oh yeah? Where you been to?'

'All over the world. You name it, I've been there.'

'Ah, you're a sailor then. Why—'

'I was a sailor,' Kyriakos cut in. 'I told you: I'm a mayor now.'

The gypsy chuckled. She shot an ironic glance towards Kyriakos's hirsute thighs. He was slumped against the pillows, bloodshot eyes ranging over the whitewashed bedroom. It was a small room, divided from the kitchen by a hanging grey blanket. Amalia's old mother slept in the kitchen but was said to be stone-deaf.

Kyriakos sat up, shook his massive head, as if trying to clear it, then reached for a cigarette. The room smelled of burning coal and unwashed socks but seemed clean enough, and pleasantly warm.

'Where's the toilet?' he asked at length, his gaze seeking out his clothes. The garments were lying in a heap on one of the chairs, next to an old vanity table.

'Outside. Across the courtyard.' Amalia sat on the edge of the bed, appraising herself in the mirror like a bored princess. Kyriakos was muttering under his breath. 'There's a jar in the corner.' The gypsy pointed. 'Use it if you like.'

Kyriakos hoisted himself off the bed. It was a large iron-framed bed, creaking under his shifting weight. At the foot of the bed stood the charcoal brazier, which in his haste he almost stumbled into. Staggering backwards, Kyriakos hit the bedside table, all but upsetting the burning candle. *'Ach, sto diablo!'*

'Watch you don't singe your *popo!*' Amalia tittered. She slid a pocket watch from under a pillow and consulted it, then glanced up at the mayor, indulgently amused, like a mother watching a young, clumsy child.

The mayor was shuffling across the room, muttering to himself. The pine floor squeaked under his feet as he stumbled to the corner and reached for the empty jar. Finally, he turned his back on the gypsy and urinated as best he could, his cigarette clamped between his teeth.

'Where are the children?' he asked, lifting the frowsty blanket as he climbed back into bed.

'Children?'

'Rozakis said you had two boys with you . . . when you came to Molyvos.'

'Ah, those were my nephews.' Amalia drew a slow hand down Kyriakos's thigh. 'My sister got sick that year,' she said, falling abruptly silent as German soldiers went by, arguing in garrulous voices.

'I drank too much,' Kyriakos said. He spoke to the ceiling, his eyes half-closed, the tin ashtray set on his hairy chest.

'It's all right.' Amalia patted his arm. 'Take your time. You've got until nine.'

'Why? What happens at nine?'

'Nothing. At nine-thirty my man comes from his evening shift.'

Kyriakos turned to face her. 'You mean to tell me you're married?'

'Yes and no. Aren't you?'

Kyriakos was silent. He gestured irritably. 'What does that mean, yes and no?'

'It means – oh, what business is it of yours?' Amalia snapped. 'You paid me for two hours, didn't you? That was the deal, eh?'

'I could pay you a little more,' Kyriakos said.

'No, you have to leave. At nine sharp, Mr Mayor.'

He cast her a sidelong glance. 'You making fun of me or what?'

'Nah,' said Amalia, shifting to free her long hair from behind her shoulder. She had loosened her plaits because he'd asked her to and now lay scrutinising her split ends with a vague sort of interest. Kyriakos watched her, frowning a little.

'How can you sleep with half the men in town if you're hitched?' he asked.

'Half the men in town?!' Amalia hooted. 'Where d'you hear that?' She swung a leg over Kyriakos's thigh. 'I only sleep with men I fancy, and there aren't that many, believe me. I wouldn't have slept with that fat friend of yours, for example. Not even for a gold-stuffed chest.'

'But in that case . . . in that case, why ask for money?'

'Why not?' Amalia was stroking his moustache, but there was something mildly taunting in her every gesture. 'I fancy men, but I fancy money too. What's so strange about that?'

'Hm.' Kyriakos rubbed his gums.

'Anyway,' she went on, 'I support my mother, I support my sister and her children . . . she can't work anymore.' Amalia sighed. In the kitchen, the old woman snored on, muttering in her dreams.

Suddenly, as if to alter the gloomy tenor of their exchange, Amalia rolled over and straddled Kyriakos, her hair surrounding him like a tent. Kyriakos raised his arms and twined them round the gypsy.

He went on embracing her, his mouth sliding down from her neck, his huge hands squeezing her buttocks. The only problem now was an insignificant one: gradually, Kyriakos's body had got pushed back and his head was pressing uncomfortably against the metal bed frame. He tried to slide down, to roll into a dominant position but, at that precise moment, a mouse came scurrying over the bedclothes – a little grey mouse crossing near the edge of the mattress, disappearing down to the floor.

Kyriakos groaned. 'You've got mice here!' he said.

'What? Oh . . .' Amalia laughed. 'Well, you didn't pay for a room at the Grande Bretagne, Mr Mayor,' she said, wrinkling her nose. She sat up and glanced at the floor, then shrugged and gave his genitals a playful poke. 'Ach, ach, ach, Mr Mayor,' she cackled. 'Looks like you've burned yourself out, sailing around the world.' She let her head drop back towards the pillow. 'I once knew a sailor from Plomari—'

'Ach, what do I care about your damn sailors?!'

Kyriakos reached over and put another cigarette to the candle. He'd rolled them earlier, arranging them carefully on the bedside table. 'I wanna celebrate. You got something to drink?'

'No. You've got only fifteen minutes left.' Amalia yawned. 'What have you got to celebrate anyway?'

Kyriakos smiled a little. 'If only you knew.'

'What?' She turned to him. 'What does a mayor do these days anyway? Aren't the Germans in charge in your village?'

'They like to think they're in charge.'

'Aren't they?'

'Yes and no.' Kyriakos laughed. He began to toy with Amalia's nipples.

The gypsy shifted her weight, drowsily curious. 'So, you haven't told me. What are you celebrating today?'

'Ah, if you only knew,' he said again. 'If the Germans knew!'

The gypsy's lips tightened. 'The bastards killed my brother-in-law,' she said, staring at the ceiling. 'Picked up a bunch of men for no reason, and . . . *bang*!'

'Is that a fact?' Kyriakos scratched his chest. 'Well,' he said thickly, 'in that case you . . . you'll be glad to know we're working on it.'

'Working on what?'

'That, *Kyria mou*, I'm not at liberty to say. But take it from me: I'm no pen-pushing . . . bureaucrat.' He chuckled complacently. 'The men here . . . your men in the capital . . . may be stuffing themselves with chocolates, but we . . . we're doing something to get rid of the bastards.'

'Oh yeah?'

'Better believe it, lady!' Kyriakos went on blustering in this manner, until Amalia slid her hand under the pillow and once more consulted the pocket watch.

All at once, she heaved herself up and swung her legs down towards the floor.

'Time to go home, Mr Mayor.' She sat for a moment, rubbing her upper arms as she looked about, vaguely disgruntled. Kyriakos stirred and reached out for her, but the gypsy shook herself free, laughing, and lowered her feet to the handloomed rug.

'It's five minutes to nine,' she stated.

The mayor lay watching her get ready. She had her back to him now. All he could see from the bed was her narrow waist, with the taut buttocks blooming out between the dark curtain of hair and the slender legs planted on the rug. 'What's time when you're in good company?' Kyriakos chortled, echoing the gypsy's own words back at the *kapheneion*.

Amalia spun round with a short throaty sound. 'Ach, you're finally waking up!' She stood regarding him for a moment, wryly amused. 'The company might be good, but a deal's a deal. Come on, mister.' She made a short whistling sound, cocking her thumb towards the front door. 'Time to go!'

There was a pegboard hanging near the kitchen entrance. Amalia yanked off her clothes, wriggling into her panties, then into her striped skirt with its elastic band. Naked from the waist up, she picked up her sweater, then stood sniffing it for a moment, her nipples seeking the ceiling. Kyriakos sat perched on the edge of the bed, his pupils dilated with longing.

'But if he's not your husband,' he ventured suddenly, 'can't—'

Amalia's eyes flashed. 'I told you, it's none of your business! You've got to go! Now!' Her hand shot out, pointing towards the entrance.

Kyriakos eased himself to his feet. He was a powerfully built man and, now that his reluctant member was reasserting itself, there was a sudden gleam in his eyes.

Amalia had pulled on her socks and was beginning to draw a comb through her hair when Kyriakos sidled up to her and tried to cup her breasts. The image was reflected in the vanity's spotty mirror: the fully dressed gypsy and the naked, hirsute man with his large hands splayed over the plump tawny breasts.

'Ach, you!' Amalia slapped Kyriakos's hands, wagging a jaunty finger. She snatched up the pocket watch and shoved it under his nose. 'There's no time!' She let out an exaggerated sigh. 'Come back another time and—'

'No,' said Kyriakos doggedly. 'I don't get to Mytilene very often. Why—'

'I said no! Get dressed!' she commanded, tightening her lips. She put on one of her shoes and began to look for the other, plaiting her hair with swift, practised fingers.

She had all but finished when she spotted her shoe behind the curtain. She snapped it up and put it on, tying up the laces. When she looked up again, it was to find Kyriakos slumped back on the edge of the mattress. He was staring at his own tie, which had slipped off the chair and lay across the floor like a silky striped snake.

'Ach, you're still sitting?!' Amalia hissed, her eyes darting fire.

'I . . . I can't leave . . . not now!' Kyriakos protested. He was about to add something, but the gypsy was no longer listening. Her chin thrust out, she headed straight for Kyriakos's clothes. She snatched the tangled garments from the chair, gathering them into a slipshod bundle: the coat and trousers, the shirt and cardigan, the shoes and socks and cotton underwear. Muttering to herself, she marched in the direction of the bed, hugging the clothes to her chest, as if meaning to fling them at their owner. Instead, with one swift movement, she threw open the window and tossed out the rumpled clothes with a little triumphant cry. Kyriakos had sprung up from the bed, but it was too late.

'*Aaaach!*' he bellowed, watching his shoes fall towards the moonlit pavement, coins and bills flying every which way. Kyriakos shot the gypsy a venomous look. He seemed momentarily torn between flinging himself at her and dashing into the night for his scattered garments.

'You better hurry up, Mr Mayor, before someone grabs your money and clothes, and then what?' Amalia threw back her head, going off into peals of laughter.

Kyriakos wheeled about and snatched a blanket, waving a threatening fist. Then he tore across the room, flinging the front door open. Soon, he was gone, his draped limbs disappearing down the shadowy corridor.

The gypsy laughed and closed the window. Braiding her second plait, she went to the door and was about to lock it when Kyriakos reappeared: a naked, menacing giant frothing at the mouth like an enraged bull. Amalia tried to slam the door in his face, but Kyriakos kicked it open, dropping his pile of clothes. He stood breathing hard, a ferocious look twisting his face but his manhood at last irrefutable.

'Fucking whore!' he hissed, smacking the gypsy's left cheek. About to slap the right, he stopped abruptly, like a man recalling something of vital importance. Spinning around, he dashed out again, pausing only long enough to collect the clothes scattered over the threshold.

The gypsy picked up the blanket, then quickly locked the door, an angry flush rising on her cheeks. She picked up the jar of urine, holding it carefully as she hastened across the room. For the second time, she threw the window open. She stood waiting. When Kyriakos appeared, still buttoning himself, the gypsy rose on her tiptoes, then flung the jar out, aiming it straight at the mayor's back.

Kyriakos was bending down to snatch up a folded note from the ground, but somehow, the jar of urine fell wide of the mark. It landed on the pavement with a crashing sound. The gypsy swore.

The mayor, momentarily frozen, glanced over his shoulder, as if expecting another assault. Then he straightened up, spun about, and thumbed his nose, hooting like a gleeful boy.

Amalia stared down for one baleful moment, then slowly closed the window. This time she was not laughing.

— 7 —

One look at Dhaniel's face and Calliope knew he had heard the news, probably from Rozakis, who had been taking his leave as she approached the clinic. The doctor was going home early. Seeing him come through the gate with his satchel, Sappho began to wag her tail. She shook her rear end. She raised her head. She barked.

Dhaniel ignored the antics. For once, he didn't look happy to see either dog or mistress. Calliope had been on her way to visit her friend Eleni, who was pregnant again, but Tomas had stopped her in the *agora*, whispering in her ear. There was a rumour that Yorgos Lyras had been captured in Mytilene. At the cinema.

'The cinema?!'

'So they say. Maybe it's not true. It could be some other Lyras.'

The doctor soon confirmed it was Captain Yorgos.

'Can you believe it?' he said, plodding away from the clinic. 'He's supposed to be lying low and goes to see a Hungarian melodrama, then gets involved in some petty squabble. In the capital!' Dhaniel shook his head, a weary man groping for comprehension.

Two German soldiers were striding towards them, carabines slung over their shoulders. Calliope waited for them to pass, reflecting that Molyviates seemed increasingly indifferent to their own fate. A few had gradually gone mad. The building contractor's mother had begun to eat paper; the *hamam* caretaker's widow had stopped bathing and cleaning her house, but continued to conduct conversations with her dead husband and daughter. Others, like Eleni's mother, had grown apathetic.

'Sometimes I get the feeling that people want – that they deliberately court danger, just to get it over with,' she said, sharing her thoughts with the doctor.

'Ach, I don't know,' said Dhaniel. He thought that men, men like Yorgos, were simply incapable of tolerating any constraints. 'I don't believe they're indifferent to their fate. But this need, this compulsion, to assert their independence . . . it just gets the better of them.' The doctor sighed, then went on to cite another recent example: Kyriakos

Himonas's entanglement with the Mytilene gypsy. 'He and Rozakis almost came to blows over it,' he added.

'*Rozakis?*'

'Yes, imagine! Two grown men falling out over a wench after risking their lives to save a foreigner!' Dhaniel shook his head once more. The sun was setting now, sliding down like a giant egg yolk. It was getting windy. 'Did you ever meet her, by the way?' the doctor asked at length, placing a hand over his flapping tie. 'She's been here a few times, selling—'

'Her?!' Calliope cut in. 'A young gypsy, with a beauty mark on her cheek?'

'Queen of Sheba in rags.' Dhaniel achieved a smile.

'I thought she looked like some rare, colourful bird,' Calliope said. She paused to let Sappho water a primrose bush, recalling the first time she had seen the gypsy, in that last spring of her father's life. How long ago it all seemed now: walking up with him after school, stopping to watch an exotic stranger chat with her father's barber. She recalled how quick people had been to blame the gypsy boys for the subsequent lice outbreak. As if they'd never seen head lice before! Recently, there had been reports that the Germans were sending gypsies to labour camps, along with European Jews.

'Doctor, doctor!'

Dhaniel glanced over his shoulder. Michalis the sexton was running after them, wild-eyed: his son was having one of his asthma attacks.

'It's a bad one! Please come right away, doctor!'

'I'm coming. I'll see you tomorrow,' Dhaniel said to Calliope.

And then he was gone, leaving her on a windy corner, halfway to Eleni's house.

Calliope hesitated, then decided to go see her friend another day. It was getting dark and she had forgotten to bring her night pass. Also, Sappho had to be moved indoors. If people were desperate enough to be eating cats, wasn't it possible someone might go after a dog as well? Mirto refused to let Sappho roam about the house, but agreed to let her sleep in the storage room, where the dog had kept Rupert Ealing warm.

Calliope headed home, hoping the Englishman would prove more prudent than her own compatriots. He was, she thought, an exceptionally able, responsible man. Still, the older she got, the more unpredictable human beings seemed to her. She saw Kyriakos almost every day, had talked to him at length after his trip to Mytilene. And no, she would never have guessed that the shrewd, hard-working mayor could get drunk enough to abandon a friend and take off with a seductive gypsy.

All this was still floating through Calliope's head as she crossed the village, Sappho trotting at her side. She had gone to the clinic in the vague hope of finding reassurance, only to have her worst fears confirmed. Dhaniel had said nothing about Yorgos's fate, but they both knew the captain was bound to be tortured. For one brief moment, the knowledge rose and hissed in Calliope's face. But then she resumed breathing and slowly, cautiously, began to back away from the portentous news, as one might do with some slumbering but reputedly vicious beast.

THREE

~ 1 ~

He was known as the Lizard. He had heavy-lidded eyes set in a narrow, pockmarked face but his voice could be as seductive, as importuning, as a lover's. Seated across from Yorgos Lyras, the German gazed at the prisoner with his reptilian eyes. His name was Heinrich Volkmann. During their first meeting, the interrogator appeared chummy, almost voluptuously relaxed, offering the prisoner a cigarette, plying him with personal questions.

This interview took place in a turn-of-the-century mansion built by a local judge. The Germans had turned the cellar into a jail, where Lyras had spent several days, surrounded by little piles of dry bones. The guards were Greek policemen appointed by the Germans. It was they who would eventually tell the story of the captain's imprisonment; how he had scoffed, entering his cell for the first time.

'If they think they can scare me with such childish tactics, they don't know who they're dealing with!' he blustered. There were several gaps between the prisoner's teeth, where the gold crowns had been, before the attempted escape to Turkey.

The guards were grimly silent. They remained silent when they heard the captain curse that night, after the resident rats had emerged, scurrying across his prone body, scouring for fallen crumbs. Lyras had eaten a thin broth at noon and two dry slices of bread in the evening. He spent the rest of the night awake, falling asleep only after dawn glimmered in the patch of sky visible through the cell window.

There was nothing to do but sleep. And battle the rats. And watch the weather change in the tiny barred window. A rainy spell gave way to a week of sunshine. Out in the garden, mourning doves were beginning to call; now and then, a starling might flutter by, or a stray cat stop to peer through the grimy window. Winter seemed to be ebbing, but the scents of spring could not penetrate the thick, musty walls.

One overcast morning, two German soldiers appeared in the cellar.

They let Lyras wash and shave, then led him upstairs, to a stark room, where Heinrich Volkmann sat waiting. There was a long table with a writing pad and a vase holding a branch of pink almond blossoms. An interpreter stood waiting.

Lyras was offered coffee, as well as bread and jam. A nod from Volkmann and the prisoner's handcuffs were unlocked; a tray was placed before him. Volkmann looked on with the indulgent air of a father watching his son wolf down a favourite treat. But finally the food was gone, the tray was whisked away. Lyras stirred and belched. Volkmann rose from the table and began to pace.

'Is it true that you've been a member of the Greek Resistance?'

Lyras looked squarely into the interrogator's face. 'Yes,' he said, 'it's true.'

'And are you willing to sign a confession to that effect?'

'I am.' Lyras turned to the interpreter. 'Tell him not to waste his time. I'm ready to sign at once. I want to get it over with. Understand?'

The interpreter rendered the request into German, making the Lizard's lips stretch in a thin smile. 'Everything in good time, *Kapitän*,' he said, sitting down. 'We're not in any particular hurry. Are you?'

Lyras muttered something incoherent.

'Would you perhaps like to share your thoughts with us?' Volkmann asked, tapping his fingers on the edge of the table. He looked like a bored school principal addressing a churlish pupil.

Lyras was silent but his right leg had begun to jerk. The room was bare except for the table and chairs. A lightbulb was aimed straight at the prisoner's face.

'It's wise of you to be so forthcoming,' Volkmann was saying. 'But we've known about your connection to the Resistance for some time, *Kapitän*.'

Lyras lifted a shoulder.

'And, well, you seem like a reasonable man. You'll surely understand that we're not offering our hospitality just so you can tell us what we already know!' He laughed, his heavy eyes inviting Lyras to share his little joke.

Silence. The caique owner kept his gaze fastened to his helplessly tapping foot.

'So.' Volkmann heaved himself out of his chair and resumed pacing, hands clasped behind his back. He had a large, rather feminine bottom. 'The first thing we'd like to know is your son's whereabouts. Your elder son, Kostas. Would you tell us what happened to him, please?'

At this, a black spark flashed in Yorgos Lyras's eyes. 'I don't know where my son is. We went our separate ways months ago!' He waited for the interpreter to translate the statement. 'Anyway, I wouldn't give up my son even if I knew.' He looked scornfully into the heavy lizard eyes and said: 'Maybe a German could do something like that. A Greek father, never!'

'Very well.' The German sat down again and steepled his sausage-like fingers. 'We'll try to respect your paternal sentiments, *Kapitän*, but there are some things you can surely tell us. Something about the Englishman, for example?'

'The Englishman,' Lyras echoed vaguely. He shifted in his chair.

'Yes. The one the Turks sent back with you and your son. Remember him? He goes by the name of Roufos but I'm told his real name's Rupert Ealing.'

'Sure, I remember him.' Lyras made a vaguely disgruntled gesture. 'But I told you: we all went our separate ways.'

'And you have no idea where the Englishman has been hiding all this time?'

'No!' The captain's callused hands flew up. 'Look, we're not stupid, you know. We make sure no one has more information than necessary.'

He stared at the German squarely. 'For all I know, he's back in England by now.'

Volkmann weighed this, studiously examining his nails. 'All right,' he said. 'What can you tell us about the truck that got blown up just before Christmas?'

'I can tell you this: the first time I heard about the truck was the day I went to the cinema. In fact, I only went because . . . because I was hoping to find out more about what happened.'

'Why?' Volkmann demanded.

'Why? Why? I'm a curious man! Ask anyone: I always have to know what's going on!'

'Is that so?'

'I swear! I had nothing to do with the explosion. I wasn't even in the capital!'

'And where were you, please?'

'I was . . . underground.'

'Someone was hiding you?'

Silence.

'Who? Who was hiding you?'

'I can't tell you that!' Lyras let out a loud Turkish curse. 'Hang me if you like, but I can't give up people who risked their lives to help me, can I?' He turned his face towards the interpreter. 'What does he think we are?' He cursed yet again.

Volkmann looked at him for a moment, then pushed back from the table. 'Very well,' he said with sudden resolve. 'That's all.'

Lyras levered himself out of his chair. He stood rubbing his jaw.

'That's all for today. But I want you to think about my questions, *Kapitän*,' Volkmann added sternly. 'Because I'm going to have more of them tomorrow and, you know, we're not so stupid either.' He grinned, exposing yellow teeth. 'I'm willing to show some understanding where your son's concerned, but I'm not prepared to believe that you don't know the answers to any of our questions.'

He paused and stared at Lyras: at his droopy eyes and stubbly jaws, the swollen veins in his bullish neck. 'Now that we've got to know each other a little, perhaps you'll permit me to be blunt, *Kapitän*: we'll expect greater cooperation from you in the future. Much greater. Is that understood?'

Lyras remained silent, his huge fists hanging at his sides.

'Take him away,' said Volkmann with sudden pique.

The soldiers led the prisoner back to his cell. They had him strip down. They left him alone. Hours passed. After supper, an officer returned with the interpreter and told Lyras he could get dressed, but would have to spend the night upright, his arms raised over his head. 'It's said to improve memory function,' he chuckled.

Lyras scrambled to his feet. He lifted his short, powerful arms and stood with his chin raised and his barrel chest thrust out. The window grew black. The rats emerged from their hiding holes. The captain went on standing. Now and then, he lifted a foot and kicked at a rat sniffing around his toes. His arms began to slide down, as if supporting some great invisible burden.

Finally, the beatings started. That evening, there was the butt of a soldier's revolver whenever his arms weakened. The following night, a whip made of ox sinews lashed across Lyras's back. The captain appeared at his second interrogation with one of his eyes puffed shut and his bottom lip split in two. There were numerous welts and bruises, invisible under his prison garb. Asked whether he had anything to say, Lyras reiterated his willingness to sign a confession. He was presented with a document attesting to his clandestine activities, along with a formal statement. *Every word was translated for me by the Greek interpreter. I have understood everything and hereby testify that this is an accurate record of my statements. The entire interview was translated for me before I signed.*

He signed the same statement day after day. He signed it after his nails were ripped out and his soles scorched with burning cigarettes. He went on signing it after his testicles had been squeezed, but had nothing new to say.

This went on for a week, then suddenly stopped. Lyras was left to languish in his cell. When he began to recover, he was made to lie prone, his feet bound with a heavy rope. A rifle was set between his feet, then slowly twisted, tightening the rope. It was rarely necessary to resort to this extreme measure, but some men were born pig-headed. That was what Volkmann said, watching Lyras through the prison bars.

The following night, a Greek doctor was summoned and did his best to help the prisoner recover from his injuries. Lyras was a stalwart man and he did recover; enough, at any rate, to recognise the two shackled men who were briefly brought into his cell a few nights later, after a surprisingly substantial meal of soup and potatoes and cabbage. Lyras had just finished eating when the men were hauled in. It was dark in the cell but one of the guards waved a torch in front of the new prisoners' faces.

The two men were Kyriakos Himonas, Molyvos's mayor, and Yannis Rozakis, the *kapheneion* owner, whose daughter, Anna, was married to Yorgos Lyras's son.

The captain of the *Eleftheria* buried his tortured face in his hands, and let his tears spill over. It was the only time anyone had ever seen Yorgos Lyras weep.

~ 2 ~

The almond trees were vaunting their richest blossoms when the soldiers came for the doctor. They arrived late in the afternoon, as if out of consideration for Dhaniel's professional commitments. There had been no military jeep screeching to a halt in the *agora*, no arrest squad sent over from the capital. The mayor and *kapheneion* owner had been promptly dispatched to Gestapo headquarters in Mytilene, whereas Elias Dhaniel was summoned by two of Captain Umbreit's men and locked up in the town hall to await Major von Herden's arrival the following morning. It was the day scheduled for von Herden's monthly visit; he was not coming expressly in order to question the doctor. Nevertheless, there was an air of courtesy to this particular arrest, perhaps even a whiff of apology on Captain Umbreit's part.

But none of this was known to Calliope when she first learned about the arrest. She heard the news from Hektor the fool, who'd come looking for her at the fortress, where she was letting Sappho have her daily run. It was St Theodoros Day and the sun was just beginning to set. There were children playing hide-and-seek below the fortress. A donkey was heard, braying in the distance.

Suddenly, Calliope spotted the Stipsianos, with his absurd yellow turban, clambering uphill with the agility of a mountain goat. The moment he made out the schoolmistress, Hektor began to flail his arms. He cupped his hands around his mouth and shouted something, but his words got snatched away by the wind. Soon, he was bounding across the fortress grounds, blubbering: '*Kyria . . . Kyria!*' He stopped, gasping for breath. '*Kyria*, the doctor, the doctor—'

'What is it, Hektor?' Calliope assumed Dhaniel was needed somewhere.

'The do . . . the doctor's in t-t-trouble!' Hektor stammered, blinking furiously.

Calliope stared. 'What do you mean, Hektor?' Dhaniel had occasionally complained of chest pains, but the cardiologist had assured him he was as strong as an ox. The chest pains were due to either indigestion or stress. 'Is it his heart?'

Hektor shook his head, vigorously.

'It . . . it's the Germans . . . the so . . . soldiers . . .' He swallowed hard, desperately hunting for words. 'They . . . they came to . . . to get the doctor. He . . . he's in jail, *Kyria* Calliope!'

'In jail!' Calliope reached out and planted her hands on Hektor's shoulders. She peered straight into his wild eyes, willing him into greater clarity. 'You mean they've taken him to Mytilene?'

Again, Hektor shook his head. He turned sharply and pointed towards the town hall, whose pink shutters could be discerned in the distance, among the slanting rooftops and curling plumes of smoke. 'He . . . he's there! The s-soldiers came to get him!' he repeated with urgent emphasis.

'The soldiers came to take the doctor to the town hall?'

Hektor nodded, blinking furiously. Sappho was sniffing something along the opposite wall.

'Hektor.' Calliope gestured towards the dog. 'Please take Sappho home for me, will you? Tell my mother I'll be home later. Can you do that for me, Hektor?'

'Y-yes, *Kyria* Calliope. Yesyesyesyesyes!'

'Thank you,' she muttered. And then she whipped around, the wind slapping at her face as she fled the fortress, street after street sweeping by while she ran towards the town hall. It was only as she passed the clinic that Calliope's suppressed dread finally exploded, sending forth heart-wrenching images of her closest friend – a handcuffed, grim-faced Elias Dhaniel – being led to jail like an animal to the slaughter.

She stopped and retched into a bush. Just a few days earlier, *Papa* Konstantinos, St Mathaios's abbot, had been arrested. As soon as the news had reached Molyvos, *Papa* Emanouil had sent an urgent message to Mytilene. Finally, just yesterday, they'd learned that both Ealing and *Papa* Ioannis had been transferred to a safe house.

Calliope crossed the village, dimly aware of the taunting splendour of almond blossoms, of villagers' curious eyes sliding to watch her dizzying progress through the winding streets. She turned a corner and, through a stinging blur, registered a former classmate with her newborn son swaddled in a blue blanket, then the mayor's father, leaning on his cane, his skull as sleek as a squash. She was close to the town hall now, but still running, fragmented voices wafting her way from shady interiors.

At the town hall, Ourania had come out to fill a jug of water, then stopped to greet the midwife and her daughter, who had been paying a name day visit to Sergeant Theodoros Floros. The three women were exchanging pleasantries when Calliope flashed by, like a breathless animal escaping its predator. She was about to open the heavy portals when Alfred Reis came out, adjusting his officer's cap. Calliope brushed past him as well. There was just the indoor staircase now. Just the one flight of stairs.

She stormed into Captain Lorenz Umbreit's office without so much as a knock.

'Is it true?' She halted in front of his desk, her heart thudding against her ribcage. 'Have you really arrested the doctor?'

Lorenz Umbreit had risen the moment Calliope appeared in the doorway. He came around with his hands spread in a vaguely helpless gesture. He glanced at her face and his jaw tightened. 'We've brought him in for questioning.'

'Why?' Calliope asked in a strangled voice. 'What's he done to you?'

'To me personally, nothing. Von Herden's coming tomorrow morning and . . . well, it seems he has some questions.'

Calliope weighed all this. 'Can I see him, please?'

'You know I can't do that,' Umbreit said. He thrust his hands into his tunic pockets. 'I . . . I'd do it if I could,' he added. 'You know I would.' *Du weisst ich wurde.*

Calliope swallowed. 'Will I be present at tomorrow's interview?'

'I . . . don't think so.' His eyes veered away from her. He stopped and busied himself lighting an oil lamp. 'I believe they're bringing the Mytilene interpreter.'

She made an ambiguous sort of gesture, at once impatient and entreating. 'But he . . . he's a good man!' she cried. 'He wouldn't harm a fly, let alone a German!'

'I know,' Umbreit said. He stood with his back to the window, fingers rubbing the back of his neck. The early evening's shadows were thickening now. In the back alley, two cats yowled and screeched, courting under the office windows.

At that moment, something seemed to snap in Calliope's head. All at once, her arms flew away from her body. She stood for a moment, holding them out in a vaguely beseeching gesture. Then, seemingly moving of their own accord, her hands drew her forward, coming to rest on Umbreit's forearms. It was the first time she had touched him of her own accord.

'Please,' she said quietly. 'Please . . . I beg you to have him released. I beg you!' Although her voice faltered, Calliope's body went on inclining forward, her glittering eyes stating the terms of a bargain she might have come across in some long-forgotten novel. *'Ich tue was immer du willst,'* she said, barely above a whisper.

At this, Umbreit stiffened. He compressed his lips and gave her a steady look, searching and bewildered. There was a moment of silence, during which his expression grew stern. He let out a long sigh, then raised his hands and gently – gently but firmly – lifted her palms off his own arms.

'Calliope.' His voice was more strained than ever. 'I understand the doctor's a close friend. I appreciate that you're doing your best to help, but . . .' He paused, his hand rubbing across his brow, his mouth. 'Do you really think I'm the sort of man who would take advantage of such an offer?' he asked, his eyes reproaching her.

Calliope averted her gaze, utterly lost for words.

'I'm sure you know how I feel about you,' Umbreit said, relenting a little. 'Nothing . . . nothing has changed there, but . . .' He held out a finger and placed it under Calliope's chin, forcing her to meet his eyes. 'When . . . when you offer yourself to me, Calliope, I want it to be because you want me, not . . . not because—'

'But I do want you!' she heard herself blurt out. 'I do!'

And she did still want him, had become so accustomed to her suppressed desire it had come to seem like just another facet of her perpetual hunger. The prolonged deprivation was so familiar she could hardly remember how it felt to go to sleep sated.

What she could not forget was the doctor's friendship. She thought she would do anything to save Dhaniel. Still, she loved the truth well enough to ask herself later whether she would have been quite so willing to throw herself at Major von Herden.

But she did not ask herself this, or any other question, that day. Her mind, her capacity for thought, had been subsumed by dread. All she could do was stand in the office, trembling, every nerve in her body feeling exposed. She wanted to fling herself at Umbreit, refusing to take no for an answer, but simultaneously longed to make him forgive her manifestly offensive offer.

'I've tried and tried to repress my feelings,' she heard herself say in a defeated voice. 'I thought . . . I thought you must have known.'

At this, Lorenz Umbreit stopped. He stood staring at her with slow, reappraising eyes. Calliope was motionless, acutely aware of her own heartbeat. Finally, Umbreit shook himself, an inarticulate sound escaping his throat. He reached for her hand. He held it for a long moment, gazing into her eyes.

'If . . . if you are sincere,' he said, swallowing hard. 'If you are sincere . . . we must, for your sake and for mine, wait a little longer. After the war . . . after the war—'

All at once, abandoned by words, Umbreit reached out and silently wound his arms around Calliope. He held her close to his chest, his lips brushing her ear. 'It can't last much longer,' he said in a barely audible voice. *Es kann nicht mehr lange dauern.* He opened his eyes, drawing back slightly to scan her face, as if to impress upon her the truth of his ardent message. *Es kann nicht . . .*

And then Umbreit stopped, his look flying over Calliope's shoulder, landing at the entrance. *'Mein Gott,'* he let out, stiffening.

On the threshold to the office stood Ourania Nakou, her hand clutching at her chest, her eyes pools of horror.

— 3 —

'I'm glad he's in jail!' Eleni said, speaking to Calliope. She was not referring to the doctor but to her own uncle, who had started molesting her shortly after she'd reached puberty. The unmarried Natis had stopped short of rape, but there was no telling where things might have gone had he not been sent to Albania.

'I know it's a terrible thing to say but it's true: I *am* glad. I hope he rots in jail!' Both Eleni's uncle and her father were serving time for the torched bakery, but this was the first time she had shared her secret. 'Do you think I'm a bad person to be talking like this?' she asked.

Calliope made an incredulous little sound. 'You, a bad person? *You?*' she said, taking her young protégé's hand in her own. The hand was small and soft, the fingers swollen by pregnancy. The girl was only nineteen. 'It's not you who should be feeling remorseful, my dear!'

Eleni was silent. She had a curious habit of rubbing her thumb and forefinger together, as if rolling a tiny wad of chewing gum between her fingertips. She sat pondering Calliope's words, her eyes casting about the kitchen. The eyes were dark and melancholy, set in a round face on which some complex question seemed to be perpetually etched.

It was Easter Tuesday. Calliope sat in Eleni's kitchen, staring at the rain pelting the windowpanes. In the firepit, a boiling kettle was hissing.

'Did you ever tell your parents?'

Eleni rose to make tea. 'He said he would sprinkle rat poison in my food if I told anyone.' She was in her sixth month and growing ample. Everyone seemed to be feeding Eleni this time around. 'He said my father wouldn't believe me anyway.' She made sage tea, set the laundry cauldron back on the fire, then went on with her story.

After her uncle had come back from Albania, as soon as he learned that she was betrothed, he threatened to tell Tomas that she had seduced him. 'He said Tomas wouldn't want to marry me, and neither would anyone else.'

Calliope shook her head, sour with her own impotence. She placed her arm around Eleni's shoulders. 'You never did tell Tomas then?' she said.

'No!' Alarm flickered across Eleni's face. 'You're not going to tell him, are you?'

'No, my dear . . . of course not.' Calliope gave Eleni's arm a tender little squeeze. They sat sipping tea. There was the burbling sound of boiling laundry, the steady patter of rain. Calliope could find nothing else to say.

'I'm glad I told you.' Eleni smiled wanly.

'Yes,' Calliope said. 'So am I, my dear.'

This conversation had come about because Eleni's imprisoned father and uncle were scheduled to be released just before her baby was due. Eleni and Tomas had moved into her parents' home. Lazaros, one of Eleni's twin brothers, had been working in his father's shop, cared for by his grandmother. After his mother died, he had only occasionally slept at home, but as soon as Eleni and Tomas moved in, he reclaimed his old room. When Eleni's father and uncle returned, she would have four men to look after, in addition to a newborn. The thought of living under the same roof with Natis, of having to wait on him, was casting a terrible shadow over her pregnancy.

'What if he comes after me again?'

'Ach, Elenitsa. He's an old man now,' Calliope said. He would be fifty-one on being released. Not quite an old man, but what could she say? She was still chastising herself for failing to probe when the incorrigibly mirthful child had suddenly grown moody during adolescence. She had written about Eleni in her journal, but what good were words if you did nothing to alleviate suffering?

'I'll make sure you are safe,' Calliope heard herself say to Eleni, though she had no idea how this might be achieved. 'We'll work on it together.'

The laundry cauldron was boiling. It made a steady bubbling sound, gently rattling the aluminium lid. It was an oddly comforting sound, though not nearly as comforting as it might have been any other day.

— 4 —

By the time Calliope's visit to Eleni took place, over a month had passed since Elias Dhaniel's arrest. The doctor was still in Mytilene, awaiting trial. Captain Umbreit had assured Calliope that Dhaniel was being treated well, but what did it mean to be treated well by the Germans? Two Gestapo officers had recently visited Molyvos. Calliope didn't know the purpose of their visit, but the skull-and-bones insignia on their caps and belts had sent an arrow of dread through her overwrought brain.

She began to dream about the doctor: a skeletal, shackled man dressed in prison garb, plodding towards the torture chamber. Two weeks before Easter, she had finally decided to brazen it out with Umbreit. He might not want to respond, might not know the answer, but she didn't think he would lie to her.

'Is he being tortured?' Calliope asked, the last word pounding her brain. *Tortured, tortured, tortured.*

'No. Rest assured he isn't.' Umbreit gazed at her for a moment, then tried to lift her spirits with a lame stab at humour. 'Von Herden wouldn't let them touch the doctor. What if he needs a good doctor again?'

Several months earlier, stumbling on a cobblestone, the major had hurt his back while visiting Molyvos. If Dhaniel hadn't happened to know a trick an old Armenian had taught him back in Constantinople, the major might have found himself bedridden for weeks.

Umbreit attempted a smile. He and Calliope had been ill at ease with each other since the day she had thrown herself at him, like stage actors arrested by an earthquake or a fire, unable to get back into the spirit of the play.

One day, he appeared in her office for no apparent reason. Calliope had looked up from her desk and found Umbreit looming there, as if about to convey something of dire importance. He said nothing, and neither did she, but her eyes welled and her throat filled with longing.

And yet, the underlying resentment was still there, throbbing alongside her wayward desire. Their one and only embrace had been brief but had left the air around them charged with significance. It was as if, the moment he had taken her in his arms, Umbreit succeeded in breaking through the mental buffer Calliope had been zealously guarding for months. *Es kann nicht mehr lange dauern . . .*

He had begun to spend most of his time in Petra, supposedly to deal with Dwinger's turbulent legacy. Reis had taken over many of Umbreit's former duties; the village council was handling urgent affairs. Calliope went on teaching. She went on liaising for the Germans. She helped Stella care for the doctor's four children. Consumed by work, she had gradually succeeded in distracting herself from the dread kindled by Ourania's intrusion. There was still, somewhere, a small knot of suppressed anxiety, but the haze of doom that had come over her in Umbreit's office began to fade when it became apparent that the shocked witness, possibly fearful of losing her job, had opted for discretion. What Ourania would do if and when Hitler's army left the village was one of many questions Calliope had learned to sweep aside.

Finally, her body began to revolt. She was starting to suffer from a chronically painful neck; sores appeared on her inner cheeks. And then her periods stopped for two months. It was a problem many women were beginning to experience. Something to do with stress and privation, the doctor had said. Calliope was relieved to be spared the monthly ordeal, but one day she registered that her mother was looking at her askance.

200

Mirto made no attempt to deny her suspicion.

'*Pregnant?*' Calliope cried, stiffening. 'Whose child would this be, Mama?'

Mirto kept her silence. She was hemming one of Calliope's skirts and would not look up from her needle and thread.

'Whose, then? Umbreit's, Ealing's—'

'How am I—'

'Maybe Pericles's – he's certainly old enough now . . . Or even the doctor's – why not? I've spent more time with him than anyone else . . .'

Mirto cast her a baleful look. She was about to speak, but the words went on tumbling out of Calliope's mouth. 'There's also the headmaster, you know. I—'

'Ach, stop . . . please stop!' Mirto rubbed her eyes. 'How am I supposed to—'

'You're supposed to trust me! You're supposed to believe me when I say I've never had relations with anyone besides Iason!' Calliope paused, a small, bitter sound escaping her mouth. 'Anyway, I'm supposed to be barren, remember? Isn't that what everyone's been saying?'

Mirto gave a sigh. 'It wouldn't be the first time people were wrong.'

'Well, you're wrong too!' Calliope tossed back. 'I could not possibly be pregnant. Please believe me,' she added, softening.

She knew her mother's nerves to be as frayed as her own, though in recent days they had both withdrawn deep into themselves. For days after the doctor's arrest, Mirto had stopped cleaning, and barely touched her food. And although Calliope herself was not fastidious about housekeeping, she had gradually begun to notice the dust angels clinging to room corners, the bird droppings left unswept on the windowsills. Hoping to provide a little cheer, she had brought a sumptuous bouquet of lilacs from the town hall and placed it in a vase. Her mother thanked her politely. A week later, the wilted lilacs were still there in their onyx vase, the odour of fetid water and dead blossoms hanging in the dusty air.

She decided not to share Eleni's secret with Mirto. But she was still brooding on it – her own culpability – as she made her way home on that drizzly Easter Tuesday. The streets looked deserted. The rain had gradually ceased but black clouds were still floating across the tattered sky and the smell of soaked earth and drenched leaves hung in the air. It was getting dark. She had not quite reached the *plateia* when she spotted several dogs sprawled on the wet cobblestones. Two German guards were poised in front of the barber's. What were they doing here? What was there to guard anyway? Every shop in the *agora* was shuttered, now that the merchants had virtually run out of stock.

Calliope strode on, fidgeting with her slipping headkerchief. She was about to pass her late husband's *pantopoleion* when, all at once, the entire rainwashed *plateia* seemed to blur, then abruptly darken. Another moment and Calliope would start howling, but in that brief black spell, all she could do was whimper, her shoulders hunched, her fists pressed against her mouth, like a child recoiling from an imminent blow.

Suspended from the dripping mulberry tree were the sagging corpses of Captain Yorgos Lyras and Kyriakos Himonas, former sailor and erstwhile mayor. The third hapless man was Yannis Rozakis, the *kapheneion* owner, who, bruised and bloodied, was dangling between his colleagues, as if ever hopeful of making peace between the two intransigent men.

— 5 —

It was turning out to be another bitter spring. Herakles the cobbler had recently died of syphilis, but not without shedding unexpected light on a brutal, almost forgotten, crime going back to 1935. He had, he confessed to *Papa* Iakovos, received his dire prognosis that year; had spent an entire evening getting drunk before heading home. When he passed the Adhams' gate, their dog for some reason went into a barking frenzy. Two days earlier, Socrates had defecated in the *agora*, just outside the cobbler's own shop. The schoolmistress had quickly collected the droppings, but Herakles had felt cross anyway. He had heard people say that Johnny the Australian had married his sister on the rebound.

That *Papa* Iakovos had shared the secrets of the confessional with his wife surprised no one who knew St Kyriaki's priest. But the *papas* himself had fumed on learning that Olympia had spread the gossip in the *agora* – all because of some petty quarrel over a shoe repair!

Shocking as all this was, the same week brought more distressing news. The doctor had been shipped off to a German labour camp, along with St Mathaios's abbot. It was by then June but full understanding was just beginning to penetrate Calliope's mental barricades: Dhaniel was not going to be released. He was not about to return home.

Although the truth about Nazi camps was as yet a well-guarded secret, Dhaniel's arrest and the death of their colleagues had left Calliope floundering. Ironically, despite all the years she had spent railing against the clergy, she was beginning to find solace in *Papa* Emanouil's company. It was St Pandeleimon's priest who had passed on the news about the doctor; who then tried to comfort her, pointing out that a labour camp was, after all, a relatively merciful fate.

Papa Emanouil was an autodidact, a former tailor who had one day decided to join the clergy so as to better feed his family. The family kept growing and *Papa* Emanouil remained a poor man – until recently, when he unexpectedly found himself a major beneficiary of Zenovia the fortune-teller's will. That Calliope was a co-beneficiary had been one of the surprising circumstances favouring their unlikely friendship.

Two days after receiving the news about the labour camp, Calliope returned to the priest's house. The *papadhia* was busy laundering clothes, but *Papa* Emanouil took Calliope to the courtyard, where, over small cups of ersatz coffee, he made an astounding revelation: Rupert Ealing and *Papa* Ioannis had found asylum in a Mytilene brothel. Calliope, who had been hunting in her bag for a handkerchief, stopped.

'A brothel?'

'So I've been told.' *Papa* Emanouil's grin was as mischievous as a boy's. Someone in the Mytilene Resistance apparently had a connection to a local madam.

'I'm having trouble imagining this, *Papa* Emanouil.'

'That's life, *koritsi mou*. You never know where it's going to take you.'

Calliope almost smiled. She only half-listened as, possibly trying to divert her, *Papa* Emanouil told her about *Papa* Ioannis, who had once entertained hopes of becoming a bishop. Since a family man could never be more than a parish priest, he'd finally decided against matrimony.

'What shall I tell you, *koritsi mou*? The poor man gave up his intended, but turned out to be too outspoken for the church fathers, so he finally became a pedagogical priest. Now, in old age, the rascal ends up sleeping in a madam's boudoir!'

Papa Emanouil's beard shook with laughter, but his wife, who had come out to hang the laundry, only wagged her head.

'This husband of mine's over seventy and still hasn't learned to talk like a respectable priest!'

'Ach, my dear,' parried her husband, 'the more you have to be ashamed of, the more respectable you must be. Me . . . I've never even seen the outside of a brothel!'

Calliope laughed, but before long, an obvious question began to clamour for attention. If the Germans arrested the doctor and the abbot, why not her or *Papa* Emanouil? Were the Germans just playing games, biding their time in hopes of catching more fish in their net?

~ 6 ~

The very next day, Calliope was summoned to Petra.

Umbreit had adopted a conciliatory attitude in Molyvos's sister village. He was far more effective at dealing with the natives than Franz Dwinger had been, but some situations made an interpreter's services indispensable. Most of the time, help was sought in Kaloni; only once had Lorenz Umbreit sent for Calliope. It was possible that her professional services were required again; that the Kaloni interpreter was ill or away on leave.

And yet, zooming down in the Germans' sidecar, wave after wave of dread kept washing over Calliope's brain. The motorcycle raced on, raising clouds of dust. There was a whiff of hot fuel, the cloying scent of wild oleander growing along the road. Halfway down, she made Reis stop so she could scramble out and empty her roiling stomach.

'I'm sorry,' she muttered, settling back into the sidecar. 'I don't know why . . .' She shook her head, giving up. 'Sorry.'

Mortified to the point of tears, she was taken aback by Reis's show of sympathy. His eyes were still watchful, still icy blue, but something had altered in them. He was offering her a clean handkerchief. Could he possibly be pitying her? Was it because he knew what awaited her in Petra?

Both Umbreit and Reis appeared to be going through some sort of internal crisis. At first, Calliope had taken Umbreit's melancholy air to be related to matters of the heart. By summer, however, even the least observant of villagers had noted that the Germans seemed to be growing dispirited. The Allies had recently begun bombing German cities. They had triumphed in Rome, had invaded Normandy. But none of these victories succeeded in arresting Calliope's grief whenever she thought of the doctor. Should she have thrown herself at von Herden? Would he have been willing to accept the bargain she had so thoughtlessly tried to strike with Lorenz Umbreit?

These questions had been gnawing at her ever since the doctor's arrest. But on the way to Petra, fear for her own safety began to pierce Calliope's marrow. What if they had finally found out about her own involvement? What would Umbreit do about it? With a part of her heart she almost felt sorry for his predicament, for if there was one thing she never doubted, it was Lorenz Umbreit's love.

She supposed she loved him too – loved him still – though it could not be denied that something had begun to sour within her after she'd stumbled upon the three corpses dangling in the *plateia*. Umbreit had been in Petra for two days, but on the third, Calliope spotted him from her desk, bounding up the Molyvos town hall's stairs. She followed him to his office, then stood at the threshold, pulsing with hostility. He motioned her to sit down, his eyelid twitching. Calliope slid into a chair. Grappling for self-control, she went on to ask the question clawing at her heart. Was Umbreit responsible for the hanging of the three Molyviates?

'No.' There was the familiar gesture involving tense hand and flaxen hair. 'They died in Mytilene . . . all three of them.' He sighed and looked away.

Calliope made an impatient gesture. 'But weren't you the one to hang them in the *agora*?'

He picked up his map pointer, held it for a moment as one might a whip, then put it down, staring at his decorative pebble jar. 'I was not the one to hang them.'

'But you must have been the one to give the order?' Calliope insisted, still hoping to be proven wrong. 'Weren't you?'

Umbreit stirred in his chair. Ever so slightly, he drew himself up. 'They were already dead. I was merely following orders.' He sat gazing at her, mute for a long moment. Suddenly, he said, 'They didn't manage to get anything out of them. I thought you might like to know.'

'What? Are you saying they tortured them but didn't succeed in breaking them? Not one of them?' Calliope was conscious of a flicker of pride or triumph. But in that case, how did the Germans find out about the doctor's involvement?

Umbreit admitted the men had been interrogated by the Gestapo. He did so with his eyes averted, like a man forced to reveal a shameful secret. 'I'm sorry,' he said.

Calliope was less surprised by Umbreit's humble air than by his willingness to discuss confidential matters. She sat still, confused, trying to prevail over her inner tumult. A part of her wanted to shake him, slap him; the other to throw her arms around his neck and comfort him in his manifest sorrow. Furious with herself, with the absurdity of feeling sorry for a German officer, she sat up with a bitter little grimace.

'It's no good, is it, being a sentimental soul?' she said, sarcastically echoing his own words back at the fortress. *Eine sentimentale Seele.* 'You don't go around killing men, then feeling sorry for them!'

'Calliope,' he said. 'I do feel for them. I do, but—' He stopped. He let out another sigh. 'I'm a Wehrmacht officer, Calliope! We are at war. I can't just—'

'Yes, I know: you can't risk your career for a handful of Greek peasants!' she said, cutting him off icily. She knew perfectly well she was being spiteful, yet something in her insisted on punishing him.

Umbreit looked stung, all his features suddenly sliding downwards. 'This is not a career I've chosen for myself, Calliope,' he said quietly. 'You know that perfectly well, yet . . . oh!' He broke off, his palms declaring the hopelessness of it all. 'It's . . . I can't possibly make you see! You just don't know, you can't understand what it means to be a soldier!'

Calliope studied him for a moment. Suddenly, she rose.

'You're right. I can't understand it,' she stated. *Ich kann es nicht recht verstehen.* And then she turned her back on him and strode out to unleash her sorrow.

All this had taken place in Molyvos, shortly after Easter. It was summer by the time Calliope was summoned to Petra, but her inner weather remained unpredictable.

~ 7 ~

The first thing she noticed on entering the Petra office was a file resting dead centre on Lorenz Umbreit's desk. It was a manila folder stamped *GEHEIM* in square black letters. SECRET. Calliope was transfixed by the German word, only dimly aware that Umbreit had risen from his chair, his right hand limply extended towards her.

'*Wie geht es dir?*' He was asking how she was, sounding gently solicitous, like a man greeting a colleague who'd suffered a recent death in the family. Despite the friendly greeting, Calliope reminded herself to tread carefully. If she slipped today, she might compromise not only herself but other Resistance members.

'How do you think I am?' she demanded, ignoring his preferred hand. 'I assume you know the doctor's been sent to a labour camp? You must—'

He cut her off, gesturing towards a chair. 'Sit down, Calliope.'

That he hadn't reverted to formality was vaguely reassuring, but something about his manner confused her. He had a large stone he had picked up somewhere. It was very smooth, very pale, the size and shape of a small child's foot. Umbreit kept toying with it; his eyes queried her, as if trying to diagnose her precise mental state.

That Umbreit had changed since arriving on the island had been clear to Calliope for months. Every time she saw him, there was something new he had found in his solitary wanderings. Little by little, he was surrounding himself with souvenirs from her own island: sea urchins and shells, pebbles and driftwood. Would he take any of it with him when he finally sailed for home?

Calliope drew herself up. 'Why am I here?'

He gazed at her sadly. 'I wanted to be the one to tell you about the doctor,' he finally said. 'I didn't realise you'd already heard.' He refrained from asking how the news had reached her, a kindness in itself. 'I know he meant – means – a lot to you.'

Calliope noted the amended tense. So the grim scene she had been dreading was not about to be played out after all. She was relieved, grateful. At the same time, some belligerent facet of her mind insisted on holding Umbreit responsible for Dhaniel's transfer to a labour camp, for not having prevented it.

'What's it to you?' she flared up. 'One Greek more or less. It's—'

'Calliope!' He half rose from his chair, then slumped back, looking defeated. It was impossible not to note that his face was sallow; that his eyes had gradually lost their childlike clarity. 'I want you to know I did everything in my power,' he said at last. There was no mistaking the sorrow in his voice, yet each word he uttered only served to further scrape Calliope's nerves. It was as if she had unconsciously resolved to adopt the most negative interpretation of his every statement, every gesture he made. Was she trying to pick a quarrel?

'You did everything in your power,' she heard herself echo. 'You mean you made sure he got sent away?'

Yes, she was trying to provoke him, if only to vent her own impotent rage. But as the hostile words came tumbling out, a new thought found its way into Calliope's mind. Was it possible that Umbreit had in fact been jealous of her attachment to Dhaniel? That he thought the patriotic doctor might try to talk her out of her unseemly friendship with a German officer? Dhaniel had, in fact, come close to doing so; had alluded to recent rumours but, finally, had stopped himself without reproaching her.

'Why was he sent to a labour camp?' Calliope asked after a long pause, striving for politeness. Her churlishness, she realised, was beginning to test Umbreit's patience.

'Would you have preferred to see him executed?'

'Why would he be executed? The man's innocent!'

Umbreit studied her. 'Are you sure?' He smiled at her wanly, almost pityingly.

Calliope was floundering. 'He's a good man. You said so yourself.'

'A good man, yes, but not an innocent one – at least not where we're concerned.' Umbreit's smile vanished, making Calliope shrink into her chair. His eyes might have lost their freshness, but they seemed no less penetrating for all that.

'Why? What's he done?'

There was a sigh, a tense raking of the hay-coloured hair. 'You know I can't go into that,' Umbreit said. 'But take my word for it: it's all been carefully investigated and documented. There's not a shred of doubt about the doctor's involvement.'

'*Involvement*? In what?'

Umbreit gave her a faintly admonitory look. *What do you take me for?* his eyes seemed to say.

Calliope shifted her weight, fresh apprehension flooding her heart. For if they really had proof of Dhaniel's activities, was it possible they did not know about her own role? Was Umbreit merely waiting for her to fall into his trap?

'But if they're so sure of his guilt,' she blurted, 'how is it he's alive?' She tossed the question at him boldly, as if to subdue the chill seeping through her bones. 'Well?' she said when no answer seemed to be forthcoming.

'I . . . both I and von Herden intervened.' Umbreit averted his eyes.

'Is that true?' she asked, looking at him intently. She knew he was not a man who would ever claim unearned credit; nor was he the sort who could utter an outright lie. The knowledge, as much as his silence and mournful eyes, made a spark of love leap back into her chest.

'Thank you,' she said after a moment.

Umbreit stirred, passing a nervous hand over his face. Calliope shifted her eyes. She let them travel around the room: over the two sunny windows, the Führer's portrait, the iron-legged daybed neatly covered in a grey wool blanket. She supposed Umbreit slept on this bed whenever he was in Petra. Someone had placed pots of fresh basil on the windowsills. It crossed her mind that if the Germans stayed much longer, they might well end up more Hellenised than the Greeks had become Germanified.

Umbreit observed her small smile and perhaps concluded that a change in her inner state might be taking place. He rose from his chair and came around the desk, his right hand briefly thrust into his pocket. Stopping before her, he unfurled his fist and reached for her hand. Her hand was at rest on the edge of the desk, but he turned it gently, dropping the green stone into her open palm.

'In the sun, it glows just like an emerald.' He smiled.

Calliope said nothing. She was staring down at the stone, as if trying to decide what it was, what she was meant to do with it.

'I keep wanting to give you things,' he blurted after a moment. 'Hardly a day goes by that I don't feel this . . . this urge to bestow something on you.' Saying this, Umbreit reached out and tenderly stroked her face, as if trying to memorise the shape of her cheekbone, the texture of her skin.

Calliope sat breathing quietly, less surprised by Umbreit's intensity than his apparent indifference to the possibility of being caught in such an intimate pose. The door to the street was kept locked in Petra, but the office door had been left ajar. Reis could be heard stirring in the adjacent office. Umbreit was a cautious man. Why was he being so careless today?

'What's going on?' she heard herself ask. 'You – both you and Reis – are behaving strangely. Reis is like . . . a different man.'

Umbreit smiled wanly. He was about to answer when Lieutenant Reis himself appeared at the door, as if sensing he was being

210

discussed. Crossing the room, he passed a note to Umbreit, then hastened to leave, saying he would return at two o'clock, ready to take *Fräu* Alexiou back.

Umbreit glanced at the note. 'My poor adjutant seems to be in love.'

'Reis?' Calliope stopped toying with the pebble. 'In love with whom?'

Umbreit folded his arms, resting his back against the edge of his desk. 'A local widow named Alkesti.' He sighed. 'I'm told her husband was a schoolmaster here.'

'*What?* The one Dwinger shot?'

Umbreit's smile evaporated. He nodded.

'*She* is seeing Alfred Reis?'

Umbreit shrugged.

Calliope went on staring, shrinking back from the news as if she'd been slapped. Her dismay was all the more acute for being incomprehensible. Why should a Petra widow's relationship with Reis appear more unseemly than her own friendship with Umbreit? Was it because Alkesti's husband had been executed by the Germans?

Yes, that must be it, she decided. But a moment later she sighed, realising that the truth was more complicated. For one thing, she had instantly assumed Reis's relationship to be intimate, whereas hers . . .

Hers, after all this time, was just a hopeless muddle. She had no idea what she wanted anymore. She wanted Lorenz Umbreit not to be German – that was all she wanted unequivocally. Everything else was subject to contradiction, anger, doubt.

Although there was no denying their ongoing attraction, Calliope's feelings towards Umbreit had grown so jumbled that when he suddenly took her hands in his own and held them, she felt half her body respond to his touch, while the other half stiffened, as if sensing danger. She was grappling with the vision of Dhaniel lugging rocks or digging ditches – whatever it was they made prisoners do in a labour camp. She felt herself starting to recoil again. 'I—'

But this time, Umbreit refused to retreat. He drew her to her feet, his arms finding their way round her waist. He held her for one intense moment in which her surprised senses began to open up like spring flowers. She was acutely aware of the trees sighing outside the windows, a banner of light dancing on the Führer's portrait. At the same time, a strident chorus was starting to make itself heard in her ears.

He would not let her go. There was the familiar smell of ink and coffee and leather as his lips touched her hair. 'It cannot last much longer,' he whispered, exactly as he had the day Ourania had barged in on them. His breath warmed her neck. *Es kann nicht mehr lange dauern.*

'It's lasted much too long already.'

Calliope had spoken bitterly – because it was true, of course, but also because he was still exploring her neck, her shoulders, her arms, raising one of them to put his lips to her pulsing wrist.

'Yes,' he conceded. 'It has lasted much too long.'

There was a time when Calliope would have given a great deal to hear Lorenz Umbreit utter these words. Now, she registered them with only one corner of her mind because the rest was intent on his warm, purposeful hands. The hands looked alien on her flesh. They *were* alien, yet she seemed utterly incapable of extricating herself.

A moment went by. She was – gently but resolutely – being propelled across the room. She was vaguely aware of this, though she had closed her eyes, listening to her own heart, to the foreign voice murmuring in her ear. When she opened her eyes again, it was in the full knowledge that her body was now dictating the terms, and that she was finally about to submit to its blind imperative. On the wall above them, over the narrow daybed, the Führer gazed at them severely, all but irrelevant.

$$\sim 8 \sim$$

Seraphim Lemos's wife spat the moment she saw Calliope. Their paths happened to cross on St Elias Day, as the contractor's wife was walking home from church, accompanied by her daughter. Going past the Adhams' house, she hesitated for the briefest moment, turned her head slightly, then spat the way old men were prone to do, clearing their throat of phlegm. The gesture bespoke both contempt and loathing but at least had the merit of being unambiguous. Two days later, at Eleni's house, Veroniki the midwife's hostility was less explicit but unmistakable.

The old woman's eyes were becoming cloudy, but the accusation in them burned as brightly as the excitement and suppressed fear in Eleni's eyes. Calliope's protégée had gone into labour a day after her herbalist *yaya* had contracted dysentery, as had Calliope's aunt, Elpida. Dysentery was another infection rampant around the island.

Eleni's contractions were coming and going. Veroniki kept reaching into her linen basket, wiping Eleni's flushed face, rubbing her legs with oil. She had given her raspberry tea and mallows to speed up labour, but the baby seemed loath to relinquish the comfort of its mother's womb. By evening, Tomas's eyes were beginning to grow hollow. His mother, who was caring for Eleni's *yaya*, came down for a spell and, fearing an epileptic fit, ordered her son away.

'Go, *pedhi mou*, go wait in the *kapheneion*!'

Nitsa Kafatou was a short, grey-haired woman whose small, gapped teeth gave her the slightly goofy appearance of an eager-to-please child. Eleni was deeply attached to her mother-in-law, who was airing about, boiling water and tea, getting cobwebs ready to staunch heavy blood flow.

'It's going to be a while,' Veroniki declared halfway through the evening. A scrawny woman resembling a furled umbrella, she had directed her comment at Nitsa, who sighed, stroking away a damp strand of hair clinging to Eleni's cheek. It was a sultry evening and, though the windows were open, the air in the room felt sodden, smelling of oil and sweat and the decaying-flesh smell of birthwort. After a while, assured that Calliope would stay, Tomas's mother decided to return to her own patient.

'I'll be back later,' she promised her daughter-in-law.

Calliope went to sit at the bedside. She took Eleni's hand. She muttered vaguely soothing words, doing her best to ignore Veroniki's pointed coldness. Eleni was gazing up beseechingly, panting between contractions. Her damp hair was drenched in sweat, her face contorted as, again and again, pain gripped her uterus.

After a while, Veroniki made Eleni pad around the room, stopping her now and then to insist on the foul birthwort juice. 'Drink, drink some, *koritsi mou*,' she murmured. 'It'll strengthen the contractions, my child.'

Eleni drank, her face warped by disgust. She sat. She stood. She kneeled down. She got up. She returned to bed. Veroniki began to slap her belly, her sallow face beaded with perspiration. It was midsummer now. Attracted by the smell of birthwort, swarms of flies had come in through the windows, buzzing around the lamps.

There were two oil lamps burning by the bed, and in their meagre light Eleni's eyes were beginning to have a glazed look. The old midwife's skin was a crumpled parchment, but her movements remained brisk and assured and faintly condescending: this was her realm, her kingdom. Speaking to Eleni, her voice was velvety with solicitude.

'Everything's fine,' she mumbled to the quivering girl. 'Everyone's fine, but it's going to be a while yet, *koritsi mou*.'

'How long?' Caliope heard herself ask, haunted by images of her young friend's previous losses.

'A while,' the midwife repeated. 'Get me more light if you want to make yourself useful!' she snapped.

Calliope hesitated, then went to the neighbours to borrow a lamp. She was beginning to worry about Sappho, who was accustomed to being walked at about this time. It was by now past ten and Mirto would be at her sister's house. Sappho was locked up in the storage room, probably whining with distress.

Soon after the extra lamp had been lit, Nitsa Kafatou returned, bustling in with her usual vigour. Calliope told Eleni she must run home and let Sappho relieve herself.

'I'll be back as soon as I can,' she promised.

Several men were making their way home from the *kapheneion*. The Germans had finally given up enforcing the curfew, retreating to their quarters to listen to their wireless broadcasts. Two days earlier, there had been an assassination attempt on Hitler's life. The Führer was virtually unscathed, but his troops appeared more demoralised than ever.

214

Calliope had her own reasons for feeling discouraged. While Sappho leaped and barked and ran circles around the garden, Calliope's mind kept returning to the mounting evidence that Ourania Nakou had tattled after all. The villagers, Aunt Elpida had reported, were becoming divided into those who believed the rumour about her and Umbreit and those who argued against it, stating that Ourania must have grown envious of the high regard in which the schoolmistress was held by the Germans. Calliope's supporters were quick to point to her close friendship with the doctor. Would a man who had risked his life to fight the Germans, a man as intelligent and upright as Elias Dhaniel, have maintained such a close friendship with a Nazi whore?

All this was still taunting Calliope as she headed back to Eleni's house.

She was almost there, had reached St Pandeleimon's, when she found herself gripped by an atavistic impulse. Darting into the deserted church, she quickly lit a votive candle for Eleni. And then another one for the doctor, astonished to find herself muttering an impassioned prayer.

She was still bemused, still chuckling to herself as, about to leave the churchyard, she spotted a knot of men sauntering by. They had been singing rowdily but broke off the moment she emerged from the churchyard. As she closed the gate behind her, Calliope suddenly recognised her brother-in-law, Vangelis. Another moment and she made out Dimitris Stephanides, Iason's best man, flanked by Ourania's son and a shadowy man she had yet to identify.

'Well, well, well, look who's here!' The olive mill owner's son spoke with mock heartiness, his voice slurring. 'If it isn't our little schoolmistress!'

'My own sister-in-law!' Vangelis threw out his arms, as if to greet a long-lost relative. He placed himself in Calliope's path, resolutely blocking her way

'Let me pass, please!' Calliope snapped. She stepped sideways, only to find her way barred again. The fourth man was a fisherman named Nilos, who lived next door to Ourania Nakou and whose son was among Calliope's pupils. The men reeked of ouzo.

'Is this where you meet your lover then?' Vangelis demanded, unsteady on his feet. 'A Nazi lover in a Greek church! Aren't you—'

'Don't be ridiculous!' Calliope spat out. 'I went to light a candle for my friend Eleni. She—'

'You, lighting candles?!' Vangelis hooted. 'Since when have you got religious?' he said, bumping her with his shoulder.

'I . . . oh, what business is it of yours?' Calliope bristled, trying to push through.

'Naturally, it's my business!' Vangelis belched. 'You're my brother's widow!'

'Exactly! So, please cut out the nonsense and let me pass. Eleni is—'

'Ach, let her pass,' interposed Ourania's son. He was called Babbis, and seemed more sober than his drinking buddies. 'She's going to squeal to her lover and get us all in trouble.'

'Is that so?' Iason's best man chortled. 'So it's true what they say . . . he's your lover, then?' He stood tugging at his flamboyant moustache, contemplating Calliope with the curiosity of a fisherman who has just found a new species of fish caught in his net.

'You're all drunk!' Calliope heard herself exclaim, her skin prickling. Babbis's neighbour was watching her closely, his hands in his pockets, his face immobile as stone. Calliope glanced at him, chaotically wishing his son were a better pupil.

'Oh, come on, admit it!' insisted Dimitris. Calliope had lunged sideways, but her husband's best man had spread his arms, barring her way.

'Admit it!' echoed Vangelis, his pirate eyes slitted with menace.

'I admit nothing!' Calliope was still trying to muscle through, but the men only laughed, like children who had suddenly grasped the point of some new, complicated game. Calliope whipped around, hoping to see someone who might intervene. To think that a bunch of drunken louts could stop her from getting back to Eleni!

All at once, she pitched ahead, thrusting her arms forward to sweep Vangelis out of her way.

'Let me go!' she shrilled as her brother-in-law's hands clamped onto her wrists. She was thrashing from side to side, struggling to extricate herself. 'Let me go, you stinking idiots!'

At this, Dimitris made a faux-astonished sound. 'Did she just call us idiots? This . . . this Nazi whore is calling us—'

'Come on now, let her go,' said Ourania's son, his voice growing tense. 'She—'

Vangelis's fist came swinging out, like a rock dislodged by a sudden landslide.

Calliope staggered, a cry escaping her throat. She was still trying to recover from the blow when Nilos struck with his fist, hitting below her breasts. This time, she went reeling backwards, crumpling onto the cobblestones as though the bones in her legs had been abruptly shattered.

'You're calling us *idiots*?' Vangelis's voice hissed in her ears. 'You, who . . . who dishonoured my brother's memory as if . . . as if . . .' Unable to find the right words, Vangelis raised his leg and brought it down viciously. 'I'll give you idiots!'

Groaning, Calliope rolled over, tasting her own blood. Blood and dust. There was a shock of pain as Dimitris's foot assaulted her ribs. The blows kept on coming. The blood went on thudding in her ears. She was being bludgeoned by a merciless horde, battered by an army of colossal boots. After a while, everything grew black. The men's voices reached her across a vast, turbulent sea. She was drowning, drowning.

Then, all at once, the blows ceased. Calliope became aware of a distant, querying shout, then the sound of receding footsteps. She attempted to get up. Dimly, she knew that she must get up. With a valiant effort, she succeeded in rolling herself onto her back, only to lie there, heaving, the sky throbbing above her, a chorus of maddened crickets shrieking in her ears.

Hektor the fool was bending over her.

'K-k-Kyria . . . Kyria . . . Calliope,' he was stammering. His face was suspended above her, its contours swaying like some water-blurred marine creature's. 'K-Kyria . . .'

'Hektor . . .' Groaning, Calliope raised herself slightly on an elbow and spat out a mouthful of blood. 'Go . . . go to my aunt,' she croaked.

Then she flopped back, and the icy stars shot out of the sky and came striking her flesh like bullets.

Hektor galloped over to Elpida's house, somehow managing to convey to Mirto that her daughter was in urgent need of help . . . that she was to be found just outside St Pandeleimon's church . . . that Mirto had better hurry.

He did not wait for her. While Mirto wriggled into a dressing gown and rushed out into the night, Hektor flew towards the town hall, where he repeatedly attempted to get past the two German sentries, possibly meaning to alert Lorenz Umbreit. The captain was spending the night in Petra, but Hektor could not have known this, even had he not been drunk, which he was. Yet not so drunk that he failed to grasp just how dire Calliope's condition was.

'*Kyria* Ca-ca . . .' Thwarted by his own impediment, Hektor began to gesticulate towards St Pandeleimon's, his eyes rolling in their sockets, his raspy voice hissing into the two guards' faces. '*K-k-ky-ria* . . .'

He blubbered on and on, standing his ground, while the sentries sniggered, trying to ward him off. Amused at first, they were becoming irritated by Hektor's foul breath and flying spit. They swore. They told him to scram. They kicked and threatened and swore yet again.

But Hektor was not giving up. He tried to insinuate himself between the two sentries, still drooling, still trying to communicate. But the only person capable of interpreting Hektor's broken appeal was just then lying in a bloody heap on a deserted street, dimly aware of her own surroundings. She was on the verge of losing consciousness when a shot resonated through the slumbering neighbourhood. A single gunshot, followed by profound silence.

Suddenly, a woman's voice rose in the night. A twisted, disembodied howl that happened to be the maternal cry accompanying a harrowing birth, but could just as easily have been the sound of an older mother's erupting grief.

And then silence reigned again, broken only by the roar of the sea, the bark of a dog, the rhythmic sound of a woman's feet slapping the cobblestones.

Mirto ran and ran through the sleeping village.

FOUR

~ 1 ~

There were two Germans in the black ink drawing; two helmeted soldiers leaning side by side over a balcony, their posture and expression suggesting hilarity. On the pavement below, three street urchins were engaged in a hectic scuffle. They looked like ordinary boys wrestling over a football, but were in fact fighting over dinner scraps thrown down by the German soldiers.

'They made us into animals,' the young artist's mother was saying. 'Wild animals.'

Olga Samiou was speaking to Calliope, who had been leafing through one of the drawing pads. It was the summer of 1945. The Occupation was over. The Molyvos carpenter's widow and her deaf-mute daughter had just arrived from Athens, where Olga had lately worked as a char, trying to save money for the journey home.

'You should have let us know. We would have sent you money,' Calliope's mother said. In the early 1920s, she had taken Olga, a traumatised refugee, under her wing, nursing her and her husband back to health in her Molyvos home. They were in Mytilene now. Mirto was preparing dinner, grating cheese, chopping tomatoes and onions. Through the open window came the voice of a hawker selling courgettes and peppers; a neighbour's radio played an Edith Piaf song.

Calliope went on leafing through Zoe Samiou's drawings, while the twenty-one-year-old artist slept upstairs, in a bedroom furnished by Dr Dhaniel's mother-in-law.

There were three sketchpads in all, their dog-eared pages chronicling

219

every heartrending aspect of the Occupation. There were drawings of homeless Athenians camped around the subway's warm air vents, of soldiers stopping civilians to confiscate jewellery, of corpse-littered pavements and skeletal children lining up for soup.

'That's the last one she did,' Olga said, her mouth a trembling wound. 'After that, she drew only on pavements and poster pillars.'

Poor Zoe had run out of art supplies, but had gone on drawing until the day her father died of pneumonia, just before the end of the Occupation. 'Don't ask what we had to do to survive,' Olga said, dabbing at her eyes.

At a loss for words, Calliope reached out and stroked Olga's arm. Her own well of tears had by now frozen over and might, she felt, never thaw out again. The hardships in the capital had been widely known for a long time, but the truth about the Nazi camps had emerged only recently. For months, Calliope had tried to tell herself that Lorenz Umbreit would never have participated in the gassing of prisoners. But then his own words would come back to taunt her: *You just don't know, you can't understand what it means to be a soldier!*

It was by now common knowledge that virtually all Salonika's Jews had perished at Auschwitz; an ancient, thriving community wiped out in a single season. Calliope was haunted by the harrowing images; tortured by the tragic fate of poor Hektor, shot while trying to save her life. Gradually, her ribs had healed, her body had learned to function without a spleen, but it was still impossible to imagine the village of her birth without poor, addled Hektor.

'Ach, those were black years,' Mirto put in with a heavy sigh. She waved away a fly, then stopped to taste the aubergine casserole simmering on the stove. 'At least we're eating again,' she added.

~ 2 ~

For months, Calliope had tried to put the Occupation years behind her; had done her best to ward off thoughts of Lorenz Umbreit even after learning that he had done everything possible to save her life. He

and, incredibly enough, Alfred Reis as well. It was Reis who had contacted Umbreit on that fateful July night, after Mirto had found him
outside the town hall, bent over Hektor's inert body.

The village fool had been shot by one of the sentries, but Calliope
was found in the nick of time. She was whisked to a Kaloni clinic,
and then to the hospital in Mytilene, where she underwent emergency
surgery.

Mirto had quickly moved to the capital. She had stayed with her
brother and sister-in-law, then arranged to rent Stella Gravari's house
when it became clear that Calliope would need ongoing medical care.
She was young and sure to regain her health, but it would take time,
the doctors kept saying. It would take time.

Calliope was growing impatient with her own body. Ten months
after surgery, her joints still ached and her bones felt fragile, as though
she were her mother's age and not a young woman who had just turned
thirty. It was impossible not to contemplate the bitter irony that it
was Molyviates, her own people, who had almost killed her, while the
enemy she had for months tried to resist had finally saved her life.

And yet, the hospital staff had not allowed Umbreit near her while
she was in intensive care; had not even told her that he'd tried to gain
admission. She had been led to believe that the late Kyriakos Himonas's
brother had brought her to the hospital in his taxi and she had seen
no reason to doubt it. Having finally heard from Umbreit, however, it
came to her that he would have surely written before the Wehrmacht's
departure. Perhaps he had left a letter with her Molyvos aunt? Elpida had
recently lost her younger son to bone cancer. Perhaps she had been too
distraught to forward the letter?

Mirto claimed to have no knowledge of any such letter, but Calliope
was not convinced that she was telling the truth. Why would Umbreit
suddenly send a letter to the telegraph office in Molyvos? Why not to
her mother or her aunt?

Whatever the reason, the letter she had received the other day was
addressed to Tomas Kafatou, Eleni's husband. The telegraphist had
passed it on to his wife, who brought it with her to Mytilene when
she came for a paediatric checkup. Ten-month-old Athena, Calliope's

second godchild, was thriving, and so was Eleni. Her errant uncle, Natis, had recently married Dora the weeper, moving into her dowry house.

Lorenz Umbreit's letter had been posted in late April, in Zurich. Since then, Mussolini had been executed by Italian guerillas, Hitler had committed suicide, Germany had formally surrendered to the Allies. Calliope was still undecided about reading Umbreit's letter. Somehow, while Olga and Zoe were there, she felt certain she would never read it. She wished they could stay in Mytilene, if only to ensure that she wasn't tempted. For months now, she had lived like this: resisting the past, keeping the future at bay. But then Olga and Zoe left for Molyvos and, unable to sleep, Calliope found herself irresistibly curious about the letter's contents.

The letter had come in an airmail envelope, bearing a Swiss stamp but familiar handwriting, familiar purple ink. On the back of the envelope, across the glued flap, a monogram had been added, possibly intended to discourage tampering.

And still, Calliope dithered. It was over between them. Over. She cautioned herself against slipping into the quagmire of her wartime past. She did so again and again.

It was midnight before the sky-blue envelope was finally slit open. Sitting up in bed, Calliope slid her hand inside, paused for a moment, then went on to extract a sheet of white onionskin. Just a single sheet, which she was soon unfolding with trembling fingers, vaguely disappointed by the brevity of the letter.

27 April 1945

My dear Calliope,

I am writing this not knowing whether my letter will ever reach you. I've been wanting to write for some time but could not find the words with which to ask your forgiveness. I have finally come to realise that forgiveness, in this case, may be too much to expect from you and your people. All the same, I desperately want to say one thing, and I beg you to believe me: I had no knowledge whatsoever of the death camps, though now that I do, I frankly don't know how to live with the truth.

I've had a nervous breakdown and am still convalescing, but hope to be going home by summer's end. I sincerely hope that you have regained your health, and that the years ahead will make it possible for you and your beautiful country to recover from the devastation we have wreaked upon you.

As ever,

Lorenz

P.S. Should you decide to answer this letter, perhaps you won't mind satisfying a trivial but nagging curiosity. The day Reis and I ran into you and your mother on the Eftalou road, there was more than wild mustard in your baskets, right? I ask this not because it's of any consequence, but because I have always wondered whether I was able to read you as well as I thought I was.

'*Panaghia mou!*'

Calliope sagged against the pillows, feeling something turn over in her chest.

Almost a year had passed since she had last seen Umbreit, but it was his note – above all, his astonishing postscript – that seemed to be dissolving the small stone lodged within her heart. She wept half the night, then drifted off with the light on, bolting awake just before dawn.

There was no going back to sleep. She rose to use the toilet, then returned to bed and read the letter all over again, finally allowing herself to contemplate a subject she had kept at bay for months: she had been pregnant the night of the beating; had lost the baby in Mytilene, never suspecting that she had conceived during her one and only sexual encounter with Lorenz Umbreit.

Calliope replaced the letter in its envelope. She lay staring at the purple monogram: LFU. The father of her doomed child and she didn't even know his middle name. She had asked him once, back in Molyvos, but he wouldn't tell her. She supposed it was some silly German name. What he didn't know about *her* was far more significant. Even after all these months, she was hard pressed to explain how she could have allowed herself to be swept away on the Wehrmacht's cot in Petra; with Adolf Hitler staring down on their heedless bodies!

She was still brooding on the past when her mother came in to wake her. She came earlier than usual because it was the day before St Calliope's Feast. Calliope was still indifferent to name days, but this year she had good reason to celebrate: Dr Dhaniel was about to return from Dachau, along with *Papa* Konstantinos, St Mathaios's abbot. Dachau had been liberated in late April, but the survivors were only now starting to return. Dhaniel was scheduled to arrive tomorrow, his safe return the only event promising to dissipate the melancholy mists hovering over Calliope's days.

The sleepless night had left her with a throbbing headache. She would stop at the pharmacy, she decided; pick up a painkiller as well as sleeping tablets. She wanted to ensure a restful sleep tonight; wanted to feel – to look – her very best tomorrow.

The pharmacy was no longer owned by the Fotiadis family, who had recently moved to Salonika. Orestes himself was no longer among the living, having been executed by the Resistance after it was discovered that he had been a Gestapo double agent, responsible for the arrests of the mayor, doctor, *kapheneion* owner, abbot. There were, of course, others involved in what had come to be known as the English Spy Case but, fortunately, Orestes Fotiadis had never found out about them.

Oddly, Calliope had learned about Fotiadis's execution from Rupert Ealing, who had left for England in the wake of the Germans' departure. Eventually, he wrote to her, expressing the hope that she might come to London some day, reminding her of her wartime promise to learn English.

Calliope had not kept her word; she'd finally asked her young brother-in-law for a translation of the Englishman's scribbled message. Pericles was preparing for university exams, but still visited Calliope at regular intervals. One day he arrived in Mytilene with the translated passage. It was the conclusion to a famous English poem entitled 'Ode to a Grecian Urn'. *Beauty is truth, truth beauty – that is all ye know on earth, and all ye need to know.*

'Beauty is truth, truth beauty . . . that's what it says?' A short, dismayed laugh escaped Calliope. The quotation bewildered her. She thought the English poet's words utter nonsense. So did Pericles, who scoffed, saying he had written better poetry when he was fourteen. Calliope didn't dispute this. She had just read Pericles's most recent poem, 'Occupation', and thought it masterful.

'But surely,' she wrote to Rupert, 'there is beauty without truth, as there is truth without beauty, though personally I don't think there can be anything more beautiful than truth – assuming one could actually find it. One can't, of course, but the search for it may be quite beautiful in itself. Don't you think?'

~ 3 ~

And then, at last, Friday morning arrived. Calliope and her mother were joined by Pericles, Stella and the doctor's children, as well as by the ageing *Papa* Emanouil, who had come to welcome the doctor and St Mathaios's abbot. Yannis Rozakis's widow and daughters were also in Mytilene: Pavlos, the *kapheneion* owner's missing son, had turned out to be alive after all, though he had been seriously wounded in Egypt.

'Ach, if only my husband could be here today!' Rozakis's widow kept saying, craning her neck. 'If only he could have lived long enough to see our Pavlaki alive!'

The white ferryboat was advancing towards the port, its foghorn blasting. It was nearly noon, but the sun was still merciful at this time of year, dancing on the azure sea. The boat was two hours late, but ferries had always been late, can't blame the Occupation for that, people kept saying.

The little joke seemed immensely funny to everyone. There was wild applause as the boat eased its way into the harbour. Then a tall priest came elbowing his way through the crowd, having spotted *Papa* Emanouil's stovepipe hat among the waiting Molyviates. It was *Papa* Ioannis.

'The Resistance priest,' Dora the weeper whispered in her mother's ear.

The two priests embraced; excited greetings were exchanged amid a cacophony of chattering relatives, droning hawkers, clamouring porters. The porters kept trying to push their way through the thickening crowd; the hawkers went on peddling sesame rolls and roasted peanuts and miniature white-and-blue flags.

At least two of the hawkers were gypsies and, for a moment, Calliope thought she recognised Amalia. But no, this woman was older and plainer, though she too resembled a tropical bird, dressed in turquoise and red and orange. Calliope bought a flag for her seven-year-old godson, then Pericles lifted him onto his shoulders so Aristides could see the passengers starting to queue up on the lower deck.

Now that the ferry had docked, there was utter pandemonium on the quay. The crowd was surging forward, reluctantly parting for disembarking vehicles. The trucks came rattling down in clouds of exhaust fumes and dust, but could barely make way through the pressing crowd. There were shouts and protests as uniformed officials attempted to keep back eager relatives. Drivers honked horns. Policemen blew whistles. Two porters started to quarrel as they stood waiting for custom. Then, at last, the gangplank was lowered and the first dishevelled passengers came shuffling off the boat, weighed down by bags and bundles.

At this point, the crowd became an unstoppable torrent. Dora the weeper let out an excited yelp. 'Look!' She pointed, waving frantically. 'There he is, Mama, look – no, not there: *there!*' Pavlos Rozakis had turned up at the top of the gangplank, flanked by Dr Dhaniel and *Papa* Konstantinos. 'Yes, of course it's him, Mama! He's just grown a beard, *kale!*'

'I see the beard,' said her mother, frowning. 'But look . . . look how thin he is! A regular scarecrow. Are you sure it's him? Why—'

'Of course it's him, Mama!' Anna jumped in. *'Panaghia mou!'* She crossed herself with theatrical fervour; then she, too, started to wave, while Dora burst into uncontrollable sobs.

Calliope witnessed all this in silence, her own eyes starting to blur. She braced her feet against the surging crowd, batting at her cheeks with the back of her hand. Dhaniel was still too far off for her to see whether he had changed. Not for the first time she thanked a god she did not believe in that the doctor had been arrested as late as he had. Who could tell how long he would have managed to survive otherwise?

'It's a miracle!' *Papa* Ioannis was babbling excitedly. 'Three of the finest men ever born on the island and all three come back alive! It's a miracle!'

No one bothered to correct the elderly priest. No one seemed to remember that the doctor was actually one of the *Turkospori* from Asia Minor. The three men were still shouldering their way through the crowd when Aristides spotted his father.

'I see him!' he shrilled, his sandalled feet kicking the air. 'I see my *Baba*!'

'Your *Baba* is a hero! A real hero!' *Papa* Emanouil stated, ruffling the child's hair. Caught up in the joyful spirit, he then announced they must all go and celebrate together; have a festive meal on the waterfront, drink some local wine.

'What, you mean today? Right now?' The doctor's mother-in-law appeared sceptical. She pointed out the passengers would be exhausted after their long journey, but *Papa* Emanouil waved it all away.

'We have to drink to the future today! The future!' he reiterated, reaching out to pat Calliope's shoulder. 'Ach, *koritsi mou*, this is not a day for tears, but for celebration. Celebration, *koritsi mou*!'

Everyone in the party nodded in agreement, but Calliope was no longer listening. She and Dhaniel were gazing at each other across the shrinking distance, tears streaming down their faces. In an hour or so, they would all sit down and repudiate the past, as one might repudiate the memory of some loutish, disruptive guest. Calliope's godson had clambered down, his matchstick arms flung towards the summer sky, as if to support its weight.

'Baba, Baba, Baba!' he kept shouting.

Calliope stood, tugging at her skirt, not knowing what to do with her own impatient arms.

1947–1959

ONE

~ 1 ~

One windy October night, two famished guerillas clambered down the balding hill slopes, as agile as mountain goats prancing through rocks and brambles. It was two days after St Dimitrios's Feast, but the smell of winter swirled in the air, spurring the men on through the whispering darkness. They had been living outdoors for months, sleeping in caves and forests. Now and then, the national army soldiers would march right by their hide-outs, singing their allegiance to king and country. A day earlier, there had been a skirmish in the Argheno hills and the older man had been slightly wounded.

'I hope the old hag knows how to change a bandage,' he muttered.

The old hag was Mirto Adham, the late headmaster's widow. She was known to be a Royalist, though her daughter was believed to harbour Leftist sympathies. The Communist guerillas had their informers. They knew that Calliope spent every Sunday night with her lover in the late fortune-teller's house, and that she always brought her dog along. It was one reason they had chosen this widow, this particular night.

The two men entered the sleeping village through a back road, as furtive and alert as pine martens stealing into a poultry shed. It was by now well past two in the morning. St Kyriaki was the younger man's own neighbourhood, but Dimitris Kapellas kept his eyes averted from his family's shuttered windows. His decision to join the guerillas in 1947 was a surprising one for such a diffident, pampered boy, even one whose postmaster father had threatened to throw him out if he didn't stop attending the Communists' clandestine meetings.

Gentle but famously mulish, Dimitris had left home for the hills, welcomed by the new Communist commander. Nikos Antipas was a fatherly man but a steely leader. Fearing entrapment, he forbade his guerillas even a brief conjugal visit, staying away from his own young wife and child. In no time at all, he had established an intelligence network all along the coast, with shepherds and fishermen reporting on the movements of government soldiers. By mid-August, the authorities had placed a 25-million-drachma bounty on Antipas's head, but the new leader remained as elusive as an octopus.

The two young partisans marched on, shivering against the wind. In the silence of the night, Dimitris's stomach began to rumble.

'I could use a bowl of *trahana* right now,' he said, his hand seeking the grenade in his pocket the way an anxious child's hand might mechanically seek a familiar toy. He was barely twenty. His comrade, Christos, was older and more experienced, having fled to the hills when the island had still been under German Occupation. His clothes were frayed, his head infested with lice, but his stride was proud and quick with purpose.

'Fuck, my tooth's acting up again!' he said.

'We're almost there,' said Dimitris.

They were approaching the widow's residence, a fine two-storey house looming on a windswept corner. In the moonlight, the two men could make out the outline of a high stone fence, a wooden gate that squeaked on being opened. The limbs of denuded trees swayed in the darkness, like the arms of old men defending themselves against invisible assailants. The guerillas glanced at the kitchen windows, then stole towards the back entrance. Behind them, the moon floated in the murky sky, intermittently obscured by tattered black clouds.

~ 2 ~

She stood framed in the doorway, clutching an oil lamp, her eyes dilated less with fear than with a sort of arrested amazement. She had on a flannel robe and long, woollen stockings. Her hair had been gathered into a wispy plait, but a few grey strands had escaped in sleep, framing her withered features. The blacksmith's son was clearly visible in the kitchen but, in her confusion, the old woman muttered something about rats, then began to pluck compulsively at her belt.

'But what . . . what do you want?' she finally asked, her entire being focused on the eye of the rifle being aimed at her chest. There was a burning candle on the pine table; a faint smell of melting wax hung in the air.

'What do you think we want?' Christos snapped, reaching into the bread box. 'Food. Food and blankets.'

'Food?' The widow stood blinking for a moment or two. Suddenly, she recognised him. She said his name twice. It came out sounding like a question the first time, but barely more than a sigh the second. 'Aren't you ashamed, *pedhi mou*? Wouldn't I have given you food if you'd asked for it?'

'Why should I be ashamed? It's you people who should be ashamed!' Christos's eyes bore into the widow's face, his mouth warped in a contempt so deep it seemed to border on pleasure. All the same, he had relaxed his grip on the rifle, shifting his feet under her gaze like an errant boy being called to task by a stern grandmother. His army boots were mud-caked, his matted hair had gone unwashed for days. Mirto Adham took all this in and her parched lips trembled, as if she couldn't quite decide on the proper response.

'I think you—'

'What's it to me what you think?' Christos cut in. 'We're not here to listen to your ideas, are we?' He gave 'ideas' an ironic emphasis. 'Come on, now. Where d'you keep your *trahana*?'

The old woman limped towards the kitchen table. She set down the lamp, then blew out the candle. There was something deliberate in all her movements, as if every step she took caused her physical pain. Now that she had identified the intruder, her face had become almost composed. She turned and lit a fire, making the shadows dance.

'The *trahana*'s in the pantry. I'll gladly give you some,' she answered at length, 'but only . . . only if you put down your . . .' She trailed off, having suddenly registered the beam of light flickering outside the pantry.

'We're not here to negotiate!' Christos barked at her. 'We do the fighting, you do as you're told!'

The widow was silent, picking and plucking at her fraying robe. Dimitris Kapellas had just emerged out of the pantry, holding a candlestick. With his clothes rumpled and hair in disarray, he might have been a boy awoken by the call of nature. 'I beg you, *Kyria* Mirto,' he pleaded. 'Do as he says and everything—'

'Ach!' Mirto Adham swallowed. 'You, Dimitraki?!' She stood gaping, face furrowed with a sort of stunned reproach. The postmaster's son was a stocky young man raised by a gaggle of female relatives. He had three sisters as well as two maiden aunts and a besotted mother, but in recent months, his plump features had acquired a lean, faintly bewildered mien. He looked like an adolescent who had slipped into adulthood without the benefit of a mirror, astonished, when one finally came into his possession, to find himself facing a grown-up's reflection.

Christos had taken off his pullover and was rolling up his sleeve to expose his bicep.

'*Panaghia mou!*' The old woman crossed herself, blinking at the blood seeping through the bandage.

'Why don't you take care of my arm,' Christos snapped, 'instead of standing there like a ghost? Go on, get a bandage or something!'

'I – I don't have a bandage. I'll have to find something upstairs. Upstairs,' she mumbled.

'Well, get it!' Christos grabbed a heel of leftover bread and bit into it savagely. 'Let's go!'

Mirto Adham picked up the lamp with a martyred air. 'It's a good thing your mother's not alive to see how you treat an old woman,' she said.

'Leave my mother out of this!'

The widow paused in her tracks.

'If you want me to change your bandage, you'd better behave like a human being.' She began to climb the stairs. Christos followed, still chewing, still gripping the rifle.

He set it down once they reached the bedroom, stopping to peel off his ratty vest. A brazier was whispering at the foot of the bed, and this is where he planted himself, a sudden look of childish glee suffusing his face. He had just discovered a wilted cigarette in one of his shirt pockets.

Mirto Adham was rummaging through a brass-studded trunk. She seemed maddeningly determined to take her time, examining one garment after another, finally bringing out a long, gauzy nightgown which she carefully inspected, while Christos stood unwinding his stained bandage.

The old woman appeared to have forgotten all about the intruder. Muttering to herself, she went about shredding the old nightgown into long, uneven strips, stopping to cast a worried glance at the rattling shutters. The room was spacious but draughty. It smelled of moth-balls and smouldering olive pips. At last she hobbled over and began to examine the wound. 'I'll have to wash it and—'

'Never mind, it's clean enough, just—'

'It has to be washed, *pedhi mou!*' she remonstrated as if addressing an impetuous child eager to run out and play. 'It could get infected and then what?'

'Well, hurry up, then!'

But she was already shuffling towards the enamel basin, lifting the jug and pouring water onto a fresh cloth. She swabbed the injured arm as gently and efficiently as a nurse, silent at last in the shadowy room, with the brazier hissing and a night bird calling, its cry muffled by the wind.

'There!' she finally said, tying up the strips of cloth around the thin arm. Christos was long-limbed, like his father, and had the same face, as alert and impassive as a bird of prey's.

'Now, get us some blankets!' he snapped, dropping his ashes onto the pine floor. 'Go on! It doesn't have to be your bridal quilts. Just get us something warm. Quick!' He settled into a small stuffed chair, alternately dragging on his cigarette and poking in his mouth.

There was an old pine wardrobe standing against the wall. Leaning into it, Mirto Adham pulled out two grey blankets, muttering about what the world was coming to: village boys dragging old women out of bed, dropping ashes onto freshly scrubbed floors. The blacksmith's son listened to this litany in silence, his eyes following the plume of smoke curling towards the ceiling. The tobacco seemed to be calming him; his voice, when he finally spoke, had lost some of its edge.

'Your sleep's not important,' he said, fixing the old woman with a long, didactic gaze. 'The revolution's what's important . . . your helping patriots like me is—'

'Patriots!' She ceased folding the blankets and swivelled to face him, her eyes flaring within their web of wrinkles. 'What makes you a greater patriot than me? Didn't I do my bit during the Occupation?'

'What makes me a greater patriot is that I sleep in a cave and fight the Fascists, while you snuggle up every night in your warm bed!' This reply seemed to give the blacksmith's son inordinate satisfaction. He rose and picked up his rifle, the cigarette dangling between his lips. 'Go on, get moving!' He gestured towards the door. 'Bring the blankets with you!'

Downstairs, Dimitris was seated in a pool of light, hunched over a plate of cold fish, his eyes dilated with greed. There was the whispering of the fire but no other sound as Christos came to a stop at the threshold.

'She's a good cook!' Dimitris blurted, lurching out of his chair.

Christos's eyes were two chips of coal. 'A good cook!' he roared. 'We're not here on a social visit . . . with polite smiles and compliments to the hostess, eh, putty-face?'

Dimitris wiped his mouth with the back of his hand. He had a cowlick which, in tense moments, he compulsively tried to push off his forehead. On the windowsill, two cats had begun to meow.

All at once, Christos seemed to relent. He looked at a loss for a moment, as if trying to work out where his anger had vanished to. 'Did you find the *trahana*?'

The postmaster's son gestured towards the divan. He had it all in a flour sack, he said. '*Kritharaki*, too.'

At this, the old woman let out a croak of protest. 'And what are we supposed to eat all winter?'

'Don't you worry, *Kyria*. I'm sure your daughter won't let you starve,' Christos retorted. The candle was guttering on the kitchen table, about to go out. 'Go on – give Dimitris the blankets.' He gestured with his head. 'Hurry up now!'

The kitchen was dimmer now, its hanging pots and drying vegetables hardly discernible on the murky walls. Dimitris was picking his way towards the old woman, holding out his arms, as if in anticipation of an embrace.

'Ach, ach, ach, Dimitraki *mou*!' Mirto said, relinquishing the blankets.

'Remember to keep your mouth shut, eh?' Christos patted his rifle, as if to make it clear it was a real weapon, not a child's toy. 'You will remember, won't you?'

'What I'll do is pray to the Virgin for you!'

'Ach, don't bother!' The blacksmith's son slung the jute sack over his shoulder. 'The Virgin helps those who help themselves!'

Dimitris was heading out, muttering goodnight in passing.

'Goodnight!' Christos echoed ironically. He cast the widow one final glance, then stalked off into the night, slamming the door behind him.

Alone in the kitchen, Mirto Adham shivered, clasping her robe about her. For a moment, she stood by the dying flames, rubbing her hip and peering into the night. The wind was still wailing, swallowing the men's footfall.

Suddenly, the old woman crumpled to the floor, like a puppet whose string has abruptly been snapped. The cats, which had briefly and hopefully trailed the two men with their bulging sacks, returned to the window, yowling and hissing in each other's faces. On the kitchen table, the oil lamp continued to burn, making protesting noises. At length, it too went out, leaving the old woman lying in a heap on the kitchen floor, clawing at the darkness, as if to grasp something that kept eluding her.

TWO

~ 1 ~

The last time he asked her to marry him had been on St Basil's Day, the first day of the new year. She had already said no on at least two occasions, but he must have hoped to find her more amenable after her mother's death.

She had not been amenable, but he had been right in sensing that she was feeling as bereft and bewildered as an orphaned child. For weeks, she had rattled around in the empty house, able to perform only the most essential tasks. She was incapable of making a responsible decision at such a time – how could he expect her to?

She seemed equally incapable of explaining her own persistent reluctance. She had, at first, tried turning it into a joke: she was afraid of becoming a Wicked Stepmother, she had said, trying for a smile. The statement had elicited a chuckle, but his eyes reproached her. Floundering, Calliope begged to be asked again on her birthday, which fell in spring. She should be able to think clearly by then, she'd stated.

And now her thirty-third birthday had come around, and though she knew Eli Dhaniel well enough to be sure that he had not forgotten, Calliope also knew that he would not raise the subject today – not while they were all reeling from the news of the Lyras family's latest tragedy.

Mimis, Calliope's old classmate and erstwhile football champion, had just hung himself. That he had not done so after his leg had been amputated, but did after a lengthy police interrogation, shocked both Rightists and Leftists; that the authorities had chosen to arrest the handicapped Mimis rather than his brother, Kostas, had not come as much of a surprise. The captain's elder son was known to be as pig-headed as his late father, unlikely to break under interrogation. No one doubted that both brothers were Communists. They had been too vocal for their own good during the Occupation. Had they been involved in helping the guerillas? Perhaps. They might have even known something about the fugitive Communist commander's whereabouts, though Nikos Antipas was related to them only by marriage.

Such was the buzz of speculation flying all over the village in the wake of Mimis's suicide. No one would ever learn the precise reasons for his detention. All anyone knew was that Captain Yorgos's younger son had finally signed the abhorrent Declaration of Repentance. There could be no doubt about that because the confessors' names were broadcast in church during Sunday services. Everyone knew that most men signed only under duress, but virtually all avoided being seen in public after the announcement.

On Monday evening – the evening of Calliope's birthday – the doctor arrived late, looking more rumpled than ever. Mimis, he told Calliope, had stopped at the clinic on Saturday after being released, complaining of persistent cough. Dhaniel had examined him, given him cough syrup, and sent him to bed. An unexceptional visit. Yet he couldn't shake the feeling that he'd missed some crucial signal; that Mimis had been trying to tell him something.

'I don't know . . . maybe I'm just imagining things.' He sighed. 'I wish I knew.'

The doctor, too, was known to be a Communist, though no one ever complained, as they did elsewhere, that he neglected certain patients because they supported the opposing side. If he was criticised, it was only for never setting foot in church, and for spending an inordinate amount of time with the widowed schoolmistress. On his occasional visits to the *kapheneion*, Dhaniel had heard both Calliope's supporters and detractors speak of her with equal authority. There were those who accused her of having been a German collaborator; others insisted that she had been in the Resistance. That both the doctor and *Papa* Emanouil were among Calliope's staunchest defenders might have silenced her critics, but couldn't she have been a double agent, like Orestes Fotiadis, their erstwhile pharmacist?

All this Eli had occasionally discussed with Calliope, but today all they could think about was Mimis's bereaved family. They were sitting in the small room off the kitchen, where Mirto used to rest of an evening, knitting or mending socks. In the corner, there was still a basket containing skeins of multicoloured wool.

Calliope was about to offer dinner but Eli requested brandy.

'Don't you want to eat?'

'Later.' He was hunched over, his elbows on his knees, his face between his hands. Sappho padded in, wagging her tail, then flumped down at the doctor's feet. The clock in the foyer chimed eleven times.

When Calliope handed Eli his glass, he shifted and drew her to him, absently trifling with her hair. His own hair was almost silver now but still abundant. His face was more gaunt than it had been before Dachau; still the face of a man listening to a joke with one ear and some melancholy tale with the other.

Calliope reached for an ashtray, then sat for a while, smoking desultorily. In her head surfaced the image of the Lyras brothers in short trousers, one fair, one dark, both given to picking at scabs, their limbs perpetually covered in bruises of various hues and sizes. The Lyras men were known to be hotheads, but Calliope was beginning to brood on a much larger question.

'I don't know what it is with our men,' she mused out loud. 'When they don't have Turks or Italians or Germans to fight, they go after each other.' Ever since the Civil War started, the entire country had become divided into Rightist and Leftist camps, pitting neighbours and family members against each other. 'Do you suppose we've just forgotten how to live in peace?'

Eli gazed into his glass as if it might miraculously provide illumination. 'I think we've forgotten how to live without suspicion and rage,' he said.

'So, how are we to go on?' Calliope asked at length. 'When will it all end?'

'God only knows.'

The response was as mechanical as Calliope's occasional invocations of the Virgin Mary. She had long since stopped being surprised by human inconsistency. Her conflicted feelings for Lorenz Umbreit had been among the first, but certainly not the last, hint of her own capacity for inner contradiction. Her love for Eli Dhaniel might seem unimpeachable, but it was no less surprising given that, for years, she had thought of him as a mentor. If anyone had ventured to tell her before the Occupation that some day she would be waiting for her mother to fall asleep so she could sneak out for a tryst with the doctor, she would have either laughed or slapped such a person's face.

Of course her mother must have guessed that she had a lover, staying out as she did till the crack of dawn. Did she know who the lover was?

Calliope had felt an occasional flash of resentment at having to steal out like a wayward maiden, though she could have easily solved the problem by marrying Eli. She loved him, she had no doubt about that, though at first she could not help comparing her feelings for him to her tortuous wartime passion.

She seldom compared anymore, but it was, perhaps, inevitable three days after receiving birthday greetings from Heidelberg. Lorenz Umbreit wrote without fail twice a year, but Calliope never answered. Her pain over their doomed affair had gradually become muted, but she would never understand how it was that men – intelligent, decent men – could serve despicable causes. There were times, she wrote in her journal, when she felt thoroughly disgusted by human folly. Could she really be turning into a misanthrope, as Eli suggested only recently? And was he right, saying that a misanthrope was just an idealist with a broken heart?

Eli's own idealism occasionally left Calliope shaking her head. That a doctor could support the Communists, while in the north, Communist rebels slaughtered every educated man they could ferret out, seemed beyond comprehension. It was one of the things they used to quarrel about, finally resolving to avoid all political discourse.

In time, Calliope understood that for Eli to lose faith in Communism might cause some sort of inner rupture. It would, she thought, be no less heartbreaking than the life of a priest robbed of his faith in God.

Eli Dhaniel was no longer the infallible man she had once thought him to be, but – and this had truly astonished her – she had discovered that a man's flaws and foibles could actually bring about a deepening of feeling. In retrospect, being with Umbreit seemed to her tantamount to feeling perpetually intoxicated, as though the Occupation had forced her to subsist not on beans and dandelions but on wine and baklava. By contrast, being with Eli left her feeling thoroughly sated, a woman who had just consumed a crisp, freshly baked roll, lavishly spread with honey. Had she been forced to choose between the two men, she would have been utterly incapable of doing so.

Mercifully, she had not been asked to make this choice, anymore than she had the choice of a *patrida*. Tortured by the spread of the Civil War, she wrote and wrote in her journal. She even tried to write poetry, as she had after losing her father, but in this she more or less failed. It fell to her more talented brother-in-law to express the rage and the anguish.

There had been no news from Pericles; not since he had been expelled from university and sent to Makronisos, a notorious prison camp for Leftist dissidents. Just before his arrest, however, Pericles had sent Calliope two poems. One of them, his latest, gave eloquent voice to a veteran soldier who, demented by the horrors of war, wounds himself with an old Turkish sword. Standing in the lush countryside, the soldier slashes his own arm, then watches his flesh bleed into a spring meadow – drop by drop by drop, tormented by the pain, unable to chuck the sword away.

~ 2 ~

The Civil War had brought a new headmaster to the village. A staunch Royalist, Leandros Tsouras had been transferred from Kaloni to replace Stamatis Miltiadis, who had been jailed after a policeman had overheard him humming a subversive song on the way to school. The song, in which the King was likened to a mule, was a popular one in Aghiassos, Stamatis's home village. He had gone there for a family wedding; had, he was to claim later, picked up the catchy tune without meaning to.

The headmaster had been the first Communist jailed in Molyvos. He was released after signing the Declaration, but his teaching days were over. A signature was a signature, the authorities had argued, but who could tell what ideas a schoolmaster might take it into his head to plant in impressionable children's heads? Calliope, who had gradually arrived at a reasonable working relationship with Stamatis, found herself doubly vexed by his successor.

Tsouras was a widower in his mid-forties, a man devoted to his books, his garden, his two magnificent peacocks. Tall and erect, he had prominent blue eyes and a heavy chin that had over the years become submerged in his neck, making for a smug, supercilious look. He had a son at university and a daughter married to a civil servant, and would have much preferred a transfer to Athens. Alas, even his son-in-law's connections had so far failed to secure Tsouras the desired post.

All this the headmaster had shared with Calliope soon after his arrival, perhaps hoping to establish a congenial footing. He kept a respectful distance in the weeks following Mirto's death but, as soon as spring arrived, had finally declared his personal interest, as bashful as a smitten adolescent. He knew there were rumours about her and the doctor but he didn't believe them, he said. Not for a single moment.

'Well, this rumour happens to be true.' Calliope almost smiled.

At this, Tsouras coloured and began to fiddle with his necktie. He seemed on the verge of saying something, but then his nostrils twitched. Another moment and he succumbed to a spate of ferocious sneezes. Calliope waited for him to stop. Reaching for a handkerchief, the headmaster claimed to have developed an allergy to chalk dust but, it would soon become apparent, was susceptible to outdoor dust as well.

There were no further indiscretions, but at some point Calliope became aware that Tsouras was watching her every move. He was a man who prided himself on his fair-mindedness. She was a good teacher, he conceded in one of their school meetings, but surely he could not be blamed for objecting to her smoking and wearing scent in class? Surely he was not alone in thinking that such habits ought to be renounced by a woman entrusted with children's education? People talked, he told her. Whatever her personal inclinations, a schoolmistress could not afford to be indifferent to public opinion.

'I am not indifferent to public opinion,' Calliope said. 'I care deeply how people feel about my teaching. And, by the way, I never smoke at school.'

'A respectable teacher must behave like one at all times,' Tsouros insisted.

Calliope sighed. 'I won't wear scent anymore,' she said.

It had occurred to her that Tsouros might be allergic to her perfume. Yet there he was now, ambling through the playground, beset by another sneezing storm. He sneezed explosively: again and again and again, seemingly unaware of the children's barely suppressed mirth.

When, at last, the sneezing spell was over, Tsouras resumed his stroll, surveying the playground with the air of a victorious general attending a celebratory parade. The junior class teacher was also out with her class, but Tsouras's gaze kept returning to Calliope. Suddenly, on a half-spiteful, half-impish impulse, she decided to play Slap the Donkey with her pupils.

The children were mostly eleven-year-olds, but the butcher's grandson was almost thirteen, having been kept back two years in a row.

'Slap the donkey!' Calliope was crouching on all fours on the dusty ground, her knotted hair loosening, her rump catching the sun.

'Slap the donkey!' the children echoed, leaping over their laughing teacher.

She had instructed them to slap between her shoulderblades, but the irrepressible Manos slapped her bottom, then remained astride, bouncing like some demented jockey. Reminded of the rules, the boy finally jumped off, bumping into the even more backward Apollon. If the sailor's son was allowed to attend school at all, it was only because of people's compassion for his mother, whose husband had abandoned the family, starting a new one in America.

Calliope, too, pitied Apollon's mother; had repeatedly resisted the headmaster's efforts to expel the unfortunate child. In the classroom,

Apollon was usually subdued, dreamily picking his nose, or doodling in his notebook. But in the schoolyard, feeling his backside bumped, the indolent boy wheeled about, blinked a few times, then slid into sudden hilarity. Soon, both he and the butcher's grandson were braying with laughter, whooping with savage glee.

'That's all! We've played enough for one day,' Calliope said, separating the two wrestling boys. She stopped to straighten her blouse, and pin up escaping strands of hair. Only then did she become aware that Leandros Tsouras was still watching them from a distance, like a large, hungry spider: expectant and venomous.

～ 3 ～

The school year was almost over when Calliope knew without any doubt: the headmaster had taken to spying on her. By the late 1940s, the school had four classrooms, each with two windows, each facing a long expanse of silvery olive groves. Below the windows, oleander had been planted; pink and white bushes that had over the years matured into flowering trees. The only creatures habitually seen through the classroom windows were the somnolent sheep grazing under olive trees, the occasional roving cat. And, of course, birds and bees and butterflies, darting from branch to branch, flower to flower, each with its particular thirst, its own imperative purpose.

But now, perhaps once a week, there was also Leandros Tsouras, probably thinking himself undetectable through the oleander. What was his purpose? The man was a born fool, but quite possibly a dangerous one. Calliope had spotted his disembodied head that morning, during class dictation; had found herself fighting a childish impulse to stick out her tongue or waggle her fingers over her ears.

'The Marathon victory galvanised the Greek nation because it demonstrated that the Persians were not invincible.' She had gone on with the historical excerpt, but thoughts of the headmaster came back to nag her later that day, on her way down to Petra. She had an early evening appointment with the notary; had, at the last moment, decided to bring her godson along so they could enjoy homemade ice-cream at a seaside sweetshop. It was an exceptionally hot day for June.

The appointment with the notary was meant to settle financial matters related to the late fortune-teller's will. Zenovia's land and olive orchard had been bequeathed to *Papa* Emanouil, her Molyvos home to 'the schoolmistress, who would be sure to put it to good use'. A codicil stipulated that Hektor be allowed to keep the garden shack, and that he be paid a proper salary for gardening and picking olives. The cats were to be poisoned after her death – gently, Zenovia implored from beyond the grave. She could not bear the thought of their suffering, nor of their having to go on living without her.

Zenovia's will had dumbfounded Calliope: had the old woman lost her marbles just before the end? In time, both surprise and unease faded, giving way to an occasional ripple of guilt. Hektor the fool was gone, the cats had gradually died off or vanished but, five years after the fortune-teller's death, it was impossible not to feel that the old woman's faith had been sadly misplaced: all Calliope had ever done with the house was use it for her own weekly trysts before her mother died.

The notary had suggested that Zenovia's house be rented before it fell into ruin. He had sent several reminders to Calliope, making her wish that Zenovia had left the house to someone else, or at least that she had said nothing about putting it to good use. She recalled a pre-war conversation in which she'd told Zenovia that the village children were in need of a library. Had that been the bee in the old woman's bonnet?

The sun was sliding towards the horizon as Calliope and her godson went strolling along Petra's seaside promenade. Aristides, who was not yet ten, stopped to watch an elderly man beat a freshly caught octopus. The Petran beat it against a rock, stopping only when some of the spurting ink splattered onto his nose. Aristides went into peals of laughter, reaching for Calliope's hand. As they crossed the street, a gust of wind rose, snatching at their hair. In the *kapheneion*, men were beginning to gather, the Rightists clustered on one side of the room, the Leftists on the other. The smell of roasting coffee beans hung in the air. The sweetshop was just opening up.

'But are you sure you really want ice-cream?' Calliope asked, tweaking her godson's nose. The child smelled like freshly picked berries. 'Absolutely sure?'

Aristides nodded, chin bobbing up and down. 'Suresuresuresuresure!'

It was only later, after they'd had their treat, that the day began to go awry. They had left the shop by then, were ambling down the promenade, when they came upon a white bedsheet hanging from a window, displaying a vivid splash of blood, the shape and size of a man's palm. Why did the housewife not wash the sheet before hanging it out? Aristides wanted to know.

'Why? Oh!' Calliope cast about for an explanation. What was she supposed to say? That some local girl must have got married the day before? That the bloodied sheet was meant to proclaim her female purity to all and sundry? She fumbled for a cigarette, muttering something about the sun bleaching out the stain.

But Aristides was no longer listening. His attention had been snagged by a legless man selling roasted seeds and nuts from a handmade cart. Calliope didn't know the former army officer, but she had heard about him in the early days of the Civil War, after Communist guerillas had reportedly set off an explosion in the Argheno hills.

Aristides was looking over his shoulder, speaking in an urgent whisper. 'But how . . . how does he get around?'

'Did you see his muscles?' Calliope blew smoke into the balmy air. 'He pushes himself with his hands and arms.' Aristides's chin had begun to quiver. 'Look!' She pointed. 'Look at the kids.'

Two barefoot boys were jogging by, rolling a metal hoop. A little girl toddled after her mother, clutching a jar with a trapped jellyfish. The mother stopped, and waited, then reached out to brush a stray curl away from her daughter's eyes. Banal though it was, the small maternal gesture filled Calliope with sudden longing for Mirto. The feeling was as intense as it was complicated, but it was nothing new.

~ 4 ~

The rain came early that autumn. It started suddenly one September afternoon, pouring down with a spiteful ferocity. Because of the storm, because her son was afraid of thunder, the Communist commander's wife put the boy to bed later than usual, after she had trimmed his hair and fed him a snack, and the rain had finally slackened.

They had been using the chamber pot all evening, but once the rain stopped, Ermione threw a shawl around her shoulders and padded to the outhouse. The privy was cold and damp as she lowered herself over the Turkish toilet, her feet on the footrests, her hands clutching at her bunched-up skirts. She then hurried back with the empty chamber pot; had just put it away and bolted the door when she heard the crunch of footsteps on the gravel path. There was a rap at the door.

'Nikos!' Ermione darted back to the entrance, fumbling with the bolt. 'Ni—'

The man who came hurtling out of the night was not Nikos Antipas but Dimitris Stephanides, the son of the late olive mill owner. He was hissing at her to be quiet.

Ermione sprang back. The intruder had a flick knife. His eyes darting about, Stephanides took in the large, cluttered kitchen: the basin of dishes waiting to be washed, the dying fire, the shadowy corners beyond the range of the oil lamp. It was only ten o'clock but the storm had caused a power outage. A laundry line was suspended from two long nails, hung with a child's underwear. On the table, next to a flower vase, lay a hand mirror, a comb, a pair of kitchen scissors.

'Where's your husband?'

Stephanides crossed the room, walking with a slight limp. He reeked of ouzo, yet was evidently sober enough to have waited for the rain to let up before venturing out.

'He's not here.' Ermione had backed away as far as the laundry line, intent on Stephanides's every movement.

'I know he's not here! *Where* is he, I asked!'

Ermione's face quivered. 'I haven't seen my husband in months!'

'Oh, go on! He couldn't stay away from you this long. Not Nikos.'

248

Stephanides chuckled. He went on scanning her face: a balding, thickly built man with eyes that seemed to be in perpetual search of some misplaced item. He was only in his mid-thirties but the magnificent moustache looked like it would have to compensate for quite a lot. Years ago, he and Nikos Antipas had been classmates. 'I hear you're such a good wife too,' the intruder said, 'washing your husband's feet and all. Isn't that right?' /

Ermione raised a shoulder, as if deprecating her own wifely devotion. She seemed about to say something when lightning filled the windows. She was a beautiful young woman, with languorous green eyes and honey-coloured hair tumbling over her shoulders. Her parents had died in Skala Sykamnias during the Occupation; her Molyvos in-laws did not approve of their son's choice of bride any more than they did of his politics.

'I suppose you're hoping to collect the reward?' she blurted out, as if the idea had just crossed her mind.

Stephanides cleared his nose. 'I'm *planning* to collect it,' he stated, looking at her with a small, crooked smile. 'Now, for the last time, where is he?'

'I have no idea!' Ermione tossed out. 'But I know you'll never catch him!'

'You think so? You think he's too smart for us, eh?' Stephanides chortled. 'Funny thing is his own father doesn't think he's so smart, does he?' Nikos Antipas's father was a staunch Royalist; he'd been heard to laugh in the *kapheneion*, hearing of the twenty-five-million-drachma reward placed on his son's head. 'He's not worth so much as a drachma, that's what his father said!' Stephanides's eyes appraised Ermione, gleaming with irony. 'What d'you say to that?'

'What do I say? I say a single one of his fingernails is worth more than the whole of you put together — moustache and all!' she added.

At this, a spark of fury appeared in Stephanides's eyes. 'You bitch! Who do you think you are? You who came here with nothing but the rags on your back! You stupid, arrogant bitch!' Saying this, the intruder gave Ermione a violent push, watching her stagger backwards. She managed to regain her balance, only to trip on a bird-whistle. She went reeling to the floor, her slipper flying off her foot.

'A Communist bitch opening her sewer of a mouth! At Dimitris Stephanides!'

Ermione levered herself on her elbow and sat hunched over her foot. She began to massage the arch, her face scrunched with pain.

'What's the matter? Has the lady hurt herself?' Stephanides tilted forward, mock-solicitous. He was about to add something when Ermione raised her eyes. She leaned forward, paused, then spat straight into the taunting face.

'You!' Stephanides looked stunned for a moment, but quickly rallied himself, growing resolute. He put away the knife. He extracted a handkerchief from his pocket, then a pair of handcuffs. He swiped at his cheek with the rumpled cloth, then stuffed it into Ermione's mouth. He grabbed her wrists and bound them with the handcuffs.

'So, where's that clever husband of yours now, eh? Let's see if we can get him to come to your rescue!'

It was raining again, the storm blowing gusts of water against the windowpanes. Ermione was weeping now, kneeling with her mouth gagged and her hands shackled, her eyes wildly sweeping around the room. Stephanides stood stroking his moustache, like a military strategist contemplating his next manoeuvre.

All at once, as if suddenly inspired, he lunged towards the kitchen table and pounced on Ermione's scissors. With a swift, brutal gesture, he swept away the child's drying underwear. He cut down the laundry line, then hastened back to his captive.

She began to jostle from side to side, her head thumping at her tormentor's chest, her whole body resisting as he went about binding her limbs. Soon, he had her all trussed up, hunched over in the pool of flickering light, with the dying embers hissing in the hearth and the rain spitting on the tiled roof. There was a rip of lightning, a ferocious roar of thunder that seemed to shake the house to its very foundations. In the absence of the customary dowry, Nikos and his family lived in an old rented house, standing all alone on the way to the harbour.

Seizing a clump of Ermione's hair, Stephanides began to hack, the scissors flashing through the thick tresses. He gripped an ear, letting the golden coils drop around the defeated body like flowers from a dying bush. He chopped on the left and chopped on the right, on top and on the bottom, in front and in the back, never so much as glancing at Ermione's face until he was done. He seemed satisfied. The young wife's head looked like the shorn skulls of female prisoners in wartime newsreels.

Only then did Dimitris Stephanides look into his victim's eyes. He lowered himself to Ermione's level and poked his face at hers, his tobacco-stained teeth bared in something between grin and grimace. 'So! Are you going to tell me now?'

The response to this was a strangled sound, a vigorous toss of the violated head. The hair was gone but not so the loathing.

'No?' He snickered. He stood up, letting his hand travel to his belt. There was a momentary hush. He let go of his buckle, then began to fumble with his fly buttons. He undid them slowly, deliberately, ignoring the muffled sounds coming out of Ermione's constricted mouth. His absorption was such that a moment passed before he registered that her eyes were fixed not on him, but somewhere beyond his shoulder.

There was no doubt about it: the child gave him pause. He stood on the threshold, a six-year-old boy dressed in a flannel robe, his bare feet peeping from under the hem, his eyes huge with terror. As the man's gaze fell on the boy, his mother let out a choked sound and appeared to grow limp, a look of pure entreaty filling her eyes.

The child was whimpering. He took a step forward, arms raised in frantic appeal. 'Mama!'

'Stay where you are!' Stephanides barked. 'Don't budge, or I'll kill your mother, understand?' He gave the child an arresting look, then shifted his attention back to Ermione. He appeared, all at once, almost conspiratorial, as if the two of them shared a secret beyond the child's ken. 'So, you ready to tell me now?'

The response this time was a strangled sound, a slow, defeated nod. Stephanides leaned forward. He yanked the gag out of Ermione's mouth, waiting while she struggled with a spluttering cough. Finally, she stopped. She remained silent.

'Well?'

'He's somewhere in the hills . . . around Vafios, I think.' The young mother looked doomed, her eyes darting towards her son. The boy's whimpering had turned into gulping sobs; a worm of mucus was sliding out of his nose.

Stephanides ignored him, searching the mother's face. He seemed unable to decide whether she was telling the truth. All at once, he reached into his trousers and whipped out his penis. The air in the room grew dense with menace. For a moment, Stephanides seemed to hesitate; then, squaring his shoulders, began to urinate all over Nikos Antipas's wife. He aimed the stream at her neck, her face, her raw scalp, like a gardener bent on watering every corner of a neglected garden. Ermione, whose face was streaked with tears, now had urine coursing down her cheeks. She kept her head angled to one side, her eyes squeezed shut, her mouth twisted with ferocious disgust.

'So, is there anything else you might like to tell me?' Stephanides had taken out his knife and was sliding it across his own cushioned palm, as if testing its sharpness. 'Where can we find your husband?'

Slowly, Ermione's eyes blinked open. She glanced at her son, then at the knife, trembling violently. She looked straight into her captor's face and shook her head slowly. There was, her gesture said, nothing else she could tell him. She was utterly at his mercy. For another moment, Stephanides stood staring at her with his restless eyes. The boy was clutching at his groin, his sobs turned to hiccups. The man looked fleetingly at a loss, like an actor groping for forgotten lines.

'Look here!' He had picked up the mirror and was thrusting it at Ermione, whose eyes were screwed shut. 'Look, I said: I want you to see yourself!'

And at last she did. She glanced at her own reflection, then raised her gaze, the sea-green eyes shimmering with accusation.

'Don't look at me like that! You're lucky it's me or you'd be losing something more precious than just your whorish hair!' Stephanides rose and tossed the mirror into the sizzling hearth. The shattered glass made a shriek escape the child's mouth, but the intruder shot him another look and the shriek faded into a whimper.

Stephanides was about to put his knife away when something seemed to strike him. Bending forward, he narrowed his eyes and held the blade to the young mother's throat. 'If you're ever tempted to talk, remember this!' he said, gazing at her creamy neck like a lover. 'Understand?'

Ermione was silent. The child was sobbing, a puddle of urine forming at his feet.

'Do you understand?'

Ermione dropped her gaze. She nodded.

Stephanides let out a long, heavy breath. He snapped the knife shut and slowly returned it to his pocket, then freed Ermione's wrists. Outside, rain was falling again, spitting on the tiled roof. Stephanides hesitated, then finally turned to go. He paused only long enough to pat the child's head as he brushed past him, as if to reassure the boy that all would be well.

— 5 —

There were those who said that Dimitris Stephanides must have finally lost his reason. He was not, after all, a stupid man. But something seemed to have snapped in him during the Black Years. Jailed for the drunken assault on the schoolmistress, Dimitris was released after the Occupation, only to find his father imprisoned for wartime profiteering. He quarrelled with his uncle, who had taken over the olive mill. He began to beat his wife.

Ermione reported Stephanides to the police, then took her son back to Skala Sykamnias. Everyone knew it was only a matter of time before Nikos Antipas got wind of his wife's ordeal. The village, as usual, was divided, the Leftists choosing to believe Ermione – what reason did she have to lie after all? – the Rightists supporting Stephanides's denials. The authorities kept a close watch on Antipas's home, as well as on Ermione's relatives in Skala Sykamnias. Stephanides was out on bail, pending trial.

Calliope didn't doubt Ermione's story, but she had her own worries that fall, having to do with Tsouras, but also with the suspicion that she might be pregnant. Her periods had been erratic for years, but in recent days, she'd had to rush out of the classroom twice, her throat clenched against rising nausea.

On the second occasion, she had run straight into the headmaster. She said nothing to Eli about the suspected pregnancy, but one Sunday night, in bed, tried to share her growing unease over Leandros Tsouras.

'He criticises everybody,' she conceded, leaning over to the bedside table. 'With me, I think . . . I think it's more personal.' She lit a cigarette, then settled against the pillows, candlelight flittering across her breasts. Holy Cross Day had come and gone but the night was still almost as warm as summer. Sappho was sleeping by the balcony; crickets could be heard, singing in the garden. Eli's foot was absently toying with Calliope's toes. He thought that she was fretting unnecessarily. Everybody said she was a superb teacher. 'I'm sure the Ministry of Education knows it as well as anyone.'

Dhaniel was able to say this with confidence because, once a year, a government watchdog appeared without warning in the nation's classrooms to monitor teachers.

'Ach, I don't know,' Calliope said. 'I just hope you're right.'

Was she making too much of the conflict? Was she blowing it out of all proportion so as to distract herself from a likely pregnancy? She mulled it over, recalling a lame joke Tsouras had recently cracked in the teachers' room, hinting that she, too, might be a Communist.

'As if I could ever support a party capable of organising a *pedhomasoma!*' she said, pulling the sheet up to her neck.

The statement had been made lightly, almost teasingly, but instantly stopped Eli's toe flirtation. For several months, there had been reports that Communist guerrillas were abducting children from Right-wing villages and sending them to be raised by Eastern-Bloc families.

'So you believe all that nonsense.' Eli sighed, shaking his head. 'I never thought *you* would fall for their propaganda.'

'How do you know it's propaganda?' Calliope flashed out. Ever since the reports began to circulate, she had occasionally found herself conjuring up the alleged horror in northern Greece: the screaming children plucked out of their beds, the wailing mothers, the trucks trundling across the border, packed with terrified children on their way to strangers.

'Ach, the things people dream up these days,' said Eli, as if speaking to himself. 'If there's one thing I'm sure of it's that no Greek would ever abduct another Greek's children,' he added at length. 'If I thought . . . if I thought for a moment such a thing was possible . . .' He waved the rest away, as if the rumour did not merit another word.

Calliope agreed that the *pedhomasoma* sounded far-fetched. On the other hand, would he have believed Communists capable of burning villages, of burying their own people alive?

The question made Eli sit up, his voice swelling.

'You talk as if it's only the Communists who commit atrocities! What about—'

'Ach, *Panaghia mou! You remind me of my pupils. He did this to me, Kyria . . . yes, Kyria, but he started it, it's his fault!'* Calliope said all this in a falsetto voice, piqued by the ease with which he dismissed her views. Because he was older, because for years she had been an adoring, naive protégée, he had a tendency to be patronising.

'You should have been there to hear Petros scream when they pulled out his nails,' he was saying now. 'Pulled them one by one, the bastards!'

Petros was the son of a fisherman coerced into collaborating with the Germans. As if to redeem his father's reputation, the son had become a staunch Communist. Although an Eftalou man had already been arrested for a similar offence, Petros had painted a subversive slogan on the long seawall: BREAD AND OIL FOR THE PEOPLE!

Calliope had seen the slogan, but she didn't have to hear Petros scream to know that the authorities were torturing suspects.

'What I want to know is what makes us different from the Germans,' she said, stubbing out her cigarette. The question had reared its head before but she had never dared air it. 'We're doing the same things they did, the very same, though—'

'The Germans!' Eli turned to face her. 'If it weren't for the British and the Germans, we wouldn't be where we are today!'

'Yes, and before that it was the Turks. Everything was the Turks' fault!' She paused and ordered Sappho to quiet down. The dog had been roused by the butcher's grandson, playing his harmonica. 'The Germans, too, had their scapegoats, you know.'

'Calliope!' Eli stared, a vein pulsing in his temple. 'We're nothing like the Germans! We're just a poor nation others keep manipulating for their own ends!'

Calliope was silent, her mind calling up Greek battalions marching across Turkey just before the Catastrophe. Well, she wasn't going to reopen *that* can of worms. 'I've had a letter from my French cousins,' she said instead. 'They're trying to understand what's happening here. I don't know what to tell them. How—'

'Tell them what I once said to your father,' Eli interposed. 'When two bulls tussle, it's always the grasshoppers that suffer.' He lay scratching his chest for a moment. 'By the time the British and the Americans and the Russians are done toying with us, we—'

'You're forgetting Tito,' she put in, faintly ironic.

'Indeed! And our other neighbours! That's what foreigners can't understand: it's not our fault we don't trust anyone – not even each other,' he added.

'Least of all each other,' Calliope said, musing on the Greek factions struggling for power, each accusing the other of having collaborated with the Germans. All at once, she was tired of it all; tired, as well as sorry to have provoked a political argument in bed. There was no denying it: she had become quarrelsome lately. She leaned over and lightly bit Eli's earlobe.

'I trust you!' she said, abruptly flirtatious. 'Even if you're a Communist.'

This was true but had nothing to do with her suddenly flaring desire. Her shifting moods were among the reasons she suspected pregnancy. And if she *were* pregnant, what would she do? She would have to arrange for an abortion, she supposed. Veroniki, the old midwife, had finally passed away, replaced by Calliope's widowed friend, Eleni Bastia Kafatou.

It was Dhaniel who had urged Eleni to take up midwifery after Tomas died during an epileptic seizure. With Veroniki gone, the doctor had struggled to cope with all the new births and ailments emerging in the wake of the Occupation. Eleni was persuaded to go to Mytilene, where she was trained in midwifery. There had not been a single still-birth since she had taken over; not one woman had died in childbirth.

So, yes, an abortion was probably the answer, Calliope reflected. Her only other option was to marry Eli, though she had finally told him she would never marry again. She didn't think she was made for marriage; that was all she'd been able to offer by way of explanation.

Banishing the subject, Calliope let her tongue run down Eli's chest, flirting with his navel. Hairless men were generally considered unmanly, but she much preferred Eli's smooth torso – Eli's and Lorenz Umbreit's – to her late husband's hirsute chest and back. In recent months, the doctor's body had begun to thicken, but his torso was still firm, his limbs youthfully muscled. She was deeply attached to his body's growing complexity. The skin wrapping his neck, with its hint of old age, moved her in inexplicable ways; the flesh of his abdomen made her want to weep, as if all the sorrows of his past had found shelter within its tender cave. She and Eli might be politically opposed, but their bodies never failed to sing in harmony.

THREE

～ 1 ～

Calliope stood surveying herself in the mirror. It was October now and the pregnancy could no longer be denied. Her breasts were swollen and tender; the odour of grilled fish made nausea tug at her stomach. She had little appetite. She had cravings for vanilla ice-cream, as desperate as an infant's search for a mother's nipple. She was pregnant! She had thought of telling Eli last Sunday; had been on the point of kissing him awake and revealing all, but finally hadn't. Why?

She didn't have the answer.

Her abdomen still looked innocent, but Calliope's inner self seemed as capricious as autumnal weather. Although she was aware that an abortion was best performed early, weeks went by in which nothing was decided, nothing revealed. She still didn't quite believe in her own fertility. *Pregnant!*

Not for the first time, Calliope wondered why it had never occurred to her that she was not necessarily responsible for her failure to conceive. It galled her that, given to questioning everything, she had failed to question the assumption that a childless marriage must be due to some defect in the wife's reproductive apparatus.

Barren. How often she had seen the word, the gleam of disdain, in other women's eyes!

The old rage was gone, but not the satisfaction of imagining the villagers' amazement should she decide to proceed with the birth. The satisfaction was a little sour but undeniable. She was beginning to recoil from the thought of an abortion. Deep inside her, a new tenderness had begun to unfurl – an exotic flower struggling to survive in an alien climate. She had never experienced such exquisite solicitude, except perhaps for her godson. Aristides's existence, however, had never been seriously threatened; she had never been called upon to decide his fate.

In late October, she received a letter from Pericles, and was distressed to learn that he was in an Athens hospital, undergoing treatment for tuberculosis. Smuggled out by a Leftist nurse, the letter was seven pages long, including three recent, very powerful poems.

All at once, Calliope longed not only to share the poems with Eli, but to finally let him in on the pregnancy. Whatever she thought of marriage, it was apparently her destiny to wed the good doctor – whom, she reminded herself, she loved with all her heart. Why her brother-in-law's letter should have dissipated the last vestiges of inner resistance was a mystery, but she decided against waiting for Sunday. Perhaps she feared she might change her mind; feared being plunged back into inner chaos? She supposed she was. It was the evening before *Ohi Day*. She would go straightaway to Eli; would explain everything, before he left the clinic.

Only Eli wasn't there that particular Wednesday. All Calliope found was a note scribbled by Olga Samiou, the late carpenter's widow, who was now assisting Dhaniel at his clinic. The doctor was attending a council meeting, Olga's note stated. In case of an emergency he was to be found at the town hall.

There was no emergency, but there *was* disappointment – even a flash of petulance – that he should be unavailable when she was finally ready to impart such stupendous news. Vexed by her own unreasonableness, Calliope considered telling Eleni, then decided against it: the baby's father must be the first to know.

And so she headed home, Sappho trotting beside her through the shuttered *agora*. She had the dog on a lead because Sappho was prone to pounce on anything edible: dead rodents, mangled birds, other dogs' droppings. Pericles's news had left Calliope's heart feeling bruised, but the season, with its intimation of winter, had always tugged at her soul. She could sleep in tomorrow. She was, these days, as greedy for sleep as Sappho was for scraps of food.

They had just passed the site of Morales's burned bakery, were approaching a neighbourhood alley, when Sappho came to a sudden halt. Sniffing the night air, she began to whine, pulling on her lead. Calliope fought to restrain the dog. She had become aware of strange, fuddled sounds issuing from beyond the stone wall running along the alley. At first, she thought it must be cats, scuffling and hissing in the dark. Then she heard muffled thumps and a faint moaning sound. Sappho let out a volley of barks, then bounded ahead, tugging Calliope along.

There was a street lamp at the entrance to the alley, where Calliope had stopped, peering into the dark. The alley wasn't long, but it took her eyes a minute to make out a shifting shadow, a blurred figure clambering to its feet. Sappho went on barking, straining on her lead.

There were, in fact, three men. One by one, they lurched into the night, their footsteps echoing down the alley. Calliope took a tentative step forward. A few feet away, against the stone wall, she had made out the contours of a crumpled body. The victim was lying in the shadows, making odd gulping sounds – the sound water made, penetrating a densely clogged sewer.

Ach, Thee mou!

Suddenly resolute, Calliope tethered Sappho to a tree, lunging towards the wall. What she saw made her bones shudder, as if reliving the nightmarish sensation of walloping boots and hammering fists on her own cringing flesh.

The battered man was Dimitris Stephanides. She would never have recognised him had it not been for his showy moustache. The face and chest were awash in blood, the stomach clobbered so savagely that, Dhaniel would later testify, his bowel had been punctured. It had been too dark to identify the assailants, but they were almost certainly Communists, avenging the assault on Antipas's wife.

The victim was making little agonised sounds, as though trying to squeeze some urgent message out of his mangled throat. Then, all at once, he stopped, becoming perfectly still among the trampled weeds.

Calliope thought Stephanides was probably past help. She was about to check his pulse when Sappho let out a sudden howl. A tingling sensation rose at the back of Calliope's neck. Something seemed to topple inside her. *I must get out of here*, she thought chaotically. *I must go to the police.*

Unable to lift her weight from the ground, she began to spew out vomit all over Dimitris's body, the tangle of weeds, the bloodwashed stones. When there was nothing left, she straightened up and released the dog, then started to pick her way out of the alley. Sappho ran ahead in the dark, trailing her lead across the cobblestones.

~ 2 ~

The pain started early on *Ohi Day*. It started low in her abdomen, as menstrual cramps did every now and then. In the hazy interlude between sleep and wakefulness, Calliope thought it was indeed her *periodos* coming on. She yawned, stretched, plumped up her pillow. The clock struck seven times. A rooster crowed and crowed in the distance.

And then full awareness struck. Pulling up her nightshirt, Calliope ran a hand over her warm flesh, mentally focused on the intermittent pain twisting her womb. She was still only in her first trimester. On the bedside rug, Sappho stirred and yawned noisily.

A few minutes passed, during which Calliope raised herself from the pillows, having become aware of wetness beween her thighs. There were two stains on the white cotton sheet, one small and round, the other elongated: a bright red exclamation mark issued by her own body. Gingerly, she slid her way towards the floor, then sat perched on the edge of the mattress, arrested by a rip of pain.

She managed to get off the bed, swaying a little.

The pain had slashed through her, but now it was over. She pulled on a robe, then shambled towards the highboy, extracting a cotton rag from the top drawer. She stuffed it into a pair of panties, her mind resisting the onslaught of questions. Thank God it's a holiday, she said to herself. She drew the curtains and rested for a moment, watching the mist rise over the mountains. Then she plodded downstairs, Sappho nosing at her heels.

The pain kept coming in excruciating waves. Shivering, Calliope used the toilet, then went into the kitchen and hastened to light a fire. The morning sun was just beginning to filter through the treetops. On the windowsill, a ginger cat Mirto had named Loula unfurled herself and meowed sleepily. The cat was visibly pregnant. The church bells were beginning to toll.

Calliope turned away, wishing that Eli were there, though she never did get the chance to tell him about the pregnancy. She had last seen him after he'd finished examining Dimitris's corpse – hardly the time for momentous revelations.

Sappho was prancing about, wagging her tail, getting underfoot. Calliope snapped at her, then wheeled and rushed back to the water closet.

Theirs was one of the few homes with indoor plumbing. There was a newly installed bathtub, as well as a separate room with a bidet and a flush toilet. Calliope lowered herself slowly, as though any abrupt movement might bring down some delicate internal dam. She thought of last night's retching in the alley, and then of her grandmother's voice warning expectant mothers against lifting heavy objects, walking past stray dogs, venturing out in storms. A snarling dog, a sudden clap of thunder, a single moment of fright and the foetus could be in mortal danger.

This was what village crones habitually told young brides, but Eleni laughed at them, saying you could no more shake loose a good egg than an unripe apple from a healthy tree. Were hers not good eggs then? Could she have taken after her mother, who'd had two miscarriages in the first two years of her marriage?

There was another twist of pain, then more blood, flowing freely now. She began to weep. Something solid and slippery had been expelled from between her thighs, dropping into the bowl with the most banal of sounds. *'Panaghia mou!'*

Hoisting herself up, Calliope saw her own hand pull the toilet chain, but it seemed like the hand of some feeble stranger, seen through a thickening mist. She did not look into the toilet bowl, did not dare to look, yet almost at once found herself overcome by a sort of blind, febrile curiosity.

But too late – too late! She had not truly wanted the child – *couldn't* have wanted it or she would not have waited all this time to tell Eli; would never have stopped to contemplate an abortion. And what sort of mother would she have been anyway? How many times had her own mother accused her of being selfish? Deep inside her, the baby must have known: she could never be a real mother!

Wobbling over to the entrance, Calliope opened the door and peered into the sunlight. A neighbour's son was ambling down the street and she called out, asking him to go fetch the doctor.

'Are . . . are you sick, *Kyria*?'

'Yes. Run, please, and ask him to come right away. Hurry!'

'Yes, *Kyria*!' The boy ran off. Calliope sat down to wait, weeping by the fire. If she had not received Pericles's letter yesterday . . . if she had not gone out in the evening . . . if Eli had been at the clinic when she got there . . . if she had taken another route home and not passed the alley . . . if the sight of Dimitris Stephanides had not made her body shudder with pained recollection, would her child still be safely nestled within her womb? Would she still be a normal expectant mother?

— 3 —

'Why didn't you tell me?'

Eli's voice conveyed unmistakable reproof. He had suppressed the question as long as he could, no doubt waiting for her to recover. He must have thought she was ready now, wearing a dress he liked, cooking his favourite fish soup.

She wasn't ready; would have, indeed, preferred never to discuss the failed pregnancy, but there was, she knew, no distracting him any longer. She had tried to prepare herself for this moment, only to find she had nothing to offer except a shrug, a sigh. 'I don't know what to say.'

She sat poking her fork at a leftover fishbone. The *psarosoupa* was the first dish she had cooked since the miscarriage. For two weeks, neighbours had come over with soup and pies, having been led to believe that Calliope had caught the mumps from one of her pupils.

263

'Please . . . I want you to level with me,' Eli was saying. 'Didn't you think I had the right to know?'

'I suppose you did.'

'But?'

'I just couldn't do it! I was too confused about what I wanted . . . I'm sorry.'

'But it shouldn't have been just your decision, should it?' He regarded her for a moment, his brow furrowed. 'You could have at least—'

She stopped him. 'I suppose I knew what would happen if I did tell you.'

'What would have happened?'

She gave him a slow, melancholy smile, as though responding to one of her godson's naive questions. 'You would have insisted that I marry you.'

'No doubt. I might have even persuaded you.'

Calliope closed her eyes. She could have said something about trying to see him the night Dimitris Stephanides died; could have made it clear that she had fully intended to tell him but he wasn't there. The council meetings were usually held on the last Monday of the month, but October's meeting had been postponed till Wednesday because the mayor had come down with the flu. Such a trivial complication, yet one that had come to seem somehow preordained.

'Eli.' Calliope spoke with tender resolve. 'I've tried to make you see. I don't think I'm meant to marry, to—' She buried her face in her hands.

He studied her for a while, rubbing his jaw. He'd told her, when he came, that he had a toothache. 'What do you think you are meant to be doing?'

'I'm not sure, but—'

He reached across the table and took her hand. 'You can tell me, darling.'

'I don't know!' She snatched her hand away and began fumbling for her pack of cigarettes. She struck a match. 'I don't know,' she repeated.

'But what do you want?' Eli demanded with quiet tenacity. 'What is it that—'

'I don't know, I tell you!' Calliope looked away, feeling the way her pupils must have felt when called upon to give an answer they did not possess. 'I keep hoping I'll find out one of these days, then maybe—'

'Find out what, exactly?'

'Why I can't be like other women,' she heard herself say, inwardly intent on Mirto's echoing voice. *We shouldn't have pushed you to marry . . . you were not born to be a wife and mother.* She stubbed out her cigarette, then, her eyes stinging, rose to clear the table. 'I'll tell you one thing,' she said at length. 'I wouldn't want to have a daughter like me.'

'No?' He looked at her with the hint of a smile. 'I would!'

'You think so?'

'Absolutely!'

She set a fruit bowl on the table, longing to tell him how, night after night, she mourned both her mother and her lost child – she, who liked to think of herself as unsentimental. Yet she said nothing. She could not discuss either her self-doubts in the weeks leading up to the miscarriage, or the devouring disappointment that followed. How could you explain so much contradiction?

'I don't think we would have been happy, married to each other,' she heard herself say at last. She sat down and reached for an apple.

'Why not?'

'Oh, my dear!' Calliope regarded him for a moment, then began to peel the apple, her eyes fastened on the curling skin as though the task demanded her closest attention. Not for the first time, she tried to imagine living with Eli's children and mother-in-law, but didn't voice the thought because Stella would probably go back to Mytilene if Eli were to remarry.

All the same, Stella or no Stella, the mental picture refused to gel: waking up to make breakfast for husband and children, having to satisfy so many conflicting demands, day after day, never having any time to think, to read, to daydream. She believed she was not equipped for this commonplace challenge; she probably *was* too selfish but couldn't bring herself to say so. He might think she didn't love his children, which was far from the truth, though she did love Aristides best. His sisters were virtually grown now, the eldest preparing for university, but Aristides still needed her.

Calliope held out half a cored apple. She said, 'Sooner or later, you would have started bossing me around. Isn't that a husband's prerogative?' The words were accompanied by a gentle smile, at once fond and ironic.

'Is it?' She was being frivolous, his gaze told her. She had picked up the apple peel and was winding it listlessly around her forefinger, like a bandage. Although the last statement had been meant in jest, it came to her that it might nonetheless be true. 'You don't really think I'd boss you around, do you?' Eli was saying.

'Yes . . . yes, I think I do,' Calliope answered, finally opting for the truth. She looked at him with unflinching eyes. 'You would have forbidden me to smoke in bed, to keep Sappho indoors, to—'

'Calliope!' he broke in. 'I'm not some kind of . . . of tyrant! I would not have been issuing orders. You should know—'

'Maybe not orders,' she allowed, growing obstinate, 'but you would . . . oh, what's the point? It obviously wasn't meant to be,' she said, staring out the window.

Loula was loping across the garden, a newborn kitten clamped between her teeth. The day Mirto was buried, Loula had sneaked into the house and tried to jump into the open casket. There had been mourners coming and going. Calliope threw Loula out time and again, but the cat kept stealing in. When the pallbearers came out with the casket, Loula followed them all the way to church, alongside the mourners.

'Please don't cry.' Eli held Calliope's fingers, his nut-brown eyes mellow with solicitude. 'I'm just trying to understand, my love.'

But the words only made fresh tears spring into Calliope's eyes. 'Oh, why must life be so complicated?' she said, swiping at her cheeks.

'Life's not that complicated,' he said patiently, as if explaining some elusive concept to one of his children. 'It's people like us that needlessly complicate it.'

'You think so?' Calliope paused, mulling over Iason's observation that she thought too much. Beyond the fence, she could hear a neighbour feeding her chickens, addressing the stupid creatures as tenderly as some mothers did a beloved child. This particular mother, though, was often heard screeching abuse at her three children, saving her tenderness for her egg-laying hens. No, Calliope decided, she did not agree with Eli. Life, she thought, *was* complicated. Human beings were complicated.

And then Eli himself changed the subject, going on to talk about two of Dimitris Stephanides's killers, who had just been arrested. One of the men had managed to escape to the hills, but the second man, a Petra barber, had been quickly nabbed. The third man was Fat Dinos, the former postman.

'They say it was Marina who denounced him,' Calliope said to Eli. She had heard the rumours in the *agora* but was finding them hard to credit. Marina was Dinos's wife. 'Do you think it's true?'

It was true. Chatterbox Evgenia had come to the clinic and confirmed the story in tedious detail. How Dinos had come home, splattered with blood; how, the very next day, Marina got up and went straight to the police station. Chatterbox Evgenia was Marina's mother. She suffered from occasional hives, and from a chronic inability to keep anything to herself.

Calliope sat thinking of poor Marina, with her scratchy voice and rabbity teeth; how her eyelids would quiver, then drop, whenever Dinos mocked her in public, sometimes in their two sons' presence. She would be in her late fifties now but the cowering look had been there for decades.

'I wouldn't have thought she had it in her to seek revenge,' Calliope said.

'I'm not sure revenge was the point,' Eli said. 'I suspect she just saw an opportunity to get rid of the bully, and grabbed it.'

'Hm,' Calliope said. 'I suppose even a mule must have its limits.'

Eli wagged his head. He smiled to himself.

'What?'

'I was just thinking: Marina may be the only woman in all of Greece to actually benefit from the Civil War.'

Calliope dimpled. Eli's inability to hold a grudge was one of the things she loved best about him.

'It's the first time I've seen you smile in two weeks,' he said.

'Is it?' Calliope's eyes followed a small lizard scuttling along the low stone ledge running below the windows. A baby lizard was supposed to be a good omen. If only she believed in such things! She was still thinking of the courage it would take someone like Marina – perhaps any woman – to walk into the police station and report that her husband had come home with Royalist blood on his clothes.

For some reason, this thought made her think of Lorenz Umbreit, sitting behind his town hall desk, gravely listening to his adjutant's daily report. She wondered whether the time would ever come when nothing at all made her think of him.

~ 4 ~

Three days before Christmas, Odysseus the beekeeper was caught red-handed, aiding and abetting the rebels. He had been arrested once before, after a mule-riding farmer had spotted a guerilla huddled under Odysseus's cow's belly, sucking on her udders like a greedy calf. The beekeeper was suspected of having deliberately let his cow loose so as to provide nourishment for the rebels. He had been interrogated in the summer but released without undergoing torture. Some believed this was because his daughter was married to the new mayor; others said it was probably due to his advanced age. Odysseus himself believed he had succeeded in outwitting the police. He had, after a drinking binge, confided as much to Calliope. His children might think he was growing dim, yet somehow he'd managed to convince the chief of his innocence.

All the same, the beekeeper had lain low for several months, devoting himself to his beehives and his youngest grandson, who was recovering from polio.

The assignment the old man eventually accepted entailed carting hand grenades to the outskirts of nearby Petri. Twice a year – at Easter and at Christmas – Odysseus would travel to surrounding villages to peddle his famed thyme honey. On that fateful December day, he stuffed the bag of grenades into the bottom of a large jute sack, piled jars of honey on top, and clambered onto his rickety mule cart. He left right after the midday meal, taking a shotgun along, ostensibly to ward off a potential attack by guerilla rebels on some mountain road.

The men who ambushed Odysseus were not partisans but gendarmes. They had sprung out from behind a clump of trees, brandishing guns, shouting at the old man to halt. Despite the great care he had taken to conceal the grenades, the flustered Odysseus lost his wits and snapped up his gun. He was aiming it at the gendarmes when two shots rang out, shattering the bucolic silence. One of the bullets went into Odysseus's left cheek and out the other; the second one hit his shoulder.

Eventually, the old man was taken to the *agora*. It was late afternoon by then and the streets bustled with Saturday shoppers and idle old men ambling about, their hands clasped behind their backs. The moment the gendarmes tossed the beekeeper out of his cart, a crowd began to gather around the *plateia*. Odysseus had been dumped under the mulberry tree, his spotted skull exposed, his turban uncoiled on the cobblestones. By the time Sergeant Floros arrived on the scene, blood was streaming from Odysseus's shoulder.

'*Ach, Panaghia mou*, is he dead?' *Papa* Iakovos's sister asked, bouncing out of the *pantopoleion*, a basket swinging from her arm.

'Nah, he's not dead,' the butcher answered. 'They caught him smuggling grenades to the guerillas.'

'Old Odysseus?!' The priest's sister shifted her basket. 'Impossible! He's been our neighbour for years, *kale*!'

'Ach, Marianthi! These days you can't trust your own mother, let alone your neighbours,' the butcher countered.

The wounded man groaned, as if in feeble protest.

This was when Calliope, who had stopped at the pharmacy, came to join the crowd. One day, when she was an adolescent, the beekeeper had found her crying after school; had taken her to his farm to see a litter of newborn puppies. That had been the beginning of the comfort she still found in dogs' company. It was Odysseus who had given her Socrates for a pet.

The moment Calliope understood who the victim was, she tried to push through the crowd, only to find her way blocked by Sergeant Floros. The policeman was a heavy-set man with small ears and a large, florid face resembling a wilted cabbage

'In God's name, what are you doing?' Calliope spurted. 'Are you going to stand there and let him bleed to death – your own compatriot?'

'Compatriot!' Floros's face twisted with scorn. 'The bastard would sell us all to the Russians, if he had his way!'

'A Communist would sell his own mother!' Lazaros the blacksmith shouted from the back. He was one of Eleni the midwife's twin brothers; the Royalist supporter.

'But he . . . he's just an old man!' Calliope said to Sergeant Floros.

'An old man he is, *Kyria* Calliope, but even a geezer can shoot to kill, you know!'

'Has he shot anyone? Odysseus?' Calliope's mind was working feverishly. She knew that Eli was in Kaloni, getting a tooth extracted, but her eyes went on scanning the crowd, until she spotted one of her pupils. She beckoned the child over, instructing him to go to the clinic for Olga, before fetching the mayor, Odysseus's son-in-law.

Floros grabbed the boy's arm. 'There's no point. We—'

'What do you mean there's no point?' Calliope cut in. 'Even a Communist's entitled to medical care!'

Floros opened his mouth to say something, but the crowd's jeers made his response redundant.

'He deserves to hang from this here tree, if you ask me!' someone shouted, spitting at the victim.

'First he lets the guerillas have milk, then he supplies them with arms!'

'Well, I for one am not surprised. I never much liked his honey anyway!'

'*Ach, Thee mou*,' Calliope murmured, still casting about for someone willing to intervene. At the back of the crowd she spotted the headmaster, but quickly dismissed any thought of appealing to him.

She stood clutching at her collar, craning her neck in the hope of seeing one of the village councillors.

'Please . . . I beg you to do something!' She was once more addressing Sergeant Floros, whose parents had moved to Molyvos from the Peloponnese, to care for his young daughters after his wife had died in childbirth. 'You have an old father yourself,' she implored. 'What if—'

'My father's not a Communist!' Floros set his jaw.

'All right, so Odysseus is a Communist! But you, all of you, are Christians! How can you all—'

'We may be Christians,' Makis, the new postman, hollered from the back, 'but Communists have no use for religion. They don't even believe in God, *Kyria* Calliope!'

Calliope did not deign to answer. The police sergeant was her one chance, if only because she had taken his daughter under her wing after the girl had lost her mother.

'Look, you can put him on trial if you have to. I just want to stop his bleeding!' Calliope pleaded. She made another attempt to push through, but Floros stopped her again, a defensive note creeping into his voice.

'I'm under orders, *Kyria* Calliope.'

Calliope rounded on him. 'Under orders to do what? Let an old man bleed to death just because you're too cowardly to act like a man?' She pointed towards Odysseus. 'He may be a Communist, but at least he wasn't too cowardly to risk his life for what he believed in!'

'Let him die for his beliefs then!' the postman shouted. He was exceptionally tall and bony, with a small head and long neck that gave him the appearance of a giraffe looming over the heads of the crowd. Beside him, Calliope spotted poor Apollon, his backward nephew, another one of her pupils. As she glanced their way, the boy raised a catapult, aiming it down at Odysseus. The stone went whistling in the air, landing on the beekeeper's blood-soaked shoulder.

'Apollon! What in God's name are you doing?' Calliope pushed her way through the crowd. 'Stop!' she shrieked, seeing the boy fiddle with another stone. 'Stop it right now, I said!'

The way the child dropped the stone, it might have been a hot chunk of coal. He buried his chin in his chest and began to blubber, his thick brows knitted together. The wounded man's moaning was growing ever more feeble.

At that moment, as if inspired by the unfortunate child, several men started to pick up stones, hurling them at the beekeeper's contorted body.

'Death to all Bolshevik traitors!'

'Down with Communism!'

'Here's to King and country!'

'Please stop!' Calliope's voice was starting to crack. 'Stop! We're supposed to be a civilised nation, not a tribe of barbarians!'

'Even civilised nations execute traitors, *Kyria* Calliope,' Sergeant Floros put in.

'If you ask me, he deserves everything he gets,' the priest's sister said in her stilted voice. She turned towards her husband, who was raising his arm to fling a stone the size of a seagull's egg. Most of the onlookers had gradually shuffled away, but others held their ground: spitting, heckling, scrabbling around for stones.

Calliope made another attempt to slide past Floros, but was stopped yet again, this time rather roughly. Shaking herself free, she whipped around and was about to address the crowd when she caught the headmaster staring straight at her. Leandros Tsouras's expression was only slightly more supercilious than usual, but Calliope's body went on recoiling from the pitiless force of his prolonged gaze. And in that moment, she briefly forgot all about the dying Odysseus because she suddenly felt as if her own flesh had just been struck by bullets, cold and victorious.

FOUR

～ 1 ～

Just before Easter 1949, there was an outbreak of chicken pox among Molyvos's children. With half her pupils away, Calliope decided to put off her lesson plan: she would spend the last hour or so on a little-known chapter from their own history. Perched on the edge of her desk, she told her class how, back in the fifteenth century, Molyvos had been invaded by Turkish troops, then rescued by a princess named Onetta d'Oria. In those days, the island was still ruled by the Genoese; an Italian prince had built the fortress still crowning their village.

'But the prince was away, the invaders were coming and, well, something had to be done, right?' Calliope paused dramatically, then went on to speak of the villagers' fear and d'Oria's despair, of people's prayers for a divine miracle.

There had been no miracle but, just as the Turks appeared in the distance, the princess astonished the crowd, appearing in full armour, crying out: 'Let's teach those marauding Turks a lesson they'll never forget!'

The children sat listening, alert and still, their chins in their hands, their eyes dilated. They were speechless when Calliope reached the triumphant ending; so quiet that two flies could be heard mating on the windowpanes.

At that moment, a knock came at the door. A note was delivered, asking Calliope to stop in the headmaster's office before going home. The request was not unusual. Tsouras often found excuses to detain his teachers. That particular afternoon, however, Calliope felt her skin tighten as she entered the headmaster's office. The moment Tsouras invited her to take a seat, she knew that she was about to be caught in a web as fatal as that of a deadly tarántula. Tsouras was running his hand over his long face, as if trying to ensure everything was in place. He addressed her formally.

'*Kyria* Calliope,' he said, stopping to clear his nostrils. 'As you know, I have always done my best, my very best, to be fair-minded. Strict, I admit, but nevertheless fair-minded.' He paused with a conscious sort of delicacy, as if offering her a chance to refute his gambit.

Calliope was silent.

'Well, as I was saying, I've done my best to fulfil my duties as far as—'

'Oh, please! Spare me the preamble, will you?'

'I beg your pardon?' Tsouras hesitated, then grew resolute. 'Very well,' he said. 'As you wish, *Kyria* Calliope. It is my duty, then – my unpleasant duty – to inform you that the Ministry of Education has reached a unanimous decision to relieve you of your duties at the end of the school year.' The words came out sounding like a rehearsed speech. Tsouras paused for a moment. 'There will, of course, be an official letter in due course, but I thought . . . I thought it only . . .'

At this point, Calliope shook herself out of her mental stupor. 'Relieve me of my duties?' she echoed. 'On what grounds?' She spoke in a cold, disdainful voice, her skin cloaking her anxiety.

'On what grounds?' He stared at her with arch surprise, as though she were an errant pupil foolishly attempting to defend herself in the face of incontrovertible evidence. 'You're a fine teacher, *Kyria* Calliope,' he stated at length. 'I know we've had our differences in the past, but all the same, I'd be the last person to deny your skills.'

This speech, too, had a rehearsed quality to it. A tiny pause followed, but when the headmaster opened his mouth again, Calliope's skin suddenly proved too tight to contain her outrage.

'What have you done – told them that I'm not a suitable role model?' It was something he had said during one of their recent encounters.

'There is that,' he said after the briefest hesitation, 'and, well, to tell you the truth, there have been complaints—'

'Complaints!' she scoffed. 'Complaints from whom?'

Tsouras let out a forbearing breath. He steepled his fingers.

'As I say, there have been complaints, but that's not the issue just now. The issue is your . . . your political dossier. As you—'

Once more, she didn't let him finish. 'My political dossier!' she erupted. 'I'm a Centrist, as you know,' she said, a glint in her eyes.

Tsouras offered a forgiving smile. 'I know that's what you've told us. It isn't what the authorities have been led to believe.'

Calliope stared, doing her best to subdue the fluttering in her chest. 'Go on.'

'The authorities have received reports that you've been listening to Sofia broadcasts. I'm sure I don't have to tell you—'

'Sofia!' she interrupted hotly. Radio Sofia was a clandestine Greek Communist station broadcasting from Bulgaria. 'That's an absolute lie!'

He stirred a little. 'It's not what your neighbours say.'

'My neighbours?' Calliope stopped, her lower eyelid twitching. She thought of the women who had come by while she was in bed, recovering from her putative mumps; of the casseroles they'd left in the kitchen; of their feeding Sappho, taking the dog for walks. She had stayed upstairs, reading or listening to the radio, while they came and went. 'It's a lie,' she repeated, striving for composure.

'Are you accusing your neighbours of malice? People who cared for you—'

'I don't know what my neighbours told you,' Calliope cut in. 'I know I'd never waste my time listening to Radio Sofia!'

'No?' He gave her a look that was sceptical yet seemingly determined to be open-minded.

'Absolutely not. I know the Communist broadcasts can lie just as shamelessly as our own government stations!'

The headmaster's lips twitched in what might have been a smile or a warning. There was a rap on the door. 'Come in!' Tsouras swivelled towards the entrance, a squeak of surprise escaping his mouth. He sprang out of his chair, beaming. A young man had just thrust his head through the open door.

'*Yassou, Baba!*' Timolis Tsouras stopped in his tracks, his gaze sliding towards Calliope. 'I'm sorry. I'll—'

'Come in, come in, my boy! Let me greet you properly!' The headmaster held out his arms, his eyes crinkling. He introduced his son to Calliope, who reluctantly offered her hand, registering the young man's beauty despite her inner turmoil. Timolis Tsouras resembled his father in colouring and height, but whereas the headmaster's eyes were pale and supercilious, his son's were almost violet, as alert and curious as the eyes of a young cat eager to explore a new domain.

'I wasn't expecting you for another hour!' The headmaster studied his son: thoroughly, lovingly.

'I found a taxi. I'll wait outside.' The young man spoke in a warm, sprightly voice. 'Nice meeting you,' he tossed out towards Calliope.

'Please excuse me for a moment.' Tsouras followed his son and stood whispering outside, while Calliope watched the afternoon light dance on the desk, the blackboard, the shelves holding attendance records and students' report cards. The windows were wide open, letting in the scents of spring, the cry of a distant cuckoo.

Re-entering the room, Tsouras strutted towards his desk and sat down energetically, pushing up his sleeves. There was a moment when something unexpected, some spark of human sympathy, glimmered between them, and then was lost, like a dying ember.

'I am sorry,' he said, composing his features into an expression of professional gravitas. 'I wasn't expecting him yet.'

Calliope shrugged, her eyes fixed on a desktop globe standing on Tsouras's desk. The room, the whole universe, seemed too cramped to contain her emotions. What would she do if Tsouras wasn't bluffing; if he really had the Ministry of Education on his side?

She stared at him, grappling for composure. 'Let me make this perfectly clear,' she finally said. 'I'm not a Communist, or even a Leftist. I am a Centrist,' she reiterated.

'A Centrist,' he echoed, as if essaying a word whose precise meaning eluded him. 'A Centrist, I believe, is someone who could go one way or another, depending on—'

'A Centrist,' she broke in, 'is someone who believes in democracy, who—'

'Democracy?' he said, with the same querying, slightly bewildered air.

'Democracy!' she repeated. 'It's the one thing I believe is worth fighting for. The one thing which neither the Left nor the Right is ready to offer us.'

'Indeed!' He cocked an ironic eyebrow. His eyebrows were greying but the hair sprouting out of his nostrils was black. It twitched as he stretched his lips in something resembling a smile. 'And yet,' he said, 'your . . . your doctor friend is known to be a Communist.' He crossed his arms over his chest. 'Isn't that so?'

'I have friends who are Communists, others who are Royalists,' she said with calm certitude. 'I don't necessarily share their political views.'

'Hm,' he said, 'I've been led to believe that all your friends are . . . if not Communists, then at least strong Leftists.'

'Well, you've been misled,' Calliope retorted. 'Olga Samiou, one of my oldest friends, happens to be a Royalist, so—'

'Olga Samiou. Is that the doctor's aide?'

'Yes.'

Tsouras continued to look sceptical, perhaps because he could not conceive of a Communist doctor hiring a Royalist who not only cleaned his surgery but served as a de facto nurse. 'All the same,' he said.

'All the same, my friends' political views are beside the point,' Calliope stated, vexed at having allowed herself to slide into an utterly irrelevant discussion. 'The point is I am being dismissed for the wrong reasons.'

'And what would the right reasons be, might I ask?'

'The only legitimate reason would be incompetence or abuse of my charges.' She paused, almost smiling. 'Which even you can't bring yourself to accuse me of.'

'My dear *Kyria* Calliope.' Tsouras let out a long martyred sigh. 'I am not an unreasonable man,' he said, looking at her with a new expression, reproachful and faintly wounded. The look seemed familiar somehow. It reminded Calliope unpleasantly of someone, but who?

All at once, it came to her: Seraphim, the building contractor! He had once gazed at her with the same air of injured pride. And though years had gone by since the German roof repair, the memory sent forth a sudden spasm of hot indignation.

'You're not an unreasonable man,' she echoed ironically, 'but you are a spiteful one!' She was beside herself now, seething with the realisation that the battle had been lost long before she entered the office. All that was left to her now was the luxury of venting her suppressed rancour. 'You tried to seduce me with your unctuous charms, and did not succeed. That's what this is all about, isn't it?'

'*Kyria* Calliope!' Tsouras's face looked patched in chaotic shades of pink and red.

'This has nothing to do with my politics but with your vanity,' Calliope continued. 'If I'd let you have your way, you wouldn't give a button about my politics!'

'*Kyria* Calliope, if you please!' Tsouras slowly massaged the back of his neck, staring at her from under his bushy eyebrows.

'What?' she said. 'You think it's a crime to breach professional decorum, but perfectly acceptable to spread malicious lies. You—'

'Ach, *Kyria* Calliope.' Tsouras sighed, a sorely tested man growing resigned. 'You seem to think that I . . . I'm out to punish you, whereas the truth . . .' He hesitated, then judiciously corrected himself. 'Or let's just say the fact . . . the fact is I wasn't the only one to witness your outburst over the beekeeper.'

'Odysseus was an old neighbour. My outburst had nothing to do with politics!'

'Maybe so, maybe so.' Tsouras glanced at her, then consulted his watch. 'I might be willing to believe you, but the decision, as I said, is not in my hands, it's the ministry's.' He spread his palms, vaguely apologetic. There was a beat of silence, during which a sheep was heard, bleating beyond the window. 'Certainly, you'll be given a chance to contest it in due course, *Kyria* Calliope.'

He waited. When she failed to respond, Tsouras reached for a sheaf of papers and, his mouth pursed, began to slide them into his open briefcase. Then he rose, ostentatiously clearing his throat. 'I was only trying to prepare you . . . I thought it only fair,' he added with a minimal shrug. 'Now, if you'll excuse me . . .'

He stood waiting, stiff with courtesy, fingertips drumming on his briefcase.

And, at last, Calliope stirred. Placing her hands on the chair's arms, she hoisted herself to her feet, then stood facing Tsouras, speechless with impotence and loathing.

'You bastard,' she said at long last. Her hands longed to scratch his smug face, but she spoke quietly, neutrally, as if this were a secret only the two of them were entitled to share. 'You hypocritical bastard.'

～ 2 ～

Was Heraclitus right, then, saying character was destiny? If so, was her reluctance to acquiesce and conform, her inability to curry favour with the likes of Tsouras, responsible for her latest predicament? She remembered reading Stendhal, asking herself whether it was possible to live in society and still be true to oneself, without hypocrisy, without the need for perpetual compromise?

Questions. Nothing but questions in the aftermath of her ignoble dismissal. Enough questions to last an entire summer, with nothing whatever to look forward to. By now, the letter from the Ministry of Education had been received, read and responded to, in the full knowledge that nothing she said, none of her cogent arguments, was going to reverse the Athenian bureaucrats' decision.

In the days following the end of term, Calliope set herself the stupefying challenge of getting out of bed every morning, mustering the wherewithal to wash, make breakfast and find a pair of fresh underwear and something with which to cover her useless bones. She had no ambitions, no aspirations, other than to get through the day. She was, she allowed, luckier than the former headmaster, who had landed in jail for humming a subversive song. But Stamatis had been a Communist and she was a Centrist. She wondered what he was doing, unemployed in Aghiassos.

And what was she supposed to do with the rest of her life – scour pots and polish cutlery? Eli had his patients, he had his family, so Calliope read more voraciously than ever, and slept more, and wrote longer letters. She wrote to Rupert Ealing, who was still working for the British government. She wrote to Pericles. She was, on at least one occasion, tempted to write to Lorenz Umbreit, but what would be the point?

She fought off the impulse by writing to her Parisian cousin instead. She had never met her French uncle's daughters, but felt close to the elder one, a comparative literature professor named Alexandra Sorel. The younger one, Marianne, had married an American and was living in Massachusetts, working as an interpreter.

One day, having received a letter from the hospitalised Pericles, Calliope impulsively sat down to translate two of his latest poems into French. Thrilled by her own efforts, she decided to send them to her cousin. There was welcome distraction in all these new activities but inadequate consolation. When her name day came around, she went to the cemetery, where she unburdened herself at her mother's grave.

One of the things Calliope could not bring herself to confess to Eli but did at her mother's grave was the weight of shame she carried that summer, as if she had been caught committing a crime and couldn't bear to show her face in public. She walked Sappho late in the evening, or in mid-afternoon, when most villagers rested. She paid the butcher's grandson to post letters and buy groceries, though she had few needs and little appetite.

One afternoon in August she went to the cemetery and encountered a woman named Stavroula Houmi. The kiosk owner's wife was a middle-aged matron with a square body and frantic eyes, one of which was staring at Calliope from within a mound of grotesquely swollen flesh, like an insect caught in a clump of fresh dough.

'Stavroula!' Calliope, who had been sitting at her mother's grave, sprang up, trapped between solicitude and a wrenching need to flee. 'What happened to you?'

Ever since her young son's death during the Occupation, Stavroula

280

had a dishevelled, harried air. Her brother, Captain Yorgos, had also died during the War.

'Ach, *Kyria* Calliope!' Stavroula's face crumpled. 'Only the *Panaghia* knows my sorrows.' She had left home wearing her apron; was nervously burrowing in its pocket while the sun taunted her greying head.

'Come.' Calliope placed an arm around Stavroula's shoulders. 'Let's sit in the shade.'

There was a bench near the entrance, under a leafy plane tree. Calliope steered Stavroula towards it, the air around them pulsing with heat and insects.

'Ach, ach, ach, *Kyria* Calliope!' Stavroula flumped down, clutching a handkerchief, her knees wide apart. She was barely coherent, but Calliope gradually gathered the problem had to do with Stavroula's husband, who had been caught with a stash of *Orizospastis*, the underground Communist paper.

'I would have stood by him, would have died with him!' Stavroula was saying, angrily swiping at a clump of hair. 'But to think he betrayed his customers! To think he would agree to sign the Declaration!'

'Ach, don't be so hard on him, Stavroula,' Calliope ventured. 'It isn't easy to say no when—'

'My brother said no to the Germans!' Stavroula flashed out. 'The bastards pulled out his nails and crushed his *ameletita* but he didn't give in, did he?' She faced Calliope with her wild eyes, one swollen, the other glinting with hot indignation. 'How can you sign something renouncing what you've spent all your life believing?'

Calliope raised her gaze. 'Not everyone is born to be a hero, Stavroula.'

'Well, I wasn't born to be a coward's wife!'

What was there to say? Calliope looked away. A few moments went by while Stavroula blew her nose, mulling things over.

'Fine,' she allowed at length. 'So he couldn't help being spineless, but what am I supposed to do? How can I show respect to a man like that?'

'Maybe you should just try to pity him?'

'I do pity him! I do! What I can't do is wash his feet and share a bed with the jellyfish! He's lucky I've been willing to cook his dinner!'

'Ach, Stavroula.'

'It's true. I served it to him, same as always, but then, when I got ready to sleep on the daybed, he flew into a rage and . . .' She pointed at her eye. 'You can see for yourself, can't you?'

Calliope sighed. 'What are you going to do?' she asked at length.

'I don't know . . . but I'm not going back to him!' Stavroula's eyes welled. She wanted to go to her married daughter in Athens, but didn't know whether her son-in-law would allow it. Also, she didn't have the money to buy a ticket.

'I can give you the money,' Calliope put in, glad to be able to offer tangible help. 'But are you sure—'

'I'm sure!' Stavroula cleared her nose. She was, Calliope thought, as bull-headed as her late brother. She even looked like him, with her jutting chin and blazing eyes. 'It's not just the Declaration,' she went on, kneading her soggy handkerchief. 'He's been beating me ever since the Occupation. You'd think it was my fault our child died.'

At this, Calliope began to massage her temples. It was one thing to reject a husband because he was no hero, but if he beat his wife? She wasn't sure what she, or even Stavroula, ought to do, given the paucity of options. The last thing she wanted was to meddle in other people's affairs.

'I could lie down with a man who beat me while drunk,' Stavroula was saying. 'I've done that, but with a sober man . . . a coward who whips me like a dog? Never!'

Suddenly, perhaps recalling the purpose of her flight to the cemetery, she fumbled in her pocket and whipped out a snapshot of her husband – a young soldier leaning against a eucalyptus tree, smiling at the camera.

'That's the man I married!' she declared, pride and bitterness vying in her voice. 'I rue the day we exchanged marriage wreaths,' she said, spitting at the snapshot.

'Ach, Stavroula. I'm sure—'

But the poor woman was no longer listening. 'I'm going to put a curse on him!' she announced. 'Maybe the *Panaghia* will hear my prayers.'

She began to scratch in the moist earth, first with her nails, then with a stick she found lying in the dirt. She seemed to have forgotten all about Calliope as she crouched in the afternoon dazzle, muttering under her breath like some demented witch. Calliope looked on with an inner shiver. Stavroula was tearing her husband's snapshot. She ripped it into tiny bits, then hunched over and, breathing harshly, buried the annihilated image in the cemetery's earth. Calliope became acutely aware of the chattering birds, the vibration of insects, the hiss of the wind taunting the sleepy trees.

Finally, Stavroula scrambled to her feet and clapped away the dirt on her hands, shooting a defiant glance towards Calliope, as if challenging her to voice an objection. Calliope slid off the bench and stood in ineffectual silence. It was going on four o'clock. She took a step forward, seeing the battered woman's features quiver, then collapse into a mask of utter defeat.

'Stavroula!' Calliope was still fighting the compulsion to flee, but found herself offering the comfort of her own arms. 'Come. Don't . . . please don't cry, Stavroula.' She began to make soothing maternal sounds, as if the distraught woman were her own daughter and not someone easily old enough to be her mother.

'But what am I going to do, *Kyria* Calliope? Where—'

'Don't worry. Come. It'll be all right,' Calliope said, abruptly decisive. She took Stavroula's arm. 'First, we're going to send a telegram. Let's see what your daughter has to say.'

~ 3 ~

Inspiration, Calliope would some day tell an Athenian interviewer, is like an apricot or a cherry pip, spat out and lying ignored on the wayside, until some sudden change in environmental conditions makes it sprout and grow into a fruit-laden tree.

The metaphor would be offered by way of explaining a life-altering idea inspired by the chance encounter with Stavroula Houmi. The salient change in her own circumstances was, of course, her lost teaching post, but there was also her nagging guilt over her mother, over the fortune-teller's neglected house. She had, she would say in the years to come, been obsessed with the need to atone for her past selfishness.

She had certainly felt selfish at the cemetery, thinking she ought to take Stavroula home with her, yet recoiling from the very idea. It was, she argued with herself, like asking a solitary monk to take in some garrulous sailor washed up after a shipwreck

And yet, she was not indifferent to Stavroula's plight. Plodding down towards the telegraph office, Calliope recalled the distressing stories she had heard from Eleni, whose work as a midwife had made her privy to married women's secrets. And now there was the kiosk owner's wife, shuffling downhill with her apron on, her face blotched by tears. Stavroula's husband was a tense but mild-mannered man. Who would have thought he would turn out to be a wife-beater?

It was sheer happenstance that the road from the cemetery to the *agora* led past the fortune-teller's house; that Calliope's inertia had not blunted her native resourcefulness. As she walked past the house's entrance, mechanically glancing at the shuttered windows, Calliope's thoughts meandered back to the old scandal surrounding the fortune-teller and her errant husband. As for Stavroula, whatever she ultimately decided, some sort of temporary arrangement was clearly called for.

Less obvious but certainly inspired was the idea of letting the kiosk owner's wife take refuge in Zenovia's house. Perhaps Stavroula's daughter would talk her husband into taking her mother in; perhaps the chastened kiosk owner, having to fend for himself, would beg his wife to return, and promise never to lay a hand on her again. At the very least, Stavroula would have gained time to reflect on her situation.

That Zenovia herself would have thoroughly approved of the invitation made it seem not only fitting but almost preordained. Not that Calliope had any desire to sway Stavroula either way. Having wired Athens, she hurried home and got the key to Zenovia's house. She showed the hand-wringing woman where bedding and towels were to be found, then beat a hasty retreat.

Within a week, the kiosk owner's wife was settled with her daughter. Calliope felt both gratified and relieved; and yet, more aimless than ever. Before her expulsion from school, she had toyed with the idea of starting a children's library, a possibility she'd intended to pursue during the summer break. That she had done nothing about it was due to the lassitude that had come over her in the wake of her dismissal. Later, it would occur to her that she might have alleviated some of the misery by setting the library plan in motion, but this had been far from her mind at the time.

Stavroula's daughter wired her thanks, but Calliope continued to flounder on her precarious mental island, comforted by Eli, distracted by her godson, her books, her ongoing correspondence. In early September, there was a letter from Pericles, whose health was reportedly on the mend. Calliope, who communicated with him through his devoted nurse, was delighted by the medical prognosis, all the more as she was able to write back with exciting news: her cousin Alexandra had sent Pericles's poems to a French literary magazine and its editor was eager to publish them!

Alexandra's surprising letter so lifted Calliope's spirits that she sat down that very evening to render Pericles's latest poem into French. She suddenly knew how a shipwrecked sailor might feel, spotting a distant light on an alien shore.

~ 4 ~

Then, one Saturday morning, the most surprising letter of all arrived. Calliope had become accustomed to receiving Umbreit's greetings at Christmas and on her birthday; had felt secretly gratified that he had not forgotten her, though she resisted the temptation to write back, and could not quite work out why he went on writing. Perhaps it was his way of expiating his guilt?

But it was only October now and, this time, Umbreit was writing to request a favour. He was teaching literature at Heidelberg University, as well as trying his hand at writing a novel. The plot was set in wartime Molyvos. He had, of course, done his research but still had questions only a native could answer. He would certainly understand if Calliope decided to reply, he said, but was nonetheless hoping that her love of books might persuade her to oblige him by answering a few questions.

Calliope read the letter but postponed making a decision because she was helping Aristides with his homework, then taking him for a swim. The boy was eleven now. He excelled in all subjects, except mathematics. He was a curious, imaginative child, but without regular tutorials might have failed some crucial exams. Dimitra, his elder sister, had the same problem, though her heart was set on studying architecture.

It was eleven o'clock when Aristides finished his assignments, dashing out to fetch a classmate named Fanny Dimou, hoping she might be allowed to join them.

The Dimous lived nearby, so Calliope knew the family rather well. She thought it a great pity that Fanny's parents would not let their clever daughter attend middle school. Knowledge was a fine thing, the father had conceded, but sending a young girl alone to Petra was just asking for trouble.

Such attitudes had rankled with Calliope ever since Eleni Bastia's educational ambitions had been thwarted, but Fanny's parents often kept their son home as well: to pick olives or do farm chores. Calliope, who happened to be reading *Jude the Obscure*, found her thoughts drifting to Fanny's brother, Gavril, who, at that very moment, was doubtless tending to farm animals, while his father sat in the *kapheneion*, drinking and arguing over politics.

All through the summer there had been talk of the split between Tito's Yugoslavia and the USSR. While Fanny sought her father's permission to go to the beach, Calliope eavesdropped on the men's rehash of the political fallout. Yorgos Roumeliotis, the new schoolmaster hired to replace her, was taking part in the argument. He was somewhere in his mid-thirties, pale and skeletal, with the vaguely resigned look of a man outnumbered and outmanoeuvred by a clique of chattering women. Calliope had yet to be introduced, but noted that he had a slight speech defect, which made his r's sound like those of a Frenchman trying to recite Homer.

'My name is Yorgos Roumeliotis and I am from Ksirokambi,' Aristides was soon aping the new schoolmaster. 'From Ksi-ro-kam-bi!' he said, spluttering with mirth. The boy had a gift for mimicking adults, delighting Calliope with the acuteness of his observations.

Halfway down to the beach, Aristides paused to inspect a fly trapped in a pine tree's sap, and then a crab spider that, he told Fanny, could change colour on moving from one plant to another. Calliope had lived in the village all her life but had never noticed this. And what would she do in a year or two, when Aristides was no longer interested in his *nona*?

The moment they arrived on the beach, Aristides and Fanny ran into the sea, while Calliope stood clutching her parasol, shouting after them to stay near the shore. She then sat down in the shade to read, dimly aware of the squawking seagulls, the rhythmic slap of waves on the pebbly shore.

By the time her goddaughter found her, Calliope was fully absorbed in Hardy, but looked up to see Athena giggling, about to squirt water from a fat sea slug. The child had her late father's observant eyes, her mother's round face and luminous skin.

Eleni had been one of the prettiest girls in the village. She was still only in her twenties, but already resigned to having been born into an unlucky family. Not only had she lost a young husband, but her mother had died of mushroom poisoning, her father of cirrhosis. Her Uncle Natis, on the other hand, seemed to be thriving, having quickly fathered two robust sons with Dora the weeper.

Eleni, too, had wept after Tomas's death; had been mute for days and might have remained in a state of prolonged mourning had it not been for her lively daughter, and the pressure from Calliope and Dhaniel to take up midwifery. Three years later, the young widow seemed to be finding enormous satisfaction in supporting herself and her only child. She had, over the years, become one of Calliope's staunchest allies.

The two women sat chatting under the trees, but Calliope's mind kept wandering in private directions. Eventually, she mentioned Umbreit's letter.

Eleni stopped and regarded her keenly. 'Are you going to write to him?'

'I don't know. I haven't decided yet.' Calliope tapped her cigarette. 'But just think, Elenitsa: a novel about our village!'

Eleni chewed on this for a moment. 'But do you really think it'll be published?' she wondered. 'I mean, why would anyone be interested in a backward Greek island?'

'I don't see why not,' Calliope said. She pinched a shred of tobacco from her lower lip. 'Why are people interested in Thomas Hardy's primitive villages?'

~ 5 ~

Having lost her own pen somewhere in her wanderings, Calliope had the nib replaced on her father's old fountain pen. She began to use it as winter set in, and there was pleasure in the memory of her father, hunched over his pupils' exams, pausing now and then to refill his favourite pen.

But the greatest satisfaction of all lay in sitting at his desk, surrounded by his books, translating poetry. If only he could see her now! If only she had known sooner the joy to be had in ferreting out the perfect word; the way each image followed another, forming a string of words as exquisite and inevitable as olives ripening on a branch. Although she still wished she had the gift to create her own images, it was the unexpected success of her literary translations that had pulled her back from the shores of professional despair. Her translations of Pericles's poems had been extravagantly praised by both her French cousin and Rupert Ealing. The Englishman had urged her to keep on translating until there were enough poems for a collection. He was sure a foreign publisher could be found some day.

The very day she received the letter from London, Calliope sat down to reply, waiting for Eli to arrive. Rupert was keen to know how the Civil War was playing out in the village, though he was occasionally in possession of relevant facts even before they reached the northern Aegean. Tito's break with Moscow had recently splintered the Greek Left. What with Yugoslavia and Albania withdrawing their support of Greek Communists, Rupert thought the Civil War had just about run its course.

It was in this letter that the Englishman confirmed what Calliope had long suspected: Greek children had indeed been transported across the border, allegedly to be indoctrinated by Communist families. Some thirty thousand children were said to have been snatched away from their homes, but there were counter rumours of children from Greek orphanages being shipped off to America, for adoption by Right-wing families. The latter reports, Rupert wrote, were as yet unconfirmed, but Queen Frederika was said to be a prime mover in this covert campaign.

The news about the queen's role was so astounding that Eli had hardly come through the door when Calliope thrust Rupert's letter at him. The doctor sat down to shuck off his shoes, mechanically fumbling for his slippers as he read the letter. He was still holding it as he padded into the sitting room, his jaw working tensely.

Although months had passed since the argument over the *pedhomasoma*, Eli had never wavered in his belief that the rumoured abductions were merely government propaganda. Now, as he reached the end of the letter, a baffled look began to take over his features: Rupert Ealing was well placed to know what was what.

'Unbelievable,' he muttered, sinking onto the faded divan. He sat for a moment, pinching the bridge of his nose. 'Unbelievable!'

Calliope had settled into an old chair, silent. There was the sound of rats scuffling through walls, of Sappho's wheezing breath. The dog lay dozing at Eli's feet, as was her wont whenever he came to visit. Sappho's ongoing devotion was bewildering, given that the doctor barely tolerated her presence.

When Eli declined to eat, Calliope sighed and didn't press him. That their German-born queen might be involved in dubious operations was distressing but believable to someone of Eli's political persuasion. The Communists' *pedhomasoma*, on the other hand, he seemed wholly incapable of absorbing.

Having fetched the brandy, Calliope tried to distract Eli with talk of her own plans. Eli knew about the children's library she was setting up in the late fortune-teller's house, but not about the tutorial service she was hoping to offer. She had been meaning to tell him for weeks, but feared some unforeseen obstacle; dreaded another failure.

The idea for the tutorials had germinated the day she had taken Aristides and Fanny down to the beach. Listening in on their chatter, she had marvelled at the girl's lively imagination. She thought children like Fanny desperately needed a library, but less gifted children might also thrive, given tutorial help. It was a well-known fact that even clever children sometimes failed to pass Kaloni's high school entrance exams. Calliope was especially interested in adolescent girls. Most men didn't want their daughters leaving the village for an education, but surely they couldn't object to their attending informal study sessions in the Molyvos library?

She was beginning to share all these thoughts with Eli, but all at once stopped, scanning his face intently. 'What is it?' she asked. 'You think I'm just floundering, don't you?'

Eli looked startled. 'Darling!' He reached out and drew her from her chair and onto his lap. 'I think it's a brilliant idea,' he said, stroking her hair away from her face. 'Whatever inspired it!' He touched her mouth with his own. 'Zenovia will be dancing in her grave,' he added. 'Dancing with joy!'

'I hope so. I sure hope so,' Calliope murmured. She started to add something, but then stopped herself, not yet ready to share a more radical idea she had been contemplating ever since she'd run into Stavroula Houmi at the cemetery. She was reluctant to voice it because she herself could foresee several obstacles; because, after all these years, she still craved Eli's approval as she had once craved her father's. Yes, she would keep it to herself for now. She had, in any case, sensed that Eli was merely making conversation, as he sometimes did to take his mind off a new case of polio or birth defects among children conceived during the Occupation.

It was only in bed that Eli seemed able to shut out his professional concerns. With dinner over and the dishes done, Calliope hauled him up from his chair and, Sappho pressing in after them, led the way up to what had once been her parents' bedroom. She slept in her own bed when she was alone, but in the matrimonial one when Eli spent the night. In truth, she slept little in either bed, having resolved to kick her dependence on sleeping pills now that she no longer had to get up for morning classes.

So she lay awake in the double bed, while Eli drifted off, his legs entangled with hers. She knew she would likely stay awake until the neighbours' rooster began to crow, but was resigned to it. She nestled against Eli's warm body, listening to the peaceful breathing of man and dog, the shrieking of a night bird. The air around the bed was beginning to grow chilly, so she sat up and fumbled for her nightgown. The clock downstairs struck three-thirty before she felt herself being towed towards sleep.

Suddenly, a moan escaped Eli's throat and his eyes snapped open. He sat for a moment, rubbing his eyes, muttering incoherently. At length, he grew lucid, sliding towards the edge of the bed. He scratched his head, then reached for the bedside torch. The power in the village was still being shut off at midnight.

Calliope stirred. 'Bad dream?'

'Mm.' He thrust his feet into his slippers, pulled on his dressing gown, then shambled across the room. Sappho had scrambled to her feet and was sluggishly padding after him.

'Bring me a glass of water, will you?' Calliope murmured. She was by now accustomed to Eli's nightmares, which had plagued him for years, ever since he escaped from his Anatolian home. Calliope burrowed deeper under the covers. Warm and sleepy, she heard the toilet flush, then the muffled sound of slippers shuffling towards the kitchen. She heard the faucet being turned on, and then the sound of Eli's footfall approaching the staircase.

There was a brief pause, as if he had just realised he had forgotten something.

Calliope was dozing off when she heard a sudden thud. Had the flowerpot on the newel post been knocked down? she wondered drowsily.

And then she was fully awake, listening. All at once, she sat up in bed, throwing off the blankets.

'Eli?' She went swishing out of the bedroom, heading for the stairs. 'Are you all right, darling?'

But even as she asked the question, Calliope could taste dread settle between her teeth. She blundered towards the stairhead, every mental cell abruptly alert. Why wasn't he answering? What happened to the torch?

'Eli?'

She was still fumbling her way down the shadowy stairs, hand gripping the banister, when Sappho let out a tentative little bark, and then a sudden howl. It was a sound that Calliope had heard only once before, on the night Dimitris Stephanides was beaten to death.

'Eli!' she screamed. 'Eli!'

And still there was no answer. Her panic seemed to reverberate through the nocturnal silence. Another moment and her voice joined the dog's, howling together in the pre-dawn dark. In the foyer, the clock's pendulum struck four times – *boom, boom, boom, boom* – as it had every night for almost half a century.

FIVE

~ 1 ~

Dear Rupert,

I am sorry I have been such a poor correspondent lately, though I did send you a note on getting your invitation and must assume that it somehow went astray. In any case, I was delighted to hear from you, and to see your grown-up son and his bride! The photos are lovely. I wish I could have been there for the wedding, even if I am something of a cynic when it comes to marriage. And I do appreciate your concern. I am quite well but busier than ever. The *kentro* continues to take up most of my time, and the rest just seems to fly away. I can't believe almost three years have passed since we lost dear Eli. The older I get, the more I understand the villagers' fatalistic attitude towards life. It used to infuriate me, especially the women's perpetual '*Ti na kanome*'? I'm beginning to see, though, that in many cases this is all we human beings can do: accept the card fate has dealt us and limp on as best we can.

What I still have trouble accepting are the primitive practices, which sometimes maim and kill through sheer ignorance. I believe in education as others believe in the Virgin's powers. It's the only thing that will take us out of the Middle Ages.

I was sorry to hear that you don't much like your new job, but will be very interested to read your memoirs. It seems the older we get the more compelling our own past becomes, and the less time there is for all the things we still hope to accomplish. I started out with the modest hope of improving our children's education but have willy-nilly become something of a social worker. Not that I can always provide adequate solutions. Much of the time all I can do is validate women's domestic grievances. It is not much, I know, but in the absence of laws, in the absence of a social support system, in the absence of financial independence, validation is a good beginning. I confess there are days when I despair of it all. What do you say to a woman whose brother has raped her adolescent daughter? What do you say to a young bride whose husband has beaten her up for not having dinner ready when he came home from work?

We have a new doctor but he is not well liked, even if he does keep an icon on his desk. We also have a new priest, but most women prefer to consult either me or the midwife. Some used to seek *Papa* Emanouil's advice, but now that he, too, is gone, the villagers seem a little like orphaned children. I had no idea there were so many wretched women around. I suppose I had just been too wrapped up in myself. You'll be glad to know that I have become somewhat less self-absorbed, and may finally be starting to atone for all my omissions and commissions.

Sappho died just before Christmas. She might have lived longer, but never quite regained her spirits after Eli's death. Pericles is well but there is no doubt that Makronisos and his long illness have left their mark. He is moodier than he used to be, and sometimes appears inexplicably restless. But he is immensely excited by the acceptance of his book, and dreams of seeing it published abroad.

Speaking of books, Umbreit's novel is about to be published in French. I think that writing it has really helped him come to terms with his role in the Occupation, though it's to his credit that he never tried to whitewash the past. I didn't think I'd ever speak to him again, but having such an ambitious novel dedicated to me has, I suppose, softened my heart – or maybe just tickled my vanity?

I suspect the Civil War also had something to do with it. Having seen the abominable things Greeks did to each other, I've come to regard all human beings with an equally jaundiced eye.

Nearly three years have passed since the Civil War ended, yet some facts are only now coming to light. Did you know that more Greeks were killed by other Greeks than by the Germans? It is mind-boggling! To think that a quarter of a million people have been left homeless, on top of those imprisoned or exiled! That Greeks could shove their own compatriots into burning ovens; could rape and kill children in front of their parents. To think that ordinary men could chop off women's nipples and turn them into worry beads!

All these atrocities took place far away from here but we, too, remain bitterly divided, even if Lesbos has come to be known as The Red Island. A Leftist who needs a table would rather eat off the floor than go to a Rightist carpenter. The carpenter won't speak to his brother, who happens to be a Communist. And so on. The government continues to discriminate against Leftists. A man wishing to start a business venture still needs a document attesting to his never having been a member of the Communist Party. I thought that with time, things might improve, but the country is so unstable, both economically and politically, that the end doesn't seem to be in sight, which is why thousands of Greeks are emigrating to the four corners of the world.

Our government, meanwhile, seems to see everyone as a potential spy. Let this be a warning to you, should you decide to return to Greece some day, as you keep promising. Not that I'd want to discourage you. It would be a great pleasure to see you, Rupert, even if it means getting my ear boxed for forgetting most of the English you taught me. Oddly enough, the only thing I seem to remember perfectly is the limerick about the loss of hair. I assume you still have your nose and your toes (one of my neighbours recently had his nose bitten off by a rabid dog), and if you've lost your hair, well, it doesn't really matter. It's what's under the hair that counts. I hope this letter finds you well. I have no immediate plans to travel to Athens, but will go next winter to buy library books, and promise to look for the Seferis then.

Yours,

Calliope

~ 2 ~

She was overdressed. Athens had been cool the previous evening, but the ferry docked in Mytilene on a morning as bright and balmy as spring. It was late February. Calliope was waiting for a taxi. She had taken off her jacket but was still too warm in her new wool pullover and trousers. The outfit had been purchased two days earlier. She had never before considered buying trousers, but the moment she spotted this pair in the shop window, she'd impulsively decided to go in, if only to try them on.

The trousers were made of a soft tweedy fabric, cinnamon-hued, with tiny reddish spots in the fine weave. Cuffed at the ankles, they had a pocket on each side and buttons in front, exactly like a man's. Only she had never known a man's trousers to have such an elegant cut and feel. Certainly, none would have hugged her hips and bottom as these trousers did.

'Imported from London.' The boutique owner had come up to observe Calliope, her head canted, an ivory cigarette holder clamped between her ruby-coloured lips. 'They look like they were made for you, don't they?'

'Mm.' Calliope contemplated her own reflection while the shop owner waited, looking arch and doubtful. The doubt may have had something to do with the price, which was exorbitant. Most of the Kolonaki shop's clients would be foreigners.

Calliope thrust her hands in the trouser pockets, vaguely intrigued by the fact that a piece of clothing could alter more than just one's outward appearance. Naturally, she looked more like a man than a woman, but the moment she saw herself in the English trousers, a more subtle transformation seemed to take place within her skin. She found herself recalling the day a tomcat had sneaked into her house while she stood signing for a parcel. Entering her bedroom an hour later, she found the cat in front of her vanity mirror, his back menacingly arched, hissing at his own reflection.

Except for the price, Calliope had no reason to hiss, but the woman staring back at her in the boutique's mirror looked like a stranger in some foreign magazine. Calliope had leafed through some of them while waiting in the bookshop on Akademias. There had been photographs of women riding horses and waving from convertible cars. Women in tapered skirts with breasts poking through tight sweaters. Women in jodhpurs. Women in striped vests and trousers.

Calliope sighed. The trousers were nothing but an expensively tailored piece of cloth, yet it could not be denied that the new image was generating a peculiar sense of empowerment. Inexplicable, really. Early in the Civil War, scores of new policemen had been transferred to the island. There were twenty new officers in Molyvos alone and, on occasion, Caliope had come across one of them dressed in civilian clothes. Oddly, though she had little regard for their position, the policemen seemed diminished out of uniform. When a man put on a uniform in the morning, did he feel instantly aggrandised? she wondered. She thought of Lorenz Umbreit in his smart Wehrmacht uniform, surprising herself with the wish that he could see her now, in this new incarnation: a strong, modern woman ready to take on the world!

The thought made her smile. It flashed on her that Umbreit, too, might lose in stature, were she to see him in street clothes or pyjamas.

The boutique owner had briefly disappeared, but was now coming back with a leather belt. She hastened to thread it through the tweedy loops, then frowned a little, staring at Calliope's lilac-hued blouse. 'You would probably want to wear a shirt or a sweater with these trousers,' she suggested, stepping back in her patent-leather shoes.

'Yes, perhaps a sweater,' Calliope said, mostly because she couldn't decide whether to buy the trousers, which bore the extraordinary price tag of two thousand drachmas. 'Do you have anything in this colour?' She pointed to the reddish spots, feeling like a child plucking off daisy petals. If they had a sweater in this colour, she was meant to buy the trousers; otherwise, she would walk out as she'd come in, dressed in skirt, blouse, jacket.

'I have an angora pullover, if—'

'May I see it, please?'

The Athenian clicked away, coming back with the most luxurious sweater Calliope had ever held between her hands: a long-sleeved pullover, the colour of persimmons. Its price was equally shocking, but the only time she could remember experiencing a leap of something like love for a piece of clothing had been back in the late 1930s, when she'd impulsively bought a French-made dress in Mytilene.

She ended up spending an average Greek's monthly salary, buying the trousers and belt, as well as the pullover. She had put them on just before she left Piraeus and was still wearing them the following morning, when she returned to Molyvos. The taxi driver dropped her off at the *kentro*, helping her with the suitcase and boxes of books before heading back to Mytilene.

Calliope picked up her jacket, then a small red valise she had bought in Athens. She occasionally had to spend the night in Mytilene, and all she owned was a large suitcase. One of the porters would have to bring that one, since her house was not accessible on wheels. The red valise was empty, except for some new toiletries.

By the time she made her way through the *agora*, men were beginning to gather outside the main *kapheneion*, drinking their midday ouzo. They had been discussing the possibility of union with Cyprus but fell silent now, watching Calliope pass with her chic little valise, her spring jacket folded over her arm. She was feeling inexplicably buoyant, like a woman coming home from an extended rest in some European spa instead of a few hectic days in the capital.

Approaching the *plateia*, Calliope stopped to greet a former pupil on leave from the army. Gavril Dimou's father had just been admitted to hospital and his mother was having problems with the admissions office in Mytilene. Could Calliope possibly help?

'I'll see what I can do,' she said. 'I'll drop in a little later.'

'Thank you. I'll tell my mother.' The Dimous lived in Calliope's neighbourhood. 'Are you sure you don't want me to help you home?'

Gavril asked as they reached the stairs. She had already told him the valise was virtually empty.

'I'm sure. Thanks anyway.' She smiled. She had just caught her elder brother-in-law staring from the *pantopoleion*'s threshold, his mother at his side. Both Vangelis and Katina had their mouths open, like children gawking at some coppersmith or knife sharpener passing through the village.

'They're only staring at you because of the trousers,' Gavril said, as if to reassure her there was nothing else anyone could possibly find fault with.

'I know.' Calliope patted the young man's cheek. She had always had a soft spot for Gavril and Fanny Dimou. 'See you later,' she said.

Then she turned and began to climb the steps, chuckling to herself.

'I think I'll wear trousers from now on,' she informed Pericles Alexiou later that day. She laughed at herself but refrained from telling her young brother-in-law that his own mother and brother had unknowingly inspired her decision. He was, in any case, working out a new poem in his head. She could tell he was because he hadn't so much as chuckled at what she'd just told him.

— 3 —

It didn't take the villagers long to discover that Calliope Adham and her young brother-in-law had become lovers. She was by then thirty-seven years old; Pericles was a decade younger. Somehow, having survived Makronisos, having triumphed over tuberculosis, he had succeeded in making Calliope forget that she had been his teacher when he was still a schoolboy in short trousers, obsessed with the names of world capitals.

At first, Calliope had feared that her sexual involvement with her husband's brother might sabotage her efforts at the *kentro*, but she soon discovered that where there is a potential advantage, people will usually find grounds for turning a blind eye.

By the summer of 1952, when Pericles had returned to the village, both the library and the tutorial service were considered an unqualified success. Molyvos children planning to attend high school were passing entrance exams with distinction; primary-school children received free tutorials after school hours.

The most ambitious program, however, was one that Calliope had initiated only recently and that was strictly intended for adolescent girls whose education had been arrested at the primary level. When Calliope had first aired the idea, Mathaios the mayor told her that most parents would consider it a waste of time. Calliope thought it over, then went on to publicise the program as highly selective: only ten girls would be chosen to participate in the study sessions. Free of charge.

Mathaios laughed when he heard all this. She was as cunning as any man, he told her.

It quickly became a matter of prestige to have a daughter selected by the *kentro's* director. Having engaged former pupils to help with tutorials, Calliope devoted herself to the study sessions, meeting two groups on alternate days, to discuss history, poetry, logic. She was careful to schedule the sessions in the late morning. This placated the mothers, who needed help with chores; the absence of boys stole the fathers' thunder. Before long, mothers could be heard boasting that their daughters were not only able to cook and embroider, but were also among 'Calliope's girls'.

Calliope's girls were known to be clever and diligent, and too busy to succumb to temptation, as the late baker's daughter was rumoured to have done with a young Athenian. The mayor had recently brought in a construction crew to restore the crumbling Genoese fortress; the baker's daughter had been seen alone with one of the workers. The only place Calliope's girls ever went unaccompanied was the *kentro*. Two years after its inception, the new enterprise was functioning so smoothly that Calliope was able to devote most of her evenings to her literary pursuits.

Mirto's sister was impressed by her niece's achievements but scandalised by her private life. Elpida had been a vivacious woman, but after the deaths of her husband and her younger son, she'd acquired the abject air of a whipped dog. When she found out that Calliope had taken Pericles for a lover, Elpida saw it as her duty to intervene on her late sister's behalf. The village might be willing to turn a blind eye but what about Mirto?

'Your mother will be turning over in her grave!' she said.

But this warning only made Calliope sigh and kiss her aunt's sagging cheeks. After all these years, she retorted, her mother surely knew better than to believe that playing by the rules and praying to the Virgin offered any sort of protection.

'From now on, I'm going to live by my own rules!' she stated.

'From now on?' Elpida chuckled, ruefully. 'You always have, *koritsi mou*. Always – as far back as I can remember.'

~ 4 ~

Another year went by. Pericles had all but recovered from his recent ordeals, but continued to write about them, living for the day when a collection of his poems might be published. He passed much of his time reading and writing; had gotten into the habit of spending his weekdays in his mother's home, his nights and weekends with Calliope.

One Sunday, they decided to have a picnic in Eftalou. It was a brilliant day in the spring of 1954. They spread a blanket next to a blossoming almond tree, in a meadow spotted with poppies, anemones, daisies. Calliope had prepared *taramosalata* and stuffed tomatoes. She had also brought cheese pies and *dolmadhakia* sent by the late beekeeper's daughter.

It was generally believed that Calliope had lost her teaching job because of her impassioned defence of the beekeeper. Though she had staunchly refused to discuss her expulsion, the family's gestures of gratitude didn't go unappreciated. Calliope had little time to cook, and Pericles was barely able to make a cup of coffee. Although he had studied literature with the intention of teaching, Iason's brother seemed content to let his mother and lover look after him, while he wandered in Eftalou, and read, and wrote poetry.

When they had finished their meal, Pericles rose and stretched, then plucked an almond blossom from Calliope's hair. 'Race you down to the beach?'

Calliope wiped her hands, scrambling up. 'Only if you don't mind losing!'

'One, two, three, go!'

They romped on the water's edge, shrieking as they chased and tickled each other with snakes of dripping seaweed. She was a carefree girl again! She could roll in a sunlit meadow, amid drifting pollen and thrumming insects; could forget all about unhappy women and their children – forget to think altogether, though Pericles never seemed to. He was like a spider, perpetually spinning the web that would catch the brilliant butterflies fluttering through his inner landscape. There was nothing that, sooner or later, did not find its way into Pericles's incandescent lyrics.

He was much the same as a lover: intense and watchful, as if committing every flicker of the eyelid, every explored patch of skin, to his greedy memory.

That Sunday, they made love in an Eftalou cove, where Pericles sometimes napped during his wanderings. The seagulls shrieked, circling the rocks; the sea murmured in the distance. And all the while, his eyes would be on her, finding rare pearls, discerning improbable rhymes. Her body, Calliope felt, did not belong to her but to some trapped, desperate creature struggling to be rescued. It bit and scratched and shrieked along with the raucous seagulls. In time, it landed on its small private island: depleted, astonished, blessed.

~ 5 ~

A month later, the long-awaited copy of *Sacrifice* finally arrived. The book had come in the morning mail and, the moment he opened the package, Pericles raced across the village to share it with Calliope. She was in the garden, reading, when he stormed through the gate. It was two days before Easter. Breathless, he stopped and held out the book, gazing at her mutely.

'Oh!' Calliope reached for the book, breathing in the heady smell of freshly printed pages, running her fingers over the smooth sea-blue cover. She opened the book as an exiled scholar might open some precious manuscript after decades away from the printed word. Pericles remained standing, watching her thumb the pages.

'You've missed something,' he said at length. 'Go back to the beginning.'

She went back. She read the dedication. She was incapable of writing a single memorable line, but standing before her was yet another man who had dedicated his book to her.

Pericles seemed on the edge of tears, gazing at the volume in her hands with the expression a man might wear on watching his wife nurse a newborn. Soon, he was hoisting Calliope to her feet, delirious with joy. Makronisos and illness had left him gloomier than he had been before the Civil War, but still given to occasional rapture.

'I want you to marry me!' he blurted, eyes bright as sapphires.

'*What?*' Calliope threw back her head and laughed. 'Just because I've inspired a poem or two?'

'Of course not!' Pericles said. He was the same height as his brother had been, but more sinewy. He loved her, he stated simply. 'I've loved you all my life.'

'Ach, don't be silly!' Calliope spoke in the tone of voice she might have used in the old days, when she had been his teacher. 'I'm ten years older than you!'

'So?'

'So, I'll feel like your mother in a few years.'

He shook his head. 'You're in the prime of life!' he stated. 'Ask any man!'

She plucked a leaf and tickled his nose. He was a man who lived entirely in the present. 'So what happens when I'm past my prime?'

'Oh, I'll probably be dead by then. All great poets die young,' he stated breezily.

'That's not true! Anyway—'

'Anyway, you're my brother's widow,' he put in, nibbling on her ear. 'Hindus and Moslems have laws requiring a man to marry his brother's widow.'

'Really?' Calliope pondered this in silence, breathing in the odour of Pericles's youthful sweat. 'Then you must thank God you're not Hindu or Moslem.'

'Why, would that be so terrible?'

She extricated herself from his embrace and reached for her pack of cigarettes.

'It would be quite wrong,' she said, regarding him steadily as she lit a match. 'You should marry a young woman some day. Marry and have children.'

He shook his head. 'I'm sure you could still conceive,' he said with conviction. She had told him about having miscarried Eli's child but not about Lorenz Umbreit's. Even Eli had not known about that.

'Maybe so, but I'm not going to.'

All at once, Calliope could feel her mouth starting to twitch. The thought of having a child with a man she could vividly recall as a boy in short trousers seemed too funny to contemplate. But then, perhaps having him as a lover was equally laughable?

It was a thought Calliope had repeatedly tried to keep at bay, but one thing she was determined to make clear once and for all. She would not allow marriage to become a bone of contention with Pericles, as it had been with Eli. The two men might be completely different but the need to possess, she was beginning to think, was possibly common to all men.

Briefly, Calliope experienced an intense need to flee. One of the things that troubled her about her young lover was his tendency to keep feeding some vague subterranean discontent. She had never known anyone capable of sliding so quickly from sublime joy into abysmal despair. He seemed to be ceaselessly trying to capture something bright and elusive. Could this be a normal aspect of any poet's soul?

The question flickered across Calliope's mind as she sat leafing through the published book, having managed to distract Pericles with a question concerning a recently revised stanza.

He didn't like to talk about Makronisos, but the poems spoke for themselves. He had been tortured in the prison camp. His tuberculosis had been diagnosed only after he collapsed one morning, cleaning the prison latrines. Half of *Sacrifice* was devoted to the Occupation, the second half to the Civil War. Calliope had no doubt that some day the book would be published in France or England; maybe even America. She voiced this thought as she stopped to re-read one of the poems, inspired years ago by the sight of a hungry child trying to shoot down a hidden mourning dove.

'May there be hundreds more where these came from!' she said with feeling.

'*Merci*. It's all thanks to you, you know.'

'Not really,' she said. She took a last drag on her cigarette.

'I would never have kept on writing without your encouragement,' he insisted.

'Nonsense!' she said. 'You could no more stop writing than I could stop being envious.'

'Envious! Are you really?' The thought seemed to delight him. He reached out and took hold of her hair, drawing her towards him.

'You seem surprised,' she said, looking into his eyes as if to gauge his sincerity. 'I'd give my soul to the devil to be able to write like you.'

He smiled with half his mouth. 'But that's just the beginning,' he said.

'The beginning? Of what – the bargain? You must tell me the rest so that—'

'The rest is obvious. The devil's not satisfied with our souls.'

'Oh? What else is there?'

He cocked an ironic eyebrow. 'What else is there beside the soul?'

'That the devil does not already possess.' Calliope smiled.

'He has it all, you see,' Pericles said, 'but not all the time, and not necessarily as much as he'd like at any given moment. That's what makes him the devil. Possessing everything, he derives his greatest satisfaction from projecting his own greed and frustration onto us poor mortals.'

'So this is it? That's what I must accept if I'm ever to write poetry?'

Pericles chuckled. 'A diabolical bargain, I agree!'

'Well, I suppose I must stick to translation then.' Calliope laughed.

Pericles whipped a pen out of his breast pocket. He opened the book to the dedication page, where two words – *For Calliope* – had been immortalised by the Athenian publisher.

The dedicatee sat with her chin resting against the poet's shoulder. She watched, silent, as he inserted a comma after her name, paused briefly, then scribbled three additional words: *my contrary muse*. He signed his name, solemnly touched his lips to the inscription, and passed the book back into Calliope's waiting hands.

~ 6 ~

2 January 1955

Dear Lorenz,

What a wonderful surprise – thank you so much! I believe I enjoyed the French edition even more than I had the original, partly because I didn't have to keep using the dictionary, but also because I noticed several things I'd missed the first time. I was sorry to hear that you are not entirely happy with the translation, but letting some stranger take over your work must be, I imagine, a little like passing a newborn infant to a wet-nurse without being sure of the quality of her milk. Anyway, just for the fun of it, I took the first page of the original and translated it into French, then compared my own version with that of Madame Desrosiers. It's astonishing, isn't it, the degree to which the translator's own sensibility informs the translation? I confess I prefer my own version, but no doubt that's sheer conceit on my part.

Your Penelope, too, is occasionally conceited, but has virtues I cannot claim to possess. For one thing, she is far more heroic than I, even if you've made her resemble me in some ways. You may find it hard to believe, but I really am a coward. If I joined the

Resistance, it was only because I have always found my own impotence more difficult to tolerate than fear.

The Nightingale's Silence made me marvel again at how well you have captured our wartime agony (you remind me of Pearl S. Buck's depiction of China). I think it's extraordinary that you manage to present both Greek and German points of view with equal sympathy and authority. It's not every male writer that can so persuasively enter a woman's skin, though Flaubert did so with stunning success, didn't he? Your understanding of village mentality is also remarkable. As Eli Dhaniel once said: 'We live with one foot in the Middle Ages, the other in the twentieth century.'

I was very glad to hear about your second Greek novel and am longing to know what it is about. If you go on like this, you may come to be regarded as a German Hellenophile, though I suppose some people might consider this an oxymoron. I am tempted to press you to tell me more, but I do understand your reluctance. I, too, am occasionally surprised to find that I am not altogether free of superstition. I spent years poking fun at my poor mother's primitive beliefs, but the older I get, the clearer it seems to me that superstition is just a universal expression of human impotence. An illiterate villager panicking at the sight of a black cat might be unable to articulate his real fear, but he somehow knows that he can no more stop an earthquake or an invading army than he can a black cat crossing his path or an owl hooting on his own roof. One of the things I especially appreciated in your novel was the Destiny leitmotif. My French cousin, who teaches comparative literature, says your philosophical background is evident in your writing, though you manage to raise serious philosophical issues without sounding in the least didactic.

I have recently read Moby Dick, and was intrigued to find that Melville, too, was preoccupied with Fate. Do you know his work? I have also read Billy Budd and found it extremely moving. I had never stopped to consider how impotent inarticulate people must feel, especially when confronted with a silver-tongued opponent. I don't know whether this is what is meant by wisdom, but I am slowly becoming more sympathetic to my neighbours' foibles and limitations. I imagine that inside every uneducated villager there is a voice desperate to be heard, unable to express itself with the longed-for eloquence, just as I am unable to find the words for the poetry I feel glimmering within me. Pericles says I am too greedy and he may be right, though he himself seems to fluctuate between thinking himself another Seferis and wanting to burn his entire oeuvre whenever he feels he has failed to capture some elusive image. Is this something you have ever experienced?

I think about such things whenever I am alone, which is not that often. My husband used to say that I thought too much. Sometimes I agree with that, other times I feel I don't have time to think nearly as much as I'd like to. Still, I am very glad to have found something worthwhile to do with myself. There are days when I can't help thinking that Zenovia Antoniou really did have a clairvoyant gift, though I've always been sceptical of such claims. But I'd better stop here. I wish you great success with your new novel, and a happy Christmas to you and your family.

Sincerely,

Calliope

P.S. You may be interested to know that we finally have electricity in the village. No telephones yet, but many of us have radios, and the road to Mytilene is in the process of being paved.

In future years, Calliope would insist that she had never contemplated rendering Lorenz Umbreit's work into Greek – not until he wrote back later that winter, urging her to try translating a couple of chapters, which his German publisher would then send to an Athenian colleague.

Although Calliope was flattered, the project seemed rather daunting. It would, she thought, take her years to translate an entire novel.

Translating German prose into Greek might be easier than translating Greek poetry into French, but she was not at all sure that she was up to the challenge.

Umbreit, however, had not lost his powers of persuasion. He pressed Calliope to have a stab at the prologue, but Easter had come and gone before she finally sat down to try it, and even then rather reluctantly.

Pericles had won a Greek poetry award. The day after the Burning of Judas festivities, he had sailed to Piraeus for interviews, leaving Calliope to her own devices. By Friday afternoon, she was out of excuses. She spent all day working on Umbreit's prologue, almost forgetting her appointment with the mayor's ten-year-old son, who needed tutorial help after his bout with polio.

Sotiris was usually tutored by Fanny Dimou, Aristides's childhood playmate. Calliope's godson was by now in high school, but Fanny had been forced to leave school at thirteen, forbidden to keep company with adolescent boys. She eventually started attending the study sessions and, more recently, helping *kentro* children with their homework. Calliope was paying a modest salary to her young tutors, ensuring regular attendance.

That Friday, however, Fanny Dimou was to be betrothed to Pavlos Rozakis, the late *kapheneion* owner's thirty-four-year-old son. Pavlos was now the owner, and though Calliope liked him well enough, she could not subdue a certain sadness, sensing Fanny's and Aristides's mutual attachment.

The sadness was still with her as she sat down to help Sotiris with his maths. She was using walnuts to demonstrate that multiplication was just a mathematical trick to speed up addition. Sotiris had no difficulty grasping the concept; his only problem lay with the zero factor. He could easily understand how $0 x 1$ must equal 0, but stoutly argued that $1 x 0$ should equal 1 and not 0, as Calliope insisted.

'But you had *one* walnut, *Kyria*, you multiplied it by zero. Zero is nothing!' he reasoned, scanning her face with his grave, dreamy eyes. 'So what happened to the walnut . . . the one walnut you already had?'

Calliope smiled at the boy. How was it that, in all these years, no other child had ever thought to ask this question? She was about to explain the necessity of mathematical symmetry but they had reached the end of the hour, so she told Sotiris they would continue next time.

It was by then past eight o'clock. Everyone had gone home and she, too, was ready to leave when the door opened and in sauntered Timolis Tsouras, son of the man responsible for the loss of her teaching job. He happened to be passing by, Timolis shyly explained, and thought that Calliope might be able to do him a favour and recommend a book for his young niece. He was going to Mytilene and wanted to buy something for her approaching name day.

'She's my goddaughter, a real book-eater . . . not like me,' he added disarmingly.

'Well, you've come to the right place.' Calliope stepped back into her office, toying with her key-ring. She was intrigued by Timolis's decision to consult her, given that she and his father were not on speaking terms. The young man had by then finished both his studies and military service. He would be somewhere in his mid-twenties. 'I'll make you a list,' she offered.

He was almost androgynous in his beauty, though there was no vanity in his manner; only the hint of a strong need for friendship or understanding. It may have had something to do with his mother's premature death, or perhaps the recent falling-out with his father. There had been the usual village gossip, but Calliope had never learned the details. And now here he was, seeking her out. Perhaps trying to spite his father?

Having established the niece's age and interests, Calliope jotted down several titles, then rose from her desk, making conversation as she prepared to leave for the day. Timolis had recently qualified as a notary.

'What are your plans now?' Calliope asked, locking up the *kentro*. They were both heading towards the St Kyriaki neighbourhood.

'I don't know – I'll stay here for a while, then decide.' He had hoped to go to America for a year, but it hadn't worked out, he told Calliope. He had a simple, forthright manner, a fetching way of tilting his head and casting sidelong looks as he spoke, smiling ever so faintly.

He would have been the sort of boy who brought flowers or cherries for the teacher and found excuses to linger after class.

'Do you speak any English?' Calliope asked.

He did. His father had urged him to study French, but he'd always wanted to go to America, and had taken English courses for several years. He had a former classmate whose family lived in New York. 'But that's not the reason. I'd just like to see something of the world, and America – well, it's the ultimate dream, isn't it?'

Calliope chuckled. She told Timolis about the travel photos she used to collect when she was a child, dreaming about the Taj Mahal, the Great Wall of China. '*My* ultimate dream was to ride a camel across the Sahara. See the Pyramids!' She laughed. 'So, what made you decide to stay in Molyvos?'

'My father,' Timolis said. He had remarkable eyes: blue, black-rimmed irises and dark lashes, as curly as a girl's. 'He thinks I should open an office here. In Molyvos.'

'Well, we could certainly use a notary,' Calliope said.

'He's afraid I'll marry an American and never come back.' The statement was accompanied by a quick, winning smile.

'It's been known to happen,' Calliope said, feeling a surge of sympathy. It would not be easy to get out from under Leandros Tsouras's thumb, she thought, but quickly cautioned herself: Do not meddle!

They had reached the parapet overlooking the sea and paused to watch the sunset, as people often did on their way uphill. Calliope's mother-in-law lived in this neighbourhood, with its fine courtyards and vast panorama. As the day waned, the primroses began to unfurl, their scent fusing with the smell of tar from the newly constructed road. The road was finally paved, cutting travel time to the capital in half.

Timolis took out a pack of cigarettes and held it out to Calliope. They leaned against the parapet, smoking companionably, watching children play. Two of the boys were chasing a ball; the youngest frolicked with a stray puppy, crowing happily. With his hazel eyes and pale hair, the child reminded Calliope of Aristides, just before his hair had been cut for the first time. To think that her godson was almost eighteen now!

They were still watching, laughing at the child and the dog, when Pericles appeared on the steps, headed for the *agora*. He had turned the corner, stopped for a moment, then sauntered down towards Calliope, smiling uncertainly. His mother was baking a cake and had run out of sugar. She had sent him to get some before the shops closed.

Pericles blurted all this, then glanced at the headmaster's son. There was, Calliope noted, a flicker of discomfort in Timolis's eyes. She stood watching the two men with interest: two sets of blue eyes assessing each other in the golden dusk.

'What were you doing with him?' Pericles was soon asking, having decided to get the sugar from a small neighbourhood grocery on the other side of the hill. Timolis had gone his own way by then.

'He stopped at the library.'

'The library? What, the man reads fairytales?'

'I doubt it.' Calliope explained about the niece, the name day, the book.

'Since when does the *kentro* sell books?' Pericles demanded.

Calliope took a long steadying breath. 'He didn't buy anything. I just gave him a few titles. He's going to Mytilene tomorrow.'

Pericles said nothing.

'*What?*' she flared up with sudden exasperation. 'What's the matter with you? Don't tell me you're jealous!'

'Me, jealous?' Pericles snorted. 'What have I got to be jealous of?'

'Exactly!' Calliope could never decide whether her lover's occasional flashes of arrogance amused or repelled her. She shot him a sidelong glance. 'But you *are* jealous. Look at you!' She reached out to touch his pulsing jaw but Pericles jerked back, lightly slapping her hand away.

'What's he doing here anyway?' he demanded then. 'Is he planning to stay?'

'For now,' Calliope said, pausing to crush her cigarette underfoot. 'He wants to go to America, but his father won't let him.'

'Hm,' Pericles said, frowning.

The grocer had been about to close his shop, but stopped and scooped out sugar into a paper bag. Through the window, a goat could be heard, bleating plaintively.

'I'll see you soon,' Pericles tossed towards Calliope, ready to head back to his mother's house. Calliope fluttered her hand over her shoulder. She strolled home in the deepening dusk, breathing in the perfumed summer air.

It was almost dark when she returned home. She flicked on the lights and headed up to her bedroom. She was about to change and start preparing supper, but suddenly stopped and, fully dressed, turned towards the vanity mirror. There were, Eleni had told her, those who said it was having a young lover that kept her looking so youthful. And, well, perhaps they were right?

When they first became lovers, Pericles had surprised Calliope, saying that her eyes and her saucy walk still drove Molyvos men wild. During his stay in Athens, he had seen a film with a young Italian actress named Sophia Loren, who reminded him of Calliope. Pericles thought that Calliope's face was more refined but she, too, made him think of a leopard in repose: golden-eyed, faintly disdainful, ever ready to leap and strike at the slightest provocation.

Calliope had never heard of Sophia Loren, but the leopard had made her laugh. Now, contemplating her own reflection, she smiled at her own recollection. Then she turned away, inwardly shaking her head.

She had recently turned forty.

SIX

~ 1 ~

8 September 1955

Dear Alexandra,

Your letter arrived on the same day as the announcement that Pericles's book won the National Prize for Poetry! He is thrilled, of course, but I worry that all this acclaim is beginning to go to his head. Perhaps it's to be expected. He is still young and will, I hope, acquire some humility once he can take success for granted.

As for my own humble endeavours, most villagers seem to appreciate what we are doing, but it's much easier to make progress with children than to change an adult's mindset. This is especially maddening with village women, who could certainly benefit from occasionally breaking with tradition. I realise this is easier said than done. Even I sometimes catch myself unthinkingly imitating my mother, and have to make a conscious effort not to spoil Pericles any more than his mother already has.

You'll be glad to hear that Eleni has finally thrown out her obnoxious brother, though only after she caught him pawing her daughter. She sent him to live behind the blacksmith's shop, but now worries about his getting bitten by rats, his not being able to look after himself, etc. Imagine: the man had no compunctions about abusing her trust, and she sits there, feeling sorry for him! After all these years, I am still astonished at the things women are willing to put up with. Last week, a sixteen-year-old girl threatened to take poison if her father forced her to marry a man twenty-two years her senior. He insisted she was just bluffing, though a Petra girl had poisoned herself under similar circumstances only two years ago. I reminded the father of that tragedy and he finally agreed to think it over. My success rate is not nearly as high as I'd like it to be. Several of the girls in my study groups complain that their own mothers treat them like slaves while their brothers sit playing cards or backgammon. So, you see, women themselves perpetuate the problem. I can't tell you how proud I am that I taught Aristides to help me around the house, exactly as I did Athena.

But now that Aristides is at university, I see him only in the summer, and, briefly, at Christmas and Easter. He has a girlfriend (ironically, one from a prominent Right-wing family) and seems to be flourishing, studying architecture like his sister, but suddenly talking about the possibility of some day going into politics. He has always been interested in social issues, though I can't imagine such a high-minded person entering politics without having his spirit crushed. But what young man has ever listened to his *nona*? He is still young enough to think he can change the world.

Political change is very slow, but at least the Marshall Plan is helping our economy recover. We finally have a paved road. It now takes only an hour to get to the capital by motorcar. This will make our lives much easier, especially in cases of medical emergency. Last month, a local woman set a precedent by giving birth at Mytilene Hospital, albeit only because her cousin had recently had 'a blue baby'.

Finally, some good news: Eli's eldest daughter works at a prestigious architectural firm in Athens, the second is expecting another child, and the youngest, who has been helping me at the *kentro*, seems to be keen on our new doctor. I am hard at work on Umbreit's novel. The Greek publisher liked the extract I'd done, so I took a deep breath and signed a translation contract under my maiden name. I am going to be using Adham from now on because that's who I feel I am. The work, though slow, is immensely satisfying. Umbreit is thinking of a Greek trilogy and is planning to come back to Greece to pursue research in the Peloponnese. For obvious reasons, he won't come to Molyvos, but I may see him when I go to Athens in spring. The publisher wants to meet me, and I am looking forward to it, though I have mixed feelings about seeing Umbreit after all this time. As for seeing you, I can only reiterate my invitation. I understand your situation, but still hope you will find it possible to come one of these days. Until then, *bon anniversaire*! I hope my gift will give you years of pleasure.

Yours,

Calliope

~ 2 ~

There are many ways to break a man, but at Makronisos, the most dreaded torture of all had been inspired by an ancient punishment once reserved for adulterous women. Pericles himself had never personally experienced the barbaric treatment, but one day he told Calliope about an uncooperative Communist leader who had been stuffed into a sack with two cats, then dumped in the sea, ostensibly to be drowned.

'Just imagine this . . . imagine the sack beginning to sink to the bottom of the sea, the crazed cats scratching every which way, the poor bastard trying to breathe, to protect his eyes, even as he feels himself beginning to drown. But, at the last possible moment, a reprieve! The sack is hauled out of the sea, the hissing cats are released, and the prisoner, streaming with blood, is given the Declaration of Repentance and asked to sign. Would you or wouldn't you?'

The question had come up in the wake of a philosophical argument over the definition of heroism. Perhaps because he hadn't experienced it personally, Pericles never attempted to write about this particular torture until one day, as he sat reading a letter from a former cellmate, one of Calliope's cats leaped into his lap. And it was at that moment, as he felt the cat's claws dig into his flesh, as he tried to slap the six-toed Tigris off his thighs, that Pericles suddenly reached for his notebook. He had the first stanza within half an hour but, a day later, was still grappling with the second, stopping every now and then to shoot a baleful glance towards Calliope.

Calliope ignored Pericles's black looks. She went on putting the kitchen in order, driven by manic energy. She always knew when her *periodos* was coming on: it was the only time she approached domestic chores without her habitual reluctance.

Pericles rose to get a glass of water. Despite his generally superb concentration, he had been restless all day, pacing the floor, scratching his head, shooing the cats away. He drank the water in silence, then fell into a chair, his lips hardening with fresh resolve. He had rather thin lips, which looked as stern as a monk's, except when he was amused. His smile, then, was as sublime as it had been in childhood. When he smiled, Calliope felt she could forgive Pericles almost anything.

He was not smiling now. When the poem continued to elude him, Pericles sprang to his feet, crumpled the sheet of paper, and tossed it into the kitchen hearth. The fire shot out a few surprised sparks, then blazed on, making hissing sounds. When Calliope failed to react, Pericles wheeled about, gave his trousers a nervous little hitch, and finally spoke.

'How long will you be gone?'

Some twenty-four hours earlier, she had informed him that she was going to meet Lorenz Umbreit in Athens, but Pericles hadn't asked any questions then; had merely withdrawn into himself, nursing his grievance in silence.

'About a week,' Calliope said, going on with her cleaning.

He stood regarding her, eyes agleam with irony. 'What are you going to do, take your German friend to the Acropolis? Show him where the swastika used to fly?'

Calliope went on working. 'I doubt it. I might go with Aristides, though.' She spoke casually, wiping the glass jars with unprecedented diligence.

'Is his wife coming?'

'Umbreit's wife? I doubt it.' She stopped to think it over. 'I really don't know.'

'Why wouldn't she come with him?'

'I didn't say she wasn't. I said I didn't know.' Calliope sighed. 'He's coming to do research. It's not a holiday.'

'So why does he want to see you?'

'Oh, for God's sake!' she finally erupted. 'I'm translating his book, remember? I have a long list of things I need to review with him.' She glanced at him balefully. 'You, of all people, should understand!'

'Will you be going with him?'

'To the Peloponnese? Don't be ridiculous! I'm going to see him in Athens, at some restaurant. We're supposed to have lunch with the publisher.'

'The publisher,' Pericles echoed. He was silent for a moment. 'I want you to know I'm not at all happy about this,' he finally said. 'I don't like you going alone to Athens, publisher or no publisher.'

She glanced up, feeling her eyelids flicker. 'Well,' she said, 'I'm going anyway.'

He went on eyeing her sullenly. 'Does it mean nothing to you that this makes me profoundly unhappy? I haven't been able to write a single stanza today!'

'You'll get over it.'

At this, Pericles raked his hand through his hair and let it stand stiffly, like a cockscomb. 'If I were your husband, I would stop you from going,' he said.

'There you are then. I always knew marriage was not for me.'

'You turn everything into a joke,' he said, 'but the truth is—'

'The truth is I wasn't joking,' she interposed. 'Why should I need your permission to go to Athens? Did you ask my permission when you had to go?'

'I wasn't going for a tête-à-tête with another woman, was I?'

'How would I know what you were or weren't going to do in Athens? Did I ever question you?' She stopped and passed her forearm across her forehead. 'For all I know, you spent every night with your adoring little nurse.'

Pericles blew into his cheeks, watching Tigris chase a cricket across the kitchen floor. The insect scuttled under the hutch and Tigris kept slapping at the wooden edge with his fat paw. 'Just tell me this,' Pericles said at length. 'Was there anything to the rumour about the two of you?'

'Which particular rumour's that?' Calliope asked the question in a breezy tone, but suddenly stopped, replaced the sugar jar, and inhaled deeply. 'Look . . .' She spoke with an air of determined patience. 'I'm doing my best not to lose my temper. I know you're jealous. I know you can't help it, but—'

'I'm not jealous!' he interjected. 'I just don't like my woman gallivanting all over Athens with a former Nazi!'

'So that's what this is all about – patriotism?'

'Among other things. Do you know any man who would let his woman—'

'I'm not *your woman*!' Calliope snapped. She regarded him for a moment. 'Look. Why can't you understand? That's one of the reasons I never wanted to marry. I can't bear anyone telling me what to do!'

Pericles detached himself from the table and went to wash the coffee cup, as she had trained him to. He rinsed it and set it on the counter. 'Would you have gone if Dhaniel had forbidden it?'

'Eli wouldn't have dreamed of dictating to me!' she said, then found herself wondering whether this was true. 'But, yes, I would have gone anyway.'

Pericles weighed this for a moment, then sidled up to her and placed a hand over her breast. 'You're so beautiful,' he muttered in her ear. 'I can't bear . . .' He stopped; she had extricated herself from his arms, reaching for a candlestick. 'So now you don't even want me to touch you.' He sounded like an aggrieved adolescent.

'Not when you're trying to manipulate me.'

'Manipulate you!' he said. 'You talk as if I never touched you except to manipulate you.'

She let out a little puff of exasperation. 'Have I ever told you how much I hate it when you shout at me?'

'Was I shouting?' He glared at her for a moment, threw his palms in the air, then whipped around and stood staring at a trapped fly beating against the window. Tigris had been joined by one-eared Loula, who was assiduously licking his underside. 'Funny how there are all these things you suddenly don't like about me,' Pericles said. 'Do you even like my poetry?'

'I think your poetry is sublime.'

'But?'

'But right now you're behaving like a bully.'

'A bully? *Me?*' Having been bullied in his childhood, Pericles liked to think of other men as the bullies. Calliope went on calmly picking wax out of the candlestick.

'Would you be happier if I'd compared you to a child having a temper tantrum?'

He regarded her with steely eyes, something new flickering in his face. 'I would be happier if you could stay home and behave like a decent woman,' he finally said.

'What did you say?' she hissed, rounding on him at last.

'You heard me.'

'Well, now you hear me! I'm not only going to Athens, I'm going to do whatever pleases me! And if that includes jumping into bed with a German, then that—' *That is what I'm going to do*, she was about to say. She knew she was taunting him – of course she knew it. And yet, when Pericles reached out and slapped her face, Calliope's mouth shaped itself into a small oval of mute amazement.

The surprise lasted no more than a moment; just long enough for the memory of Iason's slap to go hissing through her brain. Then, as if of its own accord, Calliope's right hand flew out and slapped Pericles right back, on his sharp, visibly pulsing jaw. She stood trembling with rage, thinking: *You're just like your brother!* Thinking: *I swore no man would ever lay a hand on me again. I swore it!*

But these thoughts remained unvoiced. 'Get out,' Calliope said quietly. She was striving for composure, but flared up when Pericles showed no sign of budging. 'Go!' she shouted. 'Go back to your mother! Tell her she was right all along!'

She waited, pointing towards the garden, until at last Pericles roused himself, shot her an embittered glance, and strode towards the exit. Loula stopped licking Tigris and twisted her head to watch him go out. The buzzing fly abandoned the windowpane and hastened to flit towards the fresh air. Out on the street, an old man could be heard climbing towards home, banging his cane from one step to another, tap, tap, tap, all the way up to St Kyriaki.

— 3 —

He had brought her gifts: an exquisite sculpture of a nightingale, as well as an illustrated 1904 edition of *Madame Bovary*. The first he had bought in Venice, the second in Paris, where, passing a Left Bank stall, he'd suddenly recalled Calliope's wartime longing to read Gustave Flaubert.

Calliope had hoped to avoid speaking of the Occupation, but Titos Stamoulis, the publisher, had brought up the subject at lunch, albeit only in connection with Umbreit's novel. To judge by the tenor of the conversation, by her own outward composure, they might have been discussing *War and Peace*; the woman to whom Umbreit's novel was dedicated might have been a stranger, known only to the author.

The lunch had taken place at the Grande Bretagne, where Lorenz Umbreit was staying, and in whose emptying dining room he and Calliope lingered after Stamoulis left, planning to go over the passages she had copied for consultation. But then, just as she was about to reach for her notebook, Umbreit took out his gifts and they became engaged in a literary discussion that had nothing to do with the work in progress. Calliope had read *Madame Bovary* soon after the end of the war but, she was soon telling Lorenz Umbreit, it was still resonating with her.

'Sometimes I think that if it hadn't been for the war, if Iason hadn't died in Albania, I might have easily become a Greek Madame Bovary.'

It was something she had occasionally pondered over the years but the statement only made Lorenz Umbreit smile. He was now approaching his mid-forties. His hairline was beginning to recede, his cheekbones were less prominent, but his gaze, his voice, penetrated Calliope's body like an all-but-forgotten refrain. He was shaking his head slowly, smiling a little. 'Emma Bovary was a foolish, frivolous woman—'

'Ah, but don't you remember? You yourself said I was a sentimental soul.' *Eine sentimentale Seele.* Calliope shook a cigarette out of a dwindling pack, but he beat her to the matches, something that Eli, too, was wont to do. It still made her feel like someone very young, who could not be trusted with a box of matches.

'There were some crucial facts I didn't have when I made that statement,' he was saying. She supposed he must be alluding to her Resistance activities.

'And yet,' she mused out loud, 'you were not altogether wrong.' True, she conceded, she had never shared Emma Bovary's longing for glamour and luxury. 'But when I read the novel, I suddenly remembered my father cautioning me against confusing novels with real life.'

He smiled. 'I suppose one could read *Madame Bovary* as a cautionary novel about the danger of reading novels.'

'Indeed.' She took a drag on her cigarette, waiting for a clanking tram to go by. 'Speaking of novels,' she said, 'did you ever find the time to read *Steppenwolf*?'

Of course he had. He smiled at her sadly, watching her tuck a strand of hair behind her ear. She saw him take in her earrings, round garnet jewels that had belonged to her mother and that she had put on to match her new suit. He was still interested in everything, still absorbing everything. Was that something novelists did? Calliope thought of her late husband, who would have had to be shaken to notice anything that did not have a profit potential.

She said, 'Iason was nothing like Charles Bovary, but I did feel trapped in my marriage, just like Emma. Not just the marriage, the whole social milieu, with its stupidities, its brutalities.' She waved away a puff of smoke but might have been thought to be dismissing her own youthful folly.

Umbreit looked thoughtful. 'Madame Bovary and you might have a thing or two in common,' he said, 'but she totally lacks any of your virtues.'

Calliope smiled vaguely, casting about for a response that might dispel any impression of false modesty. 'I could never decide how we're meant to feel about Emma Bovary,' she stated at length. 'Flaubert himself seems ambivalent, doesn't he?'

'As he was about himself. Did you know he wrote the book for a dare?'

'Did he really?'

'His friends challenged him to write a novel set in a dreary place, inhabited by dull characters, and still make it interesting.'

She laughed. 'I thought the novel was inspired by someone Flaubert knew.'

'Someone they all knew – a former classmate, I believe. It was his friends who urged Flabuert to dramatise the poor sod's story.'

Calliope chuckled. 'Trust genius to turn dross to gold.'

Umbreit called for more coffee. He drank too much of it these days, he confided, though he had given up smoking during a bout of bronchitis. Calliope tapped her cigarette into the ashtray, her eyes idly trailing a passing waiter.

'So you really think you've changed, do you?' Umbreit was saying. He seemed vaguely amused, but also a little wistful.

'I know I have.' She glanced at him, then looked away, thoughtful. 'I think my mother was right all along,' she said at length. 'I was – before the war, before I met you – a spoiled, self-centred girl afflicted with excess imagination.'

He chuckled at that. 'Afflicted?'

'Well . . .' She half-smiled. 'Obviously, it's not an affliction if you're a novelist, but I think . . . I think I used to spend more time inside my head than I did—'

He did not let her finish. 'It's hardly your fault that you were born where you didn't belong,' he stated.

'That's true,' she allowed, 'I didn't. Maybe I still don't, but . . .' She shrugged, unable to find the words that would convey what she saw as a profound inner transformation. How do you squeeze over a decade into one succinct statement?

Umbreit was watching her closely. 'Do you know Adorno, the philosopher?'

She did not.

Theodor Adorno, said Umbreit, was a German social philosopher. 'He wrote something you might think about: "The highest form of morality is not to feel at home in one's own home."'

Calliope pondered this, making a mental note to look for Adorno's books. She would probably like him better than Nietzsche, she told Lorenz Umbreit. 'If only because he seems to vindicate my own questionable conduct.'

The statement, or perhaps her smile, elicited another wistful chuckle. 'You're too hard on yourself,' Umbreit said as the waiter returned, bearing their coffee. 'Much harder than Flaubert would have been.'

'You think so?'

'You always were,' Umbreit went on. 'You may have been a little naive when you were young, but then, we all were.' He brushed his flaxen hair off his brow. It was the closest he would come to speaking of his own monumental error. 'Anyway, you sound happier with your lot these days – judging from your letters.'

Calliope stared into her steaming coffee. 'I'm not *un*happy. I think happiness is often a matter of simply accepting your destiny,' she said.

He gazed at her with unabashed affection, like a tired but doting godfather.

'Still grappling with destiny, I see.'

'No . . . not really. I think I've just about arrived at the point when I'm ready for total surrender.' She looked up and grinned, stubbing out her cigarette.

'Some surrender,' he said.

'What do you mean? Don't you think—'

'I believe you've found your own way of turning dross to gold.'

'Thank you!'

He smiled at her, but with such exquisite sadness that, all at once, she was desperate to get off the personal path he seemed bent on pursuing.

'Just don't get me started on the *kentro*,' she said, 'or we'll never get around to discussing your book.'

324

'I thought we talked quite enough about my book over lunch,' he said.

'Oh, no, no, no!' She shook herself, as if recalling the purpose of this congenial tête-à-tête. She reached for her bag, glancing up as a Dutch couple went by: a bald man wearing a natty grey suit and saddle shoes, and a fair-haired woman with round, laughing eyes, as blue as a child's marbles. The woman wore a pastel-blue outfit and a hat with a bunch of artificial cherries. Under the hat, yellow curls were visible, framing the pretty face. It flashed on Calliope that Umbreit's wife might resemble this sort of woman, but all she knew was her name: Alicia. Umbreit had wanted to come to Greece before Christmas, but Alicia reminded him that his sons were in a school play. He did most of his writing in the summer, but was looking forward to his sabbatical next year. The current, exploratory trip was taking place during an Easter break. Stamoulis had found an interpreter who would drive him to the Peloponnese.

'Where exactly are you going?' Calliope asked, toying with her pen.

'Kalavryta. I was stationed there before I got transferred to Lesbos.' Umbreit hesitated, then relented, saying that the plot of his second novel had been inspired by historic events in the Peloponnese, but also by the wartime execution of Makris, Petra's schoolmaster. All he needed right now was a few days to poke around town. He planned to be back towards the end of summer.

'As for your questions . . .' He glanced at his watch. 'How would you feel about discussing them over dinner? We could both rest for a few hours, then—'

'I'm sorry—' Calliope began to apologise but he quickly waved it away, as if he couldn't bear to listen to banal excuses. 'I'm expected at my godson's house around eight,' she said all the same. She was not only seeing Aristides but meeting his mother's relatives. She had a sudden, fleeting vision of the young Umbreit urging her to take the Nietzsche book she had just declined with a lame excuse. For some reason, it seemed imperative that he know she was being perfectly truthful. 'I would be happy to have dinner with you,' she said, 'but I honestly can't . . . there are other people involved.'

He gazed at her for a moment. 'How about tomorrow then?' he asked, as if testing her sincerity. 'I was planning to go to the Acropolis, but I can do that in the morning. You can even come with me, if you like . . . we could have lunch somewhere. I promise to answer all your questions.' He sat watching her closely. 'I really am very tired right now,' he added, faintly apologetic. He had flown in early that morning; had been talking nonstop all day. 'Please say yes.' He smiled disarmingly. 'I was also hoping to see the changing of the guard at the parliament. I'm told it's on at eleven?'

'That sounds about right.' Calliope had last seen the *Evzones* in Iason's company. The parliament building had still been the Royal Palace then. They had watched the ceremony, then found themselves embroiled in a fierce argument over the monarchy. 'All right.' She smiled, a little distractedly.

Umbreit's own smile was radiant. She had almost forgotten how, years ago, his smile had seemed to her like a precious gift. 'Shall I come to fetch you?' he asked.

It wasn't necessary: her hotel was within walking distance. Calliope slipped her notebook and cigarettes into her leather bag. The parliament was just across the street from the Grande Bretagne. 'I could meet you here around ten-thirty?'

'Splendid!' He beamed at her, motioning to the waiter.

He had lost some of his wartime gravitas. Was he a happier man? Calliope rather missed his former self, though she knew that beneath the buoyant exterior the wartime experience went on lurking, a capricious beast making its presence known at unpredictable intervals. So there was, she sensed, something not entirely authentic about Umbreit's new cheer, something that had more to do with manly resolve than with inner peace.

She had gradually become aware of the urban rumble outside the landmark hotel. Did Umbreit know that the Grande Bretagne had been the Nazis' headquarters during the Occupation? she wondered. He must know, she decided, letting her eyes range over the glittering chandeliers, the sumptuously curtained windows.

It was going on six o'clock. A warm amber light was sifting in through the glass panes. The waiter shuffled away, hastening to greet two heavyset men who had just materialised at the entrance. In the corner, the Dutchman said something to his pert companion, who threw back her head and laughed.

Calliope lowered her eyes, warding off a mental picture of Alicia Umbreit, laughing at one of her husband's jokes.

~ 4 ~

Lorenz Umbreit had left the Grande Bretagne's dining room and was crossing the marble-floored lobby to greet Calliope. It was Sunday morning, the first day of April. A cluster of Italians had just trooped in, prattling in front of the reception desk. In the distance, church bells began to peal. It was not yet Easter for Orthodox Greeks, but it was for Lorenz Umbreit.

'*Frohe Ostern!*' Calliope shook his hand, wishing him a Happy Easter.

'I almost said, the same to you.' He smiled back, stepping aside to let a porter pass. 'Alas, I won't be here to say *Christos anesti*!'

'You can always wish me a Happy Fool's Day,' she quipped.

'Of course! Happy Fool's Day,' he said, bowing very slightly.

'The same to you!' She laughed. 'Ready for the *Evzones*?'

'Ready! I promise not to play any Fool's Day pranks, but I make no such promises for the weather,' he said, gesturing towards the street. The day had started out warm and sunny, but now the sky was beginning to darken.

'I should have thought to bring my umbrella,' Calliope said, thinking out loud.

'*What?* See the Acropolis with umbrellas?' He laughed at the very thought, then stopped and glanced at his watch. 'Shall I run upstairs and get mine?'

It was ten-forty but there would be a crowd; they were just going across the street. 'You can always get it after the ceremony,' Calliope suggested. 'It only lasts fifteen or twenty minutes.'

'All right then. So, tell me about these *Evzones* of yours,' he said. They were waiting for a tram to go by.

Greeks, Calliope said, adored the *Evzones*, though they also liked to poke fun at their outlandish attire. The uniforms had been inspired by the garb of anti-Ottoman rebels during the War of Independence. 'They are called *Klephtes*.'

Calliope offered all this over the urban roar, but soon a traffic policeman's whistle brought the bustle to an abrupt stop, and a military band was heard, marching towards Syntagma Square. Then the *Evzones* themselves appeared, a theatrical parade of rifle-bearing men dressed in kilted tunics called *fustanellas* and red garrison caps with waist-long tassels swishing about like black horses' tails.

'In the summer,' said Calliope, 'the *fustanellas* are white and have four hundred pleats in them—'

'Four hundred!'

'One for every year of Ottoman rule.'

The *Evzones* were approaching the Tomb of the Unknown Soldier. They wore white stockings with black knee tassels, the flamboyantly kicking feet clad in riveted red clogs sporting black pompoms. There was a handful of foreigners, jostled by natives in their Sunday best, the children nibbling on chocolates and pink candy floss. Umbreit was taking photographs. His sons, he said, would be keen to see them.

As soon as the ceremony ended, they went to inspect the tomb.

The inscriptions surrounding the marble relief included quotations from Pericles's ancient funeral oration. Calliope translated, wrenching her mind away from the thought of Pericles Alexiou. She hadn't seen her young lover since their late-March quarrel.

Syntagma Square was where Athenians traditionally held their political demonstrations. It was where the first shots of the Civil War had been fired. Churchill had come to act as mediator and was almost assassinated during his short stay at the Grande Bretagne. A bomb had been placed in the hotel's sewer on Christmas Eve.

'But don't worry,' Calliope hastened to add. 'The only danger right now is our getting caught in a downpour.' They laughed. She pointed out that it didn't seem to be clearing up. They should probably go and get the umbrella after all.

Umbreit glanced at the sky, but he had just spotted an organ-grinder and his monkey on the corner and wanted to take a close-up. The gypsy was as tiny as a ten-year-old but had the wizened face of a crafty old man recalling some youthful prank. Calliope stood waiting. It proved impossible not to imagine Lorenz Umbreit back home, sharing the photographs with his family.

The gypsy was playing 'La Vie en Rose' when the monkey began to squeal. A pack of dogs was approaching the corner, trotting alongside the traffic with an air of singular purpose, as if anxious to arrive on time at some momentous rally. A plane was flying overhead. Calliope, who had not seen an aircraft since the Occupation, tilted her chin up, and at that moment, as if the shifting of her head had triggered some divine signal, the surly skies opened and rain began to pelt the strolling families, the organ-player and his monkey, the moss-green café awnings across the street.

Umbreit snapped his camera shut, shooting a quick glance towards the packed café. He gestured with his head. 'Back to the hotel?'

'Yes!' She began to laugh as they darted back, though the rain was starting to come down in sheets, sizzling down on the historic square.

Calliope entered the hotel lobby, plucking at her clinging georgette dress with one hand, mopping her streaming face with the other. Umbreit was fussing with his camera. He pushed his limp hair off his forehead. He glanced at Calliope, then looked away, casting about with his eyes, as if in search of inspiration. He gazed down at his own soaked shoes, then turned to look at hers.

'Mea culpa.' He sighed, looking undecided. 'If you like, we could go up to my room,' he finally said. 'I have a suite . . . I could perhaps . . .' He made a vague gesture suggesting the possibility of somehow drying up.

Calliope hesitated, but could think of no better alternative.

'We can see the Acropolis from my room,' he said and achieved a smile.

'In that case . . . I accept.'

He ushered her to the lifts and down the corridor, then unlocked the door to his suite and stepped back with an ironic little bow. She remembered the mock bow; was beginning to remember other things she had forgotten over the years.

She slid past him, nibbling on her thumb like a schoolgirl. There was the scent of fresh freesias and, faintly, of furniture wax.

All at once, he grew as brisk as he had been in uniform, hastening to point out the bathroom, offer his dressing gown. He picked a large towel for himself, then left her alone, striding towards the bedroom.

Clutching gown and handbag, Calliope stepped into the marbled bathroom, marvelling at the opulence. She pulled off her sodden shoes, quickly rolled off her stockings, then unbuttoned her clinging dress, hanging it to dry over a towel rack. Her bra, too, was damp. She hesitated but finally removed it and hung it up as well. It seemed somehow disingenuous to feel so ill at ease in the room of a man she had been intimate with; a man whose unborn child she had once carried.

It was pleasantly warm in the bathroom. Calliope mopped herself thoroughly, then struggled into the paisley dressing gown, snuffing the faint masculine scent. She combed her hair, then reapplied lipstick and powder, which she had only recently begun to use. Leaning into the mirror, she rolled her lips together, tightened the belt on the dressing gown, then stepped out of the bathroom, barefoot.

Lorenz Umbreit was seated on the edge of the sofa, opening a bottle of red Kalligas. He had changed into a fresh pair of trousers and a shirt with blue and dun-hued stripes, the colours of sand and sea. He glanced up and appraised her appearance briefly, with a vaguely humorous spark in his eyes but with no comment.

'Stamoulis arranged this to welcome me,' he said, pouring out the wine. She accepted a glass, then went to stand over by the window.

Only the back of the Parthenon could be seen from this vantage point, though construction laws dictated that the Acropolis be visible from anywhere in the capital. 'Too bad they couldn't come up with a law governing the weather,' Calliope quipped.

Lorenz laughed, watching her settle into a blue wing chair. She set her glass down on the coffee table and took out her notebook.

She crossed her legs; she carefully adjusted the silky gown over her knees, groping for a modicum of professional dignity. Her hair was still damp, curling loosely just above her shoulders.

She had several questions stemming from her imperfect knowledge of German; other passages she judged to be deliberately ambiguous. She wanted to ensure that she had not misunderstood his intentions. When she read the copied passages out loud, he smiled a little, as if the sound of his own words issuing out of her mouth both delighted and slightly embarrassed him. She asked a question that had to do with his protagonist's state of mind. When he said *konfus*, did he mean confused or bewildered?

Lorenz Umbreit answered her questions, interjecting an occasional comment. They sipped wine. They exchanged thoughts on the German text. She had several pages of scribbled notes, but it took less than two hours to review them all. Halfway through their discussion, he stopped to ask whether he might call room service and order lunch. Once more she hesitated; once more she agreed.

The decision seemed perfectly reasonable until, looking up from her notebook, watching Umbreit speak into the phone, Calliope inwardly acknowledged a flash of lust. She hastened to quell it by setting the wineglass down and padding back to the dismal windows. She had meant to buy cigarettes but the rain had thwarted all their plans. *What are you going to do, take your German friend to the Acropolis? Show him where the swastika used to fly?*

She was still resisting Pericles's echoing words when Lorenz Umbreit replaced the receiver and sat down again, tugging at his trousers. By the time lunch arrived, all her questions had been answered, but the rain showed no sign of abating. They could hear it pattering on the balcony, muting the urban rumble. The suite was well heated and, what with the good food and the wine, the awkwardness of the situation gradually dissipated. They began to talk about personal matters. She told him about her mother's death, which still haunted her. Umbreit's mother had also died tragically, a year after hearing that her youngest son had been killed on the Eastern front. When she first learned the news, he said, his mother went instantly blind and never recovered.

'The news of his death made her go blind?'

'It's a hysterical syndrome.' Umbreit sighed. Some people regain their sight; his mother never did. There was, he thought, something sadly symbolic about it all. 'She died believing in the Führer . . . died, I sometimes think, because she could not bear to accept the truth.'

Calliope reflected that the same might be said of Eli Dhaniel, a thought she soon found herself sharing with Umbreit.

And then they both fell silent, sipping coffee, staring at the waning afternoon. She told him freesias were her favourite flowers; he said the Kalligas was the best he'd had. They talked, then, about the Civil War, the *kentro*, Pericles's blossoming career. Umbreit must have gathered she had lived with the doctor, and perhaps guessed about Pericles as well. The longer they talked, the more vividly she recalled the feeling he had always given her: of seeing more, knowing more, than seemed humanly possible.

It became impossible, at a certain point, not to be aware that she hadn't asked a single question about his family. It seemed rude not to do so as they sat there, surrounded by the cocooning silence, the cease-less pulsing of rain.

'Do you have a photograph of your family?' Calliope smiled across the coffee table like a polite stranger, but instantly regretted her ques-tion. She had, she would eventually admit to herself, spoken from a desperate need to subdue her aroused senses. She should not have drunk so much; should have perhaps not eaten so much either. The salads and *spanakopita* had been delicious, but there was no denying the slight nausea tugging at her stomach.

He was holding out a Christmas snapshot of a remarkably hand-some family: a smiling, blond man and his two young sons, seated in front of a blazing fire. Both boys were as fair as their father, but the mother was as dark as a Greek. Alicia. Calliope studied Umbreit's wife, contemplating the fact that she bore no resemblance whatsoever to the Dutchwoman in the dining room. If there was anyone she resembled, it was Calliope herself. With a suffocating feeling, she took in the dark, curly hair, the wide smile, the steady, forthright gaze. *Ach, Thee mou.*

Calliope knew that she, too, should smile at this point; should offer the usual banal commentary. But even as the thought flitted through her mind, her throat was beginning to feel constricted. She couldn't bring herself to utter a single word. At last, she raised her gaze and looked into his eyes, still unable to rally the requisite politesse.

He did not flinch before her scrutiny. '*The heart has its reasons, which reason does not understand*,' he said, quoting Pascal with a minimal shrug. He went on regarding her wistfully, his long hands resting on his knees. Something about this pose made an odd image float through Calliope's mind: Lorenz Umbreit as an old man, seated in a rocking chair, his variegated hands on his knees, staring into the fire. It was then she found herself telling him about her wartime miscarriage.

'I lost the child soon after you and Reis left,' she said and averted her gaze. 'I didn't even know – not until much later.'

At last, it was out. But then, as if in response to the mention of pregnancy, Calliope felt her tongue thicken. Lurching from her chair, she bolted to the bathroom, where she hunkered over the toilet, heaving and retching, her very teeth aching with unleashed grief. She knew he could hear her throwing up, yet he didn't come to the door as she feared he might.

Her stomach was empty now but the blood was still beating in her ears as she rinsed her mouth, applying some of his toothpaste with her finger, then dousing her face with water. I must leave, she thought frantically; must borrow an umbrella and return it later. Yes, she decided . . . yes.

She opened the bathroom door. She watched Lorenz turn away from the window and gaze at her across the darkening room with a complicated expression in which doubt and confusion and anguish were all evident. She felt a stab of pain but remained standing, pinioned by his gaze. A room-service cart went trundling down the long corridor. There was a knock on the adjacent door, the murmur of voices.

She was about to speak, intending to say something about leaving, when he paused for the briefest moment, then took a brisk step forward. He was holding out his hands, like a supplicant before an unexpectedly opening door. Calliope's own hand was resting over her breast, in a gesture unconsciously mimicking her mother but merely intended to placate the unruly beating in her chest. There being no laws to govern the weather, the rain went on falling, as if it might never cease.

~ 5 ~

It was her own scream that woke Calliope on Monday morning – the scream and the dream that had generated it and that left her heart pounding as wildly as it surely would have if she had indeed been in Makronisos, about to be dumped into the sea with a pack of crazed cats.

The scream had woken Lorenz as well, though barely five minutes before the requested wake-up call. Another sixty-five minutes and she would be alone in an alien bed, her heart no longer beating in terror but already resigned to pain.

'It's all right.' He was cradling her in his arms, making soothing noises in her ear. 'It was just a dream.'

'I know.'

He glanced at his watch. It was nearly six o'clock.

'I'm being picked up in an hour.' He went on stroking her hair.

'I know.'

He drew back a little and scanned her sleep-rimmed eyes. 'Would you like to have breakfast with me?'

She shook her head. The rain had stopped sometime in the night.

'We could have it here if you like,' he said.

'Thank you.' She averted her eyes. 'No.'

'Are you sure you won't come to Kalavryta?' he asked, not for the first time.

She was sure, though already she could feel his absence, his body beginning to drift away from her. It was a body whose natural movements had always suggested purpose; not a single gesture was ever allowed to be wasted. Even now, in peacetime, this was a man of prudence, efficiency, foresight. That she was the one person for whom circumspection had been cast to the wind somehow seemed humbling.

She lay watching him stride towards the bathroom. No matter that he was reluctant. No matter that he would have preferred to take her in his arms and stay. She knew this was so; had never known anything with greater certainty. But there was a shower to be taken and teeth to be brushed, and all the other rituals he presumably performed at home – a place she still couldn't imagine, trespasser that she was. A chauffeured car would be waiting for him at seven o'clock. She would leave the Grande Bretagne alone, making her way slowly through the kingdom of the damned.

'Why don't you go back to sleep?' he was soon asking, getting into his trousers while she lay watching him drowsily. 'I'll be back on Friday,' he added.

'Shall I stay in bed until then?' She almost smiled.

'Why not?' A grin was accomplished. He leaned over her and put his lips on hers. 'Friday night at eight,' he stated decisively.

Well, he was German after all. Not having been raised on steady doses of Greek mythology, he would make no allowances for divine caprice. He would be ready as planned; would leave Kalavryta on Friday, knowing how long the trip would take but never stopping to consider the possibility of hailstorms, stalled engines, road accidents.

'Will you be here?' he asked, sitting next to her when it was finally time to go.

'I'll be here.'

For the moment, she, too, had forgotten all about prankish gods.

～ 6 ～

The message was waiting for her at the Attikon: 'Please phone Molyvos mayor as soon as possible. Important.'

The mayor! She had left the Attikon's number with Mathaios in case something unexpected came up at the *kentro*. And something apparently had, though it took an agonising hour for the operator to put the call through. Only then did Calliope learn that the news concerned the late baker's youngest daughter, who had just eloped.

'Marika! I don't believe it!' Calliope lowered herself to the edge of the bed, recalling a note the distraught girl had written her, pleading for support. She had been in virtual house arrest after her mother got wind of the rumours about the fortress restorer. But the rumours were unfounded, Marika had told Calliope. All she had ever done with the stranger was talk. She begged to be allowed to attend the study sessions at the *kentro*, and Calliope managed to extract Elektra's consent. As a child, Marika had been a bit of a goody-two-shoes; she had also been bright and diligent, never skipping school even after the bakery had burned down and classmates became cruel.

All this began to taunt Calliope as soon as she understood what had happened back home. 'Don't tell me she was supposed to be at the *kentro* when—'

'No.' Mathaios cleared his throat. 'No. They eloped on Saturday night.' The firm engaged to restore the fortress was Athenian, but Marika's young man had turned out to be a fisherman's son from nearby Chios.

'Ach, *Panaghia mou* . . . poor Elektra,' Calliope muttered. It was impossible not to pity the late baker's widow, but why was Mathaios calling her?

'It's Elektra. She went crazy when she found Marika's bed empty.'

'Well, can you blame her? After—'

'No, I mean really crazy. There's talk of having her sent to Daphni.'

'Daphni!' Calliope gripped the receiver, visions of the notorious asylum flashing across her brain. 'What did she do?'

At first, after everyone had left the *kentro*, all she'd done was throw stones at the windows, but this had apparently failed to provide adequate relief, so, possibly inspired by the torching of her husband's bakery, Elektra set fire to the *kentro*.

'The *kentro*! Why the *kentro*? Didn't you just say it was Saturday night?'

Mathaios sighed into the telephone. 'She kept saying it was your fault, putting notions into the girls' heads.'

'Notions,' Calliope muttered chaotically. 'How bad is it?' she finally brought out, breaking the crackling silence.

'Well, it's a stone house . . . she couldn't burn it down—'

'But?'

'Well, there's damage, naturally.'

There was a long silence as Calliope sat contemplating her options. 'Is there a ferry today – do you know?'

'There's an overnight one leaving at four.'

She glanced at her watch. 'I'll see you tomorrow morning,' she said decisively.

She went downstairs and had a quick breakfast, then sat down to write a note to Lorenz Umbreit. She would drop it off at his hotel on her way to Piraeus. That, it seemed, was what the fickle deities wanted. That was what she was meant to do.

2 April 1956

Dear Lorenz,

You may think this a ploy on my part, but I give you my word of honour: it isn't. A village woman set fire to the *kentro* yesterday, all because I wouldn't stop sticking my nose in other people's affairs. I have thought of myself all this time as a women's advocate but it seems I am nothing but a meddlesome fool. I am beside myself with worry and must return to Molyvos at once. I'll write at greater length shortly, though I doubt I'll be back on Friday. Perhaps I should have taken a talisman when I left the village, or lit a candle to St Christopher. May he be with you on your way home, my dear. I hope your trip to Kalavryta went well and promise to write as soon as I can.

Yours,
Calliope

~ 7 ~

Excerpt from Calliope Adham's journal – 2 April 1956

It is almost sixteen hours since we said goodbye. I have started to write to him three times but have destroyed all three letters. For once in my life, I don't know what to say. I keep thinking he must regret what happened and who can blame him? I blame myself. I have, it seems, not changed as much as I liked to think. I may be forty-one but I am still the selfish girl polishing off a jar of cherry preserves. Wartime deprivation might have exculpated me, but what can I say to absolve myself now?

Nothing, except perhaps this: the force that keeps propelling me towards him is a blind force, a force of utter madness, beyond will or reason. How else can I explain ending up in bed with another woman's husband? I remember telling Elpida I would henceforth live by my own rules, but this is not what I had in mind. Never. That I have broken the golden rule makes my heart cower, the way Sappho used to do after gobbling up something forbidden but utterly irresistible.

And yet, there is anger – not, interestingly enough, towards Lorenz, but towards his wife, whom my wayward heart insists on regarding as the real usurper. Perversely, I keep trying to imagine him at home, with his family. Strange, but the thought of his making love to Alicia is less distressing than imagining him calling her name, caressing her cheek, laughing over dinner. I think of her, her indisputable entitlement, and the pain is scarcely describable. I imagine him bringing flowers for her birthday, kissing her neck while she stands at the stove. I imagine him calling her '*Liebling*' and I long for something my hands might pounce on and reduce to ashes.

And so, of course, I am to be punished. My punishment may be less drastic than being drowned with wild cats, but I can't help wondering whether a part of me did not know, on that last afternoon with Pericles, what might happen in Athens. Certainly, Pericles seemed to know. Could I have been lying to myself when I agreed to meet Lorenz?

I don't know the answer, but I now realise something I was not ready to admit to Eli, or even to myself. One reason I have always been reluctant to marry is the fear that people might be right about me; that I am more like a man than a woman, and might find it impossible to be monogamous. How can anyone, man or woman, promise to love another human being – love one and only one – forever?

I ask this question though I feel sure I will love Lorenz to the day I die. So am I really less foolish, less ludicrous, than Emma Bovary? Lorenz seemed amused by the comparison, but, sooner or later, love makes fools of us all, in literature as in life. Lorenz's middle name, it turns out, is Frederick, which apparently means 'peaceful ruler'. This was why he was reluctant to reveal it during the Occupation. He told me only after I'd spent the night with him, making me laugh when I wanted to cry.

I don't feel like laughing anymore. I feel as foolish as Madame Bovary and young Marika rolled into one. I feel I'll never be entitled to the comfort of my own skin. I don't know what to say, what to write to him.

'This is not the end,' he said to me, just before leaving the Grande Bretagne this morning. There was no time for questions, for explanations. Just as well, I suppose.

And so he went off to Kalavryta, leaving me to grope my way out of a place where I had never expected to find myself. Getting past curious chambermaids was a minor challenge, but I have somehow strayed into a dark labyrinth, which my soul must now stumble through blindly.

I pray that he loves me. I pray that he doesn't.

The fire that had devastated the *kentro*'s first floor spelled the end of the girls' study sessions. The primary-school children's tutorials would eventually resume, but the news of Marika's elopement brought about a permanent change in parental attitudes. It was as if, Calliope was to write Lorenz Umbreit, sending adolescent daughters to the *kentro* would expose them to some moral contagion; as if, sooner or later, they were all bound to elope, or do something equally rash.

By autumn, the library had reopened its doors; Elektra, mostly through Calliope's own efforts, had been discharged from the asylum and allowed to join her daughter in Chios. But Calliope herself was like some of the refugees from Asia Minor who couldn't stop lamenting the day on which Constantinople had fallen to the Turks. That the fire had taken place while she had lain in Lorenz's arms made the catastrophe seem, at first, like a cruel April Fool's prank, then like a message from some stern, punitive deity. Although many villagers had pitched in to help restore the *kentro*, there had also been those who could not help but express a smidgen of satisfaction.

'When the head gets too big it can't escape punches,' Calliope's aunt had overheard someone say.

The statement about putting notions into the girls' heads was what hurt the most. Over and over, Calliope reflected on how careful she'd been never to say anything that might encourage the girls to behave recklessly in their private lives. Even while reviewing the War of Independence, discussing the legendary Bouboulina, she had not so much as breathed a word about the Greek heroine's tempestuous love life. All for nothing! She was being blamed anyway.

At the searing height of her misery, the unfairness and ingratitude only served to intensify Calliope's yearning for Lorenz Umbreit. Repeatedly, she called on God without any expectation of being heard. Her heart lacerated by guilt, she resigned herself to small consolations: eloquent letters from Heidelberg, expressing solicitude, respect, understanding. Not trivial in themselves, they seemed so when examined in the resplendent light of relinquished love.

The inner struggle continued for months.

One day, against all reason, Calliope surrendered, agreeing to meet Lorenz Umbreit again. It was by then late October. He was back in Greece on his sabbatical, going on with the research for his second novel. He had finally talked Calliope into accompanying him to Kalavryta. She had, it seemed, not only abdicated thought but managed to silence the voice of a rather exigent conscience.

They decided to visit a famed historic site. This was where the 1821 revolt against the Ottomans had started; moreover, Kalavryta was the town where one of the worst German atrocities had taken place, back in 1943.

In December of that year, the Wehrmacht had torched the town, killing every male over fifteen – over a thousand men – in reprisal against Resistance activities. One of the first things Calliope had seen on arriving here was the clock on the town's cathedral, its hands fixed at two thirty-four, when the slaughter had started.

The hands of the clock had been arrested but not so Calliope's thoughts, which kept straying back to her own village under the Occupation. It was mid-afternoon and the Kalavryta hillside was deserted because of preparations for St Dimitrios's Feast.

'There's something I've been meaning to ask you,' Calliope said at length, turning to Lorenz. 'That day in Eftalou . . . the day you and Reis ran into my mother and me. What would you have done if you'd found out I was not carrying mustard greens in my basket but live ammunition?'

The question made Lorenz pause, eyes ranging over the Martyrs' Monument.

'But don't you see?' he finally said. 'I didn't look into your basket because I didn't want to know what you had in it.'

Calliope turned this over in her mind. 'Those bullets could have killed you,' she said after a while. 'Just one of them in a guerilla's gun and—'

'I suppose I was willing to take that chance.'

Calliope glanced at him. He had been prepared to die rather than have his suspicions confirmed, and have to arrest her in Alfred Reis's presence. The thought made something stir in her chest. Walking away from the monument, she suddenly stopped, rose on her tiptoes, and put her mouth to her lover's lips.

But all the while, her mind continued to wander. December 1943, just before Christmas, was when Rupert Ealing had been transported to Mytilene. At the time Lorenz Umbreit was stationed in the capital, but what if he had never been transferred away from Kalavryta? What if he had been ordered to set the town ablaze?

'What ever happened to Alfred Reis?' she suddenly asked.

'Reis?' He cast her a quick glance. 'Didn't you hear?'

'What?'

There was a heavy sigh, a moment's hesitation. 'Reis came to see Alkesti in Athens after the War, and her brother shot him.'

Calliope stopped dead in her tracks. 'Her brother—'

'You didn't know?' He looked fleetingly baffled, but then awareness dawned. 'It was right after the War. You were probably still convalescing.'

Another moment went by. 'What happened?'

'The brother found them in bed. He—'

Calliope's hand flew up. She did not want to hear any more.

'It's in my novel,' said Lorenz. 'You'll have to read it sooner or later.'

Calliope fell silent. So he had moved the Petra love affair to Kalavryta, raising the fictional stakes by setting the story around the destruction of a town, the slaughter of its entire male population.

All at once, Calliope felt herself starting to recoil, as she had after seeing newsreels of the Nazi death camps. A decade had passed since the end of the War, but the images had not yet lost their unnerving power.

Yet there she was, an erstwhile Resistance member, strolling through this blood-soaked landscape, arm in arm with a former Wehrmacht officer. They were heading back to the centre, towards one of the town's resurrected hotels. It was late October. They walked in silence, the grim facts flapping like bats over Calliope's head, as unsettling as the lurking thoughts of Lorenz's wife and children.

He had not spoken of them, except to say that he would be going back for his son's birthday, then returning to Greece after Christmas. It had been agreed that Calliope would act as his interpreter. She had led Molyviates to believe that she was in Athens, visiting Aristides and her cousin Grigoris. She had never thought of herself as a liar, let alone an adulteress. Yet there she was. There they both were, as if the rest of the world had simply ceased to exist.

Strolling through Kalavryta's centre, they stopped at a street stall and bought pomegranates to take back to the hotel. Lorenz loved pomegranates, possibly because he had never tasted one until he arrived in Greece. Calliope liked eating the seeds, but lacked the patience to extract them. She also disliked having her fingers stained.

'I'll peel them for you.' He smiled.

'You're going to spoil me,' Calliope said. They had let go of each other on entering the centre of town.

'You deserve to be spoiled.'

Back at the hotel, Calliope ran a hot bath, trying to silence her whispering mind. Soon, Lorenz came in, bearing a white bowl full of pomegranate seeds. He sat on the edge of the bathtub and began to pop the glittering gems into her open mouth. Calliope chewed on them slowly. She reached for a bar of soap.

'I feel like the abducted Persephone,' she said and smiled.

'Ha! I had exactly the same thought," Lorenz said, filling her mouth with more crimson seeds. 'Though I'm certainly no god of the under-world,' he added, his eyes crinkling while Calliope marvelled at how frequently their minds meandered in the same direction. She thought of Hades's love for Persephone; his consenting to see her for only three months a year, letting her spend the remaining nine on earth, where she clearly belonged.

Calliope did not belong in Kalavryta. This much she knew, and the knowledge had almost stopped her from keeping her Athenian rendez-vous. Leaving Molyvos, she had almost told the taxi driver to turn back, but then changed her mind, deciding to see Lorenz after all. Take the wind as she found it.

She was finding the wind predictably stormy, though she managed to keep the internal tumult to herself, as she had her wartime suffering all those years ago. There was some element of stubborn pride in both concealments, but also an as-yet-unexamined need to spare Umbreit unnecessary torment. She was careful not to touch on the future, not to ask any questions, least of all of herself.

All the same, when, after three weeks, it was time for Umbreit to leave, Calliope handed him a symbolic sprig of basil she had impul-sively plucked on his last evening in Athens. 'This will ensure your return,' she said, trying for a smile.

He gazed straight into her eyes. 'My return? No charms needed,' he said, smiling back sadly. He slipped the basil into his buttonhole, as one might a rose or a carnation. At the hotel, he placed it in a bathroom glass. The next morning, travelling to the airport, the sprig of basil was back on his lapel.

It was still there when he turned and waved to her just before boarding. Calliope waved back, wondering what he would do with the basil once he was back in Heidelberg.

No charms needed.

— 9 —

The Owl's Cry, the novel Umbreit had been researching in the Peloponnese, was scheduled to be released in Berlin in the spring of 1958. The Greek edition would not be published for another year. Calliope was still polishing the last segment of her translation.

She had brought the manuscript with her to Athens, where Lorenz was researching the third novel in his Aegean trilogy. The last one was to be set during the Civil War; that's all he would say about it. He had been spending hours at the National Archives, while Calliope sat in the shady courtyard, reading or revising. They had rented a furnished villa in suburban Glyfada, overlooking the sea. But that late-March morning – her last day in Athens – Calliope had gone into town to buy a pair of shoes, as well as half a dozen books to take back to Molyvos.

They'd had several clandestine meetings since that first reunion in Athens, but Lorenz was flying back to Germany the following day. Again. They had fallen asleep in each other's arms after a long swim and an excellent lunch at a nearby taverna. Yet Calliope had woken from her nap feeling vaguely disgruntled. Lorenz was still dozing, so she picked up one of the books she had purchased and began to read, only to find herself arrested by the music playing on Lorenz's transistor.

The broadcast was coming from Paris. Calliope lay perfectly still, listening to the querying lament, the mournful cellos, the exquisite soprano rising towards an impassioned crescendo. The aria made her heart tremble. It was not quite over when a neighbour's dog began to bark and Lorenz opened his eyes.

'What? What did you say?' he mumbled, rubbing his eyes.

'Oh, nothing. Just cursing the stupid dog.' Calliope sighed. 'I was listening to the radio . . . one of the most beautiful songs I've ever heard.'

'Hm.' Lorenz yawned. He wanted to know who the singer was.

'Victoria de los Angeles . . . the Aria Number Five from something called the *Bachianas Brasileiras*. Have you heard of it?'

'Hm. I don't think so. I'll try to find it when I get back home,' said Lorenz. He turned off the radio when the news came on, then reached out lazily and drew Calliope towards him. The book tumbled off the bed. 'What are you reading?'

'I'm rereading *Anna Karenina*,' Calliope said. 'In Greek. I read the French version when I was much too young.'

'How young?' Lorenz yawned again.

'Not quite sixteen,' she said. 'I was staying with my aunt and uncle in Mytilene, and there it was, on one of their library shelves. I filched it, and read it, and eventually replaced it. They never even noticed.'

Calliope chuckled, idly watching a spider crawl up the wall. She was still afraid of spiders, but this one was so frail its legs were like the filaments in a lightbulb.

'Would you like me to get rid of the spider?' Lorenz asked, a smile in his voice.

'Ach, let it be,' Calliope said. He had obviously traced her gaze, but it never failed to amaze her, the things he noticed, the things he remembered about her. She thought of the huge hairy spider she had recently found in her water closet at home; of how her neighbours laughed when she ran out in her bathrobe, begging someone to get rid of it. They wouldn't laugh if they could see her now, she thought with an inner sigh. Even her Parisian cousin was not likely to be amused.

A few minutes went by. Calliope lay meditating on the fact that people were far less judgmental about fictional characters' transgressions than they were about the men and women they knew in real life. She was, of course, thinking of Anna Karenina, but when she shared her thought with Lorenz, he only shrugged, smiling a little sadly.

'*Tout comprendre, c'est tout pardonner*, as Tolstoy said.'

'Buddha,' she said.

'Huh?'

'It was Buddha who said it, though I don't suppose he said it in French or in Russian.' She dimpled.

'I'm sure I read it in *War and Peace*,' he insisted.

'If so, Tolstoy stole it from Buddha, who I believe came first.' She glanced at him, still smiling, then leaned over to bestow a kiss.

'I'll check it when I get home,' he said.

'And if I'm right?'

'If you're right, I'll never doubt anything you say, as long as I live.'

She laughed, then grew thoughtful again. 'Anyway, I think there's more to it than you suggest . . . more than just authorial sympathy. I think people derive secret pleasure from fictional characters' moral lapses. They get a vicarious thrill from them. What they can't tolerate is the thought that their friends and neighbours might be leading more exciting lives than they are.'

Lorenz laughed. 'You may be right,' he said. He consulted his watch as he spoke and the small gesture irked Calliope. He seemed to be obsessed with time; *she* always seemed to be quarrelsome before his departures. She imagined Lorenz in Heidelberg: reading the morning paper over breakfast, getting rid of a house insect, kissing his wife goodbye. She had never known self-loathing before but, oh, she knew it now!

'I've always thought of myself as rather high-minded,' she suddenly said, thinking out loud. 'I suppose I must have wanted to be.'

'You *are* high-minded,' he said. 'But, well, life can be a humbling experience.'

'Yes, indeed!' She paused and mulled it over for a moment or two. 'And I'll admit it: I *was* arrogant . . . maybe I needed to be humbled,' she added distractedly. She went on pondering his words. 'When you think about it, though, there's no point in being humbled if you haven't learned anything from it, is there?'

Lorenz ran his hand through his hair but said nothing. It was getting dark.

'All I seem to have learned is that guilt is cheap,' she said after a long silence. 'A cheap ticket to self-absolution.'

'Ah, I think you spent too much time with *Papa* Emanouil,' said Lorenz, trying for a lighter tone.

She ignored the comment, still thinking out loud. 'I mean, guilt is so disagreeable, it's such an ordeal, that we feel . . . I think we put ourselves through it as a form of punishment.' She paused. 'We punish ourselves, then keep right on blundering.'

Lorenz almost smiled but chose to keep his silence.

'Why don't you say something?' Calliope turned and looked at him keenly. 'Do you think I'm wrong? Don't you feel guilty when you get home to Alicia?'

It was the first time she had dared voice such a question, but she genuinely wanted to know. She still admired Lorenz's steely reserve, yet, oddly, she also resented it. She wanted to penetrate his inner fortress; to see it come crumbling down.

'I don't want to talk about Alicia,' he said and his jaw tightened.

'But why?' Calliope asked. Then, because she was angry at herself for not holding her tongue, because she felt excluded from his real life, she went on, with a touch of resentment. 'You can lie to your wife but you can't talk about her?'

'I talk to my psychiatrist,' he said coldly. 'My time with you is much too precious. Please let's not spoil it.'

She gazed at him for a moment. 'You're very lucky,' she finally said.

'Lucky?'

'You get to fictionalise your experience. You don't have to share any of it.'

'I'm not writing about us, believe me,' he said.

'No, you always write about things after the fact. You write when they're over.'

'That's true,' he allowed. 'I do.'

'So.' She let out a small, bitter chuckle. 'Some day, when this is over between us, this conversation will appear in some novel, and you . . . you will write a disclaimer saying it's all just a figment of your imagination. Right?'

He gave her a long, wounded look, his eyes the colour of a stormy sea. 'It's never going to be over between us,' he said. 'Whatever happens.'

'You think so?'

'I'm sure of it.'

She looked at him, struggling with her inner chaos. 'What if

347

Alicia finds out some day? What if she senses something has changed in you?'

'Nothing has changed. I've always loved you,' he said. And then, all at once, his expression faltered. He regarded her with a mixture of pain and love and silent reproach. 'Why must you torment me like this, my darling?'

At this, Calliope felt instant remorse wash over her heart. How careful she'd been, at the start, to spare him unnecessary pain. When had her attitude begun to change?

'I don't want to torment you. I just think there's something wrong with . . .' She groped for the German expression. 'Hiding your head in the sand.'

'Oh, please,' he said. 'Please.'

'Please, what? In Heidelberg, you pretend I don't exist, then you come here and pretend you have no family, no care in the world. There's nothing really to—'

He did not let her finish. 'My head is not in the sand. I'm fully aware of my own actions,' he said, staring into the distance. And then his lips turned up wryly. 'I'm quite willing to take my chances with the fires of hell,' he added. 'Just so long as I can scream in private.'

'Well, I don't believe in hell, so—'

'Oh, but you do. You just have a different name for it,' he said and gazed at her sadly. 'Hell's within us, inside each of us. It proves that we have a conscience.'

She gazed back at him for a moment. Then she smiled a little. 'And heaven? Does it exist as well?'

He reached out and stroked her cheek, with infinite tenderness. 'Heaven is here. It's being here with you.'

She pondered this for a moment, staring at the yellow freesias he had brought for her. He always brought her bouquets of fragrant freesias, yellow or white.

'Don't you like making love to your wife?' she asked, surprising herself again.

'Oh!' he said. 'I give up – I give up!' He flung the blankets aside and turned his back on her. He sighed, shaking his head slowly, but remained slumped on the edge of the bed, smoothing and smoothing his wheat-coloured hair.

'I don't know why you're doing this,' he said at length, sounding defeated. 'It's our last evening together. Why do you want to stir things up now?'

Calliope was silent. Was she trying to pick a quarrel so as to make his departure more bearable? Perhaps, even, to bring an end to things?

'Maybe I'm more troubled by my sins than you are by yours,' she finally said.

'Ach,' he said with a wan gesture. 'There you go again!'

'There I go again. The thing is you . . . you go back to your wife, your children, whereas I . . . the moment you leave, I start imagining you with your family. I start thinking we must try to—'

'Try! Try! You think I haven't tried? You think I find it easy? You think I wouldn't stop if I could?' He had turned and was regarding her with fire in his eyes. But then he mastered himself. He ran a hand over his face, then stood up and grabbed his trousers, pulling them on in grim silence.

Calliope closed her eyes. The sight of him twisted her lungs.

'Do you want to go get something to eat?' he asked after a while. His voice was neutral; his jaw went on throbbing.

'I'm not hungry,' she said.

'I am. I'll go get something,' he said.

He came back half an hour later, bearing a platter of *dolmadhakia*, *taramosalata*, tiny meatballs and stuffed courgette blossoms, which he knew she loved. He sat down on the edge of the bed and began to slide morsels of food into her mouth, as if she were recovering from some illness and was too feeble to feed herself.

'I can't bear it,' he said helplessly, 'I can't bear it when we fight.'

He looked at her, and she looked back at him, her eyes full of anguish. 'I'm sorry,' she said. 'I seem to want to punish you. For abandoning me, I suppose. Will you forgive me?' she asked.

'I've forgiven you already.'

They were silent after that, then she glanced at him, half tearful, half smiling.

'I don't want you to fictionalise this conversation. Not ever . . . not in anything you ever write.'

She was thinking of their wartime encounter at the fortress, of his having re-created, in his first novel, the conversation they'd had the night they heard the nightingale's arrested song. It was that night, he eventually told her, that he'd felt the first stirrings of the story that would one day become *The Nightingale's Silence*.

'All right.' He was saying now. 'I won't write about us.'

'Promise?'

'I promise,' he said, then resumed feeding her. He picked one of the delicate courgette blossoms, studied it for a moment, as if to ensure its perfection, then, smiling a little, leaned forward to slip it into her mouth. As he did so, Calliope experienced a current of love so powerful it threatened to crack her heart.

But this moment, too, passed. She chewed. She swallowed obediently. She was silent.

～ 10 ～

Calliope recognised her immediately. She would have had to be blind not to, having seen Alicia Umbreit's photograph, having quickly noted the physical resemblance. Lorenz's wife was a little shorter, her eyes were greener, her hair somewhat darker. If she perceived her own resemblance to her husband's translator, she gave no hint of it as she held out her elegant hand.

'I've heard so much about you.'

Calliope felt the blood ebb from her face. 'And I about you,' she lied.

The German woman's eyes measured the Greek. She flashed a smile, saying something Calliope failed to absorb as she waited for the room to stop spinning. Lorenz, who had introduced the two women to each other, stood stiffly to the side, ignored by both. Calliope went on fighting the impulse to turn around and flee.

The 1959 book launch was taking place at an Athens university lecture hall, where rows of folding chairs had been set up, facing a long, draped table on which three microphones waited. Over by the wall, on a smaller table, was a pile of *The Owl's Cry*. The title had come to Lorenz after Calliope told him about the terror she'd experienced as a child, hearing owls call in the night. For years, the eerie cry would send her shrieking into her father's arms and would, from time to time, reverberate in her dreams.

Calliope's mind was chaotically leaping into the distant past because the present left her desperately groping for anchorage. She stood casting about for something to do or say. She could feel her tongue rising, yearning to convey something of dire significance, stupefied by the acrid taste filling her mouth.

She became aware of Lorenz's eyes seeking hers, brimming with apology, yet indignation went on coursing through her veins. She suspected that Alicia had at the last moment decided to accompany her husband to Athens. Impulse or intuition?

She would never know. One thing Calliope was sure of: had he been able to, Lorenz would have telephoned Molyvos and informed her of the change in plans. Alas, not only did she not own a phone, she had come to Athens two days before the book launch, wanting to spend time with Aristides.

She had been asked to arrive at the lecture hall early and did, hoping to have a glass of wine with Lorenz before official proceedings started. The program called for introductions, bilingual readings and a question-and-answer period, followed by book signings. Calliope herself was meant to read the Greek extract, as well as to translate the audience's questions and the author's answers. Later, there was to be a reception in the author's honour. Lorenz had planned to attend the reception, then spend the weekend with Calliope at the seaside villa. Would he now be going to Glyfada with Alicia? Would she guess that he had not been alone during his recent trips to Greece?

All these questions were still chasing each other through Calliope's head when she felt a light pat on her shoulder. Titos Stamoulis, the publisher, had arrived. Greetings were exchanged, cameras kept flashing. Someone offered Calliope a glass of white wine, while she stood enveloped by haze, struggling with her inner upheaval.

In the year that had elapsed since the German release of *The Owl's Cry*, the book had become a German bestseller, with translations in half a dozen languages underway. Among the guests was a Greek–German couple, friends of the publisher, who stopped to congratulate both author and translator. Calliope had felt proud of her own achievement; had greatly looked forward to the Athenian book launch. She had not seen Lorenz since December; had never expected to find herself shaking hands, exchanging smiles, while her heart was being secretly slashed. *Alicia*.

She had just heard Lorenz say his wife's name, a name she had mentally heard him utter innumerable times, in dozens of imagined venues. And yet, hearing him say the name now, in her own presence, made something snap in Calliope's brain. The sensation briefly paralysed every muscle in her body, then she heard him speak her own name as well.

'Calliope,' he was saying. 'The photographer wants us to pose in front of the book display. Can we please . . .' He gestured towards the wall, abruptly reanimating her, like a puppeteer tugging on an indolent puppet's strings.

'Yes, of course,' she said. 'Of course.'

She was wearing high heels, as was Alicia, but the wife seemed to be having no difficulty crossing the room. Hooking her arm through her husband's, she looked as self-possessed as a duchess, turning a neutral smile towards everyone in her path. At one point, Lorenz made a lame attempt at humour and Alicia flashed Calliope a smile, then leaned over and pressed her cheek to her husband's.

Despite his air of resolute cheer, Lorenz was beginning to show signs of strain, compulsively raising his ink-stained hand to his beaded hairline. Calliope registered the purple stain and the smell of ink invaded her nostrils, as vivid as on the day he had knocked the ink bottle off his desk. She recalled the internal chaos. She recalled the pain. She was feeling it all over again now. Barely breathing, she let herself be steered across the room, a glass of wine in her right hand, a smile pasted on a face that, she felt, no longer belonged to her.

The dust jacket of Lorenz Umbreit's second novel had a splash of red against a sky-blue background. Within the red splash was the outline, barely discernible, of a stylised owl. The photographer instructed Lorenz to station himself next to the pile of books. He positioned Alicia on his right and Calliope on his left, then stepped back and gazed at the three of them through the camera lens.

Lorenz had raised his long arms, looping one around his wife, the other around Calliope. Oh, how she hated him at that moment: his impeccable manners, his apparent sangfroid! He was smiling straight at the camera, while his left hand – ever so lightly, ever so discreetly – tried to convey the depth of his private sorrow. She was sure about the sorrow, but could nonetheless feel her mind hardening against him. It came to her then that it was in her power to bring his slick performance to an ignominious end. Certainly, in that short spell, in front of the camera, she felt he deserved it.

'I'd like one of Mr Umbreit alone,' the photographer was saying and, obediently, the two women stepped away and stood side by side like sisters, watching the author pose before the pile of books, his arms crossed, smiling serenely.

Scrutinising the photograph in the years to come, Calliope would be hard put to say where the hint of inner despair lay in the captured image. Despite the smile, the carefully composed features, it was indisputably there, but where, exactly? In the steady Nordic gaze, the tender hollows framing the mouth – where?

She would never know. She would never voice the question, but it pursued her now as, steeling herself, she muttered an excuse and left the crowd before the formal proceedings started. The lecture hall was almost full as she picked her way towards the toilets, fighting the scream rising in her chest.

Opening the Ladies' door, she darted into one of the stalls and stood emptying herself into the toilet. The odour of her inner distress was even more familiar than the smell of ink. Trembling, she stepped out of the stall, shifting her gaze away from the mirror, as one instinctively would from another's shame.

Yet the shame went on roiling inside her. Inexplicably, her unguarded mind ejected the memory of the night she had been assaulted by her drunken brother-in-law and his cronies. The night she had almost died. The memory became increasingly vivid as she washed her hands. The inner trembling had stopped but her cheeks were hot and a little prickly, as with the onset of fever.

Water. She must douse her face with water before sitting down at the microphone, to face the audience's merciless scrutiny.

There was no one else about. Pushing her hair behind her ears, Calliope bent over the basin and splashed cold water all over her face. She straightened up to reach for a towel. She patted herself dry, then turned, her glance compulsively returning to the bathroom mirror. For a moment, she stood frozen, staring at her own image: the waxen skin, the dilated eyes, the mouth which Lorenz had said he could never get enough of. She was leaning into the mirror, the way a woman might do while examining her teeth or nostrils.

There was nothing to examine. Everything had been examined innumerable times and found to be flawed beyond repair. Recoiling, Calliope watched a ball of spit come shooting out of her puckered mouth, slapping the spotless mirror. For a brief spell, she felt she might lose her bearings. She stood leaning against the sink, waiting for the moment to pass.

And the moment passed. Outside, a woman's heels were approaching the toilets. *Click, click, click.*

1966–1974

'Of all human ills, greatest is fortune's wayward tyranny.'

Sophocles

ONE

~ 1 ~

Transcript of Athens Radio Interview – 20 March 1966

Interviewer: Erti Papadimitriou
Guest: Calliope Adham

Calliope Adham is the recent winner of the Hellenic Award for Excellence in Literary Translation. She is also an educator, an advocate for battered women, and the author of numerous articles dealing with women's issues.

EP: Welcome to the program, *Kyria* Adham, and congratulations on your recent award.

CA: Thank you. I'm glad to be here.

EP: *Kyria* Adham, you are considered to be the foremost translator working in Greece today, but I gather you found your way into this domain by chance?

CA: Yes. I started out as a schoolmistress, then I became a de facto social worker. I was in my mid-thirties before I started translating on a professional basis.

EP: You were born and raised on Lesbos, in the village of Mythimna –

or, as you natives still call it, Molyvos. You began teaching several years before the War, at a time when women were kept at home and most villagers were barely literate. How did a village girl get from there to here?

CA: It's quite simple: I had an exceptional father. He was the village headmaster, but had been educated in Constantinople and was besotted with books. I—

EP (laughs): Besotted?

CA: Yes! Books and ideas. And, well, I was his only child. He began to read to me when I was barely out of nappies. He taught me French and German, along with so much else. Somewhere along the way, he passed on his love of knowledge.

EP: So you, too, became a schoolmistress. And then?

CA: Then I got fired. This was during the Civil War – my father had died back in 1935. There was a new headmaster and . . . well, let's just say we did not see eye to eye.

EP: Was your father a believer in education for women?

CA: He was a believer in education.

EP: The award you have just received was in recognition of your translation of Lorenz Umbreit's Aegean Trilogy, but you have also translated Ioannis Dimopoulos's novel into French and, of course, Pericles Alexiou's poetry. Do you prefer translating from or into your mother tongue?

CA: Well, each offers its own challenges and rewards. I like translating into Greek because it is my mother tongue, but also because it introduces my compatriots to books I happen to admire. On the other hand, Pericles Alexiou's poems and Ioannis Dimopoulos's novel might not be known outside Greece if I hadn't had the time and contacts to pursue translation and publication abroad.

EP: In a 1960 interview, you said that your knowledge of German was still spotty when you took on Umbreit's *The Nightingale's Silence*. That must have been quite a challenge?

CA: Yes . . . yes, it was, though translating poetry is actually harder, especially with two languages as different as Greek and French.

EP: Pericles Alexiou is known to have been your pupil in primary school, but how did someone with a limited knowledge of German get to translate an acclaimed German novel like *The Nightingale's Silence?*

CA: To tell you the truth, I wasn't at all sure I was up to it. I got talked into trying and . . . well, it seemed I could do the job, and so I did.

EP: You have said before that you met the author during the Occupation, while you were working for the Resistance. Are you the woman the fictional character of Penelope is based on?

CA: That you'll have to ask the author.

EP (laughs): Fair enough. But Mr Umbreit was a Wehrmacht officer stationed on Lesbos during the Occupation, was he not?

CA: Yes.

EP: And his first book is dedicated to you.

CA: Yes. And there are some Molyviates who will even tell you that I had collaborated with the Germans.

EP: Really? But you were in the Resistance!

CA: Exactly.

EP (pause): May I ask why you chose to stay in the village?

CA: Well, I almost went to France when I was a young woman, but then the war came, and the Civil War . . . there were personal factors, but I . . . I've come to believe that it was my destiny to stay in Molyvos and try to improve the lot of village women.

EP: You opened the Zenovia Antoniou Centre in 1950, but you did not at first have a women's shelter in mind . . .

CA: No. All I knew was that the village needed a children's library and a tutorial centre. Some of my brightest pupils, mostly girls, had been prevented from leaving the village to go to middle school and I had nothing to do – I had just been fired – so I thought, 'Why not offer informal study sessions?' So I did and, well, the girls seemed quite keen to learn.

EP: Who was Zenovia Antoniou?

CA: Ah, Zenovia! (chuckles) She was a well-to-do village woman, a notary's wife who had thrown out her womanising husband and lived alone for the rest of her life. She was a fortune-teller. It was mostly a hobby, but she seemed to have some sort of clairvoyant gift. Anyway, she had no children, and for some reason decided to leave me her house when she died.

EP: And where did the idea of helping battered women come from?

CA: Well, you know, inspiration is like an apricot or a cherry pip, spat out and lying ignored on the wayside, until some sudden change in environmental conditions makes it sprout and grow into a fruit-laden tree. In my case, soon after I got fired, I ran into a woman who had been beaten by her husband, who had nowhere to go. The Antoniou house was empty, so I invited her to stay there and, well, that was the pip, you might say. Actually, the *kentro* in Molyvos is seldom used as a shelter.

EP: But the one in Mytilene?

CA: The one in Mytilene was specifically founded to help battered women. I am only a consultant at this point; other women run it. Anyway, it's something someone would have done, sooner or later.

EP: Because of the high incidence of domestic violence?

CA: And because women in urban centres are beginning to get educated, and to question the status quo.

EP: In a recent magazine interview – I believe it was in *Zoe* – you said that doing away with domestic violence was your most serious ambition.

CA: That, and also encouraging women to get an education, to become independent.

EP: These are two admirable ambitions but, as you know, there are many who would argue that women's independence – women joining the workforce – will undermine the stability of the Greek family. What do you say to that?

CA: I think the stability of the Greek family has largely been paid for with women's silence . . . women's suffering. When you live in a society in which women remain in abusive or exploitative situations because they have no other options, what you actually have is female enslavement. This is not a uniquely Greek situation, of course. Women all over the world are beginning to rebel.

EP: What do you think of the male-bashing that's beginning to take place in America?

CA: It just goes to show you that women can equal men in every way, including idiocy.

EP (laughs): But—

CA: I'm sorry to interrupt you – but to fully answer your question: I'm a strong supporter of women's rights, but I don't approve of militant rhetoric. I think that men are as much victims of social and historic forces as women. Both must be re-educated if significant change is ever to take place.

EP: But it's obviously going to be much harder to persuade men to change. I mean, it's never easy to relinquish power, is it?

CA: No, it isn't easy. People tend to resist change, but that's no reason to stop struggling, is it? Just because it isn't easy?

EP: No. You are right. Of course. There are those who say that you can be as tough as a man. How did you come to have such a reputation?

CA: Mostly by speaking my mind and refusing to compromise.

EP: But isn't compromise an essential part of learning to live with others?

CA: Yes. Yes, it is. I suppose that's why I live alone with half a dozen cats.

EP: Half a dozen?

CA: Yes! But to give you a serious answer: compromise may be an inevitable part of human coexistence but I'm sure I don't have to tell you it's usually women who have to do all the compromising. In fact, I don't think compromise is quite the right word.

Self-abnegation is probably more accurate. Most women who want to marry have to be prepared to humble themselves every day of their married lives.

EP: You were only in your late twenties when you were widowed. If I may be permitted to ask a personal question – did you make a conscious decision not to remarry?

CA: Well, you know, I haven't exactly been celibate since my husband died, but as for marriage, I think it debilitates women. I just turned fifty-one and I think that had I not been widowed, had I had children, I would not be sitting here with you today.

EP: So you—

CA: But – excuse me again – I don't want to give the impression that I think raising a family is not an important achievement. It may be the most important of all, but it's not for everyone. I think people – men and women – should have the option of choosing what to do with their lives. Greek family laws are, in my view, egregiously antiquated and must be revised.

EP: For example?

CA: For example, our laws permit a father to marry off an adolescent daughter without her consent. A social system that permits this, that makes it impossible for women to escape exploitation and abuse, is a system we must fight to reform if we are to evolve into a modern society.

EP: But don't you think that feminism is likely to bring about a backlash?

CA: So? Let there be a backlash! What do you expect from a revolution? Anyway, could things be much worse for women than they are already?

EP: Well . . .

CA: Look, it's like I said: people resist change. They always have. But when you really want to get somewhere, even a haycart will eventually get you there.

EP: Or we would still be huddling in caves, I suppose?

CA: Exactly.

EP: All of which goes to say, I guess, that we must be prepared to deal with huge disappointments and setbacks. What has been the worst setback in your own professional life?

CA: Oh . . . probably the day a village woman decided to torch our *kentro*, holding me responsible for her daughter's elopement.

EP: What did you have to do with it?

CA: Well, I'm tempted to say 'nothing', but it wouldn't be quite true. I was responsible for getting the girl in question out of virtual house arrest and, in general, for encouraging the young women who came to the *kentro* to think more deeply about serious issues, and that came to include reflecting on their own lives, I suppose.

EP: So the *kentro* had to be rebuilt?

CA: Not from scratch, but restored, yes. All the books in the library had gone up in flames. It was very demoralising, especially as the girl's mother ended up in an insane asylum.

EP: What about village men? Has there not been any negative reaction from irate—

CA: Oh, to be sure. One fisherman whose wife sought shelter at the *kentro* several years ago tried to break down the front door, but this was one development I'd actually foreseen, so I had the door reinforced and barred. The husband stood on the street, screaming abuse, but even that backfired. He became a laughing stock and . . . well, no one tried anything like that again.

EP: *Kyria* Adham, you are clearly a woman of exceptional willpower and strength. I am sure many women will be wondering about both your resilience and . . . well, your youthful looks. What's the secret?

CA: Chocolates and young men.

EP (laughs): That's it?

CA: Well, it's not likely to be dusty bookstacks, is it?

EP (laughs again): I suppose you must know your way around bookstacks, but do you think that a well-read but plain woman could have accomplished as much as you have?

CA: If you're asking me whether appearance makes a difference in life, of course it does. Sometimes it offers an undeniable advantage, but it can also be a hindrance . . . even a source of pain.

EP: Really?

CA: Absolutely.

EP: Well, you seem, if I may say so, to wear both your suffering and your accomplishments very lightly, but I imagine the accomplishments give you enormous satisfaction. What are you personally proudest of? Is it the award you have just received or—

CA: I am proud of that – I love translating good books – but I am far prouder of the fact that today, most Molyvos girls remain at school past the primary level. My own goddaughter, whose mother was not even allowed to attend middle school, is about to graduate from university! I can't tell you how happy this makes me.

EP: So, what is the next challenge for *Kyria* Calliope Adham?

CA: It's the same old challenge – the struggle to end oppression: political, personal, educational. It's all part of the same process and it certainly won't end in my lifetime.

~ 2 ~

One summer day, not long after the radio interview, Calliope was at her window, writing letters, when she heard *Papa* Iakovos's wife answer a Mytilene relative's question about the fine house overlooking the public fountain: Calliope's house. Although the fountain had fallen into disuse, women continued to stop there on their way home, to rest or exchange gossip. Olympia, a woman bloated with virtue and secrets, was not one to resist an opportunity for a tantalising digression.

'She's had more lovers than cooking pots, that one!' she was saying, standing directly under Calliope's window. 'She's like a man. She takes what she wants!'

Ever since Calliope had first put on trousers, there were those who said that she was just a man trapped in a woman's body. It explained everything, especially her scandalous love life. After Eli's death, a rumour had begun to circulate that the doctor's death had been caused by sexual exhaustion. Eleni had heard it said that the poor man's heart had failed after making love seven times.

One day, she found it impossible to resist sharing the rumour.

'Seven times!' Calliope burst out laughing. 'How do they know it was seven?'

Eleni grinned. 'They seem to think you're insatiable.'

'Not nearly as insatiable as they are for gossip!'

There was no lover in Calliope's life that summer, but there had been several after Lorenz Umbreit, chief among them Timolis Tsouras, the former headmaster's son. The headmaster was no longer in Molyvos; his son had married and emigrated to the United States. But there had been a time when the young notary provided Calliope with much-needed distraction, if inadequate consolation.

That she had allowed herself to become sexually involved with the headmaster's son had surprised Calliope no less than it had his father. There was Timolis's age. There was his indifference to books and ideas. But there was also the sour satisfaction of spiting both Leandros Tsouras and the villagers' double standards. Pericles – who finally married his Athenian nurse – had once told Calliope that his mother used to give him a brothel allowance, and that other women did likewise with their sons, even the married ones.

It was generally assumed that men's sexual appetites had to be secretly indulged, since no decent woman could satisfy a husband's baser needs. Could there really be an innate difference between the sexes? Calliope had found herself wondering. The foreign novels she'd read had left no doubt that men enjoyed sexual encounters without suffering either guilt or regret; certainly without the tragic consequences of a Bovary or Karenina. Were women incapable of pure physical pleasure?

This question teased Calliope in her early forties. Years would go by, however, before she could bring herself to acknowledge that her involvement with Timolis might have had a whiff of the experimental about it. And yet, she had gradually grown fond of the young notary. When, after two years, he became the object of a visiting Greco–American girl's fancy, Calliope sadly but resolutely ended her own affair. The young man was bound to marry sooner or later and this was an opportunity he must not be allowed to forfeit.

By then, Leandros Tsouras had been transferred to Athens and Molyvos had a new headmaster. There had been a brief reconciliation with Pericles; a tumultuous relationship with a Mytilene journalist; then a brief, lighthearted affair with an Athenian actor.

The last time Calliope had seen the actor was in spring, the day after her radio interview. She had looked forward to visiting Athens, but her week-long stay was to mark the end of what she would thereafter refer to as her 'protracted hedonistic period'. It was as if broadcasting information about her private life had unexpectedly appeased some dormant rebellious spirit, she would some day tell Rupert Ealing.

The Englishman had come to Greece just before Easter. He was going through the final stages of a divorce – a rather civilised one, he had told Calliope in one of his recent letters. Once in Molyvos, however, he would put it differently: 'A goodwill divorce is like having all your teeth extracted and having to smile.'

It was late March 1966. Ealing was in his mid-fifties – one of those ordinary-looking men who somehow come to look more attractive with age. Over two decades had passed since he and Calliope had last seen each other.

'Well, your hair's still there!' She laughed, scanning his face after a warm embrace. He had a greying beard and shaggy hair, which gave him the slightly eccentric look of a man who had spent much of his life alone. This wasn't the case, but Ealing never lost the air of an adventurous boy preparing for some exciting field trip. His body was no longer wiry but retained an aura of perpetual eagerness, as if he might at any moment take it into his head to hop onto a mule's back or dive into the sea. 'Actually, you have more hair than before,' Calliope stated.

Except for the physical changes, Rupert Ealing seemed much the same, though he was beginning to contemplate early retirement. What he longed to do was travel and write his memoirs, he told Calliope soon after his arrival. He had come to Molyvos for a holiday, with a vague recollection of a defeated village he had glimpsed mostly through cellar windows. The flamboyant beauty of spring on the island, the panoramic views of mountains and sea, the fragrant, starry nights, quickly cast their spell.

Calliope's house was undergoing renovations, but she had arranged for Rupert to stay with one of the foreigners, an artist friend of her cousin's. Thierry Brabant was spending a year in Greece, renting an old mansion he called The Mausoleum. The house was neglected but had spectacular views. The Frenchman had fallen in love with a local boy. His Hellenophilia, Calliope cautioned, must therefore be taken *avec un grain de sel*.

Greece was becoming a popular holiday destination but, in the mid-60s, Lesbos was still a largely bucolic island. After a four-week stay in Molyvos, Rupert returned to London, feeling at least as enthralled as Thierry Brabant.

But of course there were some negative aspects to village life, which Olympia's comments by the fountain only served to underline as Calliope sat answering Rupert's surprising letter: He had, on returning home, decided he would like to write his memoirs in Greece. Why not? For the first time in his life, he was free to do as he pleased and, right now, nothing would please him more than a prolonged Aegean sojourn.

Calliope had no wish to discourage Rupert, but she did have doubts about his expectations. She reminded him of the pervasive malice, the banality, the endless hypocrisy and gossip. But then she added something of a disclaimer.

'I suspect you would find all this in any village, even an English one, but I do think you should come here with your eyes open or risk being disillusioned. To be sure, Molyvos is much more pleasant than it was during the Occupation, but you have seen it at an especially ravishing time of year. It is not always spring here, and the sea, which you are so enamoured of, often swarms with jellyfish. If, after reading this, you still want to come,' she concluded, 'I'll be delighted to see you. Thierry says an American acquaintance is also thinking of coming, so who knows, this may be the beginning of a small expatriate community. I, for one, would certainly welcome it. Alexandra will be here at the end of the summer. Her husband died last year, after a long illness, so she is finally free to travel. She'll be staying until late September, so if you arrive before that, you will get to meet her.'

And with this, Calliope signed the letter, sealed the envelope, then stood up and stretched. She was going to post the letter to Rupert, along with a note to her cousin. She had, over the years, trained herself to avoid dwelling on the past. But, as she crossed the village, her mind meandered towards the winter evenings when she and Rupert had sat in the cellar, singing nursery rhymes and reciting limericks. She recalled

Mirto's fretting, her reluctance to leave Calliope alone with a married Englishman.

The memory made Calliope smile. Some two decades after the end of the Occupation, she had not quite learned to resist the past's mysterious allure.

～ 3 ～

'I think Plato was absolutely right. Love is a grave mental disease,' Calliope said, smiling a little sadly. It was late August and her French cousin was finally in Molyvos, ensconced in the guest room. 'Don't you agree?'

'Oh, I suppose. Though it's a disease I wouldn't mind contracting again,' Alexandra said, smiling as well.

Approaching fifty-five, the Parisian academic had the brave air of an ageing ballerina, a woman determined to be, if not quite a merry widow, then at least an upbeat one. Her hair had recently been tinted for the first time; her eyebrows plucked. She was tall and trim, with a long neck and an elegant carriage resembling Calliope's.

The patrician physique was not the only thing the women had in common. Within hours of Alexandra's arrival, Calliope was as taken with her cousin's ways as she had been with her letters. Alexandra was the sort of person whom nothing ever seemed to escape. With her wistful, deeply observant gaze, she seemed capable of penetrating the very depths of one's soul. In this, she strongly resembled Lorenz Umbreit.

Calliope had not seen Lorenz for seven years, and was surprised, soon after Alexandra's arrival, to find herself speaking of their doomed affair. Almost at once, she regretted it; not the disclosure itself but the precipitate dive into stormy waters. Reluctant to dwell on past griefs, she gradually steered the conversation away from Umbreit's Aegean Trilogy to Greek politics. The country was still unstable, she told her cousin as they sat sharing a dish of stuffed eggplants. There were frequent strikes, demonstrations, riots. Leftists were still persecuted in the public sector; their children were denied university admission.

'You're talking about former partisans, I suppose?'

'No.' Most partisans had long since fled to Eastern Bloc countries, Calliope said. She was talking about ordinary folk with Leftist leanings. 'There's a dossier on every one of us . . . they know where each of us, each family member, stands politically.'

Alexandra shook her head. 'On the other hand,' she said at length, 'think where you'd be now if the Communists had won the Civil War. You'd be where your Bulgarian and Yugoslav neighbours are, and the rest of Eastern Europe.'

'No doubt,' Calliope said. 'Whoever won the war, Greeks were bound to lose.'

They were still talking, still finishing supper, when Eleni came calling. She had been on her way to visit her mother-in-law but stopped by to deliver a letter. It was customary for the postman to pass on letters to friends or neighbours, saving himself the steep climb to St Kyriaki.

Eleni was spending the summer in Molyvos. She had been living in Athens for the past few years, partly because of her daughter's studies, but also because the new road to Mytilene had brought a virtual end to home births. As soon as the road was completed, most village women had decided they wanted to be *moderni*. They began to have their children delivered in hospital, though there were still men who forbade it, insisting on taking their wives to an old midwife in Kaloni. In the summer, when Eleni was back in Molyvos, there would still be an occasional request for her services.

The letter Eleni had delivered was from Rupert Ealing, who was writing to say he would not be able to travel before mid-October.

'Pity. I would have liked you to meet him,' Calliope said to Alexandra.

'Maybe next time,' said her cousin. 'I'm going to be back, that's for sure!'

It was almost ten o'clock when the two women finished washing up and headed upstairs. Calliope had discovered a young Greek author whose short stories she had recently begun to translate into French. All she had so far was the title story, but she thought it brilliant. Would Alexandra like to read it, by any chance?

'But of course!' She was reading Simone de Beauvoir, but had only a few pages left, Alexandra said, entering the room that had once been Philippas's sanctuary and now served as Calliope's study. There was a recent snapshot of Calliope's godson on the desktop. *'Oh la la,* how I wish I was young again!' Alexandra exclaimed.

Aristides Dhaniel had been captured with his fair hair flopping over one eye, his thumbs thrust into his jeans pockets. He was twenty-seven, completing his doctorate in Athens. His grandmother Stella had passed away; his youngest sister had married a doctor and moved to Patras. The middle one lived in Mytilene and had three children.

'Only Dimitra is still unmarried,' Calliope said, manuscript in hand. Dimitra was the architect, much sought-after professionally. 'Greeks don't like their women to be quite so successful and independent.'

'Not only Greeks,' Alexandra said, speaking distractedly. She was studying another photograph now. Taken during the launch of *The Owl's Cry,* the photo showed Lorenz Umbreit poised next to a pile of books, looking straight into the camera. On the author's left was a tentative-looking Calliope; on his right a somewhat younger woman, smiling demurely.

'That's Alicia . . . his wife,' Calliope said, glancing over her cousin's shoulder.

'Really? German?'

'Swiss. With an Italian ancestor somewhere down the line.'

'I see.' Alexandra stood gazing at the photograph. 'She could be your sister.'

'I know. That was the last time I saw him,' Calliope said, her voice faraway. Across the moonlit water, in the distant hills, lights were flickering like fireflies. 'It's a terrible thing, you know. The heart is surely big enough to love more than one person at a time, yet we're forced to choose. We must always choose,' she stated and sighed.

'Ah, yes. The road to hell is paved with repented choices,' Alexandra said, trying for a smile. 'Did she find out about you?' she inquired at length. She was replacing the photograph on the desk but suddenly stopped, looking wry. 'Am I being indiscreet again?'

'Yes! But . . . oh, never mind.' Calliope squeezed Alexandra's shoulder. She already knew that her cousin shared her own difficulty in censoring thoughts. 'No, she never found out. At least I don't think so.'

Alexandra studied her for a moment. 'Do you want to talk about it?'

'Oh, I don't know.'

With sudden resolve, Calliope pulled out a desk drawer and riffled through it until she found what she wanted. It was a carbon copy of a letter she had sent Lorenz shortly after the book launch in Athens. She had begun to keep copies of their letters when it occurred to her that posterity might be interested in their correspondence.

'I couldn't go on with it after I'd met her,' she said quietly, as though explaining it to herself. She glanced down at the book-launch photograph, and smiled to herself. 'I've kept it here, where I can see it every day . . . just in case I'm ever tempted to stray.'

Alexandra chuckled, lapsing into thought. 'Do you think you'll ever see each other again?' she asked after a long silence. 'I suppose—'

'No. No, I don't think so,' Calliope put in. 'I do hope we'll continue to write each other, though,' she added. 'It means so much to me!'

'Hm. I'd have preferred a clean break, I think,' Alexandra stated.

'Well, to me it's a consolation . . . like a dummy offered to a hungry baby,' Calliope said, making her cousin smile.

They both fell silent then, idly watching the curtain stir in the summer breeze. It was a gauzy white curtain made by Mirto just before the Occupation. It billowed for a moment or two, then, with a kind of shudder, straightened itself and rested.

~ 4 ~

As if to signal the fact that life on a Greek island would not be the blissful idyll of Rupert Ealing's imaginings, the sea passage had been tempestuous. Rupert and Thierry Brabant's American friend had chanced to catch the same boat, the only foreigners sailing to Mytilene on that stormy October day. They had not known each other before boarding the ferry, but fell to talking shortly after their departure from Piraeus. Within half an hour, Rupert knew that Ed Bell (Belinsky) was an aspiring writer with a background in advertising; that his grandparents had been Russian aristocrats who'd managed to escape the Revolution; that he had met Thierry Brabant in Paris in the late 1950s; that he was in his mid-thirties and recently divorced.

The American liked to talk. He'd been sitting by the bar with *Newsweek* when Rupert Ealing walked into the lounge in search of a drink. As the Englishman approached the bar, a small chortling sound escaped Ed Bell. He was reading an article on the newly founded National Organisation for Women. The American, Rupert quickly learned, blamed the women's liberation movement for the failure of his marriage. They tossed the subject between them for a while, then went on to talk about Vietnam. In the morning, Rupert introduced Ed Bell to Calliope Adham.

Although she was aware of her own tendency to make snap judgements, Calliope decided the young foreigner had the eyes of a child unable to decide whether to sulk or throw a temper tantrum. Either way, he seemed the sort of man who wouldn't rest until he got what he wanted. Fortunately, he was catching the early bus to Molyvos. Rupert would go back with her in the afternoon.

Calliope had come to Mytilene to meet the ferry, as well as to see an optometrist. All at once, it seemed, she needed reading glasses. It was going on nine o'clock. Having deposited Rupert's suitcases at the taxi office, they picked their way through the *agora*, looking for a quiet café. It had rained much of the week, but by Saturday the sun had triumphed, bathing the capital in a golden autumnal light.

Rupert remembered Mytilene as a bleak, shuttered place, its twisted streets patrolled by armed soldiers. By the mid-1960s, hawkers' voices were wafting from pavements overflowing with fresh produce; farm carts trundled by, sending shoppers scampering away like pigeons. Rupert kept glancing about him, as avid as a country bumpkin on his first visit to town. The scent of fresh cheese pies hung in the air.

'Would you like a *tiropita* by any chance?' Calliope asked in French.

Rupert darted a quick look towards the bakery. What he really craved, he said, was a bowl of *rizogalo*, made with goats' milk. He'd had it when he first arrived on the island, before milk had become a luxury. 'Do they still make it here?'

'What modest cravings you have!' Calliope smiled. 'Come. I know just the place.' She stepped aside to let an old man with a sesame-roll cart push by. Rupert pointed out the street where he had been sheltered by *Papa* Ioannis. The priest had passed away, but the brave madam was still running her brothel. Rupert had brought a gift for her. Perhaps he could drop it off while Calliope had her eyes examined?

'Yes . . . yes, why not?' she replied vaguely. A fair-haired young man was waiting to cross the street. He reminded Calliope of Aristides, whom she had not seen since July and would not see again until Christmas. She missed her godson fiercely. Sometimes she wondered how generations of mothers had endured seeing their sons go off to war; why there had never been a historic mothers' revolt.

It was quieter on the seaside esplanade. A cluster of men in wool waistcoats were playing backgammon at an outdoor café. Rupert lit a cigarette, then turned to watch a ferry sail away. All around the harbour, oil-slicked rainpuddles were just starting to dry.

'It's been raining chair legs all week,' Calliope said. She was smoking as well.

'Chair legs?'

'That's what we say around here.'

'Really? In London, it rains cats and dogs.' Rupert sat grinning. He had small, gapped teeth; a child's teeth in the face of a bearded, middle-aged man.

'Are you going to insist on teaching me English all over again?' Calliope said, withdrawing her elbows. Their waiter had arrived, bearing coffee and rice pudding.

'Of course. How else are you going to read my memoirs?'

A gypsy came threading her way among the tables, a bale of shawls draped over her arm. She stopped here and there, speaking in a slow, scratchy monotone. No, she didn't need a shawl, Calliope said, barely glancing up. When the gypsy stood her ground, Calliope looked up, scowling. The hawker was a middle-aged woman, round-shouldered, heavy around the hips, with a nutmeg-hued face going flaccid. Her long plait was filigreed with grey threads.

Early on in her marriage, Calliope had occasionally found her attention caught by gypsy women resembling the beguiling Amalia. By the time Rupert arrived in Mytilene, some twenty-five years had passed since Calliope had last seen Amalia, but something about this ageing stranger's eyes – the eyes and the beauty spot on her left cheek – made sudden recognition flood through her. The gypsy was still wheedling.

'Is your name Amalia?' Calliope asked, cutting into the sales pitch.

The gypsy appraised her, her face revealing nothing. 'Do I know you?'

'You came to Molyvos a few times. Before the Occupation.'

'Ach, Molyvos!' The gypsy beamed, a gold tooth glinting in the back of her mouth. 'Beautiful village, Molyvos. Very beautiful!' Her eyes slid towards Rupert, who was smiling blandly; they returned to scan Calliope's face, her pearl necklace, her tailored suit. 'You live there?' She sounded sceptical.

'Yes,' Calliope said. There was something she wanted to say or ask, but what? The words refused to cohere. She couldn't even identify her own emotions, except for a vague sense of compassion as the memory of the young Amalia, sprightly and colourful as a tropical bird, flitted through her brain.

After the Germans had arrested the doctor, Kyriakos Himonas had told *Papa* Emanouil that the Mytilene whore must have ratted on them. Who would have thought that Orestes the pharmacist had been the one to betray them? Now, all three men were dead, and the alluring Amalia was on the cusp of old age.

'So, *Kyria mou*,' she was saying, 'are you going to buy one of these fine shawls? I'll let you have one for forty drachmas, since you are from my favourite village and have such beautiful golden eyes.'

Despite herself, Calliope smiled. 'I'll give you thirty drachmas.'

'Thirty-five,' Amalia said.

'Thirty-two. That's my final offer.'

The gypsy contemplated her for a moment. 'All right, I accept!' She began to peel a black shawl from the top of the batch, holding it out for Calliope's inspection. 'Handmade wool,' she said. 'Beautiful, eh?'

'Not bad.' Calliope was burrowing for her wallet. She had no need of another shawl, but she paid the gypsy and placed the folded shawl in her lap. She would give it to her housekeeper, for St Basil's Day.

'The Virgin's blessings upon you!' Amalia darted another look towards Rupert, then shuffled off, a stray dog sniffing at her ankles.

Calliope stared at the gypsy's retreating back, fighting an urge to run after her, as if the stranger had walked away with something that did not belong to her.

'I don't know what made me buy it,' she said at last, half-speaking to herself. 'I have enough shawls to last me a lifetime.' It flashed on her then that, having left for England as soon as the Occupation ended, Rupert had probably never heard of Himonas's wartime adventure with Amalia.

She told Rupert what she knew of the story.

'So that was her? The gypsy *femme fatale*?'

'That was her.' Calliope sighed, her thoughts meandering to Amalia's earlier encounter with Iason, back in 1935. A few months after they were married, Iason had confessed to Calliope that he never would have found the courage to ask for her hand had the gypsy not planted the seductive idea in his head.

This story, too, Calliope shared with Rupert.

'I sometimes ask myself, what if he hadn't been at the *kapheneion* that day? What if she had decided to read someone else's cup?'

'But my dear, so much of life is like that!' said Rupert. There was Albert Camus, who had purchased a train ticket to Paris, then, at the last moment, accepted a lift, only to be killed in a freak automobile accident. For that matter, there was Rupert's own brother, who had missed a train to Oxford, then took the next one, on which he met a man who would become his mentor, inspiring him to become an archaeologist rather than a solicitor, as planned.

'I know, I know.' Calliope exhaled, shredding a paper napkin. She had always had trouble accepting the randomness of life; could never quite come to terms with the fact that a rainy evening, a gypsy's decision to seek shelter in a *kapheneion*, could decide the fate of two unsuspecting individuals.

She pondered Rupert's words for a while, then slowly raised her gaze. 'What about you? What made you decide to become a spy?'

'I was never exactly a spy, you know.' Rupert's tongue picked up a stray bit of rice on his lip. He had actually worked for the Special Operations Executive, a secret British organisation whose mandate was sabotage and support to the Greek Resistance.

'But that's just as dangerous,' Calliope put in. 'You had a family. What made you want to do it?'

'Good question.' Rupert's glance drifted away. 'I had always assumed I'd be an academic, you know. Act in amateur theatricals, have a family – a perfectly ordinary life. I certainly didn't think of myself as an adventurer.'

'No Lawrence of Arabia?'

'No. At least I never thought so.'

Calliope dimpled, bringing her cup to her lips. 'And then?'

'Then the war broke out and . . . well, by then I knew my marriage was a mistake. I also knew I wasn't brave enough to end it; not with three young children.'

'What was wrong with your wife?' Calliope asked. She thought: I am just as indiscreet as my cousin!

'Nothing. Absolutely nothing. We were just wrong for each other.'

Calliope was silent. She was thinking of Lorenz Umbreit's wife. Was Alicia wrong for him? Somehow, she sensed this was not the case. Did it follow then that she herself would have been wrong for him? Oh, she had long since given up trying to unravel the mysteries of the human heart!

She glanced at her watch. 'Ready to go?'

'Mm.' Rupert took a final sip of coffee. 'Now I am.'

They were strolling away from the waterfront when Rupert asked whether she'd had a chance to look into housing. It was something he had requested in his letter, but after one or two enquiries Calliope had thought it best to wait for his arrival. With all the emigration in recent years, there was no shortage of empty houses.

'Don't worry, I'm not about to stick you in the cellar,' Calliope said.

Rupert reached out and lightly tweaked her nose. 'You might be tempted to when you hear just how far my snoring can travel.'

'You can stay in the downstairs guest room. It's a big house . . . there's no rush.'

They walked on. A beggar was sitting cross-legged on a street corner. Calliope took out her wallet and brought out a few drachmas for the blind old man. They made a merry, jingling sound as they fell into the tin can, like the coins children received on singing their annual Christmas carols.

~ 5 ~

Evanthea, the housekeeper, reported that Calliope and the foreigner were *not* sleeping together. Their rooms were not even on the same floor, she informed the occasional sceptic. And, yes, both beds looked slept in, she was quick to add. The Englishman had all his clothes in his own wardrobe. He kept his radio and reading glasses on his own bedside table. Downstairs.

After weeks of feverish speculation, it was finally concluded that Ealing must be an English homosexual. Everyone seemed to know he cooked and cleaned; had, the postman reported, opened the door wearing an apron!

What the villagers did not know was that Rupert had made himself so indispensable that five-and-a-half months after his arrival in Molyvos, he appeared to be permanently ensconced on Calliope's ground floor. Being an early riser, and too restless to write for more than four or five hours a day, he was only too happy to handle domestic chores. He claimed they helped him think, and offered more immediate rewards than his daily scribbling.

Calliope and Rupert spent much of their time writing or reading in their respective quarters, but they usually dined together, and passed many an evening going for walks or chatting in the garden. The arrangement offered so much mutual satisfaction that, writing in her journal, Calliope was hard pressed to explain their strictly chaste relations. Only one thing seemed clear: her attachment to Rupert deepened in the course of that first winter. When he flew to London for Easter, she wrote in her journal that she could hardly bear the empty rooms, the pervasive silence.

Rupert was gone for three weeks, but came back in time for Greek Easter, meeting up with Calliope's godson in Athens. The two men quickly took to each other, both being keen on history and politics, both given to playful mimicry. Later, speaking to Calliope, Aristides marvelled at Rupert's knowledge of Greece. Foreigners, he went on to observe, seemed to appreciate the Aegean islands far more than most natives did.

He had occasion to reiterate the statement a week later, at Thierry Brabant's birthday party. Calliope liked Thierry, but she had gradually discovered, somewhat to her own surprise, that she didn't much enjoy the expats' get-togethers, if only because of the foreigners' propensity to poke fun at her compatriots. It might be a natural thing to do – she supposed she would do the same if she were transplanted to a French or English village – but, listening to their table talk, she felt obscurely disloyal to her own people. That she herself had expressed similar sentiments in the past only seemed to compound her unease. She could not have known, during that lighthearted French party, that her vague disgruntlement was about to be eclipsed by far deeper concerns.

~ 6 ~

The historic events began to unfold four days after Easter, on the morning of 21 April 1967. Preparing breakfast that day, Calliope turned on the radio, bewildered to hear nothing but military marches on both local and Athenian stations. No news. No announcements. Nothing but military marches. Rupert was out, but Calliope went into his room and tuned his short-wave radio to Deutsche Welle.

At two in the morning, while much of the country slept, a Right-wing coup d'état had taken place in Athens. The conspirators – a group of army officers under the leadership of Colonel Yorgos Papadopoulos – had declared martial law, encountering virtually no resistance. The official pretext was an imminent Communist threat.

All this was soon confirmed by the BBC.

'They say Leftists are being arrested all over Athens,' Rupert reported after listening to the English news. He was a man who usually found humour in any situation. He found none that day.

'I'd better phone Aristides,' Calliope said later that afternoon.

Rupert consulted his watch. 'Yes. I should probably call London too.'

He managed to get through, but Calliope kept finding the Athenian circuits engaged. At length, she gave up. She sat with Rupert, listening to speeches about a new social order; to promises of peace, stability, justice. *From now on, there will be no more Rightists, Centrists, or Leftists, only Greeks who share a faith in Greece!*

'Stability and justice! Oh, I can't wait to see that,' Calliope said.

In the early evening, a child arrived with a message from the mayor, asking her to come to the town hall as soon as possible.

'Aristides called,' Mathaios said the moment she entered his office. 'He asked me to tell you he's all right. He's gone into hiding.'

Calliope received the news with a sigh of relief. 'Did he leave a number?'

'He said you won't be able to reach him. He just wanted you to know he's safe.'

'Nothing else?'

'Only that students had been stopped that morning and ordered to go home. No one bothered to explain what was going on, but Aristides took one look at the soldiers and slipped underground. He said not to worry,' Mathaios reiterated.

~ 7 ~

That night, Calliope and Rupert went for a stroll and found themselves hailed by Thierry Brabant. It was a beautiful night and the expats had gathered in the harbour, at what used to be Fotini Paschalou's *kapheneion*. The nondescript building had recently been transformed into a small hotel, thanks to an inheritance from a childless Australian uncle. It was called the Orpheus's Head Hotel. Legend had it that, having been severed and thrown into the Hebrus River, Orpheus's head had floated into the sea, eventually surfacing on Molyvos shores.

The hotel had a restaurant facing the wharf. This was where the foreigners were seated, served by the widowed Nikki Paschalou, Johnny the Australian's sister, who had emigrated to Australia with her husband, but eventually returned to Molyvos with her two daughters. Artemis, the younger one, was working the tables alongside her mother. She was in her early twenties and said to be as contrary as a crooked staff, having recently rejected a marriage proposal from a young policeman. Artemis's uncle, who had encouraged the suit, said he wouldn't speak to his niece until she came to her senses.

Calliope admired the girl's spunk, but, sitting with the foreigners on that late-April evening, it suddenly came to her that Artemis's wilfulness might have something to do with Ed Bell. She had just seen the American wink at Nikki's daughter, while the jukebox played 'The House of the Rising Sun'. Swishing past their table, Artemis had smiled at Ed and tossed her head, theatrically mouthing the American lyrics.

A wink and a smile didn't necessarily signify anything. Artemis was a vivacious girl and Ed was given to flirting with attractive women. Still, glancing across the room, Calliope observed that the silent exchange had not been lost on Artemis's uncle.

Mandras Paschalou was sitting against the wall, drinking with his police mates. They were discussing their rather aloof chief, who had been recently transferred from Salonika. At the other end of the room sat several fishermen, among them Captain Yorgos's elder son.

Although Kostas Lyras was far from being the only staunch

Communist in the village, he had a way, especially when drunk, of provoking Right-wing extremists. If people tolerated his occasional outbursts, it was only because an aura of patriotic martyrdom still hovered over the Lyras clan.

As soon as the foreigners stopped playing their American hits, Kostas strode to the jukebox and punched in his own selections, including a popular Theodorakis song. Mikis Theodorakis was a renowned Communist, but his music had yet to be officially banned. Nonetheless, the moment the rousing song began to play, Sergeant Floros leaned across the table and asked Mandras to stop the jukebox.

Mandras glanced up towards the fishermen's table. He was a middle-aged man who, like all the Paschalou brothers, had thick black eyebrows joined above the bridge of his nose. The eyebrows were knotted as he rose from the policemen's table. Hitching up his trousers, he crossed the restaurant, said something to his mother, then stooped and yanked the jukebox plug out of the wall.

'Hey, what d'you think you're doing?' Kostas Lyras yelled, leaping from his chair. 'I put in—'

'Relax.' Mandras made a placating gesture. 'I'll give you your money back.'

'But you've got him in your jukebox! If you didn't want—'

'Am I supposed to know every song in the jukebox?' Mandras said, counting the change in the palm of his hand. 'Artemis is in charge of the music. She—'

'I don't want my money! There's no law against my listening to the music of my choice, is there?' Saying this, Kostas flicked at Mandras's extended hand and sent the coins flying. Old Fotini glanced up from the onions she was peeling and abandoned her task. She hobbled over from one direction, while Sergeant Floros, leaping out of his chair, approached from the other, his cabbage-like face pinker than ever.

'As of today, there's going to be new laws! You'd better learn to behave!' The policeman paused, then ordered the fisherman to go back to his table. When Kostas stood his ground, Floros clamped his fingers on the fisherman's arm, simultaneously urging Fotini to calm down. The old woman was shrieking through her toothless gums. The foreigners, who had been arguing about the likelihood of American involvement in the coup, had all fallen silent.

The policeman might have simply intended to lead Kostas back to his own table, but his firm hold made the fisherman swing out with a furious motion, catching Floros smack across his mouth.

And that was all it took on that momentous day.

Seeing the blood gush out of Floros's split lip, his two colleagues leaped up and lunged for the fisherman. The sergeant was gingerly dabbing at his bleeding mouth.

Kostas's own mouth was twisted with loathing. Struggling to extricate himself, he thrashed about, tossing out a string of profanities, while everyone watched in impotent silence. Calliope had half-risen from her chair, but slumped straight back, restrained by Rupert's hand. It was time to go home.

As they left the harbour, Rupert told her she could have easily found herself locked up along with the hotheaded Kostas.

'I know,' Calliope said. The starry sky offered no consolation that night. 'Now you're starting to see the other face of Greece.'

'Well, you did warn me.' Rupert sighed. A few hours earlier, he'd learned that his elder daughter, who had been trying to conceive for years, had suffered a miscarriage.

He was still looking dispirited when they returned home. Calliope considered a nightcap, but they had already drunk far too much. Ready to head upstairs, she reached out on impulse, meaning to offer the solace of a hug. An occasional friendly embrace was not unknown between them, but on that spring night, some mysterious barrier came unexpectedly crashing down.

By the following morning, the village – the entire nation – began to absorb what it was in for under the new regime. Not even Evanthea the housekeeper would have been interested to know that the Englishman's bed had not been slept in that night.

TWO

~ 1 ~

19 December 1967

Dear Lorenz,

One of our foreigners is posting this letter for me because I believe that my mail is passing through state censors' hands. Your last letter took over a month to get here, so I think you should write c/o Ed Bell until further notice. Ed is an American, but he hates Papadopoulos as much as he does Lyndon Johnson (his brother is serving in Vietnam). It's hard to know whether the coup had CIA backing, as you suggest, but the Americans certainly have a hand in shaping our foreign policy, and there are Greeks who hate them more than they do the Turks. They accuse the USA of subsidising prison camps like Makronisos to promote American interests, which may well be true. But if there's anyone the authorities are not worried about right now, it's the Americans, so Ed will handle my mail from now on, in exchange for domestic olive oil.

A few days ago, some Royalist diehards in the military attempted a counter-coup, but failed. The King has fled to Rome with his family, along with the Prime Minister. The cream of our intelligentsia has also gone into exile. Aristides is still underground but refuses to leave Greece. He thinks it his duty to stay and work towards toppling the regime, though six thousand Greeks were arrested on the night of the coup alone. Captain Yorgos's elder son has been sent to Youra, Pericles is in internal exile in western Greece, and I won't be surprised if they come after me as well one of these days. Fortunately, our new police chief seems like a decent man. Last month, he stopped me, urging me to be more discreet about listening to Deutsche Welle. He has a daughter in Salonika who is a schoolmistress, he told me, as if to explain his kindness.

The extent to which the regime controls our lives is unbelievable. We are all expected to attend church, but other public gatherings are prohibited. Last week, some parents took their children to a puppet show, only to have the room stormed by policemen. The only ones who protested were the disappointed children. People are terrified to speak up, especially those who need permits to own a shop, a truck, a caique. Rozakis must be turning in his grave at having Papadopoulos's portrait hanging in his son's *kapheneion*. I am thinking of writing an article under a pseudonym. I think it's important for the world to know the full extent of the *junta*'s reach. If I write it in German, would you be willing to edit it and see that it's published abroad?

I was interested to hear about the feminist magazine your friend is launching, and am flattered that she wants to include me in the international women's issue. My French cousin says that my life resembles a novel more than most novels resemble life. I hope that's not why your friend is interested in me! Two new women's shelters have been opened in Greece, inspired by our success in Mytilene. I am hoping to spend less time at the *kentro* and more at home, translating works that can no longer be published here. My goddaughter has recently graduated from university and works at the British Council library in Athens, so I have persuaded Eleni to move back and take over the *kentro*'s administration. She never much liked Athens, so it was not difficult to talk her into returning. The hard part will be for me to relinquish control, but the *junta* has brought about an unexpected shift in my priorities.

Speaking of books, a German couple came looking for me one

day, after reading your trilogy. They wanted to do an interview for some German magazine ('the real-life Resistance fighter behind the wartime story') but I told them it was out of the question without your permission. A month later, two Frenchmen were also asking questions in the *agora*. Maybe we should put up a plaque at my entrance?

I was sorry to hear Alicia has been unwell, but trust she is back on her feet by now. How is your new book coming along? You'll be interested to know that my new year's resolution is to study English. Maybe some day I'll be able to read your books in yet another translation!

With best wishes for Christmas and the new year.

Yours,

Calliope

~ 2 ~

In spring, Calliope's aunt came down with pneumonia. Calliope moved Elpida to her own parents' bedroom, then nursed her with Evanthea's help through two relapses. Towards the end of the year, Elpida died in her sleep, aged eighty-one. It was a wonder she had lasted this long, given the griefs she'd had to endure. Her younger son had died of bone cancer; her elder son, unable to see eye to eye with his father, had for years avoided visiting Molyvos.

By the time his mother passed away, Grigoris Metrophanis was in his late fifties, a widower with two sons at Cambridge. To Calliope, he seemed like a virtual stranger, despite the familiar Mussolini jaw. He was bald now, his mouth fixed in an expression of perpetual irony. Calliope thought this had something to do with the political manoeuvres a shipping magnate must have had to finesse under a Right-wing regime. Papadopoulos avidly courted ship owners: extending concessions, demanding loyalty.

Grigoris had studied law, then married into a prominent shipping family. He had to return to Athens two days after his mother's funeral, and needed to ask a favour. His parents' property had been neglected in recent years. It would require not only thorough cleaning but extensive repairs. Would Calliope take care of this for him; perhaps find someone interested in renting the house on a long-term basis?

Calliope said she could certainly try.

'I am deeply indebted to you – for everything.' Grigoris stood scanning Calliope's features, as if searching for his childhood playmate in the middle-aged face. It was the evening before his departure. 'Is there anything I can do for you?'

Calliope thanked her cousin. There wasn't a thing she needed, except perhaps an explanation, she added, looking into his eyes. She recalled a long-ago conversation in which Grigoris said she was the only family member with whom he could have a frank political discussion. She was curious to know how a man who had once shared her own political views could become a *junta* supporter.

'It's called survival, my dear.' Grigoris almost smiled. He was no longer so foolhardy as to think he could change the world; certainly not heroic enough, he stated. He had a deep, sonorous voice; a manner that made even trivial opinions sound like indisputable pronouncements. He regarded her for a moment, as if trying to decide whether there was any point in continuing. 'My mother once said you had what she called "lofty aspirations". But take my advice, my dear, be sensible—'

'Ah, sensible! That I can't promise. I believe I lack what it takes to be sensible.' Coming out of Calliope's mouth, the last word sounded almost pejorative.

Grigoris sighed. He held his hand inside his waistcoat, as if to keep it warm. 'Well, at least be careful.' He touched his lips gently to her cheek by way of goodbye. He said her eyes were still marvellously golden; they hadn't changed at all. 'Call me if you need anything. I'm always there for you.'

'Thank you.' He looked, Calliope thought, tired but sincere. Perhaps his conscience was whispering in his ear? She had invited him for dinner but Grigoris declined, saying he had things he needed to finish before his departure. He and Rupert had not taken to each other; they had nothing in common except, perhaps, an impatience with broody women. Heading to Ed Bell's house to pick up a letter, Calliope recalled Mirto saying that Grigoris was not an unfeeling man, but one afraid of feeling too much. Could this still be true? she wondered.

Ed was renting a house just behind the town hall. On her way over, Calliope ran into the mayor. Mathaios was widely admired, but there were those who considered him a *junta* collaborator, if only because he had chosen not to step down after the 1967 coup. Some twenty months later, the mayor wore the woebegone look of a chastised child. Coming upon Calliope, he stopped and glanced about, then dropped his voice. He would have the forged ID ready next week, he promised.

'Oh, thank you . . . thank you!' Calliope whispered, though it was Wednesday evening and the shops were closed, their shutters rattling drearily in the wind. 'I'm going to deliver it in person,' she added.

~ 3 ~

She came home to find Rupert whistling, busy preparing a wild mushroom dish. His retirement had turned Rupert into an enthusiastic chef. When he was in high spirits, he always wanted to cook, and tell jokes, and make prolonged love. Calliope had long since observed that when men felt pleased with themselves, they were often overcome by a strangely possessive impulse. She was nonetheless astonished to hear Rupert suggest that they might as well get married. The proposal was made in bed, when she was all but ready to be whisked away into the realm of sleep.

'But why?' she asked, abruptly awake. 'Why now?'

'Why not? We could get married at the British Embassy, or you could come to London and finally meet my family.' He knew she would never agree to be married in church. They had discussed the possibility of her coming to London for Christmas, but never of tying the knot.

'What's this all about?' she asked now, searching his face. A thought occurred to her. 'Don't tell me your children don't know we're living together!'

'Of course they know.' He grinned at her, sheepish. 'They also know something you have yet to discover.'

'Which is?'

'Which is that deep, deep, deep inside, I'm both conventional and possessive,' he stated, smiling into one cheek. He had a way of disarming her with his forthrightness, his willingness to expose himself.

'Full of surprises today, aren't we?' She regarded him for a long, bemused moment. 'Give me one good reason why I should get married at the age of fifty-three.'

'Oh, you think that's too young? I suppose we *could* wait for a year or so.'

She laughed. 'Seriously. I don't understand what it is with you men. Why—'

He didn't let her finish. 'I don't understand, either,' he said, 'but I do know it will make me happy to die knowing you were my wife.'

'Was it my aunt's funeral? Is that what this is all about?'

He lifted a shoulder, his eyes landing on Mirto's iconostasis. 'Had we but world enough and time,' he declaimed, quoting Andrew Marvell.

'Oh, Rupert, I'm not there yet!' exclaimed Calliope, who was still mastering basic English. 'What are you mumbling at me?'

'I'm mumbling some profound truths about time and mortality.'

'Ah.' She smiled vaguely. The wind was whistling through the trees in the garden; the room was pleasantly warm. There was the smell of freshly washed bedsheets and burning charcoal. 'But why?' she repeated. 'Do you really think it will change anything?'

'I hope not.' He flashed her a quirky grin, then grew serious. 'I honestly don't know why it should matter,' he said. 'I do know that none of your reasons against marriage apply anymore.'

'You mean I no longer have to worry about cuckolding you with some young Adonis?' Calliope smiled. She had, long ago, confided her fear that she was innately promiscuous. He was the only man with whom she had shared this secret anxiety.

'I mean you no longer have to worry that marriage will steal your thunder. You're your own person. Marriage is not going to change that now, is it?'

She stopped to mull this over. 'Rupert,' she said. 'I haven't been so . . . so content for a very long time. Why can't you be satisfied with that? It's totally irrational, what you ask of me. It's—'

'Atavistic, I know, but can't I be irrational from time to time, like the rest of humanity?'

She smiled at that. 'Is it really that important to you?'

He nodded, still sheepish, like a child confessing to having eaten biscuits reserved for guests. She reached out and stroked his beard. It was almost all grey now, yet his energy, his indomitable spirit, often humbled her.

'I'll think about it,' she finally said.

He kissed her, abruptly exuberant. 'Thank you!'

'Don't start celebrating yet,' she said. 'All I said was I'd think about it!'

'Fair enough,' he said.

~ 4 ~

There were helmeted soldiers at Athens Airport, grimly alert, shouldering submachine guns. Rupert was flying to London but would be back in time for New Year's Eve. Calliope had decided against accompanying him. A few days earlier, she had been summoned for questioning by Molyvos's police chief. Louizos had been courteous, stopping her in the *agora*, asking her to drop in at her convenience. When she entered his office, he rose and shook her hand. He was under orders to enquire about her godson's whereabouts, he said.

'Would you happen to know where he is these days?'

Calliope shrugged. She said she hadn't heard from Aristides in months. One of his sisters had written, asking whether it was true that Aristides had fled abroad. 'Unfortunately, I have no idea.' Calliope opened her bag and took out a handkerchief. 'If you find out where he is, please let me know. I've been sick with worry.'

This much was true, but the letter had actually been sent as a ruse, after some of Aristides's classmates had been questioned by the police.

Louizos had looked persuaded, but Calliope wasn't taking any chances. She had arranged to meet Aristides at a party her publisher was giving on his wife's name day. There would be some twenty guests, but Calliope worried that she might be followed. Having seen Rupert off, she strode towards the airport toilets, carrying an old suitcase. She glanced into the mirror, then slipped into a stall, where she changed from her trouser suit and loafers into heels and a snug woollen dress. Inside the large suitcase nestled the small red valise she had bought in Athens back in the 1950s. She had also brought a hat to conceal her auburn hair. There was the cascading sound of flushing toilets, the hum of hand dryers. The arrival of a flight from Brussels was being announced. An elderly woman urged a child to hurry up and pee.

Calliope put away her travel outfit, adjusted her nylons and slipped on a pair of sunglasses. She stepped out of the stall, dropped the battered suitcase into the waste bin, and clicked away in her narrow suede shoes. All she had now was her red overnight valise. It was late afternoon. A few snowflakes drifted languidly in the crisp air, melting on the roofs of crawling taxis. Calliope raised a hand. She stepped off the kerb, glanced over her shoulder, then slid into the back of a cab.

'I'm going to Kolonaki,' she said, peering out as the taxi lurched away from the airport. The day was quickly fading. She tugged at her dress, then leaned her head against the backrest with a long exhalation.

Twenty months into the dictatorship, Athens wore an unfamiliar face. The soldiers were ubiquitous, as were the commercial billboards: American Express, Siemens, Coca-Cola. Calliope had recently tried a Coke and thought it as foul as cough syrup. What she needed now was a glass of wine. She needed to see her godson.

Sighing, Calliope yanked off her shoe and rubbed her slightly arthritic toe, vaguely wondering how Rupert was doing, up among the clouds. The cab had stopped for a light, and she glanced out again, her eyes lighting on a large propaganda poster: *Long Live the Twenty-first of April!*

Her toe throbbed and throbbed.

~ 5 ~

She had hardly recognised him, with his hair dyed black, his horn-rimmed spectacles. Gone was the blond lock of hair that had for years flopped over his eye; gone, too, the moustache he had sported in recent months. But he was still quick and purposeful and deeply self-contained. There was a certain resemblance to his father – the chiselled, sharp-boned face, the luminous eyes – but something about Aristides's movements, his keen, attentive air, reminded Calliope of the young Lorenz Umbreit.

She had brought the promised ID, along with a new leather jacket. The name in the forged document was Konstantin Katranides. It was the name of a distant cousin on his mother's side. Aristides's hair had been dyed by his elder sister. The hair had been straight in childhood but had unexpectedly begun to curl during puberty. It was still curly but was now cropped short. He was almost thirty.

Calliope reached out and impulsively ran her hand through the black curls. Aristides sipped his wine, then stopped to remove his spectacles. He kept putting them on, then taking them off, his fingers seeking the shaven moustache.

'Keep your spectacles on!' Calliope said. 'You have to get used to wearing them as if they belonged to you.'

'Yes, yes.' Aristides exhaled. 'I look like a book-eater, don't I?'

'Book-eater's good! What you don't want is to look like Che Guevara.'

Calliope reached for an ashtray. They were seated in Titos and Anasthasia Stamoulis's living room, chatting in a quiet corner. It was a vast room, with Persian rugs on the varnished floors and bookcases looming around the marble fireplace. At one end, over by the kitchen, stood a buffet covered with a white damask cloth. Aristides said there was enough food on the silver platters to feed a small African tribe. Anasthasia – Tasia to her friends – was a busy doctor. She had a full-time maid from Cyprus, reputed to be a fine cook. Aristides got up to replenish his plate.

'Why aren't you eating?' he asked. 'You should eat – it's excellent food.'

Calliope went on smoking. 'I'm not hungry.' She observed her godson chew for a moment. He was still eating like a lion, she said, chuckling. The only thing Aristides left on his plate was a long green pepper, which he had gingerly tasted, then pushed aside, scowling. He still got nosebleeds whenever he ate a hot pepper, he said.

Calliope smiled. 'At least you've stopped sticking peppercorns up your nose.'

'I'd gladly do it again if it would only block the colonels' stench,' Aristides said.

The hosts' spaniel came up and sniffed at his crotch. Aristides scratched the dog's head. He would have to be going soon, he said, then got drawn into a discussion of the recent referendum on the new constitution. From there, they went on to talk about Alexandros Panagoulis, a fiery dissident who had tried to blow up Papadopoulos's limousine. The attempt had failed. Panagoulis was arrested, tortured and recently sentenced to death, amid international outcries for clemency.

Aristides glanced at his watch. He really had to go, he repeated.

'Please promise me you'll be careful,' Calliope said, watching him zip up his new leather jacket. He was wearing only a sweater and a scarf when he arrived; had tried on the jacket immediately, delighted to find it a perfect fit.

'Goodnight, *nona*.' Aristides pecked his godmother's cheek. 'Thank you.'

Calliope took her godson's head between her hands and kissed his forehead, her eyes misting over.

'No Panagoulis heroics, please!' she said, holding onto his arms, willing him to listen. 'Promise me!' she pleaded.

He flung his scarf over his shoulder. 'Fine, *nona*, I promise.' He gazed at her for a moment. '*What?* I promised, didn't I?'

'Don't forget,' Calliope said, pressing her cheek to his.

He pulled back and gave her a mock salute. '*Yassou, nona!*'

He left then, his new ID in his jacket pocket. The cousin he was impersonating lived in Mytilene. He had briefly studied medicine in Athens but had returned home after failing his exams, to work in his father's pharmacy.

Calliope returned to the party. The guests huddled in small, ani-mated clusters, eating, arguing, laughing. Titos had introduced her to some of the guests, but she felt obscurely anxious. All around her, there was talk of recent educational reforms, of new language laws and revised textbooks. The room was warm, hazy with cigarette smoke. Among the hosts' friends was a couple whose son had been arrested during George Papandreou's recent funeral. The former Prime Minis-ter, whose anticipated re-election was widely believed to have triggered the colonels' coup, had died under house arrest, his funeral attracting half a million mourners.

University students represented the most ardent opposition to the regime. There was, Aristides had told Calliope, a *junta*-appointed campus organisation whose members spied on Leftist students. His girlfriend had an uncle working for the Security Police. The uncle had tried to talk Dorothea into becoming one of the campus spies but she had declined, claiming a heavy workload.

It was almost midnight. Calliope refilled her wineglass and sat down by the fire to chat with her publisher. A dapper, bilingual man, Titos had been educated at the Sorbonne, then returned to Greece to start a prestigious publishing house. He was the sort of man who could carry on an intense conversation with one person while still following everything else going on around him. Getting a forged ID had been his idea.

'Are you all right?' he was asking now.

Calliope made a vague gesture. 'I'm worried about Aristides,' she said. Her toe was aching, clad in the stylishly pointed shoe.

Titos regarded her for a moment. 'Is there anything I can do?'

'Ach, I don't know,' Calliope said. 'I doubt it.'

They talked about this and that: books Titos was interested in but couldn't publish under the new regime; an outspoken nephew's expul-sion from the Bar. Calliope had yet to finish work on a novel Titos hoped to publish. She was vaguely thinking of translating a German memoir by an SS officer's son, she said.

At this, Titos leaned back, a subtle change taking place in his tired features. The room was hot. He slid an index finger into his turtleneck and stretched it away from his throat. 'Have you heard from Lorenz lately?'

'Yes.' Calliope's eyelids flickered. She hadn't had a word from him for months but had finally received a letter, just the other day.

Titos dragged on his cigarette. 'Did he tell you about Alicia?'

'Yes. It doesn't sound good, does it?'

'Tasia says ovarian's the worst.' Titos exhaled. Lorenz had been planning a trip to Athens, to research a nonfiction book about postwar Greece. He had cancelled the trip for the second time, after hearing his wife's dire prognosis.

Calliope sat smoking, staring into the fire. The flames crackled, spitting against the blackened screen. 'I have to write to him,' she said at length. 'I don't know what to say . . . I have nothing to offer but platitudes.'

Titos confessed to having the same problem. He'd intended to phone, but kept putting it off. 'Such a nice woman,' he muttered. 'They were thinking of buying a house here . . . somewhere by the sea.'

'I know.' Calliope fidgeted with her mother's ring. She was musing on her encounter with Alicia Umbreit: the German woman's easy grace; the endearing way she had of wrinkling her nose at her husband's occasionally heavy-handed humour. Eager to change the subject, Calliope reminded Titos of his promise to visit Molyvos.

'One of these days.' Titos smiled. 'Maybe over Easter.'

Calliope was expecting a German interviewer at Easter but was sure they could manage. 'Do come,' she said, idly stroking the spaniel. 'I'd like you to meet Rupert.'

Titos levered himself out of his chair.

'I'll speak to Tasia and let you know,' he said, returning to his social duties.

Several guests were preparing to leave. A baby, who had been sleeping in the guest room, was howling in the hallway. Calliope thought of Aristides squalling in her arms after being baptised; of the first time he'd asked her why he had a *nona* but no mother. She told herself she should be going as well. All evening, there had been the distant rumble of street traffic, but now she registered the honking of arrested cars, the wailing of a passing ambulance. Not for the first time, she decided she really wouldn't want to live in the city. She much preferred crickets' songs and night birds' cries to the frantic sounds of the ever-expanding capital. All that awaited her this evening were the anonymous streets, the empty hotel room with its mothball smell.

All the same, it was time to go.

~ 6 ~

The *junta* had been in power for nearly a year when Klara Reinhardt arrived in Molyvos. Calliope took her guest down to Orpheus's Head, where they sat conversing in German over ouzo and *mezedhes*. It was Klara's third day in the village. A portable recorder was whirring on the edge of the table; a camera in a brown leather case lay beside it, its strap coiled like a sleeping snake.

The feminist magazine's international feature was meant to profile women who had distinguished themselves in various parts of the world. Calliope was pondering a question that Klara had put to her. Had there been a key event responsible for awakening her feminist consciousness?

'No . . . I don't think so,' Calliope answered after a thoughtful pause. 'I believe it was a cumulative set of events, of insights.'

The first thing that came to mind had taken place when she was about twenty. It was the year she'd begun teaching; the year one of their neighbours – a young, battered wife – had come to cry on her mother's shoulder, only to go back to her husband because she had no other options. 'And then, over the years, there were other things . . . things that occasionally made my blood boil.'

'Such as?'

'Oh.' Calliope exhaled. 'So many ordinary yet significant things – bedsheets, for instance, hung out to flaunt a bride's virginity.' She smiled at Klara's apparent disbelief. 'You might not come across this in Germany,' she said, 'but the fundamental issues are the same – they are universal.'

'I know.'

A Berlin journalist, Klara had come to Molyvos for a week, combining a spring break with an interview for *Sie* magazine. She was a sturdy-looking woman, taller than Calliope, with emerald-green eyes and straw-coloured hair that sat on her head like a helmet, gleaming in the sun. She was in her late thirties and an unabashed lesbian.

The thought of making love to a woman intrigued Calliope, though she couldn't quite imagine it for herself. Whenever she tried to, she found herself giggling, like a schoolgirl stumbling on the secrets of matrimony. Foreign women, she had observed, shaved their legs and armpits. Did they shave their pubic hair, too? And was it possible for a woman's body to thrill at the sight of another woman's breasts or buttocks?

Calliope thought of Lorenz, who was a friend of Klara's and whose body – the mere thought of his body – could still tug at her heart. Klara had not asked about Lorenz. They talked about Greek society, about the inequities of the dowry system.

'The thing about tradition,' said Calliope, 'is few people think to question it. But once you do, once it occurs to you, it's as if the scales have fallen from your eyes.'

One day, she had attended the blessing of a former pupil's newborn. 'It's an ancient religious ceremony,' Calliope explained. 'It takes place in church, when the child's forty days old.' She had been to such ceremonies countless times, but somehow had never stopped to question the fact that a male child is borne by the priest all the way to the Holy Portals, whereas a female is taken only as far as the narthex.

'Oh?' Klara blinked at Calliope greenly, like a curious cat. 'Why is that?'

'The Holy Portals lead to the altar. A newborn boy gets to be displayed before God, but not a girl. Never!'

This statement, too, elicited a small chortling sound. Klara sat for a moment, staring out to sea, then picked up her camera and snapped a fisherman puttering about in his boat. Half-a-dozen rowboats were moored to the quay, bobbing in the water. From the kitchen wafted the smell of wine-braised octopus.

'Anyway,' Calliope continued, 'I think that was the day I began to see the connection between the child-blessing ceremony and the fact that there had never been a woman on the village council.' She waited for Klara to finish making a note before taking her to the beach. At a nearby table, a former pupil was having a tête-à-tête with a Swedish tourist.

'Ready for coffee?' Calliope asked.

'Yes. No sugar, please.'

Calliope signalled to Nikki, then found herself wondering whether her former classmate had heard the rumours about her daughter's involvement with Ed Bell. Artemis was nowhere to be seen, but, walking up from the harbour a little later, Calliope and Klara ran into Ed himself. He was on his way to the harbour, but had stopped by the sea wall to scribble something in his notebook.

Everyone knew Ed had taken a year off from his advertising job to write a novel about his Russian grandparents, but eighteen months later he was still in Molyvos, still whipping out his notebook at every opportunity. He was tall and thin, and had an odd habit of frequently licking his lips, like a man trying to solve a complex problem, contemplating an impossible set of options.

Calliope introduced her guest, then she and Klara meandered down to the beach. The sea was still too cold for the natives, but Klara insisted on swimming, until she spotted jellyfish floating on the cresting waves. She had once been stung so badly her arm had swelled like a balloon, she said.

The beach was deserted, except for Dora the weeper's sons, who liked to hang around their aunt's seaside kiosk. The feta had made Klara thirsty. Did the kiosk sell soft drinks? she asked.

Calliope smiled. 'Even Coca-Cola.'

They bought a lemonade, then Klara snapped a few photographs of children playing in the adjacent playground. Two schoolgirls were seesawing, while a younger boy waited, his hand pressed to his genitals. Instead of swimming, Calliope and Klara went to sit on a park bench, watching seagulls glide over the darkening water. Dora's sons were climbing up a tree, laughing when they reached the top. All at once, Calliope's mind conjured up the memory of little Aristides playing by the sea. She thought of the day he had chased her up and down the beach, mock-threatening her with wet seaweed. And then of the day he had trapped minnows in a *gliko* jar, then, overcome by pity, tossed them back into the frothing waves.

The thought of her tender-hearted godson brought sudden tears to Calliope's eyes. She fervently hoped he would keep the promise he had made at Stamoulis's party.

~ 7 ~

Excerpt from Calliope Adham's journal – 20 December 1969

They had hoped she would last at least until Christmas, but it was not to be. Lorenz's letter was brief, his anguish unmistakable. I don't know what to say. What can a former mistress possibly say at a time like this? Am I even entitled to offer comfort for the death of a wife I myself have wronged? Once more, I seem to be swimming in very stormy waters, partly because of Lorenz's grief, but also because I can't help feeling culpable.

And then there is Aristides, who is neither writing nor calling. I can't sleep nights, brooding on Alicia and Lorenz, and worrying about Aristides, who still refuses to go into exile. I have pressed him to accept Alexandra's invitation, though I confess to feeling very old, finding myself more concerned with safety than with lofty ideals. Would the woman I am now have jeopardised her life during the Occupation?

I don't know the answer, but there is no shortage of courageous people. Louizos, the chief of police, has been demoted for 'nonfulfilment of official duties'. It seems he did not arrest as many people as expected. I don't know him well, but he seems almost relieved not to be in a position of authority anymore.

I also had a letter from Alexandra, saying that her American nephew has fled to Canada, dodging the draft. I suppose that if I were living in the USA, I would be taking part in anti-Vietnam demonstrations. Aristides hates the Americans, but at least they have not taken away the right to protest. The most difficult thing about being underground, he says, is not being sure whom to trust. I don't know what I'd do without Rupert's devotion and sense of humour. I'm looking forward to finally visiting London. It will be good to get away from Greece for a while, though I still dread the thought of flying – or is it the thought of tying the knot?

No one else seems to share my deep reservations about marriage. Eleni's daughter is getting engaged. Her future husband is a Cretan archaeologist, whom she met when he came to borrow a library book. Alexandra, too, has met someone she likes – a recent refugee she refers to as her Melancholy Hungarian. He is, she says, given to 'black moods', but who can blame him, given recent events in his country? I have my own black moods, but am grateful to have work that continues to interest me. I have decided against translating the German book for now, in favour of a Greek novel set in Mykonos. It is the first Greek novel depicting the social changes brought on by mass tourism. A funny, thought-provoking book.

We lag far behind Mykonos but seem to be attracting our share of homosexuals. Thierry's lover has just got engaged to a local girl and has left Thierry, who is heartbroken, planning to return to France before the year is out.

Meanwhile, a homosexual Australian artist and his lover have been staying at Orpheus's Head. The Australian, who has been studying in Paris, loves it here and is hoping to come for a longer stay. Ed Bell says it's because of all the sex-starved soldiers, but who knows? Ed himself is in love with Artemis but it seems they can't get married: He is half-Jewish and will not convert. I hope they have the sense to elope to Cyprus for a civil marriage, though I would then have to find someone else to handle my post. Ed is self-centred and talks too much, but has turned out to be a decent enough guy.

As for Uncle Mandras, he spends much of his time rooting for Papadopoulos, ranting about the decadent example foreigners are setting to our girls. Poor Papadopoulos: he wants to attract more tourists but only if he can make foreign men cut their hair and women leave their miniskirts and bikinis at home before coming to enjoy our beaches. I would love to wear a bikini myself, but I've put on weight lately. Rupert claims to love what he calls my 'Rubenesque curves' but Rupert is saintly. I think he would love me even if I grew warts all over my face.

Nonetheless, I am so overwrought these days that even Rupert occasionally irks me. Is this something brought on by hormonal changes? I am ridiculously piqued by the love-hate relationship Rupert has with his writing. There are times I think he'll never finish his memoirs; that he doesn't want to finish! There is about him a subtle, exquisite sort of fragility. It is even there in his facial features, though I can never put my finger on just where this lies. His eyes are those of a man determined to engage in serious pursuits, but his mouth threatens to give him away, perpetually hovering on the edge of laughter. He hides his sorrows well but I have stumbled upon them from time to time – dark caves of melancholy beauty I feel privileged to have glimpsed, though far less frequently than the green hills of his childlike joy.

Right now, I am waiting for him to return from Mytilene. We are flying to London on Tuesday, but I can't stop thinking about Alicia. I don't know—

Someone is at the door.

～ 8 ～

'Here's your post,' said Eleni. She paused, frowning a little. 'Am I too early?'

'No, no. I'd just lost track of time. Ouzo?'

Eleni nodded, peeling off her sweater. They were well into December but the morning had swept in with a springlike sunshine. Half a dozen cats could be seen, lolling in the garden; a mourning dove called among the denuded fruit trees. Eleni smiled, watching a half-grown kitten chase a ball of yarn. 'Rupert not home?'

'He had to go to Mytilene. He should be back any minute.' Calliope headed to the kitchen, where a meatball casserole was simmering. She put her journal away. 'So much to do before we leave,' she said. It was Wednesday, a day on which the two women routinely got together, to share a meal and discuss *kentro* business.

'Are you excited?' Eleni was scratching the edge of the divan, trying to attract the kitten's attention.

'More anxious than excited, I think.'

'Really?' The kitten leaped up and arranged itself in Eleni's lap. 'Why?'

'Oh, I don't know.' Calliope settled beside Eleni, picking up the post she had dropped in passing. She hated not being able to speak English properly; dreaded meeting Rupert's family and sounding like a child. 'I'm also afraid of flying. Don't tell Rupert,' she added, riffling through the mail. 'It's so irrational. We take our lives in our hands every time we go to Mytilene, don't we?' The serpentine road to the capital required vigilance at the wheel, but taxi owners often drove with their heads twisted backwards, carrying on heated political discussions.

'I thought you had no secrets from Rupert,' Eleni teased.

'Just one. I insisted on keeping at least one.' Calliope's eyes crinkled above her reading spectacles. She was separating Rupert's post from her own but suddenly stopped and exclaimed, drawing *Sie* out of its envelope.

She had not expected the January issue before Christmas, but there it was, with Klara's article as one of its main features. Calliope studied her own polychromatic image, making an ambiguous sound that might have been interpreted as either disdain or satisfaction. She held it out for Eleni to see. 'What do you think?'

'Oh, Calliopitsa, a foreign magazine!' Eleni ran her hand over the glossy page, the way a woman in a fabric shop might do with a bolt of velvet.

Calliope chuckled, glancing once more at her own photograph. 'Rupert calls this my Joan of Arc look,' she said, making Eleni smile.

Klara had captured Calliope with her chin in the air, a sun-tanned woman with shoulder-length hair, her unflinching eyes fixed somewhere beyond the camera. She had been carefully posed in front of the sparkling blue sea. A second photograph showed her in the *kentro* library. There was also a snapshot of the village, picturesquely perched on its fortress-crowned hill.

Eleni was trying to read the bold black caption. 'What does it say?'

'It says . . .' Calliope essayed a deep, theatrical voice. '"Calliope Adham: The Power to Decide".'

'Decide what?' asked Eleni.

'Oh, it's just something I said during the interview. I was quoting Napoleon: "Nothing is more difficult, and therefore more precious, than to be able to decide."' She shrugged, casting the magazine aside. 'Did you say ouzo?'

'Yes. Aren't you going to read it?'

'Eventually.'

'Oh, come on, read me something. I want to know what it says!'

'What for? You know me better than Klara Reinhardt ever will.'

'Please?' Eleni's eyes grew crafty. 'Does it say something critical?'

'What? Of course not!' Calliope had been about to get up but stopped and plucked the magazine, rather huffily. 'You want to hear about me or my amazing accomplishments?'

'You. And your accomplishments.'

Calliope sighed, mock-forbearingly.

'Here – a typical magazine passage.' She began to translate. '"Calliope Adham possesses an idealistic, supremely rational character. She gives an initial impression of being somewhat reserved, focused on her own inner life. And yet, one senses a secret fire just below the surface. In conversation, her face is animated, her gestures at once elegant and extravagant. She seems less like a woman raised in a Greek village than one of those complex aristocrats inhabiting nineteenth-century Russian novels."' Calliope raised her gaze. 'Enough?'

'No!' said Eleni. 'I want to hear more!'

'Sorry, it's enough for me.' Calliope made a face, playfully tossing the magazine at Eleni's chest. She got to her feet then and opened the door, letting the kitten's mother in from the garden. Eleni was still protesting but Calliope ignored her, going into the pantry to fetch a bottle of ouzo. 'Everything all right at the *kentro*?'

Everything was fine, Eleni said, though she was a little tired, having been awakened after midnight to deal with an obstetrical crisis. She rose and moved to the table, the kitten clinging to her skirt. She was about a decade younger than Calliope but growing heavy around the hips.

Calliope set down two glasses and a dish of olives. 'Who was it this time?'

'You wouldn't know them,' Eleni said. The husband was a young shepherd living outside Vafios. They had two daughters but desperately wanted a son. 'By the way, are you still looking for someone to clean your aunt's house?'

'Yes. You know anyone?' Calliope had tried to help her cousin but finding a cleaner wasn't easy now that everyone had enough to eat. She had asked her own housekeeper, but Evanthea had her hands full. Eleni said the shepherd's mother, Pelaghia, might be interested.

'Good. Ask her to come see me.' Calliope checked the time, only half-listening as Eleni digressed, speaking of a problem Pelaghia's son was having with his flock.

'I wonder what's keeping Rupert,' Calliope said. 'He should have been here by now.' She lit another cigarette. There had been a road accident the previous month. A three-wheeler had slammed into a Petra taxi, landing the driver in intensive care.

Eleni popped an olive into her mouth. 'Sometimes they leave late,' she said.

'Yes.' Calliope began to beat eggwhites for the sauce, adding a slow stream of lemon juice. The meatballs were getting overcooked. She stirred the sauce into the pot, then took out a fresh loaf of bread.

She had just finished slicing it when she finally heard the garden gate open. Turning, she saw Rupert plod through the garden, lugging two shopping bags. He looked sick, or just unbearably tired. He pecked her cheek, then stepped indoors, dragging his feet. Calliope had an odd feeling that he was avoiding her eyes, like a man coming home with a guilty secret. He set the shopping bags down, greeted

Eleni perfunctorily, then sank onto the divan and began to unlace his shoes.

'What is it, dear? What happened in Mytilene?'

Rupert began to speak, then bent over to shuck off his shoes. He sat for a moment, bleakly watching a cat chase a lizard outdoors. He tugged at his collar.

'I just ran into Mathaios,' he finally said. 'He was on his way to see you—'

'Mathaios the mayor?'

Rupert reached for Calliope's hand. 'They've arrested Aristides,' he said.

'Aristides!' Calliope clutched at Rupert's hand like a drowning woman. 'How?'

'I don't know. Dorothea phoned. She'll wait for your call around six o'clock.' Rupert leaned in and kissed Calliope's cheek, his glance meeting Eleni's stricken eyes. 'Mathaios said you can phone from his office.'

'From his office,' Calliope echoed. She got to her feet, intending to do something of vital importance but unable to recall what it was. She felt light-headed and unbearably warm. She needed to lie down. 'Yes. Yes, I'm going to . . .' she managed to bring out.

The rest of the statement slipped away from her. The floor was heaving under her feet. For a moment, Calliope continued to stare at the dust motes dancing in a shaft of light, could hear Rupert's voice speaking across a widening distance. But then her knees gave way and his words, too, began to fade, caught in a web of thickening darkness.

~ 9 ~

They had been on their way home from the fortress and there, lying under a pomegranate tree, was a dead baby owl. Aristides would have been about three years old. He had gone down on his haunches and was studying the limp, stunned-looking carcass.

'What's the matter with the baby owl?'

'It's dead,' Calliope said, glancing at the setting sun.

'Why?'

'I don't know. Maybe it fell out of its nest.'

'But why is it dead?'

'I don't know . . . everything dies sooner or later.'

'*Kyria* Maria's baby son died when she wasn't looking.'

'Did he? He must have been very sick.'

Aristides took Calliope's hand. 'I get sick sometimes.'

'Everybody gets sick from time to time.'

'But I don't want to die!' Aristides wailed. 'I—'

'Oh, you won't die,' Calliope said, bending to kiss the child's peach-soft cheek. 'Not until you are an old, old man with a cane and a long, grey beard.'

'I don't want to grow a beard!'

'You won't have to. It'll be up to you.'

A moment went by. The sun went on sliding behind the mountains.

'Will I still have to die?' Aristides asked, his face tilted towards hers.

'Without a beard? Well, maybe not.'

The memory ensnared Calliope's thoughts in Athens, as she stood outside the grim edifice housing the General Security Headquarters. She had stationed herself across Bouboulinas Street, gazing at the barred windows. It was impossible to know which floor Aristides was being detained on, let alone whether he was being tortured. Dorothea had said that his being held at Bouboulinas, rather than at the notorious military police headquarters, was something to be grateful for, but Calliope had heard that torture took place at Bouboulinas as well.

She had no idea what her godson had been arrested for, or even which underground organisation he belonged to. Someone who had been with him, who had managed to escape, had left a message for Dorothea, telling her about Aristides's arrest.

The General Security Headquarters was behind the National Archaeological Museum. Years ago, Calliope had visited the museum with Iason, never suspecting that one day she would be standing a stone's throw away, her heart clogged with dread.

Dorothea had not been able to see Aristides either. Only legal counsel was granted admission at this stage of the process. Calliope and Rupert had taken the night ferry to Piraeus. They arrived around eight o'clock, going their separate ways. It was a crisp winter morning, with a sun so brilliant it seemed like a personal taunt. They had arranged to meet Calliope's cousin later, but Rupert had headed straight for the British Embassy, to see whether he could pull any strings. Aristides was not a British subject, but Rupert knew someone who just might have the right contacts.

'*Junta* or no *junta*,' he said, 'this is Greece. I'm sure personal connections still work wonders around here.'

Calliope could only hope that Rupert was right. Grigoris had promised to make enquiries at his end; Dorothea was trying to get further details. She was to meet Calliope at eleven, at a café across from the museum. It would be their first meeting.

A face appeared at one of the prison's upper windows, peering through the bars. It was impossible to identify the man, but as she stood there, eyes riveted to the window, Calliope felt her private sorrow explode. Of course, it was unlikely to be Aristides, yet she couldn't shake the feeling that she had succeeded in summoning her godson with the sheer force of her grief; that he could see her now, peering up at him, and might draw some small consolation from her proximate presence.

She raised her right hand in a wan gesture, then let it drop, swept by fresh desolation. Sobbing, she turned and headed towards the café. If only she knew what her godson's crime had been! She had, at first, resisted contacting Grigoris – she disliked appealing to anyone indebted to her – but finally made the call. For Aristides, she would contact the devil himself if need be.

The café was spacious, with half the tables already occupied. Calliope threaded her way towards a corner table. She took off her coat and eased herself into a chair, facing the entrance. The room hummed with conversation. She lit a cigarette and was still smoking, lost in reflection over a cup of tea, when Dorothea came in, with the breathless air of a woman trying to catch a departing bus.

It was well past eleven. Dorothea paused at the entrance, squinting, eyes sweeping the room. She whipped out a pair of spectacles, placed them on her nose for a moment, and finally recognised Calliope. Aristides had kept a photograph of his godmother, next to one of his parents.

Calliope had her hair gathered into a clasp and was wearing a tweed suit, a barely ironed blouse; Dorothea wore a short red jacket. She was a long-legged young woman with striking eyes, large and earnest, the colour of an overcast sky. She would have been beautiful if not for her prim mouth which, set in a rather heavy jaw, made Calliope think of a censorious abbess. Aristides had told Calliope that Dorothea was a brilliant student, who hoped to become a judge some day. The girl apologised for being late. She had been detained outside the campus and questioned, not for the first time.

'Why?' Calliope crushed out her cigarette. 'They don't know of your connection, do they?'

Dorothea shook her head. The Security Police often did random checks around the university. The classmate she had been with looked a little scruffy. 'Fortunately, we both had the right backgrounds.'

'Thank God.' Calliope wondered whether Dorothea's Security Police uncle would have the power to intervene if she were arrested. They sat leaning towards each other, pale and intent, speaking in hushed voices. Security Police agents wore civilian clothes, blending into crowds, eavesdropping on private conversations.

'I have the information you wanted.' Dorothea burrowed in her bag, still squinting, still reluctant to wear spectacles. At length, she retrieved a folded note, sliding it across the table. Scrawled across the lined sheet of paper was the name of an Athenian lawyer. Angelos Solomos. 'I just hope they don't know who Aris really is,' Dorothea said. 'I don't think they do.'

Calliope looked up from the note. 'What makes you say that?'

'Oh . . .' A middle-aged man who had been reading a newspaper was getting up to leave. Dorothea waited for him to pass. 'If they did, he would be at the ESA,' she said. The ESA was the military police headquarters, a prison reserved for the staunchest dissidents. Calliope set her cup down.

'So you do know what he's been up to?'

Dorothea hesitated. 'Yes,' she said, and her face quivered.

'But you're not going to tell me?'

'Sorry,' Dorothea said, dropping her gaze. 'I gave my word.'

Calliope sighed, then sat silent for a long moment, her tongue probing a mouth ulcer on her inner cheek. She was fighting a small surge of resentment at knowing less about her own godson than this young, earnest stranger.

Dorothea, too, seemed to be striving for composure. 'My father would kill me if he knew I was still seeing him.' She sat staring bleakly at the window, the dead leaves drifting off tree branches. Another silent moment went by. 'I love him so much!' she blurted then, as if to justify turning her back on her own family.

Calliope didn't know what to say. 'Do they know where you stand politically?'

'Not really. They like to think I'm ambivalent. Which is . . . well, it's not exactly a lie. There are some positive things the *junta* has achieved,' Dorothea said, pausing to blow her nose. 'You may despise their tactics,' she continued, 'I despise them myself, but you can't deny they've brought both economic growth and stability.'

'Oh, but think of the price!' Calliope exclaimed.

She was nothing if not familiar with Right-wing arguments: the *junta* had promoted international investment, unemployment was at an all-time low, inflation was down, farmers were prospering thanks to government grants. It was true, in its way, but the last thing she had expected was to hear such talk from Aristides's girlfriend.

On the other hand, Dorothea was saying, she could not begin to accept the brutality, the disregard for civil rights. She spoke dispassionately, like someone reviewing the facts in her own mind, striving for objectivity. Calliope had a sudden vision of Dorothea sitting on a judiciary bench, dressed in a judge's robes.

She lit another cigarette. 'But you're not involved in student politics, I take it?'

'No. I'm too much of a coward to risk my own neck,' Dorothea said.

The young woman seemed a little rigid but, disarmed by her candour, Calliope went on to ask about her plans for the future. They talked about

Greek justice for a while, until Calliope, glancing at her watch, signalled for the bill. She was meeting Rupert at Grigoris's office at one-thirty. Dorothea wanted to know how long they planned to stay in town, but Calliope couldn't say. They had already cancelled their flight to London.

'Are you going to contact the lawyer?'

'Probably, though my cousin is looking into the arrest. What do you know about this lawyer?'

'He's excellent. Unfortunately, his services don't come cheap,' Dorothea said.

'Ach, don't worry about that.' Calliope made a dismissive gesture. She would gladly give up all her assets to see Aristides released. All night, she had been haunted by images of crushed testicles and ripped fingernails and cigarette-burned soles. She had woken up, screaming, just before dawn.

'Will you let me know what your cousin says?' Dorothea was asking.

Calliope promised. She took down a telephone number. It was not Dorothea's parents' number but that of a close friend; someone Aristides trusted.

'You can leave a message for us anytime,' Dorothea said.

Calliope put the note away, then jotted down Grigoris's number for Dorothea.

'Goodbye . . . I'll be in touch.'

Dorothea was going back to the campus, but Calliope stopped on a windy corner, trying to hail a cab. She looked at her watch and lifted her arm, her nostrils shrinking against the toxic fumes.

At that moment, she felt something brush against her hair. A golden leaf had been blown off a large plane tree and was fluttering down towards the pavement, clinging briefly to her outstretched sleeve, as innocent and beguiling as a butterfly.

~ 10 ~

Grigoris Metrophanis had invited Calliope and Rupert to come to his office, proposing to take them out to a nearby restaurant. By the time

Calliope arrived, though, Rupert had left a message, saying he was going to dine with his embassy contact and would see her back at the hotel. Grigoris related the message with a resolute sort of cheer. A large man with a hearty voice, he led Calliope into his office, trailing the scent of the cologne he had been wearing for decades. He had good news, he stated without preamble.

'Good news? Really?' Calliope lowered herself into a leather chair, her eyes fastened on her cousin's face. Grigoris had always been given to hyperbole, especially when it came to his own achievements. But he was also the sort of man who seemed to derive satisfaction from others' appeals for help. It was, she recalled, *not* being able to help that Grigoris could not abide.

'Very good news.' Grigoris settled himself behind his desk, stopped by a knock at the door. 'Come in!'

The office boy entered, bearing a tray suspended from brass chains. He offered Calliope a cup of coffee, discreetly placed a cup on his employer's desk, then turned and padded, bow-legged, out of the office. The room was sunny and elegant, in a ponderous sort of way. There were photos of ship liners on the walls; a model of a new ferry rested on the massive desk.

'So, as I was saying, it looks good. It seems the police don't know who he is.'

'Oh! Why then . . . what's he supposed to have done?' Calliope asked.

She had noticed that Grigoris's tie was askew and this small detail in so fastidious a man unexpectedly touched her, suggesting as it did neglect of his personal affairs. Somehow, within the folds of florid middle-aged skin, the bald pate and whiskery ears, a familiar, boyish face seemed to be hiding, eager to assert itself.

'I don't know about Aristides Dhaniel,' he was saying, 'but Konstantin Katranides will probably be found innocent.' Grigoris tugged at his shirt collar. 'It seems he just happened to be at the wrong place in the wrong company.'

The alleged Katranides had stopped for a drink with the former editor of a student paper, a man suspected of organising the distribution of subversive pamphlets.

'And? Did Aristides have anything to do with the pamphlets?'

'Who knows?' In his formal statement, Konstantin Katranides claimed to have run into the editor at Omonia Square, deciding on the spur of the moment to go have a drink with him at a nearby *ouzeri*. The editor's name was Michalis Orphanos.

'Is Orphanos the one who managed to get away?'

'Yes.' Aristides had been sitting with his back to the entrance when the Security Police agents came in. Orphanos instantly recognised them and bolted towards the toilets, vanishing through a service entrance.

'So that's all there is to it?' Calliope was gingerly approaching the beckoning light of hope. 'They have nothing on him except a drink with a suspected activist?'

'So I'm told.' Grigoris sipped his coffee. 'They fingerprinted your godson and found no match to the pamphlets.' He put his cup down and briefly pondered his own words. 'Naturally, they're going to check out his story, but . . . well, I gather the editor had indeed been a class-mate of Katranides. So that's good.'

Calliope sat digesting all this. 'How reliable is your source?' she asked at length. 'I was thinking we should—'

'Highly reliable,' Grigoris cut in. Angelos Solomos was a personal friend, he said; one of the top lawyers in town. He had already been in to see Aristides.

'Angelos Solomos! He has met Aristides?!'

'What, you know him?'

Calliope explained about Dorothea, then re-weighed the facts, childishly buoyed by the coincidence. 'So, if his story checks out, they're going to let him go?'

'Probably. Solomos says his background's impeccable.'

He was, of course, alluding to Aristides's putative background. Any knowledge of his true parentage would have instantly doomed him.

Grigoris's private line began to ring. He spoke laconically, while Calliope sat smoking, watching spokes of light play on the walnut desk. Grigoris said it was not a good time; he was busy now. 'I'll call you back,' he said, looking vaguely peevish.

'How long do you suppose it'll take?' Calliope asked.

'Who knows? Our bureaucrats think they get paid just to kill flies.'

Calliope sighed. She was reaching for an ashtray, about to frame another question, when Grigoris decided it was time to eat.

'Shall we go?' He clapped his hands on his knees, hauled himself up, then came around the desk, smoothing down his few remaining strands of hair. 'Stop worrying: Solomos promised to call me tonight.' He gave Calliope's shoulder an avancular squeeze, then strode towards the coat tree. The restaurant was in the neighbourhood, he said, stepping out into the winter dazzle.

They crossed the street and picked their way through a small park, keenly watched by a hunchbacked woman feeding a swarm of pigeons. She had reached into a paper bag, but now stopped and gave Calliope and Grigoris a suspicious look, as if they might take it into their heads to pounce and steal her bag of birdseed.

The cousins exchanged thin smiles. It was almost Christmas, but chrysanthemums were still in bloom around the flowerbeds; oranges peeked out of the green citrus foliage. Calliope's mind kept wandering.

'Have you had any luck with the house?' Grigoris asked after a long silence.

'Yes – I'm sorry, I meant to tell you.'

An Australian artist wanted to rent the house, but not until March, Calliope said as they entered the restaurant. The smell of lamb and okra wafted out of the kitchen.

'March is fine, I suppose,' said Grigoris, scanning the crowded room. All he cared about was preventing the house from going to wrack and ruin, he added. Calliope pointed to an empty table.

'I think I've also found a cleaner,' she said at length. Half her mind had retreated, the other half was relieved to have stumbled on a suitable topic. Now that Aristides's case had been hashed over, there wasn't much to talk about. Family politesse had been exhausted, politics was taboo, they had few interests in common. And yet, she had fond memories of their shared childhood.

Grigoris asked who the cleaner was.

'Oh, a widow named Pelaghia. I don't think you'd know them. Her son's a shepherd . . . somewhere outside Vafios.'

'I see.' Grigoris's eyes kept roaming around the humming restaurant. He was looking bored, Calliope thought, and sighed. Soon, she latched onto the story Eleni had told her about the reclusive shepherd. Pelaghia's son had been at his wits' end because of a mysterious ailment afflicting his flock. Three sheep had died one after the other and the shepherd was convinced they had been hexed by the evil eye.

Grigoris reached for his spectacles, shaking his head. 'The Americans are sending men to the moon and we're still ruled by the evil eye,' he said.

'Yes, indeed.' Calliope chortled. 'The evil eye in the countryside and evil ears in the capital,' she quipped, mechanically opening her menu.

But then her eyes shot up, flying towards the neighbouring tables. Oh, there she was again: a fifty-five-year-old woman still blurting out things like a reckless child!

'I'm sorry,' she muttered, flushing, utterly stricken. 'Sorry . . . I wasn't thinking.'

Grigoris kept his silence, though his Mussolini jaw had visibly stiffened on hearing Calliope's words. He, too, glanced at the adjacent tables but quickly returned to his menu. It was a large menu and he studied it with a desperate sort of intensity, as if his very life depended on his picking just the right dish that day.

THREE

~ 1 ~

Dear Alexandra,

Your letter reached me only yesterday. Please forgive me for not keeping my promise, but the three weeks Aristides spent in jail have taken their toll. Somehow, I managed to keep going until he was released, but, a few days later, I came down with bronchitis and have had a hard time shaking it. We were back in Athens for Easter and I am only now settling back into my routine. The bronchitis forced me to give up smoking, but I've become addicted to chocolate, which I hugely enjoy but which does nothing to calm my nerves.

I can't believe three months have passed since Aristides's release. Why is it that the older we get the faster time seems to fly – can you tell me that? By now, Christmas is a blur, so I'm not sure how much I told you on the phone. Aristides was freed only because they never discovered his true identity. He had not been tortured, but they did rough him up ('You will talk here, or we'll make you spill your mother's milk!').

One day, they made him witness a suspect's transfer from the torture chamber. This unnerved Aristides, but not for long. There was a point when I thought he might cave in and finish his dissertation in Paris, but a few days later he changed his mind again. I don't know how much his girlfriend has to do with all this. I tried to find out how serious he is about her, but he seemed evasive. One thing I know: he was very lucky they thought him small fry and did not bother to dig too deeply.

For better and for worse Aristides is an optimist and his success in escaping their clutches has only reinforced his faith in his own invulnerability. If only I could share this faith of his; if only I believed in the power of prayer! Rupert says he's just about ready to start lighting candles to the saints – to keep Aristides out of harm's way, but also to ensure that we finally make it to London next Christmas. We spent part of Easter with Aristides and Grigoris, then with my goddaughter and her fiancé. His Cretan parents and Eleni were all there, but I'm so glad to be back at my desk!

I was happy to hear that things seem to be working out between you and Tibor. For what it's worth, I think you should go ahead and let him move in, if that's what you want. Your children will just have to accept your decision. But here I am, meddling again! I'd better stop right now and go do something productive. Lorenz Umbreit will be in Athens this summer for his new book, but I am behind with everything.

My best wishes to you and Tibor. And, once again, thank you from the bottom of my heart for offering to help.

Yours, Calliope

P.S. A telephone network is being set up on the island. The *kentro* has been promised a connection soon, but I'm not holding my breath.

— 2 —

Calliope said, 'Umbreit is coming to Athens next month, to research his book.'

'The political book?' asked Rupert, a soup ladle at his lips.

'Yes.' Calliope paused for a moment. 'The thing is, he'd like to come to Molyvos for a short visit. Would that be all right with you?'

'I suppose,' said Rupert after the briefest pause. He reached out for a lid and covered the simmering pot. 'Are you thinking of having him stay here?'

'No. He wants to be by the sea. At the Delphinia.'

'In that case, he doesn't need our permission, does he?'

Calliope swallowed. 'But he's asking anyway. He—'

'I wonder that he's not worried about the villagers' reaction. They're not going to welcome him with open arms, are they?'

Calliope hesitated. 'He doesn't think anyone will recognise him, after all these years. He's much older, he's grown a beard.'

'Still.'

'It's been a quarter of a century, Rupert! German tourists are everywhere now.'

'If you say so. I shouldn't want to come back if I were in his place. Coffee?'

Calliope nodded, staring out the window. It was only mid-morning, but the laundry she'd hung already looked dry. She thought she should go get it before the birds left their mark.

'Why does he want to come here anyway?' Rupert asked after a moment's silence. 'I should have thought he'd try to avoid any reminders of the Occupation.'

'I think he's just hoping to get over his writer's block,' Calliope said. 'It's been a year since his wife died . . . he hasn't written a word since then.'

'I see.'

'He's afraid he'll never write another novel. He's started this new book because he's interested in our politics, but . . . well, he's a novelist. It's what he loves to do.'

'Of course.' Rupert stood watching the coffee pot. 'Well, it just might work,' he said after a moment's reflection. 'Coming back after all this time . . . it's bound to shake him up, I suppose.' The coffee rose, frothing, and Rupert poured it into two demitasses. 'How long is he planning to stay?'

'A week, I believe,' Calliope said, then paused to reflect. 'He won't come if he thinks it's going to cause any problems, Rupert.'

'Well, as I said, he might run into a problem or two if he's recognised.'

Calliope shrugged. 'I guess he's willing to risk it. He really is quite depressed,' she added, taking a sip. 'I just wanted to make sure it was all right with you.'

'It's fine with me,' said Rupert. 'Thank you for asking.'

They lingered over their coffee. It was the last Sunday in July. Not for the first time, Calliope found herself marvelling at Rupert's fair-mindedness. She recalled Pericles trying to stop her from meeting Lorenz in Athens and her chest dilated with gratitude. She had told Rupert everything about Lorenz, had made it clear that their romance was over, but that Lorenz would always have a place in her heart. For reasons she didn't quite understand, she found it easier to be perfectly forthcoming with Rupert than she ever had with Lorenz. She supposed it had something to do with all the subterfuge brought on by the Occupation.

They began to clear the table, but all at once Calliope stopped. 'Rupert,' she said. 'You know I would never deceive you, don't you?'

He looked a little startled. 'Yes, of course,' he said.

'But something is still bothering you. What?'

He paused. He dropped into a chair. 'I was just wondering,' he finally said, 'how much Lorenz has to do with your doubts about getting married.'

'Rupert!' Calliope, too, sat down. 'I had doubts about getting married when I was nineteen! I've always had doubts,' she reminded him.

Rupert said nothing. He seemed to be pondering her words.

'Look,' she said, 'my doubts have nothing to do with how I feel about you. Nothing at all! I wish you'd believe me.'

'And . . . nothing to do with Umbreit?' Rupert spoke very gently, studying her face with a sad sort of benevolence.

'Absolutely not!' Calliope said. 'Anyway . . .' She fell silent.

'Anyway what?'

'Anyway, Lorenz could never take your place. He could never live here. I could never live in Germany.'

Rupert sighed but remained silent.

'Look,' said Calliope. She paused. She, too, sighed then made a vaguely disgruntled gesture. 'If you're going to be reading things into it, things that aren't there, I'll do it! I'll marry you, all right?'

Rupert raised his gaze. 'Oh, I wouldn't want to twist your arm,' he said. His lips almost smiled; his eyes looked inscrutable.

'All right. Let me make myself perfectly clear,' Calliope said. 'I think marriage is pointless. I honestly do. But, at this stage, it seems even more pointless to resist, since it apparently means so much to you.'

Rupert shrugged. She went and sat on his lap, looping an arm around his neck.

'I don't want this coming between us,' she said tenderly. 'We'll get married, all right?'

'Excellent,' said Rupert. 'See that you keep your word, my dear.' He reached out and gently tweaked the tip of her nose. 'Otherwise, I'll have to find me a young wench who'll wash my feet and bring me breakfast in bed,' he added.

But now, at last, he was smiling.

~ 3 ~

By the end of August, the countryside was a parched landscape of bleached rocks and desiccated gorse, of shrilling cicadas and tiny lizards darting in and out of dusty olive groves. It was late afternoon but the sun was still high. Calliope was wearing a pale yellow headkerchief, Lorenz Umbreit a beige cotton hat and dark sunglasses. His hair was cut well below his ears; his beard was mottled with grey.

They had spent the afternoon in Eftalou but were heading back towards Molyvos. Lorenz stopped to take a snapshot of Calliope picking wild figs, then a flock of sheep huddling around a leafy walnut tree. He lingered in the shade, greedily sniffing the air, clutching his new Exakta.

'If only this camera could capture the sounds and smells!' he gushed.

The air smelled of sea salt and dry algae, of fig syrup and wild herbs and sun-ripened berries. There was the tinkle of sheep's bells in the breeze, the incessant droning of insects. The waves came and went, splashing against the hot rocks.

The road between Eftalou and Molyvos was still unpaved. Halfway to the village, two farmers looked up from a roadside grapevine, one of them a young man whose left arm ended at the elbow. Calliope could not recall his name but she knew the boy had been crippled shortly after the Civil War, playing with a hand grenade during a Clean Monday picnic.

The hand-grenade accident was the only mishap to take place in recent years, but to wander about the village was to see Greek history grimly personified, she told Lorenz as they ambled on. There were still Anatolian refugees around, one of them a man who'd had his eyes gouged by the Turks. There were men wounded during the Civil War, others born with birth defects during the Occupation. There was even an old man down in the harbour who had lost both feet in Macedonia.

All this, Calliope said, had happened within her lifetime. And now there was the *junta*. 'It goes on and on and on. A national nightmare with no end in sight.'

Lorenz was silent. They strolled on through the shimmering countryside. Calliope had just stopped for some wild blackberries when the late beekeeper's brother approached on his ancient mule cart. Nikiforos was shortsighted, but eventually recognised Calliope. He whistled at his mule, pulling on the reins. '*Yassas!*'

He was a peevish old man, with a look of perpetual bewilderment in his eyes, as though he were trying to work out the cause of the unsightly growths that had one day appeared on his face, like dark treacle hardening as it dribbled down his cheeks.

But this was not what he'd stopped to complain about. It was his stomach that was bothering him, he said sourly. 'I woulda stayed home today, but it's time to extract the honey, eh?' Nikiforos and his wife lived in Calliope's own neighbourhood so she was all too familiar with his ailments.

'I thought you were going to see the doctor last week,' she said, watching the old man squint in Lorenz's direction. The villagers were curious about the visiting foreigner, whom they took to be Rupert's relative. Lorenz had stepped aside to photograph a bird he had spotted on a nearby branch.

'The doctor, the doctor!' Nikiforos was saying. 'I did see him, but he wouldn't listen to me! He kept telling me to try some new medication, but you know how it is, *Kyria* Calliope, the doctor has his ideas, but we know what we know, don't we?'

'What exactly is it we know in this case?'

'I have worms! I told you last time I had worms!'

'So, what happened? The doctor didn't agree with your diagnosis?'

'Of course he agreed! Could a man be wrong about his own stomach?'

'So what's the problem?'

'The problem, *Kyria mou*, is the medication. Didn't I just say so? He wants me to take medicine to get rid of the worms. I couldn't make him understand: stomach worms are good for the digestion! Everybody knows that!' He gave her a disgruntled look, let out a vaguely resigned sound, then raised his whip as he said goodbye.

After he had gone, Calliope translated the exchange into German. 'And you thought I was making things up.' She chuckled. The scent of fresh pine sap hung in the air. The pine wood was where Calliope had been kissed by Johnny the Australian; where she'd almost got caught, lugging her basket of live ammunition. She was sure the same thought flitted through Lorenz's mind. They were silent, entering the village.

'Oh, there's Zoe Samiou!' The deaf-mute artist was perched on a cement step, absorbed in sketching three black-clad crones huddled in a doorway. She had, years earlier, been sent to Mytilene to study icon painting, but had quickly returned, turning her back on sacred art forever. Day in and day out, she drew village scenes, though no one showed the slightest interest in buying her work.

The three women were busy making *manestra*, cackling amiably at a French couple who had stopped by to take photographs. The foreign wife was watching the three villagers roll dough between their fingers, the rice-like pellets spilling into their enamel bowls in a steady stream. Her husband stood across the street, following Zoe's progress. He and his wife were lawyers, but art was his passion, he was soon telling Calliope. When his wife joined them, they both fell to praising Zoe's *art naïf*.

The artist was deaf-mute, Calliope told the foreigners. She was the daughter of refugees from Smyrna and had been drawing since the age of three. 'She has some fine paintings at home if you're interested,' she added, on a sly impulse. 'I could take you there, if you'd like. It's not very far.'

The foreigners exchanged glances. They saw no reason not to.

They left the three widows hunched over their pans and Zoe over her drawing pad. Lorenz wanted to have a beer and a shower. He headed back to his hotel, leaving Calliope alone with the foreigners. They were both ardent Hellenophiles; Molyvos, they said, was one of the most picturesque villages in all of Greece. Was there anything they should see while they were here? they asked, crossing the *agora*.

Calliope reflected. 'Have you been to the Theophilos Museum?' There was a new museum just outside Mytilene, dedicated to the work of a local folk artist named Theophilos. The painter had died in his thirties; ironically, Calliope said, just as a celebrated Greco-French critic was beginning to establish his reputation abroad. There was a time when Molyviates would mock the peripatetic Theophilos, cursing as they whitewashed the murals he used to paint on his hosts' walls. He died homeless, impoverished, friendless. Now the paintings were on exhibit in museums and fine art galleries all over Europe.

The foreigners hadn't yet been to the Varia museum but they'd heard Theophilos referred to as the Greek Henri Rousseau. It was a pity, they said, that artists were so often unappreciated in their own lifetime.

'Yes, indeed. Posthumous recognition doesn't fill an empty belly, does it?' Calliope sighed. 'I think our Zoe will turn out to be the next Theophilos,' she added, waving at a small child who had stopped to stare at them while toying with a wobbly tooth. 'I have two of her paintings on my own walls and I love them. I cherish them.' She offered her most radiant smile.

'And how do you come to speak French so well?' the French wife asked. She was an ample, red-haired woman named Manon; her husband was called Yves.

Calliope said she was a literary translator. 'My friend – the one you just met – is a German author. I've translated his novels. One of them is set right here, in Molyvos.'

'Really?' Yves scrutinised Calliope's profile. He asked the author's name.

'Lorenz Umbreit.'

'Has he been translated into French?'

'Oh yes,' Calliope said.

'Hm. I must try to find him.' Manon glanced at her husband. 'Remind me when we get back,' she said.

They had by then arrived at their destination. Calliope stood knocking at the Samious's door, a hot breeze blowing at her neck.

'Coming!' Olga Samiou appeared at the entrance, an old woman wiping her hands on her apron, peering at the strangers through a web of wrinkles.

Calliope introduced the couple. 'The foreigners are French,' she said. 'I think they might buy a painting. Show them the ones upstairs, Olga.'

'What, right now? The house—'

'They're not interested in your housekeeping, Olga *mou*! They want to see the paintings. I'm telling you, they are going to buy something! Go on, show them what you have. Tell them you won't accept less than six hundred drachmas.'

'Six hundred!'

'Well, bring them to me when you're done and maybe I'll let them bargain me down to five.' She turned, showing her dimples to the foreign couple, while Olga stood wringing her hands, gazing from one to the other with her sad clown's eyes.

'As you can see, she's not eager to sell,' Calliope said. 'She has an idea that the work will be worth a fortune some day.'

Yves exchanged glances with his wife. 'Tell her we'd just like to have a look.'

'Yes,' said Manon, beaming at Olga. 'Ask her if she has anything with fishermen or shepherds. Something rustic—'

'See for yourself,' Calliope said, motioning towards the stairs.

426

'Maybe we can talk her into letting you have something. I'll wait in the garden, in case you need me.'

'*Merci!*' they said, speaking in unison.

And then they trudged upstairs, trailing the heavily perspiring Olga. Calliope stepped outdoors and sat in the shade, fanning herself. It was an ordinary August afternoon, but she would always remember that summer of 1970 as the year when Lorenz Umbreit had returned to Lesbos, and when Zoe Samiou finally began to sell her paintings. Before he left, Lorenz himself bought three of them, though no one would ever discover the foreign art lover's real identity.

— 4 —

Molyvos was beginning to attract foreign artists. One of the new expats was a Belgian photographer named Hendrik Van Woert. Obsessed with doors, gates, portals, he had spent two months photographing entryways around the Aegean. He was interested in them, he said, because of their rustic beauty, but also because they so often tweaked his imagination. He could never pass an interesting door or gate without feeling the urge to stop and mentally conjure up the interior.

He was showing Calliope a collection of photographs, one of which instantly captured her interest. All it showed was a wrought-iron door and one stone step leading to what had once been an entrance. There had been a house here, a beautiful house, but it had crumbled in a long-ago earthquake. Intrigued, Calliope studied the exquisite door, the flat, empty plot of land stretching beyond it. A perfect metaphor for the threshold to the realm of the imagination, she said to herself.

'Do you think I could have a copy of this?' she asked, turning to Hendrik. He was a multilingual Belgian in his late twenties, as fair as a Viking, but with brown, almost oriental eyes peering from under bristling eyebrows. Calliope was planning to frame the photograph and send it to Lorenz, for his approaching birthday. She was sure it would speak to him.

She was far less sure of what she would say in response to a letter she had just received from Heidelberg. It was by now autumn; Lorenz had surprised himself by writing two short stories after his Molyvos visit. He was a great admirer of Chekhov, his letter said, but somehow had never considered writing short fiction. The stories he had just penned were set on Lesbos, one of them inspired by Nikiforos, the beekeeper they had encountered on the Eftalou road.

Calliope was relieved to hear that Lorenz had finally overcome his writer's block, but it turned out not to be his only psychological challenge. For some time, he had been racked by the conviction that it was his divided love that had led to Alicia's death. He had obviously let his guilt override his reason. All the same, exorcising his demons had seemed almost hopeless before his return to Lesbos. He was deeply grateful to Calliope and Rupert for making it possible, he said in his letter. 'I feel I'm finally beginning to regain my emotional equilibrium.'

Calliope had long believed that one could love more than one person at a time, though probably with different facets of one's psyche. She loved Rupert, but was nonetheless deeply attached to Lorenz and would, she felt sure, remain so to the end of her days. She had finally learned to accept the fact, but Alicia's death had made it impossible not to contemplate the irony of their current predicament: Lorenz was now in Heidelberg, widowed, and she was in Molyvos, attached to another man.

How the gods laugh at us! Calliope thought.

Lorenz had been indescribably moved by his return to Greece; had found both peace and enchantment in its bucolic splendour. The day they had spent in Eftalou would be etched in his memory forever, he wrote in his letter. As soon as he returned to Germany, he had found himself longing for a rustic Greek cottage; was once more contemplating buying one somewhere by the sea. Molyvos itself was too noisy, but Eftalou might be ideal for the summer; perhaps even an annual Easter visit?

Calliope had recently shared all this with Rupert, surprised to learn of his anguish over the time she'd spent with Lorenz back in August. Rupert had chosen to keep his distress to himself, partly because he liked Lorenz – had greatly enjoyed a long talk he'd had alone with him – but also because he considered jealousy a deplorable emotion. He was, he confessed, ashamed to find himself capable of it.

'I feel I should be able to master it, but it seems I can't. I'm sorry!'

'Rupert!' Calliope stared, oblivious to the diminishing cigarette stub in her hand. Both she and Rupert had gone back to smoking after Lorenz's visit. 'Why didn't you tell me?'

'Why, why!' Rupert stopped midstride to the fridge. 'What was the point? He was here for a week, he was leaving soon. How was I supposed to know he would suddenly decide to buy a house on our turf?'

Calliope closed her eyes. 'I'm so sorry.' She stubbed out her cigarette and went to bestow a kiss. Rupert was not given to emotional outbursts. And who could blame him for being jealous, given the circumstances?

'I don't know what to do,' she finally said, sinking onto the divan. They had just finished dinner but the dishes had yet to be cleared. 'How can I stop him from buying a house if that's what he wants to do?'

'What can I say?' Rupert sat down, staring ahead bleakly. Calliope wanted him to look at her. She took one of his hands.

'You know I never did anything I'd want to keep from you, don't you?'

'I do.' He sat up, sighing. 'But that . . . that only makes it worse.'

'Makes it worse?'

'Makes me feel even more unreasonable. I hate feeling possessive!' he reiterated, as if sheer repetition might help him exorcise his unworthy emotions. They were silent for a while. The fridge hummed, the drain in the sink gurgled.

'Why don't you tell him the simple truth?' Rupert asked at length.

'What? Tell him that you're insanely jealous?'

'You won't have to spell it out, surely? He's a mature man . . . an insightful one.'

'He is,' Calliope said.

The problem, she reflected, was not making Lorenz understand, but learning to accept the vagaries of fate. That she was being offered an opportunity to see Lorenz for two months every summer; that she was being asked to turn down this unexpected gift! Had Rupert been more strident, she would have fought him over this; would have insisted on her rights, on Lorenz Umbreit's right to live wherever he pleased.

But Rupert was not Pericles. 'I'm not saying you mustn't see him,' he was saying now. 'I would never presume—'

'I know, my dear,' she said. She was wondering what Lorenz would have done in Rupert's shoes; how he would have acted had Alicia presented him with such a thorny dilemma. She thought she knew him well, yet she wasn't at all sure of the answer.

One thing she was sure of. As she eventually wrote to Lorenz, destiny had not been on their side, his and hers; it had merely enjoyed sporting with them. She explained the situation as tactfully as she could, taking care not to paint Rupert in a negative light. All the same, after much thought and with great reluctance, she decided she must honour Rupert's request. It was an extremely difficult decision, she wrote in her letter; she hoped with all her heart that Lorenz would understand and try to find a suitable cottage in some other village.

So there it was, black on white, but her own words so distressed Calliope that she put her unfinished letter aside for three days, while her inner battle began anew.

She hadn't permitted herself to acknowledge it back in August, but Lorenz's brief stay in Molyvos had made the summer seem somehow luminous. It had been a thrill, she admitted to herself, but making Rupert suffer for two months every summer would be downright cruel. The decision before her was heart-breaking, but she knew how her letter to Lorenz must end.

'Maybe in a decade or two,' she wrote, 'when we resemble what Yeats called "a tattered coat upon a stick," we will sit by the fire and chuckle at our youthful madness. But we are not there yet, are we, my dear? There is nothing I would like better than to see you, but as I told you once at the Grande Bretagne, I have all but stopped resisting the dictates of fate. I hope with all my heart that you will understand.'

She promised to see Lorenz once or twice a year, in Rupert's company.

She sealed the letter, then sat up half the night and smoked, and was still groping for clarity when the roosters began to crow. She made herself coffee, then went to see Ed, hoping to catch him before he left for his morning stroll.

It was the most peaceful time of day, but peace proved elusive that morning. It was only October, but already the incandescent summer was beginning to seem almost like a dream; the scent of approaching autumn tugged at her bruised soul. As she approached Ed's house, a stray dog approached from an alley, tentatively wagging its bedraggled tail. Overcome by pity, Calliope stopped to pet the rawboned mongrel, stroking its spotted, quivering haunches, swiping at her own weary, mutinous eyes.

～ 5 ～

It was by sheer chance that Hendrik Van Woert was in Mytilene when a local woman immolated herself in protest against her son's incarceration.

A high school history teacher, Theodoros Philippou had been arrested in Athens in February 1971 and, seven weeks later, was still in Athenian custody. The mother, a schoolmaster's widow, journeyed to the capital, only to be told that no visitors were allowed until after the preliminary interrogation. No one would tell her when this would take place, or indeed what her son's alleged crime had been. She went back twice, telling the gatekeepers that her husband had been shot by the Germans, her son was all she had, he had never been involved in politics, it was all a mistake.

It was all in vain. Returning to Mytilene, the fifty-four-year-old widow appealed to two local priests but neither was willing to intercede. She was referred to a lawyer, but his fees proved prohibitive. Two other lawyers were contacted but were too swamped to take on any new cases.

On Good Friday, just before the traditional Easter procession, Katerina Philippou stationed herself outside Mytilene's cathedral and, possibly inspired by the recent immolation of a young Greek student in

Italy, set herself ablaze. The date may or may not have been intention-
ally symbolic, but the venue had clearly been meant to draw attention
to what many regarded as the church's collusion with the *junta*.

Katerina Philippou lived a stone's throw away from St Symeon's
church, but had chosen to stage her protest at the more imposing St
Athanasios. The sixteenth-century cathedral's crypt held the relics of
St Theodoros of Byzantium – the patron saint of Mytilene, as well as
of Katerina Philippou's son. During holy days, the church was packed
with worshippers from all over the region. Hendrik Van Woert, who
had been invited to spend Easter with local acquaintances, stood at the
back of the crowd, waiting to photograph the traditional candlelight
procession.

The priest had just finished blessing the parishioners when a sudden shriek rose outside the church. The priest went on chanting, but
several men at the entrance dashed out, Van Woert following on their
heels.

'Mother of God!'

'It's Philippou's mother! Go get blankets or something. Hurry!'

The crowd was quickly swelling. There were those who shouted,
those who sped back into the church, colliding with others pushing
their way through the open portals. There were those who watched,
weeping or crossing themselves, and those who had taken off their
jackets and were trying to extinguish the leaping tongues of flame.

Hendrik Van Woert had also rushed out to help, but quickly gave
up and aimed his camera, photographing the live torch that was Katerina Philippou. She was swaying weakly, her hair burning around her
face like some hellish crown. Her face was twitching, her arms rising
and falling, as though she might soar towards the starry skies in a blaze
of flames.

Two men had come running out of the church, dragging an
embroidered standard. The sexton was galloping after them, clutching
a scarlet tablecloth.

'Use this, use the tablecloth, for God's sake!' he shouted.

It was too late. Van Woert snapped the desperate attempts to rescue
the dying woman, then turned and took to his heels. It occurred to

him, he would later tell Molyvos's expats, that there might be police-men in the crowd, and that one of them might take it into his head to confiscate his film.

Katerina Philippou's husband had been among the ten civilians who, back in 1942, had been executed by the Germans in retaliation for the attack outside the Mytilene brothel. In the days following the sensational immolation, Greek authorities would insist that the poor woman had clearly been deranged by her husband's execution. This was not implausible but, having managed to raise a son on her own, she must have had her wits about her all these years, Calliope pointed out on hearing the tragic details. She praised Hendrik Van Woert for keeping *his* wits about him. He had been right to suspect that his film would have been confiscated.

'We must find a way to publicise it,' she said, thinking feverishly.

Hendrik reached for his camera. 'Do you have any media contacts?'

'I do, but no one in Greece will touch this. I'm thinking of foreign media.' From Rupert and Alexandra, Calliope knew of Greek exiles' efforts to expose the *junta*'s oppressive rule. It was hoped that, at the very least, foreign pressure might improve the treatment of political opponents.

'We must get the pictures out of the country.' Calliope waited for Hendrik to finish rolling the film. 'I'm going to phone Mytilene right away. I know someone who might be able to help.'

At the town hall, she placed a call to a man she had once loved, a prominent political journalist named Arghiris Economides. Their affair had ended on a somewhat sour note, but Calliope was sure her former lover would be glad to cooperate, and was soon proven right. Arghiris knew an airline stewardess who might be persuaded to smug-gle the package abroad. When could he expect the film?

The very next day, Calliope travelled to the capital and handed the film over, along with a typewritten commentary and three foreign contacts. At the top of the list was Rupert's son-in-law, who worked for the BBC and would do his best to get the photos shown on British television. Also included were phone numbers for Alexandra in Paris and Lorenz in Heidelberg. One of the three was bound to succeed, she told Rupert on returning home.

'*Tu es formidable!*' Rupert said, touching her cheek. 'The colonels are going to roar when the photos appear on foreign TV.'

'They say a picture is worth a thousand words,' Calliope said.

She had managed a smile, though she was still feeling somewhat distracted. When she wasn't brooding about the hapless mother, her thoughts would return to the house Lorenz had recently purchased on the northeastern side of the island. It was all in a letter he'd sent her just before returning to Germany. Skala Sykamnias was not as picturesque as Molyvos, but Lorenz said he and his sons were looking forward to spending their holidays by the sea, in their little rustic cottage.

He had been gracious and understanding about Calliope's domestic dilemma, and she felt deeply grateful. And yet, there was no denying the web of lingering sadness, or the obscure resentment she still felt on occasion. Resentment towards whom? She could not say. The spiteful gods, perhaps.

She had become both moody and irritable in recent weeks, as overwrought as she recalled being only during adolescence. The black mood generated by Lorenz's letter and the Mytilene tragedy persisted for days, fading only when news finally arrived that Hendrik's photographs were to be aired on the BBC.

The heart-wrenching images of Katerina Philippou's death would never be aired in Greece but several foreign stations would eventually show the grieving mother going up in flames, causing the colonels to roar, exactly as predicted. The international outcries would be swift in coming, leading to the release of several innocent men, among them Theodoros Philippou, who promptly left for London, never to return.

~ 6 ~

It was in order to reciprocate an invitation from Van Woert that Calliope decided to celebrate her name day by throwing a dinner party for Molyvos's foreigners. It fell in early June, some nine months after Lorenz's visit. The Australian artist renting Elpida's house arrived with a French boyfriend from Marseilles. The Australian was called Michael, his new lover was named Michel.

'M and M', the Australian laughed, shaking Calliope's hand.

Hendrik brought a Canadian girl named Sylvie, who was interested in international dance. Unlike Molyviates, they all came casually dressed, bearing bottles of wine and ouzo. The atmosphere was less stodgy than at traditional name day parties, but it was dampened by an astounding piece of news: Ed Bell had just been arrested on suspicion of espionage. The authorities had received reports that he was in the habit of wandering in the countryside, scribbling in his notebook.

'You have to understand,' Rupert said, uncorking a bottle of wine. 'Going out for an aimless walk in the hills is incomprehensible to Greek villagers; making notes is more suspicious than reading Trotsky.'

Everyone laughed.

'He's not joking,' Calliope said, though she herself believed the arrest had more to do with Artemis's charms than with Ed's wanderings.

Sylvie wanted to know who Artemis was and Hendrik explained, his hand on her suntanned shoulder. Sylvie was a winsome French-Canadian girl with avid eyes and an enigmatic smile hinting at delicious thoughts.

Calliope said, 'I think they're just trying to get rid of him, now that her uncle's found out about them.'

The affair had come to light after children had stumbled upon Ed and Artemis making love in an Eftalou cove.

'So now they've arrested him? Because he makes love to a Greek girl and walks in the hills?' Sylvie spoke with a strong French accent. She had come to Greece with an anglophone boyfriend, but they'd quarrelled and ended up going their separate ways.

Rupert said Artemis might have had something to do with Ed's arrest, but the authorities were genuinely paranoid about the disputed islands off the Turkish mainland. A few months earlier, a local forest had burned down and everyone suspected Turkish arsonists. Could Ed have been spying for the Turks or Russians? He didn't really look like an American, Rupert had overheard someone say at the barber's. He could be a Turk for all anyone knew.

All this was rehashed over a dish of stuffed courgette blossoms, while birds chattered in the trees and a dry-cleaning messenger from Mytilene did the rounds, hoarsely announcing pick-up services. It was a radiant afternoon and they dined in the shade, surrounded by several drowsy cats. Now and then, a breeze came from the sea, dappling the tablecloth. The smell of grilled fish wafted from the outdoor firepit, swirling in with the scent of ripening fruit.

Rupert kept refilling the foreigners' glasses. They had drifted from a discussion of Greek dance to an eager exchange of droll personal observations. Michael said he'd seen an old villager try to staunch a bleeding wound with tobacco. Sylvie wanted to know why young village men kept touching their genitals in public. 'As if to make sure everything's in working order,' she said, eliciting howls of laughter.

Calliope exchanged looks with Rupert. Although they both enjoyed meeting new people, there was no denying the hostility she occasionally felt in foreigners' company. She was especialy dismayed today because she had quickly grown fond of both Hendrik and Sylvie; had indeed been the one to introduce them and thought they made an exceptionally handsome couple. Listening to Hendrik, Sylvie's upper lip would lift slightly, giving her a tender, tentative look which Calliope found so captivating she briefly considered the possibility that she might possess a lesbian streak after all. It took her a few days to realise that what she really felt was simple envy for Sylvie's youth and vitality. The Canadian girl made her feel old. Old and jaded.

Sylvie Leroux was twenty-six, the exact age at which Calliope had first met Lorenz Umbreit. She was well into middle age now, but in her mental visions she was always young when she was with Lorenz; young and, somehow, luminous. Oh, she supposed that she was still, despite all her protests, *Eine sentimentale Seele!*

The thought made Calliope smile to herself. And then it made her sigh. She rose from the table and reached for the water jug.

'Coffee, anyone?'

~ 7 ~

Friday was Eleni's day off, the only full day Calliope habitually spent at the *kentro*. One Friday morning in August she arrived at eight, to find Varvara, the demoted police chief's wife, waiting at the entrance. She was accompanied by her six-year-old granddaughter, who was visiting from Salonika and wanted to look at picture books. Or so Varvara said.

'Eh, *poulaki mou*, you love books, don't you?'

The child nodded vigorously, her wide smile complicated by missing teeth and pink bubblegum. She skipped across the threshold and into the library, where Calliope seated her at one of the low tables built for young children. The library assistant would be there in the afternoon, after school hours.

Calliope placed a stack of picture books before the child, pulled up a chair for Varvara, and turned to go. 'I'll be at my desk if you need me.'

'Actually . . .' Varvara cleared her throat. 'I'd like to speak to you – in private.'

Calliope paused. 'Shall we go into the office then?' She supposed some domestic problem had arisen, possibly related to the visiting daughter. It soon became clear, however, that Varvara had come to warn Calliope of her own imminent arrest. She had been sent by Louizos, instructed to stress the urgency of the situation.

'They will probably come for you on Monday or Tuesday,' Varvara said, fidgeting with her fingers.

Calliope sat staring at Varvara, not a single muscle moving.

'What am I alleged to have done?' she asked impassively. Could this be a trap? she wondered, but quickly dismissed the notion.

Varvara was gazing at her with earnest intensity, tiny beads of sweat spreading above her lip. She was a woman in her middle years, with huge, haunted eyes.

'It's something to do with the American – the one they suspect of spying.'

'Ed Bell? What's it got to do with me? He's just an acquaintance.'

Calliope had spoken matter-of-factly, but maybe the police had found out about her foreign correspondence? Since she didn't think the authorities really believed Ed to be a spy, this possibility had never crossed Calliope's mind. She sat for a moment, staring out, idly contemplating an old man who was ambling past, reading a newspaper. Her father used to look just like that, walking home from the *kapheneion*.

'*Kyria* Calliope,' Varvara was saying. 'I'm here to help you.'

'But I haven't done anything!' Calliope blurted, snapping to attention. She could always say she had asked Ed to handle her mail because she did not wish her private life exposed to the censor's scrutiny.

'They found his journal, *Kyria* Calliope. They've read it . . . they know everything.'

Calliope held herself very still, outwardly calm, inwardly aware of the slow chill seeping into her bones. 'But what can they possibly know?'

'They say you were responsible for smuggling out the Philippou photographs . . . you or your godson. They know you've been in touch.'

Calliope stiffened. She was silent for a moment, weighing Varvara's words.

She knew that Ed was in the habit of scribbling notes for his novel, but not that he kept a journal. How stupid, how irresponsible of him to even mention her! she said to herself. But then it came to her that if Ed was innocent, he would have had no reason to expect the authorities to take an interest in his daily scribblings.

'They don't really think Ed's a spy, do they?' she said, turning to Varvara.

'I don't know. Anyway, it's beside the point. The point is you should be thinking about leaving, *Kyria* Calliope. Today, if possible. The new chief is in Mytilene, but when he gets back, they will come for you. Please believe me.' Varvara touched Calliope's wrist. 'There's no time to lose.'

'What are you saying, *Kyria* Varvara? You expect me to flee? Abroad? Just like that?' Calliope said, her breathing arrested.

Varvara's voice grew tighter, as if she were being forced to reason with a dim-witted child. Everybody knew how the authorities felt about the smuggled photographs, she reminded Calliope. 'But . . . it seems they're also hoping you'll lead them to your godson. My husband says to go while you still can,' she said, fidgeting with her rings, her nails.

Calliope closed her eyes. She greatly appreciated *Kyrios* Louizos's concern, she said at length, but it was simply out of the question. She couldn't possibly leave everything from one day to the next!

'*Kyria* Calliope.' Varvara spoke severely. 'My husband respects you. He's risking his own neck because he knows how serious this is. You have a passport, don't you?'

Calliope nodded.

'There's a ferry leaving this evening. Take it – you and *Kyrios* Rupert. Take it! And don't tell anyone you're going,' she added with emphasis. 'That's all I've come to tell you.' She pushed her chair back and rose, sighing, then reached again across the desk to squeeze Calliope's hand. 'The Virgin be with you,' she murmured.

~ 8 ~

Calliope drifted through the house, eyes darting from one mute object to another. She knew that her life as she'd known it was probably over. If only she could think. Think. Countless artists and intellectuals had fled abroad following the coup, yet waves of indignation kept thwarting her volition. She felt she should have been given fair warning. It was Rupert who pointed out that a warning was precisely what she had been given.

'You're wasting time, Calliope!' he said, pacing back and forth, his hands thrust into his pockets. He stopped for a moment. 'You trust Louizos, don't you?'

'Yes.' She did trust him; both him and his wife.

'In that case, there's no time to lose,' Rupert said, echoing Varvara. 'For all we know, they're issuing an arrest warrant as we speak.'

'But—'

'There are no buts here, Calliope! We must leave this evening. We'll be in Athens in the morning, then—'

'But Rupert, be reasonable! You expect me to go into exile as if . . . as if I was going on a shopping trip!'

Rupert puffed out his cheeks and stood rubbing the back of his neck. When he finally spoke, his voice sounded hollow.

'Do you know what they'll do to you in Athens?' he said, looking at her intently.

Calliope continued to bite her knuckles, groping for clarity. 'How can I possibly leave?' she said, speaking to herself. 'The chimney needs repair, the *kentro*—'

'Good God, Calliope! I don't seem to be getting through to you! There's no time to think about anything but saving your skin . . . you'll have to deal with everything else later.' He regarded her for a moment, his mouth a grim line. 'Start packing!' he said, abruptly decisive. 'Then go arrange for a taxi.'

He was marching towards his room when something snapped in Calliope's head.

'It's easy for you to say!' she blurted after him. 'What's it to you? You're just going to be flying home. You may even be secretly—'

'Calliope!' He had spun to face her, his face hardening with reproach. 'You should be ashamed of yourself!' he said. He started to add something, but thought better of it.

It was only when his back was turned that Calliope did feel a wave of remorse. She darted after him. 'I'm sorry, Rupert. I don't know what came over me!'

He turned and briefly stroked her cheek. 'Go,' he said, softening. 'Start packing.' Then he wheeled about and strode towards his own room. There was a spell of silence, during which a neighbour was heard beating a pillow over the balcony.

'I'm sorry,' Calliope murmured, blotting her eyes. Like a rebuked child, she blundered towards the master bedroom – the room where she had been conceived and where her father died. A room in which she had changed nothing since Mirto's death, and where she now stood scanning the bed, wardrobe, curtains, her parents' wedding photo, her mother's iconostasis. It was a brilliant summer morning and the windows were wide open, the room flooded with sunlight. A bumblebee buzzed in and out of a window. A farmer came lumbering up the street, hawking aubergines.

She had made it this far but suddenly stopped, overcome with grief, her eyes on a large ant carrying another ant's corpse on its back. She was like someone thrust into a dream landscape, where everything is familiar yet governed by unknown imperatives. She could hear Rupert stir below and, after a while, she roused herself and crossed towards the wardrobe. She threw open its doors, then stopped and drew back, mutinous, collapsing onto the edge of the mattress.

'Rupert!' she wailed. 'Rupert!'

He came stumbling up the stairs.

'I can't do it, Rupert!'

'Darling! You don't understand, do you?' He seized her shoulders, his voice fraying. 'Listen to me! If you don't want to think of yourself, think of Aristides! They will torture you, just to find out where he is. They—'

'But I don't know where he is!' she cut in, mulishly obtuse. 'How can they get it out of me if I don't know?'

'They'll get you to tell them about Dorothea. Believe me, they will! Then they'll work on her and get her to talk, tooth by tooth, fingernail by fingernail!' He stared at her darkly.

'All right!' she suddenly yelled. 'All right!' She turned away from him, conscious of an intense need to shove her fist through the wall. 'I want a cigarette!' she said, sounding pathetic even to her own ear. 'Give me one, will you?'

'I don't have any.' He sighed: they were both trying to quit smoking again. 'You know perfectly well I don't.'

'All right. Go. Go! I'll start packing,' she finally said, defeated.

He hesitated, then turned and made for the stairs, leaving her to face decisions she felt incapable of making. How do you prepare for a journey when you don't know its duration? They might be gone for a few months, or for the rest of their lives!

Calliope's first impulse was to pack everything she cherished. But after she hauled her suitcases out of storage, after she began going through her bedroom drawers, a peculiar but tenacious notion took hold of her brain. If she packed everything she valued, her departure would be final, irrevocable. If she *didn't* take anything of great significance, her stay abroad would be temporary. Sooner or later, she would be back, as if her abandoned possessions had the power to effect her return.

That this line of reasoning was absurd Calliope knew perfectly well. She forced herself to do what had to be done, going through notes, books, accessories. She folded the clothes she expected to use in London. She packed a book she was planning to translate, and the manuscript she was working on, a political satire written two years after the coup d'état. She took her journal and her translation award, along with her favourite dictionary. She took her best jewellery, in case the house was broken into while they were away. Everything else she would leave behind. It would all be there, waiting, clamouring for her return.

Eventually, she went to arrange for a taxi. She returned home and sat down to write a note to Eleni, and another to Evanthea. The house-keeper would find the two notes when she arrived in the morning. Her eyes blurring, Calliope sealed the two envelopes and left them on the kitchen counter. She set about making sandwiches.

Rupert came down and they picked at their food, desultorily dis-cussing purely practical matters. There was a mobile bank that came once a week from Mytilene, but its arrival was somewhat erratic, so both Rupert and Calliope had cash stashed away; it would be enough until they arrived in Athens.

Calliope was about to return upstairs when Rupert took her in his arms.

'This won't last,' he said, tenderly putting his lips to her neck. 'One day, Greeks will have had enough.'

He spoke with calm certitude, reminding Calliope of Lorenz whis-pering similar assurances about the end of the War. That he had been right, that the Occupation had in fact ended soon after, seemed to lend Rupert's words greater authority.

She was still trying to comfort herself hours later as she stood at the kitchen window, waiting for the taxi. Dusk was coming on when a lone kitten emerged out of the bushes, meowing plaintively. Calliope picked up the tiny creature and stood cuddling it, breathing in the familiar scent of her beautiful garden. The night promised to be calm. There would be no cancelled departures, no reprieve. It was not yet dark but the evening star was rising and the moon emerged to stare down at her, complicated by smoke from a neighbour's chimney.

Suddenly, seized by an irresistible impulse, Calliope released the kitten and vaulted upstairs. She snatched three nightingale souvenirs Lorenz had brought her from his travels, then several photographs: pictures of her parents and of Aristides, of Eli and his daughters, of Rupert and herself lounging in the garden, of Eleni and Athena, of Alexandra in Eftalou, and of a smiling Lorenz Umbreit, one arm resting around her shoulder, the other around his wife. She plucked all these photographs out of their various frames, then stopped and looked about the room one last time.

'I'm fifty-six years old,' she said to herself, 'and I'm about to become a fugitive.'

The words went jangling through her head, and she paused and waited for them to pass, the way one waits for a noisy cargo train to go by, spewing foul fumes into a blameless sky.

～ 9 ～

It was easy to spot the soldiers and uniformed policemen but impossible to identify members of the Security Police. Calliope knew they could arrest anyone they deemed suspicious: without a warrant, without so much as an explanation. She had heard of people being jailed for months without formal charges. Now and then, dissidents disappeared, their families unaware of their whereabouts. She thought of her godson, whom she was about to leave behind. She closed her eyes and drew a long breath, backing away from her inner anguish.

She was standing in an airport queue, waiting to check in with Rupert. Unreasonably, she had drifted from a bullish reluctance to leave, into a dread so intense it felt like foreknowledge: she was going to get caught; would, at the last moment, be prevented from making her escape, and end up in a torture chamber. Whether or not the authorities had actually been alerted, some bored Security Police agent might still take it into his head to detain them. Rupert, with his shaggy beard, could easily be mistaken for a member of the Greek intelligentsia.

For years, Calliope had been praised for her inner strength, her ability to tackle problems large and small. Yet now, about to leave her homeland, she was vainly groping for solid ground on which to rest her feet. She had been lucky during the Occupation, if only because Lorenz had been swayed by his feelings for her. She did not think she was likely to be so lucky again.

Back on the ferry, Rupert had done his best to dispel her anxieties. It was Saturday, it was August, it was when public servants took their annual holidays. 'You know how efficient your Greek bureaucracy is,' he said. 'Even at the best of times.'

'What worries me is that Himonas's wife might have said something.'

'What if she did? She doesn't know why we're in Athens, does she?'

'No.'

'There you are. Stop fretting.'

Calliope sighed. Rupert was right: even assuming that word eventually got around, that every village policeman knew that her name was on an arrest list, she would have to be very unlucky for news of their flight to reach Athenian authorities in time to stop her departure. It was possible but unlikely. Extremely unlikely.

The queue went on inching its way to the check-in counter.

'They're doing spot-checks,' Rupert whispered a few minutes later. The customs agents were there to prevent the smuggling of Greek currency and subversive pamphlets. And that was all, Calliope told herself. There was nothing to worry about, unless they decided to read through the manuscript she was translating. All she had to do was make sure she didn't foam at the mouth if they questioned her.

'They're running late,' she said quietly.

Olympic Airlines departures were notoriously unreliable, but BOAC had been all booked up. Fumbling for a cigarette – she had taken up smoking again on the ferry – Calliope watched as the customs agent singled out a lone passenger, asking him to step aside with his bulging suitcase. It flashed on her that the choice might not be random. What if there was something they were trained to detect: some facial flicker, some telltale cue she might not even be aware of displaying? What if they were under instructions to alert the Security Police?

Calliope put her hand to her brow. Neither she nor Rupert had slept much on the boat. The sea journey had taken nearly fourteen hours, leaving just enough time to pick up cash and tickets, and catch an early-afternoon flight to London.

Rupert was looking peaky. Calliope, too, had bags under her eyes but was hiding them behind dark sunglasses. Now that she was finally at the airport, her dread of an arrest was beginning to fuse with her fear of flying, while waves of a new sensation – something akin to shame – kept sweeping over her. She felt as if she were guilty of a grave moral lapse, of some appalling betrayal: a mother turning her back on her needy child, a cowardly captain deserting his sinking ship. When a burly man sauntered by, giving her and Rupert the once-over, she felt her skin tingle, as with the onset of fever.

The airport was crowded and hot, the stale air reeking of floor-cleaning detergent and human exhalations. Sighing, Calliope drew her damp hair into a clip. She kept replaying Rupert's assurances, reflecting that equanimity came more naturally to an Englishman. The thought was faintly rancorous, as if the English had been given some small but unfair advantage in coping with life's travails.

Although tourism was said to be on the downswing under the *junta*, the check-in queue included several foreigners. They seemed quiet and aloof, while all around them native families argued, laughed, scolded rowdy children. Rupert stood brooding next to Calliope, his legs apart, a finger stroking his beard. He glanced at his wristwatch, then bent from the waist to slide his suitcases forward. At that moment, the customs agent looked up.

'Step this way, please, sir.'

Calliope stopped, fighting a sudden urge to flee. The agent was a thin, pale-faced man whose right eyebrow was slightly higher than the left, fixed in an expression of permanent scepticism. He appeared bored, stifling a yawn, waiting for them to heft their suitcases up for inspection. Calliope swallowed hard, prepared to do the talking.

'How long are you planning to stay abroad?' the agent asked, unzipping a suitcase. He had a thick moustache and slitted eyes, like slivers of black liquorice.

'Until St Basil's.' Calliope slipped her carry-on bag off her shoulder and onto the inspection table. The agent looked rather sour, like a man with heartburn.

'What's the purpose of your trip?'

'My fiancé is English,' Calliope said, gesturing towards Rupert. 'We're going to be married in London.'

The agent glanced from Calliope to Rupert. His eyes were unreadable. He asked whether they had any currency to declare and seemed satisfied with the answer. 'Are you taking printed material with you?'

'Yes.' She was a translator, Calliope explained, and hoped to finish a book while she was abroad. She had a deadline to meet, had to keep working, she babbled. The agent continued to look preoccupied. Tight-lipped, he riffled through her suits and dresses. He peered into the suitcase's inner pouches, into bags, boxes, folders.

'That's all for my work,' Calliope said, achieving the vaguely put-upon look any woman might wear, watching a stranger paw through her carefully packed possessions. The agent was beginning to look like someone who just might decide to skim through her manuscript. When he came upon the translation award, he stopped and examined it, glanced at her briefly, then grew perfunctory.

Rupert watched all this impassively, fidgeting with something in his pocket. When the agent finished with Calliope's suitcase, Rupert stepped forward to help her reorganise her belongings. A second agent had meanwhile emerged from the back, coming towards them with a jaunty swagger. He paused, popped a Chiclet into his mouth, then briskly went about inspecting Rupert's luggage.

Calliope's mouth felt parched. She was saying she needed a drink when a public announcement came on, instructing passengers to proceed to passport control. There was a sudden flurry in the crowd, a spate of rising voices. A blond child, who had been twisting a long balloon, gave it one final smack and spun to follow his parents, sending Calliope's thoughts straight back to Aristides.

She stood gazing after the child, perspiration spreading between her breasts. She was wearing a light, short-sleeved summer dress, but the heat was like gauze clinging to damp skin. The second customs agent was more cursory, as well as more cordial than his older colleague.

'Have a good trip!' he drawled.

~ 10 ~

'It's a good thing they didn't find my copy of Trotsky's *Defence of Terrorism*,' Rupert said, winking at Calliope. They were approaching the passport control queue.

'Shhh!' Calliope hissed. 'They might take you seriously!'

She squeezed Rupert's hand. The public address system was announcing the departure of a KLM flight to Amsterdam.

'This must be the only European airport without air-conditioning,' Rupert said, waggling his shoulders.

Calliope was silent, peering about. If they were going to be stopped, it would most likely be here, she said to herself. In something like ten minutes, she would know her fate: imprisonment or exile. She pulled off her sunglasses, swiped the bridge of her nose, then replaced the shades. In front of her, a foreign woman was gently rocking a fussing baby nestled in a corduroy carrier. A French pilot and crew went by, laughing, the stewardesses' heels clicking across the floor.

'Won't be long now,' Rupert said, clutching both their passports. The queue was creeping forward. The foreigner ahead of them tried to slide a dummy into her child's mouth, only to see the baby's agitated fist knock it down to the dirty floor.

'Next!' The passport inspector was poking in his ear, casting a languorous glance towards the fidgeting passengers. He was a fat man with scant hair and prominent eyes that took in Calliope's voluptuous curves with an air both weary and speculative. His fleshy lips turned up slightly, promising a smile, if only it weren't so hot, if he weren't so worn out.

He glanced at her passport photo, then raised his gaze and studied Calliope more closely. She reminded herself: he was merely comparing her to the photograph, in which her hair was loose and her eyes exposed, carefully outlined with kohl. She raised her hand and theatrically whipped off her sunglasses, smiling straight into the glass booth. The inspector paused for a moment, and finally smiled back, slapping the passport shut. He shifted his gaze towards Rupert.

Calliope stepped forward, conscious of her throbbing temples and her swollen feet. She was wearing flats, but by the time they entered the departure lounge, her legs refused to carry her weight. She slumped into the first vacant seat, a hazy feeling settling over her as she waited for their flight to be announced. There were no soldiers or policemen about, but her fear had yet to release its clutches. It was only after boarding, after the jet had taken off, soaring in the radiant sky, that she felt the last vestiges of dread start to dissipate.

The relief was short-lived: a stewardess was preparing to demonstrate an emergency landing. Calliope threw her head back and closed her eyes, flexing her feet. She sat chewing on a mint for the next few minutes, dimly aware of the rumble of engines, the distant clatter of china. Somewhere in the back, a baby whimpered, then broke into a prolonged wail. Rupert took Calliope's hand and squeezed it. It was all right, the demonstration was over, he said. The stewardess was yanking the oxygen mask off her face.

Calliope turned towards the window, taking in the bleached-looking houses, the blue sweep of glittering sea. She sat gazing out for a while, struggling against a flood of grief. All at once, her face puckered and she twisted away from the vanishing view. She had made up her mind not to complain once they left the village. Yet there she was, burying her face in Rupert's shoulder, her chest heaving.

'I can't bear it!' The words had erupted against her will. 'I can't!' she repeated.

Rupert had no comforting words to offer. Unbuckling his seatbelt, he cradled her in his arms, mutely stroking her scalp. The jet had reached its flying altitude but the infant went on shrilling. Calliope was weeping quietly, her thoughts leaping back to the night her father died. Thirty-six years had gone by, yet she could still recall her father's stubbled jaws and sunken eyes, could smell the acrid odours of his illness as vividly as the nauseating cologne drifting her way from across the aisle.

Ach, Thee mou. The old memory was twisting her heart but, perversely, she went on sheltering it as she felt herself being whisked away, through an endless realm of fleecy clouds, towards unfathomable exile. She said the last word to herself in Greek, then repeated it in both French and German, as if comparing the taste the two foreign words left on her tongue. It came to her then that she did not know the English word and, flying as she was to London, this tiny linguistic setback suddenly flared into the ultimate outrage.

FOUR

～ 1 ～

London
15 December 1971

Dear Eleni,

How wonderful to hear from you! I can't tell you how much your letters mean to me, even if I must dispel some of your romantic notions about the English capital. I was amused to hear you say that my descriptions of English life made you feel as if you were here with us. I hope you will come for a visit soon but, believe me, it's not anything like the novels you've mentioned.

London remains a fascinating city, I suppose, and, as you say, it is interesting to explore a radically different society, but there are many days when I feel I am languishing in this grey kingdom. In some ways, it is a truly dismal place, especially at this time of year. Don't think I have forgotten how miserable winter can be in Molyvos, but back home, there were always brilliant days to break the gloom, whereas here, there are weeks when it seems as if the sun will never come out again. Sometimes, on rainy days, I find myself longing for the sound of the sea, the smell of burning wood, of salt-scented air. Last week I had an intense craving for *hahles*, like a woman in the grip of a tormenting pregnancy. It's astonishing, the things one can get nostalgic about! That I should prefer roosters' calls and the bleating of sheep to the mayhem of urban traffic is perhaps understandable, but how can I explain the absurdity of going to the cinema and missing men's whistles and cat calls? At times, I miss the very things I used to complain about! I can't help admiring British civility, but there are days when I find the English intolerably insipid. I sit opposite them on the underground trains and their faces are as blank as fresh sheets of paper. There is so little human warmth, or humour, or charm, and even less joie de vivre. I can now see why Rupert fell in love with our island, and why Lorenz keeps needing to get away from Heidelberg.

He is back in Germany now, reportedly hard at work. I, too, am busy, trying to finish the book I told you about. I am working at twice my usual speed because the French are eager to publish it, and because I know it's bound to open the international community's eyes to Greek realities.

I am also working on my English. It seems to be improving, but I still feel handicapped, if only because it's hard to be clever and amusing in a language you haven't mastered. Rupert likes to say that he contrived to get me exiled so as to force me to perfect my English, but no linguistic triumph is worth the homesickness I feel. How, I wonder, was he able to abandon his home and people and settle in Molyvos? Flattering but incomprehensible. It seems that, no matter how well you know someone, there are things about them you will never quite understand.

Which brings me to a piece of news I have saved for the last: Rupert and I finally tied the knot so I am now a respectable English lady. But, please, don't congratulate me. Congratulate Rupert, if you like, if only for having persuaded me to do something I consider totally unnecessary.

I try not to think about my Molyvos home, especially the chores I have saddled you and Evanthea with. I miss you and Athena but was happy to hear you are all doing well. Rupert is trying to arrange an exhibition for Zoe at a local gallery and says it looks promising. I have sent you something under separate cover and hope it reaches you in time for St Basil's. Please write again soon and let me have more Molyvos news.

Love and kisses,

Calliope

～ 2 ～

Every spring, there would be the penetrating smell of whitewash, of burning firewood and roasting lamb, and the scent of wisteria mingling with the smell of the sea. By the time Easter arrived, every house and privy would be scrubbed and whitewashed; every courtyard decorated with fresh flowerpots. Beyond the walls and gates, children would screech and chickens cluck, and birds warble among blossoming fruit trees. On Easter Saturday, the women would queue up at the butcher's for fresh lamb, laughing and gossiping, while the men chaffed each other, collecting firewood.

Such were the things for which Calliope found herself yearning during her first spring in London. The Greek exiles exchanged the traditional *Christos anesti* greetings; they celebrated the Resurrection with the usual candles and incense and *maghiritsa*, but the scents of an Aegean spring permeated Calliope's dreams, making the English reality seem not only inadequate but rather pitiful, like the efforts of a conscientious but manifestly dull pupil.

She was as busy in London as she had been in Molyvos, still engaged in literary translation or writing for the Greek branch of the BBC. There were political meetings aimed at toppling the *junta*, pamphlets to be edited, immigrants to be helped at the Hellenic Centre. Although her campaign for a battered-women's shelter had fallen on deaf ears, she had at least managed to establish a referral service. Rupert was teaching an advanced linguistics course at London University. They had English and Greek friends; they had a fine house in Hampstead; they had Rupert's children and grandchildren. And yet, everything about her life seemed provisional to Calliope, as if she were merely biding her time, waiting for the dictatorship to fall.

On 21 April 1972, the *junta* would be celebrating the fifth anniversary of the coup, but in London, a demonstration was being planned in front of the Greek Embassy, followed by a film and lecture at the Hellenic Centre. In late March, the evening following Orthodox Easter, a panel discussion took place on Greek Radio. Calliope had been invited to chair it, only to find herself caught between the Leftists and Rightists, the Monarchists and the Trotskyites, all trying to outshout each other.

Wearying of them all, she headed straight home after the broadcast, caught in a sudden downpour on the way from the underground. The following evening, she was meant to attend a meeting to discuss strategies for publicity and fundraising for a Greek library, but by noon was complaining of a headache and a scratchy throat. She had made it her habit to watch the Greek news in the evening and the English broadcast during lunch with Rupert. The day of the meeting, they sat down in the kitchen, turned on the television, and heard about the murder of a local child.

Nine-year-old Meredith Yealland had been on her way home from school; had stopped to buy a lollipop and was never seen or heard from again. Now her body had been found on Hampstead Heath, a stone's throw away from the Ealings' residence. This in itself was shocking enough; then the girl's parents were interviewed in their Knightsbridge living room, a golden retriever slumped at their feet.

'I can't believe it!' Calliope exclaimed halfway through the interview. She said it in French, the language they still spoke at home.

Rupert glanced at her. 'Dreadful business,' he muttered. The child had been molested and strangled, then dumped behind a clump of trees.

Calliope shook her head. 'Look at the mother, though!'

'What?' said Rupert.

'She's made up like a movie star! Look at her: she's been to the hairdresser's, for heaven's sake!'

Rupert sank his teeth into a sandwich but did not reply. The Englishwoman was speaking of her daughter's accomplishments. She was impeccably dressed, powdered, dry-eyed.

'You'd think this was an interview about some medal the child has won!'

Rupert remained silent. A spring wind was flapping through the garden, rustling in the chimney. Calliope pushed her plate aside. She rose to get the kettle, her thoughts meandering to a distant day when an Eftalou fire had swept through several olive orchards. She recalled the village women's grief at seeing their trees gone; income-generating trees that had been in the family for generations, but still only trees.

'You should have seen those women!' Calliope said to Rupert. 'They wept and shrieked and flung their arms around the scorched trunks. How can a mother sit there and talk about her murdered child and not shed a tear? How can she be thinking of going to the hairdresser's, I ask you?' Calliope dropped into a chair, shaking her head. If she spent the rest of her life in London, she still wouldn't understand the English!

This sentiment being all too familiar, Rupert kept his thoughts to himself. He had given up explaining that the English took pride in mastering their emotions.

'But the heart's not an electric switch!' Calliope had argued in the past. 'It's not something that can be turned on and off at will, is it?' The newscast was making the ache in her throat feel worse. Molyvos had its faults, she conceded, but at least no child had ever been murdered there. It was unthinkable.

The newscast was over. Rupert finished his tea, wiped his mouth, and returned to his memoirs, which he was now rewriting. Calliope had planned to tackle her correspondence. She had letters from Aristides and Lorenz to answer, as well as an urgent note to Varvara, whose husband had recently been shipped off to Athens to stand trial for insubordination. Calliope had been in contact with Angelos Solomos, offering to pay Louizos's legal fees. She wanted to let Varvara know the lawyer was looking into her husband's case. She went to her study and composed the note, then thought of the fundraising meeting and decided to take a nap.

She awoke to find it raining again – raining cats and dogs, as Rupert would say. She was often vexed by the English language, whose idiomatic expressions left her feeling utterly defeated. At a university party, she had heard Rupert say 'I'm pulling your leg' to one of his students. Her English cleaner had spoken of 'spilling the beans', leaving her thoroughly mystified in her own kitchen.

The rain was coming down in torrents, lashing at fresh tulips and tender-stemmed daffodils. Calliope washed her hair and made up her face, gratified to find that the nap had cleared up the shadows under her eyes. She dressed carefully, observing that only her face seemed to be benefitting from her English lifestyle, no doubt because of the clement sun and superior cosmetics. At fifty-seven, she was more attentive to her looks than she had ever been back home, partly because of her age, but also because she wished to distinguish herself from the ill-clad, overweight immigrants she met at the Hellenic Centre. She weighed herself daily, and fussed over her appearance, as if its neglect might leave her inner self doubly vulnerable.

The Hellenic Centre meeting was scheduled for eight o'clock. There were a few blocks to the underground but Calliope had recently acquired a raincoat and black vinyl boots. Dressed in her waterproof outfit, she rather enjoyed walking in the rain: the play of neon lights in the puddles, the muted sounds of traffic. By evening, the rain had slackened but the streets remained virtually deserted. There was a bookstore Rupert frequented, and a pastry shop Calliope had gradually learned to resist. There was a restaurant they occasionally ate at, and an art gallery with paintings Calliope thought vapid. Outside a brightly lit snack bar, two Africans stood in their paint-splattered clothes, waiting out the storm. Huddled deep into their skimpy jackets, they had been laughing, but stopped and stared at Calliope from under the green awning.

Calliope walked on, feeling a pinprick of obscure guilt. She had almost arrived at the underground, was about to turn the corner, when a lone man came up the steep street, carrying a black umbrella. Approaching her, he flicked his cigarette into the gutter and peered at her in the light of a street lamp.

'Excuse me,' he said. He was some sort of foreigner, a youngish man wearing a shabby coat and scarf. He was looking for Urquhart Street, he said. He pronounced it *Your-cart*.

'Is it around the heath?' Calliope asked. She had noticed how the English avoided contact with foreigners, reluctant to stop even in broad daylight.

He hesitated. 'Maybe I don't pronounce it right,' he suggested, with a small, crooked smile. 'I show you.'

Saying this, the stranger made as if to retrieve a note from an inner pocket. Instead, with a quick, flamboyant motion, he tugged at his belt and flung his coat open, pinning Calliope with the intensity of his gaze.

Except for the scarf, the man was stark naked under the coat.

Trapped by surprise, Calliope shrank back, her mind chaotically fighting to grasp what the man was after. On first exposing himself, the stranger had made an odd guttural sound; now he was staring at her with dark, smouldering eyes. Calliope knew nothing about exhibitionists. Was this meant to be a seductive gesture, a lonely man's attempt to impress her with the goods on display?

The goods were impressive. The stranger was powerfully built and magnificently erect. But later, telling Rupert about it, it would come to Calliope that she had been transfixed by more than shock. Although some facet of her mind understood that she was probably meant to react with horror, what she mostly felt was a muddled blend of pity and curiosity. Many hours would pass before she could clarify her own feelings, but one thing she knew: the spasm of pity had something to do with the man's foreignness. This was a city that could drive anyone crazy, she would think much later, burrowing under her warm quilt.

The encounter with the stranger seemed interminable, but could not have lasted more than a minute. They stood face to face in the light of the street lamp, the rain throbbing around them, the cars slithering by. The moment he had exposed himself, the man's eyes had grown bright with challenge. He stood clutching his umbrella, the rain drumming on the taut canopy, while Calliope's skin tingled. The odd mix of astonishment and fascination and fear somehow felt familiar and, as a truck came trundling by, her mind suddenly flew back to her wedding night.

A little hiccup of nervous laughter accompanied the surprising thought. Calliope stepped aside, helplessly shaking her head. She was starting to walk away, only to find herself vehemently spat at. The stranger was staring at her with unmistakable loathing.

'English bitch!' he flung at her retreating back. At least that's what he had meant to say. The words had actually come out sounding like 'English beach'.

Calliope continued walking. The realisation that she could now be mistaken for a native, could pass judgement on a stranger's English, only compounded her inner distress. It was all a muddle and for some reason it seemed to bruise her soul as she approached the underground. Behind her, the rain went on falling, pelting the thwarted streets.

～ 3 ～

Nineteen-and-a-half months later, in November 1973, Calliope was admitted to hospital with acute peritonitis, thus missing news of a momentous event taking place in Athens. The surgery lasted four hours, the hospital stay two-and-a-half weeks. On being discharged, Calliope received a package from Lorenz, containing Deutsche Welle footage. It was an edited record of a Greek student strike that had unexpectedly turned into a massive protest against the regime.

'If you look carefully,' Lorenz wrote in the accompanying letter, 'you will spot me on the sidelines, but you won't have to look very hard to recognise your godson.'

Umbreit had flown to Athens on the second day of the protest, when it became apparent that the event might warrant coverage in his new book. Calliope had arranged to have the documentary shown at the Hellenic Centre. Seated beside Rupert, she watched intently as the black-and-white images began to flicker across the screen.

Athens' Polytechneion was the most prestigious engineering and architecture school in Greece (one that Papadopoulos himself had attended without ever graduating). The students had barricaded themselves behind the gates, their makeshift radio crackling all over the capital. It was Wednesday morning, 14 November 1973.

'This is the Polytechneion, this is the Polytechneion, the standard-bearer of the struggle against the dictatorship and for democracy!'

The Athenian student's voice made Calliope shiver in her English auditorium seat. The room smelled of wet umbrellas and damp footwear, an odour she would forever associate with exile. The Polytechneion student was appealing to Greeks from all walks of life to unite in the liberation of their country.

'Citizens of Greece: we are unarmed. Our only weapon is our faith in freedom!'

The school was situated on one of Athens' busiest thoroughfares but all city buses had come to a stop, with waves of passengers impulsively joining the crowd. Soon, students and workers and farmers were marching together to the sound of the national anthem, waving flags and banners, brandishing placards.

'Down with the *junta*!'

'Bread, education, freedom!'

'Fight against the bloodsuckers!'

By Friday, the crowd numbered in the thousands but, as Umbreit eventually wrote in his letter to Calliope, Aristides Dhaniel was easily recognisable. The camera had caught him by the school gates, clutching a megaphone in his left hand, the right raised in a victory salute. He flashed a joyful grin, then turned and mounted the platform to introduce one of the key speakers. In London, Calliope and Rupert watched in silence, their knees grazing in the dark. The rest of the audience was silent as well. There was an occasional cough, a clearing of the throat. The rain kept drumming against the windowpanes.

The Athenian speeches continued. The demonstrators went on waving fists and placards. Just outside the school gates, a policeman was caught wrestling a demonstrator into a headlock. The rousing music played on.

When the riot police arrived, the camera shifted focus, and this was when Calliope spotted Lorenz, one of several men running down the street. A Norwegian tourist had been hit by a stray bullet and that was where Lorenz seemed to be heading. Meanwhile, two Greek girls were shown dragging an injured student into a hotel. The hotel owner,

Lorenz told Calliope, had been going around with platters of food, exhorting the students, 'Eat, eat, you can't fight for freedom on an empty stomach!'

The police went on thumping, harassing, arresting.

'Down with Papadopoulos!'

'Down with the USA and the CIA!'

All this was still going on when army vehicles stormed the scene, spewing out troops in battle fatigues.

'Please don't shoot your own brothers!' the broadcasting student beseeched the soldiers. 'Please do not spill Greek blood!'

The khaki-clad men appeared to be listening; some could be seen sheltering protesters from the club-wielding police. The bullets went on flying. In the background, there was the wail of sirens. The student was urging doctors and surgeons to come forward. The electrical lights flickered. The municipal power plant had been shut off but the engineering department had its own generators. At midnight, a tank could be seen, steadily rolling towards the illuminated Polytechneion gates.

'Brothers in arms!' the student's choked voice continued. 'Do not obey the orders you've been given! Do not raise your weapons against your own brothers!'

He kept imploring the tank to stop, to heed the voice of the people, but the only response came from a military officer, who leaped out of the tank, shouting: 'The Greek army will never negotiate with anarchists!'

It was a moment Greeks would never forget. In London, Calliope grew limp, sagging against Rupert's shoulder. The army officer had disappeared from view, but the tank went on creeping towards the school gates. The Polytechneion student started on the national anthem. Calliope slid down in her seat, her breathing arrested.

The student was still singing when the tank blasted its way through the gates, trapping the students but inexorably moving on. Although everyone knew how the documentary would end, a tiny squawk of protest escaped Calliope's mouth as she watched the historic event reach its tragic climax. Her hands were still clutching at her hair when the radio fell silent.

Soon, the film, too, came to an end, but Calliope remained in her seat, bitterness rising from her knotted gut. Within days of the Polytechneion protest, over two thousand students had been arrested; hundreds had been wounded. The number of dead was unknown, and would be debated for decades to come.

Aristides, it initially seemed, had managed to escape. While Calliope was still in intensive care, he had phoned London, telling Rupert he was underground, unscathed. Discharged from hospital, Calliope had called her godson's sisters. She kept calling his aunt, his cousins. No one knew anything about his whereabouts. By December, Papadopoulos had been overthrown, but there was still no word from Aristides. Calliope had made several attempts to contact the number Dorothea had given her. One evening, an unknown woman finally answered.

'Is Aristides there by any chance?'

'Aristides? No!'

'How about Dorothea? May I leave a message for her?'

'Sorry, it's not possible.'

'Why not?' Calliope persisted. 'Is Dorothea—'

'She's not here, she's not coming back.'

'But why? What happened to her?'

There was a brief pause, during which the line crackled a little. The Athenian woman let out an exasperated sound.

'Please don't call here again,' she snapped. And then the line went dead.

Calliope hovered by the phone all night, waiting for it to ring. Out on the street, a young man could be heard whistling cheerily, as only young men ever do in the small hours of the morning.

~ 4 ~

13 January 1974

Dear Lorenz,

My beloved Aristides is behind bars again. Somehow, he had managed to evade both police and tanks, sheltered by an architecture professor whose daughter had been involved in organising the protest. It seems Aristides spent the second night of the demonstration with this girl, and that Dorothea had somehow got wind of it. It's even possible that he told her himself; perhaps he had decided to break up with her – I don't know but, as Rupert says, 'Hell hath no fury like a woman scorned.'

To make a long, tragic story short, Dorothea ended up betraying Aristides. I suspect she acted in a moment of terrible pain and confusion and may well be repenting her own vindictive impulse. Alas, neither my cousin nor Angelos Solomos can do anything this time, especially not with Brigadier Ioannides at the helm. Aristides's sister tells me that, in comparison with this thug, Papadopoulos could almost be considered a benevolent dictator. He, at least, liked to pretend that the suspension of civil rights was just a temporary measure; he might have even believed it. Ioannides makes no promises and does not bother pretending. His henchmen are everywhere and Athenians are in a state of terror so deep that the atmosphere in the capital, people say, is like that of a graveyard.

Oh, my dear, I can't tell you how impotent I feel, trying to carry on with my safe English life, while everything inside me cries out for action! That I can do nothing to help – can't, even, speed up the process – fills me with impotent rage.

I have another sad piece of news: Louizos, the former Molyvos police chief, has died of a heart attack and I can't help feeling that I have contributed to his premature demise. Rupert has a Jewish friend who says that he was brought up with the dictum, 'Where there is no upright man, you be the upright man.' I suppose this was how Louizos felt, and why Aristides has been willing to risk his life for his beliefs.

This is one of the most harrowing periods I have ever known. I've always found it hellish to deal with uncertainty and don't know how I'll endure the next few weeks or months – however long it takes before we get any news. Yesterday, some local clairvoyant left a leaflet in our mailbox and I ended up dreaming about

Zenovia Antoniou, the Molyvos fortune-teller. I woke up thinking of a long-ago day when she offered to read my coffee cup. Iason was fighting in Albania at the time, but I flatly refused. I did not believe in destiny, I remember saying. Well, I believe in it now. I also understand the desperate need for hope that keeps crystal-gazers in business.

Thank you for the American postcard. I was interested in your impressions of New York and will look forward to hearing more when we see you in the summer. I am also looking forward to finally meeting your sons. To think that one of them is about to graduate from university!

Rupert and I had planned to go to Paris for Easter, but will stay put for now. In any case, we expect to be here in July. It's good to know that your book is virtually finished. I myself am between projects. I spoke to Stamoulis just before Christmas and he tried to interest me in a new Greek novel, but I am not up to it – not while I sit here, biting my nails. Titos and Tasia send their regards, as does Rupert. I hope your American visit continues to fascinate and inspire.

Yours,

Calliope

— 5 —

What she remembered most vividly was the pervasive feline smell; an intense, clinging odour that would catch at her throat every time she stepped into Zenovia's hallway. It was the winter of the Albanian campaign and the fortune-teller had come down with one of her frequent colds. Calliope, delivering a plate of Mirto's cheese pies, had followed the old woman into the kitchen. It began to rain. The room was in chaos, as cluttered as Mirto's kitchen could only be during spring cleanups.

'Sit down, sit down, my child.' Zenovia set about making coffee. She drew an ivory comb out of her dishevelled hair, then reinserted it with a heavy sigh. They talked about the news from the front. They talked about the Germans' likely involvement, and the women's determined efforts to keep homes and farms going.

Calliope sipped her coffee. When the rain had stopped and she was ready to leave, Zenovia reached into her sleeve and pulled out a none-too-clean handkerchief.

'Would you like me to read your cup?' she asked, dabbing at her reddened nostrils. 'I'll do it for free.'

The offer was received with a smile, a quick shake of the head. Staring into her cup, Calliope heard herself voicing a question that had come to her one day when the old woman's clairvoyant gifts were being discussed in the neighbourhood.

'I've always wondered,' she said, 'what do you tell people if you ever see some misfortune in somebody's cup – an accident or death, or some dreadful illness. Do you tell people the truth?'

The old woman cackled. 'People are right about you,' she said, wagging her head. 'You and your questions! No one else has ever thought to ask me this, my child. No one.' Her face screwed up in a strange little smile.

Calliope waited. 'So?' she said when no answer seemed to be forthcoming.

'So!' There was a barely perceptible shrug but still no reply. Zenovia sat casting about the room with her rheumy eyes, seemingly lost in reflection. After a moment, both she and Calliope began to speak, their words colliding between them.

'I'm sorry,' said Calliope. 'You—'

'No, no, my child. Please go ahead and say—' She coughed into her hand, her eyes watering. 'Whatever you were about to say.'

Calliope hesitated, nettled by the fortune-teller's apparent evasiveness. She decided to amend her question. 'I was going to ask . . . do you think that some people are born lucky and others unlucky?' She looked into Zenovia's eyes. 'And . . . how is it possible that the dregs in my cup would have anything to say about my destiny?' she added, conscious of a vaguely spiteful impulse.

At this, Zenovia began to pluck lint off her woollen sleeve. She sat plucking it for a long moment.

'I don't know about luck,' she finally said. 'Sometimes I believe there is such a thing, other times – well, as I said, I'm not sure.' She shot Calliope an appraising glance, then smiled obliquely. 'I can tell you one thing,' she said after a moment. 'I don't need to look into your cup to know that yours is not an ordinary destiny, my child.'

'An ordinary destiny!' echoed Calliope. 'So, you do believe there is such a thing as destiny!' she blurted. 'And if you believe in destiny, then—'

But Zenovia did not let her complete the question. 'I'll tell you what I believe,' she said. 'Only . . . well, it's not at all an original thought. Who said it – character is destiny – do you know?'

'Heraclitus, I believe,' answered Calliope.

'Well, whoever said it was probably right, don't you think?' Zenovia asked.

'I suppose,' said Calliope vaguely.

'And you.' Zenovia dabbed at her dripping nostrils. 'Do *you* believe in destiny?' she asked, watching Calliope with her probing eyes.

'No,' said Calliope. 'No, I don't.' It was in her to add that to believe in destiny was to resign oneself to things one might well be able to change; things that ought to be changed but that people accept from sheer fatalism.

Zenovia made a soft sucking sound. 'But if you don't believe in predicting the future, and don't believe in destiny, why are you afraid to have your coffee cup read?'

'I don't know!' Calliope laughed. 'My father used to say that no human being can be rational all the time. I suppose he was right.' She shrugged, her eyes sliding towards the window.

It was dark outside. In the garden, Hektor the fool stood alone in a pool of light, under a hurricane lantern suspended from a branch. He was chopping firewood in the slanting rain, while the wind kept gusting around him, strumming through the bare tree branches. Some of the wind-blown leaves fell on Hektor's turbanned head; others whirled a bit, then landed softly around the garden, amid the pots of scraggly geraniums, the soggy beds of dying chrysanthemums.

~ 6 ~

They said he had jumped out of a detention-room window. It was something they often said in those days, something that Calliope could not imagine Aristides doing, but who could say for sure? How could she possibly know what they had put him through once they discovered his true identity?

In years to come, the date of the Polytechneion protest would be ardently observed as a national holiday, but in the summer of 1974, when Lorenz Umbreit and his sons stopped in London on their way to Lesbos, the brutal Brigadier Ioannides was still wielding power. In late June, there had been a sensational attempt to assassinate Cypriot President Makarios, but the coup d'état had been foiled, leading to a massive Turkish invasion, with thousands of Greek Cypriots fleeing for their lives.

The political chaos was rehashed daily on Greek radio, but Calliope had lost interest in the news, as in so much else. The day she received word of Aristides's death, she crawled into bed, secretly contemplating her memory's finest gems, like a solitary old woman in perpetual fear of being robbed. Between late February and the end of May, she spent every day under her duvet: weeping, trying to read, listening to requiems, eating few meals but huge quantities of chocolates. Asleep and awake, she dreamed of summer skies wanton with stars, of the hum of insects on hushed afternoons, of a child's bare feet running across cool marble floors, and bedroom curtains stirred by gentle sea breezes. Above all, she dreamed of the sea, mist-shrouded in the early morning, silvery in the moonlight. She was, she told Rupert, living for the day she would see democracy restored to Greece. She could finally go home then. She would die in peace.

And then Eleni arrived from Greece, grey-haired but bright-eyed as a girl, invited by a despairing Rupert to come and celebrate her fiftieth birthday in London.

In Eleni's company, Calliope felt free to unleash her grief without regard for English restraint. She wept copiously, uncontrollably, sharing her private conviction that Aristides would still be alive if she had been there to marshal help, if she had never left for England. The feeling might be irrational, she conceded, yet it seemed imperative to hold on to both guilt and anguish, as if to let them go would be tantamount to turning her back on her godson's memory. She did not voice the thought that she was also being punished for other, unrelated sins.

Days went by. Then, roused by a nagging sense of duty, Calliope rallied herself and took Eleni to Oxford, to Stratford-upon-Avon. Eleni was flushed with excitement, but Calliope herself showed little interest in the sights, or even in sharing details of her English life. The only way to animate her, Eleni told Rupert, was to share some amusing piece of Molyvos gossip, especially if it involved one of her former pupils.

It was on the way back from Oxford that Calliope first heard about Pavlos Rozakis, Molyvos's *kapheneion* owner, who had turned down a marriage proposal for his daughter because the suitor belonged to a Right-wing family.

'When will it all end, I ask you?' Calliope said, seated next to Eleni on the homebound train. 'Are we ever going to be a normal, undivided nation?'

'My son-in-law says it will take at least two generations,' Eleni replied.

Eleni stayed in London for a month. There was her own birthday, and then Calliope's name day, but also a great deal that had been neglected on the domestic front. Eleni had quickly taken charge and, a little ashamed, Calliope ended up participating in the belated spring cleanup. Her regular charwoman had repeatedly offered to do the job, but Calliope had put her off, wanting only to be left alone. She might have, after Eleni's departure, crawled straight back into bed, but it was by then summer and she was beginning to look forward to another visit.

Lorenz was coming to London. With his two sons.

~ 7 ~

He had recently returned from America; had arranged to stop in England on his way to Greece. It was late July. Still given to unpredictable crying jags, Calliope had marshalled all her inner resources for this long-anticipated visit. She'd planned an elegant menu, had taken a dress to be altered, polished the silver, ironed a tablecloth. Rupert would be at the university all day but everything was proceeding according to plan. The creamed almond soup had been prepared the day before, as had several appetisers. The fruit and vegetables had been washed, the Cornish hens marinated. She was going out to have her hair cut, pick up her dress from the cleaner's, buy an Italian cake. And flowers; she had not bought flowers since Eleni's visit.

Walking away from the hair salon, Calliope stopped at the cleaner's and florist's, purchased the cake, then hurried home to get ready. She had hoped to serve dinner in the garden, but one look at the surly sky and the plan was scrapped. She could hear the phone ring as she unlocked the door, but it stopped before she could reach it. The house seemed becalmed and smelled unusually sweet, scented by the fresh flowers.

Moving briskly now, Calliope arranged the roses, then carefully flipped the halved hens in their herbed marinade. When Rupert called to remind her to refrigerate the wine, she assured him everything was under control. She was going to set the table, then have a leisurely bath. Rupert said he should be home before five.

'Take your time. They won't be here before seven-thirty,' Calliope said.

It was beginning to drizzle. She hastened to end the call, darting out to collect a bra drying on the line. Then she made her way upstairs, vaguely disgruntled by the dismal weather. In Molyvos, rain in late July was a rare event; a quickly passing shower when it did occur.

It was time for a bath. She turned on the faucets, added fragrant oil, then paused to study her new haircut in the bathroom mirror. It was the first time in months that she gave any thought to her appearance. Not having weighed herself all this time, she had been shocked to find that none of her dresses fitted anymore. After Eleni's departure, she had worn a housecoat much of the time; sometimes, a pair of loose trousers with an elastic waistband. She had put on the same trousers that morning, but now peeled off her tired clothes, reaching down to test the bathwater.

Not quite hot enough. She used the toilet, turned off the faucets, and was about to step into the bubbly bath when she heard the telephone ring.

'*Ach, sto diablo!*' Darting out of the steamy bathroom, Calliope almost tripped over a bedroom slipper. She managed to right herself, then lunged for the telephone, surprised to hear Lorenz Umbreit's voice. It seemed her heart could still dilate at the sound of his voice, though she had spoken to him only yesterday, after he had landed at Heathrow. She supposed he was phoning to say they were running late.

'Calliope!' He sounded like a man calling across a bustling street, trying to catch a passing friend's attention.

'Lorenz! Is everything all right?'

'You haven't heard, have you?' He spoke breathlessly, the news rippling out of his mouth before she could utter a single word. 'They're gone, Calliope! They—'

'What?' Calliope could feel her armpits grow hot. She had, in recent months, found herself feeling mentally sluggish. 'Who are you talking about, Lorenz?' She sat staring at her yellowing toenails. His sons – was he talking about his sons?

'Oh, my God! The *junta*, Calliope! I tried to phone earlier, but—'

'The *junta* is gone?!' There was a small, barely audible, gasp. Calliope went still, clutching the receiver. 'How—'

'They've finally thrown in the towel. Karamanlis is being recalled from Paris. It's all over, my dear!'

'All over,' Calliope echoed. She was conscious of a blossom of happiness beginning to unfurl within her – a wild flower, almost immediately snatched off its fragile stem. She covered her eyes with her hand and sat on the edge of the bed, shivering, forsaken by words.

'Calliope? Are you there?'

'Yes.' She tried to steady her breath. 'I'm here.' Had he, had anyone, called her with this news before February, she would have danced, naked, with utter abandon; would have sung the Greek anthem from her Hampstead balcony.

'I can't believe it,' she muttered into the mouthpiece.

'You can go home now!' Lorenz made a soft sound: something

between a sigh and a chuckle. 'I'm so happy to be the one breaking the news!'

Calliope swiped at her eyes. 'Oh, Lorenz!' she said. 'Lorenz . . .'

'We're going to celebrate tonight!' His gaiety was like a sea breeze sweeping through musty rooms. 'I'm going to bring champagne.'

'Yes, that'll be nice,' she said – a polite, slightly distracted hostess. 'Thank you.'

There was a brief pause. He had, it seemed, finally grasped the nature of her inner tumult; had no doubt failed to do so sooner because of his own unbridled excitement.

'Would you like me to come now?' he asked, abruptly solicitous.

'No . . . no, I'm not ready,' she said, her nostrils detecting the smell of her own stale sweat. 'I must phone Rupert and let him know,' she added after a moment. The rain was steadily gaining force, pelting the dismal garden.

'I'll see you later then,' Lorenz said after a brief hesitation. He was about to hang up when, all at once, the news shook Calliope's brain.

'Oh, Lorenz!' she cried, tears spilling out of her eyes. 'I still can't believe it!'

'Believe it, my dear!' He let out a deeply familiar laugh, at once tender and melancholy. A car was coming up the street, crawling to a halt under the bedroom window. In the garden, crows could be heard, bickering noisily. The English world went about its usual pursuits, damp and grey and impervious.

At length, they said goodbye. Calliope replaced the receiver. She paused for a moment, picked up the phone once more and began to dial. But then she glanced at her watch and hung up again. It was almost five. Rupert would be on his way home. She told herself she should hurry and have her bath, but instead groped for the remote control and, perched on the edge of the bed, aimed it at the television screen.

Just in time for the five o'clock newscast.

The news would be all over the world by now, duly disseminated by scores of foreign reporters whose professional prerogative seemed unreasonably vexing. The BBC report was being transmitted from

Greece by a young, hoarse-voiced correspondent clutching a mike with an air of particular urgency. He had stationed himself in front of the parliament grounds, surrounded by a crowd of jubilant, sun-bronzed Athenians.

'*Dimokratia!*' they chanted: kinetic, delirious. '*Di-mo-kra-ti-a! Di-mo-kra-ti-a!*'

The camera swept the historic square, zooming in on a pack of frisky stray dogs. The dogs were scampering down the broad marble stairs, briefly catapulting Calliope's thoughts towards a distant but vividly remembered day; the April Fool's morning when she and Lorenz had been caught in a sudden downpour. On this very spot. In retrospect, the subsequent turn of events seemed rather predictable, but who could have guessed that one day, she – Calliope Adham – would find herself in a London bedroom, childishly hugging a velvet cushion, while, back home, her own people celebrated a historic triumph?

If the thought of Aristides was inevitable, so was the slashing pain. It took enormous skill – skill as well as steely resolve – to get through the most ordinary of days, feeling all the while as if some crucial organ kept ceaselessly bleeding within your body.

This was no ordinary day, but one that nonetheless made banal demands. Calliope reached for a tissue. Turning the TV off, she levered herself from the bed and padded across the room, her bare feet sinking into the plush carpet. Out on the street, a car door slammed and voices were heard, muted by rain. The day was quickly fading. The telephone rang again, but this time she did not stop to answer. She went on shutting the windows while the telephone shrilled on and on, and finally fell silent, looking vaguely reproachful.

A faint floral scent was wafting out of the bath, but the rest of the house, the entire throbbing universe, seemed to smell of nothing but rain; punitive English rain that might go on falling for days now, its sole allegiance to verdant parks and pastures.

The bathwater was lukewarm. Leaning over the claw-footed tub, Calliope refilled it, listening to a Barbra Streisand song playing at a neighbour's. Then a motorcycle went by, its roar setting another neighbour's dog off. The vehicle quickly vanished but the dog went on barking on the open porch. Soon, a man's voice was heard, snapping at the dog; a child broke out in a sudden wail. Was the world always so intrusive, so egregiously noisy?

The thought was accompanied by a heavy sigh. The music at the neighbour's was turned off, but the child's sobs sounded muffled, as if blown across a great, unforgiving moor. The boy cried on and on, and the dog, briefly chastened, soon resumed barking in a frenzy of apparent commiseration.

Calliope was fully immersed in her hot bath before both crying and barking finally ceased, and it was only then that she became aware that Rupert had arrived. He was fumbling outside the front entrance, sliding a key into one lock, and then into the other. She heard the front door open, then close again: gently, quietly.

It was almost evening now. The rain was still whispering. In two hours, under the same alien sky, Lorenz Umbreit would be on his way over, bearing freesias and, almost certainly, another nightingale sculpture. She supposed there would be more of them in the years to come; she could almost see them now, vividly displayed on the massive desk in her Molyvos study.

A rare collection of annual souvenirs, fragile and eloquent.

HIGHLIGHTS OF MODERN GREEK HISTORY

1821–29   War of Independence following four centuries of Ottoman rule.

1832   European powers officially recognise Greece's autonomy.

1843   Greece becomes a constitutional monarchy.

1897   Greco-Turkish War over Crete. The island would not be incorporated into Greece until 1913.

1910   Eleftherios Venizelos is elected Prime Minister, ushering in a controversial twenty-five-year political era, marked by the hope of recovering Ottoman territories long inhabited by ethnic Greeks. This would become known as Venizelos's Great Idea.

1912–13   Balkan Wars bring about a partial realisation of the Great Idea. The island of Lesbos becomes independent.

1914–18   Venizelos and King Constantine clash over the advisability of maintaining neutrality in the First World War. This conflict (known as the National Schism) marks the beginning of intense political upheaval, dividing the Greek nation into Venizelist and Royalist camps. Allied pressure, however, forces the King into exile. With Constantine's younger son, Alexander, on the throne, Greece enters the war and gains several new territories after the Ottoman Empire is carved up by the Allied victors.

1920   Venizelos survives an assassination attempt but is defeated at the polls. King Alexander's unexpected death from a monkey bite leads to a national referendum. King Constantine returns to the throne.

1921–22   Encouraged by Allied promises, Greek troops invade Asia Minor, only to be abysmally defeated by the Turks. This event is thereafter referred to as the Great Catastrophe.

1922   King Constantine abdicates and is succeeded by his elder son, George II.

1923   The League of Nations orders Greece and Turkey to undertake a formal exchange of their ethnic populations, uprooting ancient Greek and Turkish communities. Forced to absorb 1.5 million Anatolian refugees, Greece finds itself in economic ruin, beset by prolonged political upheaval.

1924   Proclamation of a Greek republic. Venizelos has returned from exile but is once again defeated at the polls.

1924–35   This period is notable for its dire economic conditions and violent political strife, with coups and counter-coups taking place, eventually resulting in the restoration of the monarchy. The nascent Communist Party gains in popularity.

1936   National elections result in a hung parliament, with the Communist Party holding the balance. Ioannis Metaxas, a former Royalist general, becomes Premier and, with the King's support, establishes a dictatorship.

1939   Having occupied neighbouring Albania, Italy demands a right of passage through strategic Greek territories. Greece refuses and, despite the threat of a German invasion, goes into battle against the Italian aggressor.

1941   Germany invades Greece and, along with its Italian and Bulgarian allies, occupies the country, while the Greek government goes into exile. In the mountains, several resistance groups are formed, some Communist, others anti-Communist, but for now sharing the same patriotic goal.

1944   End of the German Occupation; the Greek government-in-exile returns to Athens.

1946   Civil War between Communist and Royalist supporters breaks out.

1948   The Soviet Union breaks off relations with Yugoslavia, forcing Greek Communists to choose between Stalin and Tito. When the majority opt to side with Moscow, Tito closes the Yugoslav border and disbands guerilla camps inside his country, causing internal conflict within the Communist Party.

1949   General Papagos launches a fierce anti-Communist campaign, further weakening an already splintered Communist Party. A formal treaty brings an end to the Civil War.

1954   Greece becomes embroiled in Cyprus, the majority of whose population is ethnic Greek.

1955   Constantine Karamanlis, a Royalist supporter, is elected Prime Minister, dominating Greek politics for nearly a decade.

1964   George Papandreou Senior, an opponent of the monarchy, is elected Prime Minister.

1967   Right-wing army officers, led by George Papadopoulos, stage a coup, ostensibly to prevent an imminent Communist takeover.

1973   The monarchy is abolished and Greece becomes a presidential republic.

1974   A failed coup in Cyprus brings about the downfall of the military *junta.* Constantine Karamanlis is recalled from exile to form a new government.

1975   A presidential democracy is proclaimed.

1981   Andreas Papandreou is elected Prime Minister, heading the first socialist government in Greece.

GLOSSARY

agora – village or town centre
ameletita – testicles (literally: unmentionables)
Dimitris – demotic version of Dimitrios
dolmadhakia – stuffed vine leaves
eleftheria – freedom
gliko – fruit preserves
hahles – biscuits made of *trahana*
hamam – Turkish bath
kale – a common, untranslatable vocative (literally: good one!)
kalimera – good morning
kalispera – good evening
kapheneion – coffee shop selling coffee, alcohol, and appetisers
kentro – centre
koritsi mou – term of endearment (literally: my girl)
kritharaki – a type of homemade pasta
Kyria – Madam/Lady/Mrs
Kyrios – Sir/Mr
maghiritsa – a traditional Easter soup made of lamb offal
manestra – rice-like pasta
mezedhes – appetisers
mou – my
nona – godmother
Ohi Day – holiday commemorating Metaxas's rejection of Italian demands (literally: No Day)

ouzeri – a bar specialising in ouzo and appetisers
palikari – young chap (literally: a brave)
Panaghia mou – Holy Virgin
panakia – rags used to absorb menstrual flow
pantopoleion – general store
papadhia – priest's wife
patrida - homeland
pedhi mou – term of endearment (literally: my child)
pedhaki mou – diminutive form of above
pedhia – plural of *pedhi*
pedhomasoma – literally: the gathering of children
Pendozali – Cretan dance
phile – friend (vocative case)
plateia – town square
popos/popo – backside
poulaki mou – term of endearment (literally: my little bird)
psarosoupa – fish soup
rizogalo – rice pudding
St Basil's Day – first day of the new year
spitogatos – domestic cat
stifadho – meat and onion stew
Stipsianos – a native of Stipsi
sto diablo! – To the devil!
taramosalata – fish roe spread
Thee mou! – My God!
ti na kanome? – What can we do?
tiropita – cheese pie
trahana – a blend of cracked wheat and yoghurt, fermented and dried,
    served as soup or porridge
tu es formidable – you're amazing (French)
Turkospori – seeds of the Turks
vassilopita – traditional Christmas cake
yassas – hello (plural or formal); also, goodbye (literally: to your health)
yassou – hello (singular); also, goodbye (literally: to your health)
yaya – grandmother

ACKNOWLEDGEMENTS

This novel was years in the writing and could not have been completed without considerable help from friends, strangers, and the work of other authors. In one way or another, I am indebted to all the following:

Andrews, Keven, *The Flight of Ikaros*, Weidenfeld and Nicolson, 1959.

Argenti, Philip P, *The Occupation of Chios by the Germans and their Administration of the Island*, Cambridge University Press, 1966.

Blum, Richard and Eva, *Health and Healing in Rural Greece*, Stanford University Press, 1965.

Borg, Susan and Laskor, Judith, *When Pregnancy Fails*, Bantam Books, 1989.

de Bernieres, Louis, *Captain Corelli's Mandolin*, Martin, Secker and Warburg, 1994.

Dunmore, Helen, *The Siege*, Grove Press, 2002.

Gage, Nicholas, *Eleni*, Ballantine Books, 1983.

Kazantzakis, Nikos, *Freedom and Death*, Faber and Faber, 1956.

MacSkimming, Roy, *Out of Love*, Cormorant Books, 1993.

Matesis, Pavlos, *The Daughter,* (translated by Fred A. Reed), Arcadia Books, 2002.

Mazower, Mark, *Inside Hitler's Greece*, Yale University Press, 1993.

Meek, James, *The People's Act of Love*, Canongate Books, 2005.

Tsalikis, Yorgos, *Katohi*, Athens, 1977.

Vardaros, Leonidas, *All of Us*, Efendi (telefilm, Athens, 1998).

Zinovieff, Sofka, *Euridyce Street,* Granta Books, 2004.

I am deeply grateful to Eleni Eliadis and Toula Karahaliou for their countless contributions, and to Nina Bawden, Louis de Bernieres, Maureen Freely, and Nicholas Gage for their early encouragement. For information pertaining to the Civil War and *junta* years, I would like to thank Yannis Karafillis, Alkman Granitsas, Leonidas Kallivretakis, Theodoros Adamopoulos of the Greek Film Archives, and Despina Zervon of ERT Television Archives; many thanks to the Athens News and to all the Molyviates who answered my endless questions; to Kate Quarry, Eva Stachniak, Ben Yarde-Buller, and Sofka Zinovieff for their helpful suggestions; to Yorgos Kaklamanos, Roger Taylor, Christos Velentzas, Montreal's Westmount Library and Goethe Institute for help with my research; to Manya Baracs, Margot Granitsas, and Margaret Rumscheidt for translations; to Patricia Strutz and Andrea Shepherd for triumphing over my techno-woes; to my publisher, Alex Craig, for editing and championing this book, and to Ranya Karafilly and Ben Camardi for their insights, humour, and warm support. Last but not least, to Thomas and Elaine Colchie, my agents, for devotion beyond the call of duty.